T0346623

THE MAN
FROM
BASHMOUR

THE MAN FROM BASHMOUR

Salwa Bakr

Translated by Nancy Roberts

The American University in Cairo Press
Cairo New York

First published in 2007 by
The American University in Cairo Press
113 Sharia Kasr el Aini, Cairo, Egypt
420 Fifth Avenue, New York, NY 10018
www.aucpress.com

Dar el Kutub No. 3298/07
ISBN 978 977 416 109 4

Dar el Kutub Cataloging-in-Publication Data

Bakr, Salwa
    The Man from Bashmour / Salwa Bakr; translated by Nancy Roberts. —
Cairo: The American University in Cairo Press, 2007
      p.   cm.
      ISBN 977 416 109 2
      1. Arabic fiction   I. Roberts, Nancy (trans.)   II. Title
      813

1 2 3 4 5 6 7 8 9 10 11 12   12 11 10 09 08 07

Designed by Sally Boylan /AUC Press Design Center
Printed in Egypt

TRANSLATOR'S ACKNOWLEDGMENTS

I would like to extend thanks and appreciation to the following individuals for their patient and generous assistance in the process of researching elusive terms encountered in the translation process: Dr. David Grafton (Coordinator of Graduate Studies, Evangelical Theological Seminary, Cairo), Ms. Nazli Rizk (Cairo), Father Baniameen Morgan Basily (St. Mark's Church, Giza), Father Laurence Mancuso (founder and former abbot of New Skete Monastery in Cambridge, New York), Arthur Miller (Academy of Languages, Baltimore, MD), my husband, Dr. Amin Odeh, and last but not least, the book's author, Salwa Bakr.

v

PREFACE

In August 1998, the Egyptian publisher Dar al-Hilal, which had been
due to publish Part I of *The Man from Bashmour (al-Bashmuri)*,
called a halt to the publication process after sectarian strife broke
out in Upper Egypt, particularly in the town of al-Kusheh, and which
had repercussions so broad that a committee from the U.S. Congress
came to Egypt to investigate the events. For my part, I argued that the
novel's release at that time in particular could help to clarify the profound commonalities shared by Muslims and Copts in Egypt. Though I
am a Muslim, the novel is an attempt to offer an objective reading of the
events of history without regard for specifically religious or ideological
considerations. Fortunately, the publisher agreed to release the novel,
stipulating the omission of certain phrases that they feared could cause
offense to some Muslims or Copts, a proviso to which I agreed.

When Part I of the novel was finally published in the fall of 1998,
it was met with mixed responses in Egypt. A contributor to *al-Ahram*
newspaper criticized it, saying that it stood to foment sectarian strife
between Muslims and Copts.* Similarly, some Egyptian Copts viewed
the novel as unwanted interference in Coptic affairs. However, a semi-
nar in which the work was discussed was attended by clergymen and
theologians who praised the novel as a significant document that offers
a re-reading of aspects of early medieval history that had heretofore
been passed over in silence.

---

* Fahmi Huwaydi, *al-Ahram*, November 10, 1998.

The novel shocked many due to the fact that it reexamines the so-called historical constants related to the Arab conquest of Egypt and the relationship that existed between Muslims and Copts during that time period, since historical accounts written by Muslim or Coptic historians have tended to be based primarily on religious perspectives and beliefs, while the cultural and civilizational facts have tended to be concealed behind this history, particularly in connection with Egypt's predominant religions and languages before the latter shifted to Arabic.

The text of the novel contains six languages: ancient Egyptian, Coptic, Syriac, Greek, Farsi, and, of course, Arabic. These languages are distributed over a large number of passages scattered throughout the novel and are taken from writings from the Middle Ages. What becomes apparent through such passages is that these languages were often used together within a single text written in Arabic, a phenomenon which reveals the extent to which different cultures and civilizations have intermingled and interpenetrated in the Middle East since time immemorial. An example of such interpenetration on the linguistic level may be seen in a passage taken from al-Qazwini's, *The Wonders of Created Things* which contains the names of varied species of fish and birds, and which was written in Arabic, Farsi, Coptic, and Greek.

The novel rests upon the events of history. However, it only concerns itself with such events in their capacity as a vehicle or receptacle for civilizational and cultural meanings that challenge the notion of a cultural or civilizational 'purity' for which so many have striven and continue to strive. Hence, for example, the novel speaks of monks in Egyptian monasteries who are punished for reading the books of the Sabeans and the Mu'tazilites, while in Baghdad we find ancient Greek culture to have enjoyed a powerful presence within a deeply Islamic culture.

The novel is set in a partially antiquated geographical context as a necessary condition for a reading of ancient history and its cultural-civilizational manifestations. As such, it makes mention of cities—such as Tanis, Atrib, and others—which no longer appear on the map due to changes, both cultural and otherwise, that overtook them with the passing of time. In this and other respects as well, the novel rearranges historical centers and peripheries, as it were, in a manner that is at variance with traditional categories. For reasons at once practical and religious, the peasant revolt witnessed by the Nile Delta, or marshlands, took place on the outer margins of Coptic and Islamic history. However, the novel places it center stage in the scheme of historical events, viewing it as the most significant link in the evolution of Egypt's cultural-civilizational history. After all, from the time when the uprising was quelled, it was the Arab culture and language that came to give the country its predominant direction and hue.

The effort required to translate this novel owes not only to the difficulty of the text on the linguistic plane—given the fact that it was written for the most part in Arabic with a Coptic tint, which called for adherence to the spirit of this language throughout in an attempt to embody it in the English rendition. Rather, it owes likewise to the process of academic inquiry into the huge store of information contained in the novel having to do with histories, cultures, and civilizations extending over the region in which the novel's events are set. It is my hope that this sincere effort will speak well for me in the event that there are slips or errors in the text that escaped my notice.

Salwa Bakr
Cairo, November 2006

THE MAN
FROM
BASHMOUR

PART 1

I was still kneading the dough for the Eucharist bread, working on getting it just right, with the intention of leaving it after that to rise. I had washed the earthenware kneading bowl in ritually pure water, as well as the lid and the sieve. The priest was standing over me, reciting the Psalms and making the sign of the cross. As he came to the psalm of praise and began to chant, "Make a joyful noise to the Lord, all the lands! Serve the Lord with gladness! Come into His presence with singing!" and as I was carefully kneading and shaping the dough to make sure it turned out the proper consistency, Thawna the deacon came up to us hurriedly, then stood beside us in a calm, respectful silence. When the priest had finished his recitation, I covered the dough with the lid that I had purified along with the mat, the sieve, and the stamps for the Eucharist bread. Then, as I was about to head for the furnace, which I had heated in preparation for the baking with hard charcoal in keeping with ceremonial regulations, Thawna approached me and whispered in my ear, "Budayr, finish your work quickly, then go see Father Joseph right away."

This took place one day in the month of Paona, which many lay people still pronounce *Pa'wni* as in the ancient pagan tongue, and the year was AM 506, or perhaps 507.

I quickly cleaned off the dough that clung to my hands and forearms by washing them in some water from the large clay jar used for ablutions. Before long my skin had become visible again and one could

3

see the lion tattoo with its bluish tint on the inner side of my right fore-arm. Assured that no one had noticed it, I rolled down the sleeves of my clerical robe, then ran out toward Father Joseph's residence on the opposite side of the church courtyard. I climbed the three basalt steps that had recently been laid in place of the old limestone ones. They had been presented as a gift by an upstanding servant of the church from Hermopolis, who had removed them from an ancient temple ruin in the old city, then brought them all the way here on his two donkeys in faithfulness to a vow he had made to himself. As I reached the top of the stairs I entered the eastern corridor, at the end of which His Eminence's lodgings were located. When I arrived, I found him in a meeting with the priest, the archdeacon, and all of the other deacons, including Thawna, the one who had summoned me. Awed, I delivered the appropriate cer-emonial greeting, then quickly lowered my head in reverence for all these distinguished ecclesiastical personages. I remained standing at the door without saying a word. Father Joseph looked at me pensively for a moment or two as though he were undecided regarding something that had to do with me. However, it was not long before he raised his hand, in which he held a crucifix, and made the sign of the cross.

Speaking in clear Bashmouri Coptic, he said to me, "Budayr, good-hearted servant, the Lord has chosen you for a sacred ecclesiastical mission. You must carry it out with sincerity and loyalty in the man-ner required of you, and do neither more nor less than what you are instructed."

Responding to him in the tongue in which he had addressed me, I murmured in a low, meek voice without looking up, "There is no resist-ing the will of the Lord, Blessed Father."

There followed a silence so thick you could have heard a sparrow's breath until he added, "You will be going with Deacon Thawna to the marshlands, where the Bashmourite tongue is spoken, and your task will be to translate for him as much as possible. As you know, he only speaks the Coptic dialect of Akhmim, as do most of those here in this church. You must be of assistance to him in every step he takes during your jour-ney there. To you he owes brotherly affection and respect, and to him you owe obedience to his every word. You are to remain by his side no matter what should happen. Do not forget that the brotherhood born of

4

baptism can never be broken till the Day of Judgment, and it is the Lord, now and forevermore, who preserves us and calls us to account."

I nodded my head without speaking this time. The mere mention of the phrase "the marshlands" filled me with distress, and my heart began fluttering like a bird flying through the seventh heaven. Images from the past began calling each other forth in my imagination, taking on flesh before my very eyes. Memories of my place of birth, scenes from my childhood and adolescence, the seasons of my erstwhile tragedy and my first tribulation roiled within me. I was gripped by an anguish so terrible, I nearly cried out, "No! I beg you by your Lord, sir, you who will know greatness in the Lord's kingdom, spare me this mission—a mission that will torment my heart, and which my spirit will not have the strength to bear!" However, I feared being accused of insubordination or disobedience. Hence, I just stood where I was, speechless and motionless, like one of the iniquitous inhabitants of Sodom and Gomorrah after the curse had descended upon him and he had turned into a pillar of salt. Father Joseph seemed to perceive my perplexity—I who had lived years outside the church, wretched and straying from the kingdom of the Lord, and who had stood before him on numerous occasions in the early days of my service to the church to confess my sins and iniquities.

Addressing me reassuringly, he said, "It is the church that sweeps away sins and iniquity and which purifies the heart. It is the church that sweeps out the 'house of the soul,' and the house of the soul is the body. The portal into enmity and discord is the mouth, and its cleansing can only come about through the recitation of the Psalms, which issued from the Person of the Holy Spirit, to Him be glory, on the lips of the blessed David after he had purified his tongue of slander, backbiting, and attempts to sow the seeds of discord among his brethren. The sense of hearing is cleansed by listening to the Holy Gospel with its Christian teachings, warnings, and exhortations. The sense of sight is purified by looking upon the Holy of Holies and the icons that depict the likenesses of the saints, and by a zealous desire to learn about their lives and to emulate them in their spiritual struggle. As for the sense of smell, it is sanctified by breathing in the incense whose fragrance ascends in the name of the Holy Trinity. And as for the sense of touch, it is sanctified

5

by kissing the glorious crucifix and the books of the Lord and touching one's forehead to them. Hence, let every person sweep his sins away with his prayers, and let the iniquity of the iniquitous be purged through the kingdom of the merciful Lord."

Then he repeated his instructions to me that I should obey Deacon Thawna, be regular in my prayers, and recite frequently the Psalms and prayers of supplication. He asked that I not persist in asking questions about things that were of no concern to me and, if I did ask, that my questions be such as to edify my faith and be of benefit to Christ and His cause. In addition, he instructed me not to anger or tire the deacon but, rather, to minister to him and care for him throughout the length of the journey to the Bashmourites in the marshlands.

We were to depart from the church at daybreak the following morning, and I still had many tasks to complete before then in my capacity as the church sexton. Hence, after leaving our Reverend Father's quarters, I washed down the church floor, which was made of the finest Byzantine tile. It had been brought from Caesarea thanks to the generosity of a God-fearing man who had lived for some time under the influence of the Chalcedonian uncleanness, not knowing the way of truth. Then God had brought him back into the fold through the efforts of Father Joseph. Being a rich and influential man, he had given our church this tile. I also wiped the dust and soot off all the church's lamps with the linen cloth that I had reserved for this purpose. I did this in preparation for lighting the lamps at nightfall with a torch taken from the Lamp of the East in the sanctuary, which is not permitted to go out either by day or by night lest 'strange fire' enter the church or the sanctuary, since the first sacrifices used to bring down fire from heaven that would consume them.

As soon as I had finished with the lamps, I turned to make sure that the fourteen instruments of priestly service at the altar had been arranged in their proper places. I cleaned those that needed to be cleaned, after which I examined all of them and straightened those that were out of place: these included the stone tablet, which is placed there as a symbol of the tomb; the paten which serves as a symbol of the manger in Christ's infancy; and the wooden chest, or ark, that holds the books and the two consecrated cloths, one of which is under the paten and the other of which rests under the chalice, which symbolizes the urn of manna. The second cloth corresponds to the grave clothes associated with death and burial, as well as the swaddling clothes in which the body of our Master—glory be to Him—was wrapped in the manger. In addition, there was the consecrated spoon for distributing the wine of the Eucharist among the people, both men and women, since they do not partake of the chalice as the priests do; and the ibrasfarin, that is, the consecrated stone that symbolizes the one that was rolled away from the mouth of the Master's tomb. I also examined the seven unconsecrated instruments, which include the candelabrum, the small clay jug, the plate holding the manna, the censer, the incense drawer, and the stand upon which the crucifix and the chalice are placed. All of these together are placed in the new Holy of Holies. After completing these tasks, I crossed myself three times and withdrew in quiet reverence. Then I proceeded to what remained of my assigned tasks in my capacity as lowly servant and sexton. I went on working diligently all day, and by the time of the late afternoon Mass I had finished all my tasks with God's full blessing. I also checked on the oblation, which consisted of incense made from a mixture of four ingredients: frankincense of the type that the magi offered as a gift to the Savior; sandarac, because it has never been offered to the satanic pagan gods; aloes, since it has the power to cast out demons; and benzoin, because of its pleasant fragrance and because God only offers that which is lofty and majestic. I limited the amounts of other types of incense and of storax resin also, since it attracts demons. The Eucharistic wine that I had prepared was among the finest, most delicious varieties. I had made it myself at the church and it was free of any sort of impurity. It was abraka—which is the Greek word that refers to wine that has been made from the first fruits of the vine. This was something I had been taught once by the learned deacon Thawna. The grape wine was dedicated to use in the Mass, whereas other types—wines made from figs and other fruits— were available for the priests to drink.

I placed the bread—which I had made from the finest, purest flour in the church bakery—in its sacred place. I had taken the utmost care to make sure that it contained no cracks, since cracks in the Eucharist bread are unacceptable, and in accordance with church regulations, I had ground the flour from the first wheat to be harvested. As soon as the Ninth Hour Mass began in the late afternoon, I rushed to stand in my designated place. Facing East in reverent silence, the priests were standing in two rows in front of the holy sanctuary. No one was permitted to be distracted from the prayer by the person beside him or by engaging in idle conversation. Consequently, no one was to speak even about necessities during the Mass. Rather, if something was needed he was to communicate it—no matter what his rank—through some sort of nonverbal signal, be it a wink or a gesture of the hand, which is more fitting for such a sacred, majestic place.

All the clergymen were clad in the prescribed ecclesiastical vestments, having placed woolen hoods around their heads and donned the alb, that is, a floor-length linen robe adorned with images of the holy cross both back and front, around the hemline, and around the edges of its sleeves. Father Joseph's alb was the only one whose crosses had been embroidered with precious stones, including sapphires, emeralds, diamonds, and carnelian, whereas those worn by the other clerics had all been embroidered with silk thread as is customary. As for the kerchief, it was held by the priest, since no one with the rank of deacon or lower was permitted to hold it at any time. It was also customary for the priest to wear a ghaffara, which—since the Arabs' tongue has become the most commonly used language throughout the land—has come to be known as a jubba or 'abaya.

Unlike those in some other churches, we did not follow the practice of wrapping our heads in a long band of white linen. Rather, we would just wear silk sashes around our waists and drape a band of linen over our shoulders, whereas the clerics—the priests, deacons, and Father Joseph—wore stoles that hung down over their chests. Decorated from top to bottom with crosses and pictures of the twelve disciples—six in each row—they looked exquisitely beautiful and majestic. At the top of each of these two rows, the text of consecration was inscribed in gold thread. It was customary for the priestly stole to be made of the finest blue silk. As for me and my fellow sexton, we would wear vestments which, like the priest's stole, had a neck opening, but without being decorated with crosses and sacred images of the disciples as his was. As for the priest's special sleeves, Father Joseph was not wearing them on that day, since it was the time for the altar service. However, I used to love to look at him when he was wearing them. They would cover his forearms entirely, blousing out at the elbow and becoming narrower toward the wrist. They were made of crimson velvet embroidered with stars, crosses, and a picture of the Virgin Mary and the Christ child worked in thick silver thread. As for their lower edges, they were adorned with sacred sayings embroidered with the same thread. One such saying was, "He who labors for the Kingdom of Heaven. . . ." It is said that a righteous Coptic man from Shata had made these sleeves in the days of Clement of Alexandria and had adorned them in this skilled manner, then presented them as a gift to the church, and that they were still being used to this very day. Even so, they were in such good condition you would have thought they had just been made. This, of course, was thanks to the assiduous care that had been taken of them on the part of all the pious fathers who had come after that time.

Father Joseph began praying as he usually did from the Coptic Prayer Book. As he did so, we were carried along with him in our hearts and spirits, taken up wholly into the prayer and distracted by nothing. For it had happened once that a deacon by the name of Elia had whispered something into the ear of the person beside him as they stood together in the choir, and Father Joseph had punished him by demoting him from his rank for three weeks. He was punished for what he had done because he did not attend the prayers regularly and had fallen into frivolity and empty talk. As for feeble, elderly clergymen and those who were not strong enough to remain standing, our custom was for them to be seated on the Western side of the church.

We had all washed our feet before the prayer service in the copper vessel containing water for purification which stood atop the Holy Thursday ablution site. Testimony to this practice is born by the Torah, since in the outer and inner sanctuaries there was a copper pail for purifying the feet of the priests before they entered the Holy of Holies in the tent of meeting.

Passages from the ancient Psalms were read, then Father Joseph chanted the glorious theotokias in the most beautiful way while we chanted after him, singing praises to the Holy Virgin and themes from the book of the Lord to poignant tunes that fill one's heart with longing and open one's soul to faith. Like the sound of a plover soaring through a cloudless sky, Father Joseph's voice was pristine and filled with such reverent humility that it reached right into people's hearts. I began listening to him as I stood there celebrating the Mass with those around me, knowing that my work in the church was not the same as prayer. After all, prayer is prayer and work is work, and although work for the church might yield some bodily sustenance, it could never take the place of prayer itself.

After the Mass was over and all the people had dispersed, I went around with a lamp in my hand checking to make sure that all the doors in the church were secured, lest—when those inside were asleep or inattentive—it be trespassed upon by anyone who would otherwise be forbidden to enter, including outlaws, rapacious wolves, or other animals such as unclean dogs or stray donkeys. As I went about my tasks, dusk began to fall, so I hurried to finish mopping the courtyard floor, and I did the same for the corridors and foyers. When I had completed that task, I cleansed myself with ritually pure water seven times, all the while calling upon the Lord for protection from Satan. Then I went to Thawna the deacon, who had signaled to me with a slight nod of his head during the prayer as he was wont to do when he wanted me for something. After walking the length of the corridor on tiptoe for fear that someone might hear me, I tapped lightly on his door for permission to enter. My quarters, which were located at the opposite end of the corridor, were a good distance away from his. When I heard him answer, I pushed the wooden door open, taking care not to let it creak lest I draw someone's attention, then went in and sat down opposite him on his pallet, which lay spread on the floor.

Thawna had been one of my closest friends in the church since I had entered it six years earlier. He had come to the Lord's kingdom after being cleansed of a sin about which I knew nothing, though it had been rumored of him—a native by birth of Antoniopolis—that he had originally been a heretic who professed the Gnostic view that the knower can achieve union with the Known. However, he had come into the Lord's fold after repentance and purification. The truth had become manifest to him through a God-fearing monk by the name of Abba Moises. Thawna had become mentally deranged for a period of time for some reason of which I was not aware. However, the Abba had recited scripture and prayers over him and anointed him with Palestinian oil, and he was healed instantly. After recovering, he pledged himself to the cloistered life of a monk in the well-known Monastery of Abba Bakhoum. However, after he had lived there for some time, Father Joseph requested that he come to our church in Qasr al-Sham' in Old Cairo to depict the Virgin Mary and the saints in icons from which people could receive instruction and edification when they saw them on the church walls. Deacon Thawna had become well known for his icons and his mastery of the art of depicting the early saints and martyrs. It was also said that before he became deranged and entered the monastery, he had made his living drawing people's pictures on caskets, which they would put away and keep until the time of their deaths. Rumor had it that in return for his skilled labor, people would pay him in bread, cheese, wine, and grains that enabled him to live like a king in the town in Upper Egypt from which he had come to the church.

I loved Thawna because he had shown me so much compassion and because, even though I had never seen him laugh, his face bespoke kindness. After all, laughter is not compatible with the life of asceticism and piety inside the church. Thawna was sociable by nature and simple in his dealings, both with me and with others who, like me, were of lower rank than he. Add to this the fact that he was a man of vast knowledge and learning. He spoke the Coptic of Akhmim and good Arabic, as well as Bihayri Coptic like that spoken by the Copts of Alexandria and Maryut. However, he was not familiar with the Bashmourite dialect despite his knowledge of Greek, which he told me once that he had learned in school. Moreover, despite the fact that his virtue and good works were clear for all to see, and particularly in the area of medical treatment and the preparation of medicaments, there were some there in that holy place who kept trying to besmirch his reputation with rumors and lies. They had branded him at times as a sorcerer, and at other times as an atheist. They had begun circulating such notions in secret, yet without being able to produce any evidence in proof of their claims. As for me, of a truth I say that Thawna was a profoundly good man whose mouth had never uttered a dishonorable word, and who had taught me a great deal.

Our mutual affection was sealed from the time when he was working on an icon of Saint Kalta the wise physician, whose right hand grasps a rod with which he is pointing to his physician's chest. The lid of the chest stands open to reveal six compartments for ointments and medicines. I was helping him during this process and the two of us together had spread a cloth over the wood in order to prevent it from cracking. On top of this I spread a layer of gesso which I made thin and delicate as he had asked me to. After it had dried and was holding together properly, Thawna covered the gesso with a layer of gold which he had prepared by mixing Arab gum imported from the land of Yemen with a small amount of water, the yolk of a Sudanese duck's egg, and some fragrant embalming substances such as musk, scented powder, sandalwood, ambergris, and camphor for the blessing it would bring. It was through this that I realized Thawna's extraordinary method of drawing, which he told me was among the ancient methods passed down from one generation to another among Coptic artists. Its distinguishing mark, he said, was the placement of the colors of the dusts of known metals such as iron, copper, and zinc in their respective places in the pictures over the layer of the gold preparation that covers the entire surface. After the colors have been pulverized in granite mortars set aside specially for this purpose, the artist mixes each one with ritually pure seawater to the desired thickness. The frame will have been prepared beforehand, and the icon's features are chiseled out with an iron nail of the type made by the nomadic gypsies in the land. This, he said, was how the cross on the right side of the picture and the long golden shepherd's staff on the left side retained their gold color.

I maintain that Thawna was a man with good faith and abundant knowledge, whose mouth never uttered anything but the purest of speech. The reason I say this is that while we were producing these pictures, I asked him a number of questions that were on my mind, especially when I saw him drawing Saint Kalta in glowing health, with a beautiful, radiant face and clad in brightly colored, elegant clothing.

Releasing something I had long kept pent up inside, I said to him, "I want to ask you, dear Thawna, about a matter that has always preoccupied me: Once, in a church belonging to the heretical Melkites in a town near my village, Tarnit, I saw depictions of Hell that were filled with frightening demons and instruments of torture. In the same picture, the

Master appeared in a state of terrible weakness and emaciation. He had been crucified on His cross, blood was flowing from his body, and on His head was the crown of hideous thorns. As for his face, it overflowed with such pain and sorrow, I knelt under the picture and started to cry in pain and sorrow myself. So why is it that we Copts only draw the Virgin Mary and the Master, to Him be glory, with the most beautiful, joyous appearances? I do not think I have ever seen a depiction of Hell or demons on the walls of any of our own churches. Tell me, my dear Thawna, I beg you: Is this a matter of doctrine that separates our Jacobite Coptic Church from that of the Melkites?"

Without turning his head or looking up from the part of the saint's robe that he was painting blue, Thawna replied evenly, "No, Budayr. This has nothing to do with secondary doctrinal differences, as is the case with the Eucharist, for example. And no council has ever been convened to discuss the issue. As you may know, the Melkites cut the Host into a round shape when they celebrate the Mass over it. However, when Christ gave His immaculate body to His disciples on the night before His sufferings and crucifixion, He did not cut the loaf into round shapes. Rather, the Holy Gospel says that He took bread, blessed it, and broke it, then gave it to His disciples. It does not say that he took part of a loaf, then blessed it and gave it to them after it had been cut with a knife in the way they do. We have no right to do anything but emulate Him: Everything He did, we do likewise. As for the matter of pictures and whether they inspire dread and fear, or longing and desire, this has to do with individual differences among people and variations in tastes from one place to another, depending on how they were raised and the kind of treatment they have grown accustomed to. The purpose of depictions of the saints is to serve as a reminder and an exhortation to try to be like them. As for pictures of Christ—to Him be glory in the highest—and His mother, the Blessed Virgin, their purpose is to encourage people to preserve both of them in their hearts. The ppatriarchs of the church have adopted the practice of marking each of these pictures in several places with holy oil in order that, when people seek the intercession of Christ or the Virgin Mary by means of them, their petitions will be granted. And this is because the corporeal or concrete is only conversant with that which is likewise corporeal or concrete."

Then he continued, saying, "We depict the saints, as well as Christ and the Virgin Mary, in the manner which we believe to be the best and most beautiful in order to inspire people's hearts with longing for them and to fill them with faith. We also do this in order for the power of their faith to be manifested to people so that if people's faith grows weak or their beliefs are shaken under the force of time and its tribulations, their fortitude will be renewed and they will receive strength to endure patiently whatever it is they are suffering. Know of a certainty, Budayr, that the Melkite Chalcedonians depict the demons and the angels who thrust the damned into Hell in order to frighten people and fill them with dread of the afterlife, and in this way, to strengthen the hands of those who wish to tyrannize them in the name of the Lord. However, to us Jacobites, the possessors of the true religion, the afterlife is the source of bliss, and our depiction of the saints in a state of exaltation and glory at the time of their triumph is an expression of our belief that asceticism and piety are a path which we travel to a blessed, joyous end. For example, you see how Mar Girgis is always pictured mounted on his steed and crushing the infernal dragon with his lance. You may also have noticed that all the iconic depictions in our churches are lovely and gilded, highlighting the most sublime states of purity and happiness thanks to the loyalty of the righteous, the followers of Jesus."

Yet, despite all of this upright faith, abundant knowledge and goodness of heart, there were some who continued to dog brother Thawna relentlessly and watch his every move. Their ambition was to pin some charge on him that might lead to his destruction and expulsion from the Church, thenceforth to depart from the Lord's kingdom and the fold of the righteous and go back to being a sheep lost in the wilderness far from the flock. Knowing all these things, I entered his quarters with the greatest of caution lest anyone see me coming to visit him, then spread rumors that we were engaged in some sort of plot or accuse of us of Sodomite uncleanness and depravity.

Once I had assured myself that no one had seen me enter his room, I caught my faltering breath and whispered to him nervously, "Thawna, my dear one, why did you call for me, when it is already decided that I will be going out with you tomorrow morning to the marshlands as Father Joseph instructed us?"

Paona's full moon in its pristine, clear sky had graciously bestowed some of its light upon us through the room's narrow window, which Thawna had opened to let in some air. We were in the final months of spring, and the hot breezes had announced the impending arrival of the searing summer months. Thanks to the gift of moonlight I was able to make out one side of his face.

Looking careworn, he said, "I called for you in order to tell you to take precautions. Our journey tomorrow to the Bashmourites' territory is not going to be easy, Budayr. The marshlands that we will be crossing will soon be inundated by floodwaters, which will make movement difficult. We might encounter things we had not been expecting, not to mention the war that is raging there between the governor's soldiers and the people of the land. The government's forces are defeated whenever they make a foray against those peasants, and no one knows what might happen. I suspect that Father Joseph is going to send me with a letter to deliver to the Bashmourites' leader, since he told me before his meeting with the clerics that he was going to employ me as his messenger in connection with some important matter today. I have also heard that two days ago, he went to meet with the caliph's governor in Fustat based on the latter's request. The governor may have asked the Father to act as an intermediary with the Bashmourites again in an attempt to persuade them to retreat from their position and pay the kharaj. They've chosen me in particular for this mission because its outcome is so uncertain, and consequently, it may represent an auspicious opportunity for some of them who would like to get rid of me. As you know, they have insisted ever since I came here that I remain in the lowest ranks of deaconhood despite my earnest service. As for you, they would never find anyone more knowledgeable of the Bashmourite tongue, which is your tongue by birth, or the paths leading through the marshlands. This is why they want you to accompany me and be my spokesman with the Bashmourite leader when necessary."

I was aware that Thawna had met with a great deal of disapproval in the church, and that if he had been wealthy and influential like the Deacon Serapion, who donated his money to the church from time to time, he would have risen quickly through the ecclesiastical ranks and become an archdeacon with authority over all of the deacons and acolytes, and with the right to carry the patriarchal staff. However, in spite of his long years in the church, his vast knowledge, and the piety that was instantly recognizable to anyone with eyes to see and a heart to perceive, he had yet to be promoted to a higher clerical rank. Even so, he patiently endured, remaining steadfast in prayer, fasting, recitation, celebrating Mass, reading, and going deep into matters of theology. Evidence of his scholarly endeavors could be seen in the papyrus scrolls and gazelle-skin parchments written in the Akhminite, Arabic, and Greek languages that filled his room. Thawna never wearied of fasting every Wednesday and Friday as was customary among monks. And in keeping with his rank, he carried the chalice containing the Eucharistic wine that, through consecration, had been transformed into the blood of Christ, as well as the spoon for distributing the precious blood to the people of God. It was also he who would do the Gospel reading from the pulpit if it had not been read by the priest. However, he would say Byaoticon rather than Keeyaoticon, the latter of which was the sole prerogative of the priest, since it is only the priest, not the deacons, who can convey blessing to the people.

Thawna took his pastoral role with great seriousness as it related to visiting the sick, orphans, widows, and those in prison, and in order to do so, he would even cross the Nile when it was at its highest point during the flood season. In the month of Misra, with the sun beating down mercilessly, he would go out on a small boat to Giza to visit the errant inmates at the Yusef Prison despite the danger posed by the floodwaters at that time, and once there, he would console them and distribute gifts and blessings. On one of these visits he encountered a group of people, among them women, who had been arrested for celebrating pagan rites in an ancient temple located some distance out into the Heliopolis desert. The state guards had seized them and taken them to the prison on charges of sorcery, making talismans, and working with chemistry and alchemy, and the prison warden had been torturing them and making life generally unbearable for them in the belief that they had brought money and gold out of the temple with them. In any case, when he realized he was not going to get anything out of them, he left them without water or food until they were about to perish. However, it so happened that during the time when these events were taking place, Deacon Thawna was on one of his visits to the prison as was his custom on the Day of Pentecost. So he fed them and gave them to drink of what he had brought with him for the prisoners, as a result of which they were restored to health and repented of what they had done. Then he paid the prison warden some money and delivered them from his clutches. One group of them he sent on their way and another group he brought back to the church, where he put them to work. Some of them went to work on the olive oil presses and others in the numerous orchards nearby that belonged to the church. Hence, they not only survived—they thrived—and blessing came to our church thanks to the good deed that had been done by that God-fearing deacon, Thawna.

I began looking at him intently, trying to discern in the moonlight what lay behind his kindly features, which looked as though they had been clothed in a kind of pristine luminosity and tranquility born of faith. Then suddenly I began imagining some harm befalling him along the way, and it was as though my heart had been placed in a vice. For I loved and revered him; nay, more than that, there were times when I saw him as my only refuge, especially when I was overwhelmed by grief and remorse over the godless life I had lived before. My pain would be so unbearable that I would weep bitter tears, preferring death to life, especially when I thought back on my family and others and the things I had experienced with them.

I made the sign of the Cross of Mercies. Then, wanting to set his mind at rest, I said, "Why do you assume that we are going to perish on the way, Thawna? And why do you say that they want to be rid of you? I know the marshland paths well. After all, I was born there and lived there all the years of my life before I came here. And now you and I are brothers in baptism, which means that everyone we encounter along the way will see us wearing clerical robes. As a result, they will not try to stop us or do us harm. The Muslim governor in Fustat will surely have given instructions to his guards not to prevent us from passing, but instead to offer us assistance as long as we are on a mission that concerns Father Joseph. Would you not agree with me, dear Thawna? And do not forget that we will be carrying no money or gold, so no one will be suspicious of us and we will not be in danger of being attacked by thieves or highway robbers. As for the

Bashmourites, they are Copts just as we are, and none of them would harm us. At the very worst, my dear friend, if they do not believe us, we can roll up our sleeves and show them the tattoo of the lion on our forearms, and they will be reassured that we are no different than they are."

In the dim light I thought I saw Thawna's lips part in a cynical, apprehensive smile at the mention of the tattoo. He remained silent and said nothing for some time. Finally, however, he heaved a bitter sigh and said, "The issue is not the perils of the journey, Budayr. Those we can deal with. Rather, the problem is with the Bashmourites themselves. You know that since the time when prices started to rise in these parts, they have gone so far along their chosen path that it would be hard for them to turn back. And you know that the rising prices are still causing people to suffer. The price of wheat recently reached five whibas for a dinar, and untold numbers of women, children, infants, elderly, and youths have died of hunger. The kharaj collector is still harassing people everywhere, and most of the Bashmourites were being tormented so mercilessly that they sold their children in return for being relieved of the tax. They would be tied to mills and beaten to a pulp like so many animals. The one who was persecuting them was a man by the name of Ghayth, and when they could bear it no longer they gave up the ghost. So when the Bashmourites saw that they had no way of escape, that no military force could pass through their land due to its many sloughs, marshes, and quicksand, and that no one but they knew its highways and byways, they began dissembling, refusing to pay the kharaj, and scheming and colluding in their defiance."

Thawna went on, saying, "The country's caliph-appointed ruler sent his military forces against them, attacking them suddenly and killing the innocent as though they were criminals, and it finally got so bad that as soon as he laid eyes on any of them he would strike him dead. He also killed a group of Christian leaders in every location he reached. Hence, the Bashmourites carried out their scheme, making arms for themselves, waging war on the sultan and thereby protecting themselves from having to pay the kharaj. If anyone approached them in an attempt to mediate between them and the state, they would rise up and kill him. After all, things had come to the point where they no longer recognized any authority, nor did they fear anyone. When Father Joseph became aware of the situation, he was grieved for these weak and oppressed people who had no way of standing up to the sultan. He could see that by choosing the path of resistance, they had, in effect, chosen destruction for themselves. Hence, out of his concern to deliver his faithful people through the truth, he began sending messengers to them and reminding them of what would befall them if they failed to repent of their ways and retreat from the path of resistance to the ruling authority. They have yet to retreat despite the fact that Father Joseph and his messengers have told them—as the Apostle Paul once declared, 'He who resists the authorities resists what God has appointed, and those who resist will incur judgment.' And now he is sending me to them with yet another letter! Perhaps you are aware that they have abused and beaten the messengers who went before us. They nearly murdered the Bishop of Asanta when our Father sent him to them and, in fact, they have assaulted messengers and plundered everything they had with them, after which the messengers came back to our Father and reported what had happened to them. You do not realize what hunger can do to a man: it can turn him from a human being into a beast. Our Father is greatly angered over this, and has said that if they do not come to their senses and turn back from what they are doing, destruction will not be far behind. Indeed, it will be unto them as the Prophet Isaiah declared: 'I will destine you to the sword, and all of you shall bow down to the slaughter; because when I called you did not answer. When I spoke, you did not listen, but you did what was evil in my eyes. . . .'

"Because of these woes and tribulations, Father Joseph was not able to write the synodical letter he had intended to write to his partner in ministry and faith, the Patriarch of Antioch. He has been more concerned about this than the trials he himself has gone through, and he has not been at ease for a single day. He is saddened and afraid for these powerless unfortunates who do not realize the consequences of their actions. Consequently, when he heard that the governor would no longer brook the Bashmourites' stubbornness and insubordination, that they were still unwilling to back down from their position, and that the governor had written to the caliph in Baghdad to inform him of what had happened, Father Joseph realized that a major catastrophe was in the offing. After all, if the caliph comes personally, he will have no mercy on them, and he will not withdraw from the battle until he has finished them off to the last man. This is why our Father is sending us to them tomorrow with a letter of warning, calling upon them once again to obey the authorities and pay the kharaj. But the problem, Budayr, is that the Bashmourites might behave foolishly toward us. They are so full of rage and distress, they might murder us, and if they do that, those who do not want me here in the church will have fulfilled their most cherished ambition."

Listening to Thawna's words with rapt attention, I did not move a muscle. He continued, "In fact, Budayr, to my knowledge, the Bash-mourites do not believe what Father Joseph says. They think that all he cares about is keeping the churches safe and protecting their property. This is what they have said openly to all the messengers our Father has sent to them thus far. What makes the situation even more dangerous is that many of the Arab tribes have begun revolting in the country's western regions, and some of them have begun join-ing the Bashmourites in the area known as Asfal al-Ard. You may have heard what happened to the Arabs. Some tribes of al-Qaysiya and al-Yamaniya have risen up just as the Copts have and refused to pay the kharaj. These people came to Egypt along with other Arab tribes, then began working in agriculture and settled on our lands. As a consequence, the kharaj is imposed on them just as it is on the Coptic farmers. So when the kharaj collector became more and more unreasonable to the point where they could no longer tolerate it, they all rose up together, and the emir of the land was obliged to send an army out against them. The army encamped in the area of Belbeis and fought them there after those in Asfal al-Ard had risen up. I have heard them talking here about how the Muslim caliph is up in arms over the situation and furious with the emir of the land on account of these events. He has even threatened to make him wear white as a punishment and to rescind his governing authority over the province assigned to him, since he took no precautionary measures and thereby caused this whole revolt. It is said that in his reply to the emir's letter, the caliph stated:

None of these grave developments would have transpired were it not for your own actions and those of your subordinates. You authorized them to impose on people more than they could bear, then kept the news from me until things had raged out of control and the entire country was in turmoil!

There are reports to the effect that the caliph has decided to put an end to all of this himself. In fact, some say that he has left Baghdad and is marching his army all the way to Egypt to find out exactly what is going on, put a halt to the rebellion, and pursue anyone who has been identified as an agitator even if it means that large numbers of people have to die, especially in view of the fact that he has announced far and wide that he will only collect the kharaj in the most equitable manner. What this means is that the kharaj will under no circumstances come to more than 4,257,000 dinars."

Having said this, Thawna jumped up suddenly and opened a small door in the wall of his room. Quietly and cautiously, he rummaged about inside it without making the slightest noise that might be heard from outside. When he returned, I saw him holding a small dagger whose blade glistened in the moonlight. He presented it to me, then said breathlessly, "Take this and hide it quickly under your clothes. Keep it with you when we depart early tomorrow morning and make absolutely sure that no one sees it."

I took the dagger from him with a trembling hand, then sat pondering it for a few moments in the celestial light that was filtering into the room. It was short, solid, and slightly crooked at the end like the San'ani variety the Muslims were often seen carrying. Agitated, I thrust it quickly under my clerical belt and inside my clothes, then placed my hand on it. I suddenly felt out of breath, as I imagined that I had heard the swishing of a robe and the footfall of someone clad in light sandals in the corridor outside the room. Thawna and I fell silent, then he went and peeked out the door into the corridor. When he was certain that no one was there, he came back and whispered, "Listen, Budayr. If you have any possessions that are precious to you, bring them with you. The journey will be a perilous one, and we need to be ready for the unexpected."

Feeling uncertain, I said, "Danger is everywhere now, Thawna. Everything is in turmoil, and nobody knows his head from his feet anymore. Things that just yesterday you could see with your eyes and touch with your hands seem not even to exist anymore, or maybe their features have just changed so much that it is hard to recognize them. May the Lord have mercy on us, dear Thawna."

Responding hurriedly as though my words had touched an inner wound and compelled him to release something buried deep inside him, he said, "That is right, Budayr. These are difficult times. Everything is in a state of warfare and strife. The Bashmourites have escalated their mutiny, and they send the governor's forces away in defeat time after time. Meanwhile, the Arabs fight among themselves, and even our church is vulnerable to internal conflicts. The Byzantines, followers of the Chalcedonian sacrilege, constantly speak ill of our church and pay bribes to the Muslim governor in the hope that he will hand our churches over to them so that they can seize their property and gain the upper hand over all followers of religion in the entire land. At the same time, paganism continues to run rampant. This is especially the case in areas far from the city. I have heard repeatedly that there are those who still hold pagan temples as sacred. In some districts there are still Magians who worship fire, and who have remained in various countries since the time when the Persians arrived. As for the people of Nubia in the Sudan, I've been told by knowledgeable people who have been to their territory that among them are people who acknowledge the Creator, glory be to Him, and draw near to Him through the sun, the moon, and the stars, while others do not know the Creator and worship only the sun and fire. Still others, they say, worship any tree or beast they find good.

"You are also aware, my dear, of the state of our church as it relates to the followers of the Arian heresy, as well as those in the Melkite churches who adhere to the Chalcedonian blasphemy and who strive against us and against the true faith, doing their utmost to bring our church down before the rulers and authorities. Truly, if it were not for the bit of faith I have to protect me, I might be totally confused and helpless. Even as it is, I am tossed this way and that by passions and scattered by the thoughts of my heart, with a raging, stormy sea within."

"Yes, indeed, my dear Thawna," I murmured with a sigh as I prepared to depart. "May the Lord have mercy on us and protect us from these difficult days and the unknown days to come."

Now at the door, I bid him goodnight, and as I was walking down the corridor on tiptoe again lest anyone hear me, I seemed to hear the rustling of a robe again and irregular breathing in the place's pitch-black darkness. Trembling, I crossed myself as I thought back on Thawna's words, "I am tossed this way and that by passions and scattered by the thoughts of my heart, with a raging, stormy sea within."

I spent that night anxious and wakeful, worried about the morrow's journey to the marshlands. The source of my fear and apprehension was the return to my village, Tarnit, the place of my birth and childhood, after having left it as a fugitive. So great was my sorrow and distress over the state of the world, I had gone out wandering aimlessly, leaving my father, my mother, and my entire family behind. This was after my father in the flesh had sought to marry my older brother to that beautiful one whom my heart had always adored, and the taste of whose enthralling, passionate affection had never left me. He knew nothing of what had transpired between us or even of my desire for her. Hence, when the beloved—whose name was Amuna—destroyed herself by hurling herself into the vast, murky salt marsh, allowing it to pull her under until she disappeared beneath its liquid mire, I lived for some time in agony over her loss. Little by little, despair consumed my spirit until it had consigned me to perdition. I was a teenager at the time, seventeen years old, and I began telling myself that this life is useless and without meaning, that it is a lie, devoid of certainty or security. No sooner has it shown us a happy face than it turns again to reveal a face of the most abject misery. This is what I used to say as I thought back on all the sweet times we had spent together, especially before life had taken us by surprise with events for which we had no desire.

We had been meeting for long months before my father asked Amuna's family for her hand in marriage to my brother. And never in my life will I forget my last tryst with that precious beloved before we heard the grievous news. We had been working together in my father's taro field, since Amuna and her family all used to work on lands owned by my father, who was among the more well-to-do farmers. I did not

23

take my eyes off her for a second as she bent over to gather grass and clean the field. I could not distinguish between the color of her lovely rosy cheeks and the color of the taro blossoms scattered here and there. My feelings in an uproar and wanting her so badly I could not contain myself, I came up and whispered to her, "Amuna. My darling Amuna. Let us get far away from here, quickly. I want to be with you right now. I will leave first, then you follow me so no one will notice."

It was around noon, and the humidity had risen to the point where people's bodies were clammy. When she met me inside the enclosure where we used to meet far from other people's glances, I pulled her toward me and began kissing her over and over until she began to laugh at me, saying, "You are kissing me as though you were doing it for the first time, or as though you were never going to do it again. Have you gone crazy today?" Then she laughed again, and I said to her, "Aaaah, yes, I have gone crazy," whereupon I proceeded to kiss her madly on every part of her body my lips could reach. Meanwhile, my hands began gradually removing the dress from that succulent dahlia. When the fire of my longing spread to her, igniting her own longing with a blaze even fiercer, we fused until our live coals had burned down to ashes. We stayed where we were, motionless, not a sound around us but the whispering of a sparrow in the distance and the throbbing of our two young hearts.

Then we pledged to belong to each other forever, for better or for worse. This was the pledge we took upon ourselves every time we met, and our agreement was that I would approach my mother about the subject of our marrying, so that she could speak to my father on my behalf and ask for his blessing on our union. However, I had sensed for a long time that my mother preferred my older brother to me and that she bore him a special affection. And in fact—may the Lord forgive her—it was not long before she had chosen Amuna to be my brother's wife and had approached my father about the matter. Amuna's appearance was so striking, it would not have been lost on anyone who had an eye for beauty and who perceived the Creator's signs in human beings. Even so, when I learned of it, I could not believe my ears. I felt as though a huge comet had sent its infernal flames against me and struck me down as with lightning. For days I was bedridden with a fever, yet for no identifiable reason. My body had nearly expired, and my spirit was about to make its exit. In fact, my father got my coffin ready with everything needed for my funeral. He removed the coffin's wooden lid, which bore a picture of my face looking its most radiant and framed by my luxuriant black hair. Then he placed it beside my bed as my mother instructed the hired mourners to be ready to come the minute they heard the news of my passing, at which time they were to bring indigo with which to spatter their loosened tresses. My mother had begun mourning my death from the time the last doctor brought in by my father left my room saying, "There is no hope." The fever had gone so high that my heart would not be able to bear it much longer, and none of the drinks I took or the herbs I swallowed had yielded the hoped-for results. Our priest did not leave my side from that time onward out of respect and appreciation for my father, who had been very generous toward the church, especially in view of some furniture he had donated, including a stand for the Holy Gospel that was decorated with exquisite shapes and designs inlaid with ivory and which included a slanted holder where the Bible could be placed. It was adorned with crosses on all sides, and the open shelf under it held the offering trays, the cymbals, the triangles, and the little bells that were rung with small rods. My father—who was a wealthy man—had also presented the church with a portable, dragon-shaped candelabrum. A candle had been mounted on it to be lit in front of the church door during the three final days of Holy Week, and a dragon-like snake held the candle in its mouth.

However, God willed what He willed, and three days later I recovered from the fever. When I thought about how ill I had been and what a close brush I had had with death and perdition, I praised God for where I had come and made up my mind to accept my lot. I would relinquish Amuna to my brother, endure the will of the Lord with patience, and keep the matter to myself out of respect for my older brother and my father's choice. I promised myself that Amuna would be my first love and my last romance, and that I would never touch another woman as long as I lived. And in fact, my heart has never been smitten by another as it was by that precious girl. Once she became my brother's wife, I said, let her be a dear sister to me. However, after what happened, and after she threw herself into the miry salt marsh to perish for all time,

I lost all control over myself, and the world became as nothing in my eyes. Having come to loathe life and this earthly existence, I left my village to wander in the wilderness, where I roamed about aimlessly without food or drink, lost to myself like one gone mad. I would look upon beasts of prey without batting an eyelid. In fact, I used to pray to Heaven that one of them would hunt me down, or that some monster would slay me. However, God wills what He wills. And I kept on walking until I lost consciousness and was on the verge of death and perdition. It was then that I was happened upon by some people from the church at Qasr al-Sham', among them Thawna, who had come out to gather herbs for his medical treatments and painting. He took me with him back to the church and treated me, and when I regained consciousness I thanked the Lord for His perfect blessings to me and dedicated myself to the service of the church, where I had remained from then on.

There was nothing I feared more than going back to the marshlands once again. I dreaded the thought of meeting up with someone from my family, especially my father and mother, since I was sure they must have discovered my affair with Amuna after her death and my sudden flight from the village. Besides which, it would be difficult for me to go back to the place that held such painful memories for me. I thought to myself: What a terrible thing it would be if Satan got the better of me and I began weeping and wailing over my departed beloved and my long-gone earlier life.

Many were the tears I shed as I sat in my room watching the dawn break over the black horizon. The sky had clouded over that night in a way that was unusual for the hot month of Paona, and the moon had disappeared from view. The river was calm and motionless, with nothing audible but the sounds of creatures that generally remained concealed in its depths but which liked to come up to its surface in the latter watches of the night. I started to imagine what it would be like to be seen by some of my former classmates in the village school. They would be sure to stare at me, condemn me for my affair with Amuna, and describe me as an evil omen, especially given the fact that the calamity took place at the time when Amuna was to marry my dear brother. Like my family and everyone else in the village, these cohorts of mine had been ecstatic with joy as they marched down the street in two large, separate processions, the bride in one procession and the groom in another. We had been singing and dancing to the tunes being played by the musicians that I had brought in. I had been told by a friend from the city of Aksir Nakhusi that they were some of the best and most famous players in the country. The contract for the musicians to play at my brother's wedding was still in my pocket when I left home, and I still kept it among my meager possessions in my quarters at the church. It was the only token I had left from my old world in Tarnit, so whenever nostalgic longing would well up inside me and I felt homesick for my family and friends, I would get it out and look at it, sighing over what I had lost, and still missed, from the life I had once known.

As I sat there, I began thinking back on that contract and how, as we were finalizing the agreement, I had started bargaining with the leader, Orleus Onferis, to get him to bring down the fee. I kept after him until he agreed to eighty loaves of fenugreek bread, nine jars of wine, and four half silver pieces for each of the musicians with him—Tassius, Afungans ibn Heracles, Kubrus, and Arsinawi. I had hired the musicians as a wedding gift for my brother despite my sorrow and anguish over the fact that, in keeping with the wishes of my father in the flesh, he was going to marry the one girl my spirit loved and for whom my soul longed. I did not dare utter the word, "No!" or object to what he saw as best, nor did I reveal the love in my heart for Amuna. After all, a father is a father, and a brother is a brother, and a father's word must be obeyed to the letter. So, suppressing my grief, I began dancing with those who danced and singing with those who sang, and we paraded down the streets escorting my brother's procession to the door of the church, where it was to meet the bride's procession. Following this we were all to come in and conclude the wedding ceremony in accordance with the will of the Lord and His ordinances.

We celebrated rapturously, singing heartily along with Orleus Onferis and his melodious, heart-rending voice. However, the closer we came to the moment of our entry into the church, at which time the bride and groom would be joined in eternal, holy matrimony, the more miserable I felt. My tears began to flow, and I found myself wishing that something would happen to prevent it because, in spite of myself—may God forgive me—I could not imagine Amuna as anyone else's wife. However, everyone who saw me at the time assumed I was weeping from joy and excitement. When we reached the door of the church we were received by the acolytes who, with the priests, were carrying candles and bells and chanting, "Blessed is he who comes in the name of the Lord." Our procession, which was the groom's procession, had arrived at the church first as wedding custom requires. Then the acolytes led my brother to the front row, chanting all the way. They continued chanting for some time as they waited for the bride to arrive and be received at the door, at which time they would begin repeating the tune, "Hail Mary!" and lead the bride to her place in the women's section. All the clergymen were decked out in beautiful white vestments, and all the ritual objects needed for the wedding were ready and waiting on the front row: a golden cross, the gold ring, the belt, and the incense on the silver platter. And, also in keeping with established custom, my brother had presented the Patriarch with an 'abaya as an offering on the occasion of his wedding.

When everyone had been waiting for a long time and the acolytes had grown weary of repeating the tunes, those present began to feel uneasy over the bride's tardy arrival. Amid a crescendo of whispers, people began craning their necks in the direction of the church door in hopes of catching a glimpse of the delayed bride and her procession. A few moments later, a black crow glided in through the top of the church door. It seemed strange for it to be flying in at a moment such as this, so people took it as an evil portent, and the sexton rushed over to shoo it out. This was soon followed by the sound of screaming and wailing, and everyone rushed to see what the matter was. One of those screaming said that the lovely bride Amuna had taken her family unawares and thrown herself into the huge salt marsh just outside the village.

When I heard it, I was beside myself. I felt as though a ghastly dragon like the one that the saint and martyr Mar Girgis once fought was crouching on top of my chest, and I could hardly breathe. I tried to gulp down some air by opening my mouth as wide as I could, but to no avail, and soon I was helpless, like someone who has no say in his own fate, and I was sure I was about to give up the ghost. My body shaking, I screamed with those who were screaming and rushed with those who were rushing out to the ill-fated, miry bog. By the time we arrived they had extricated her body, and we found the precious beloved lying next to the waters. When I looked at her—now nothing but a lifeless corpse laid out on the ground—I was beside myself again. I shrieked from the depths of my being, then collapsed at her feet in tears as I looked upon her beauty. Someone had removed the mud from her face and neck in search of some sign of life or breath in her, and she looked even more lovely than I had imagined her to be, with her thick black braids cascading onto her fair neck. Everyone wept just as I had when they saw her, and there was much wailing and beating of breasts. My older brother remained at her head, mourning and wailing, while I did the same at her feet till we had run out of tears. Then people began leading us away from her—we who, in our helpless desperation, could do nothing for ourselves.

All these events were swirling about in my imagination as I sat there in my secluded habitation, thinking about our imminent departure for the marshlands. In alarm I wondered: How will I be able to face what I am afraid to face, and which I have been running from for years? What will become of me if one of the people who were with us at the wedding recognizes me? I began to cry, wishing God would take my spirit before I had to endure such a thing, and wishing I never had to go back to Tarnit. I was compelled to go out of reverence for Father Joseph, my spiritual father in the church, obedience to whom was a duty. Even so, I had never confessed to him the sin I had committed with my precious beloved Amuna. Rather, whenever I went for communion and confession, I would take care to tell him that I had left my village after stealing some jars of honey from a neighbor of ours since, when I was discovered, I was afraid of a scandal and ashamed to face my father. Thus it was that I lied every time I confessed to this kind-hearted father, not daring to divulge my sin and tragedy in Tarnit. There had been one occasion when I sensed that he suspected me of not telling him the truth. "Are these really all your sins?" he asked. "Is it only on account of having stolen a few jars of honey that you abandoned your family and friends and are still afraid to go home? Did you murder someone? Did you commit fornication?" But when I began stammering and bowed my head, overwhelmed with pain and remorse, he would look at me with tenderness and compassion, then recite the words of the Lord, "Let not your hearts be troubled; believe in God, believe also in Me. In my Father's house are many rooms. If it were not so, would I have told you that I go to prepare a place for you? And when I go and prepare a place for you, I will come again to take you to myself, that where I am, you may be also. And you know the way where I am going."

I wept when I heard these words.

"No, Father," I said, "I did not murder anyone. But I did steal. I took what did not belong to me, and I will regret it as long as I live. And now I believe that the honey of the Lord is sweeter and more to be desired than the honey of life. So I ask you to bless me, Reverend Father, and may the Lord receive me in His abundant mercy."

And thus it was that I never had the courage to confess to the truth. Yet may the All-Forgiving One grant me pardon, and enfold me in His benevolence and bounty!

The next day at dawn, Thawna and I left Qasr al-Sham' at the Babylon Fortress immediately after the matins, which is the first of the seven daily prayers in the Coptic Church. We had prepared ourselves for departure before the prayers, and had donned our yellow robes. All the clergy came out to see us off at the last gate, which leads to Fustat. The first one to say his farewells was kind-hearted Father Joseph, who consecrated us for the journey with his staff, the symbol of baptism. After kissing the Father's blessed hand, we took leave of them all as tears filled both our eyes and theirs. However, as an expression of courtesy and respect, we did not get on our mounts until after they had shut the gate behind us. Our mounts were a couple of good young mules out of a total of three that had been brought once to the church by a believing man known as Seramits from the city of Lycopolis, who had offered them as a gift to Father Joseph after he healed a son of his. The boy had been afflicted with an illness that persisted and continued to get worse, so the man had brought him to the church for Father Joseph to administer last rites to him. However, Father Joseph gave the boy some medicine and anointed him with Palestinian oil, then recited sacred texts over him, whereupon he recovered immediately and stood on his feet.

Based on a law imposed by the Muslim governors since the time they had taken over the Church of Old Cairo and Qasr al-Sham' during the time of the blasphemous Chalcedonian heresy and the rule of Qayrus, also known as Muqawqis, Copts were not allowed to ride horses. Hence, Thawna and I went out on the two mules, carrying with us provisions of salted fish, oil, cornbread, and cakes, as well as some dates and a jug of wine. We passed through Fustat on our way out toward the orchards beyond it—Fustat being the city built by the Muslims after they seized Fort Babylon. As we were passing through the city, Thawna told me that he had read in some books that the Islamic state had begun with the transition from the air triad, which is the sign of Gemini, to the sign of Cancer and its water triad. Hence, he said, when exactly 6,345 years, three months, and twenty days had passed since the time of the first conjunction, which occurred in the beginning of movement (that is, the creation of Adam, upon him be peace), the Islamic state had come into existence, and within this triad, there occurred a conjunction associated with the Islamic religion at four degrees, one minute from the sign of Scorpio.

He also told me that he had read in the same book that the migration of the Muslims' Prophet had begun on a Thursday in the beginning of their month known as Muharram, which is the beginning of their history, and that between this and the flood that took place in the days of Noah there are 3,735 years, ten months, and twenty-two days.

I had never seen Fustat from the inside before, and I was awed by its many neighborhoods and the height of its dwellings, which were unadorned and rose to four and five stories. Thawna informed me as we passed through it that some of the houses we were seeing were inhabited by as many as two hundred people, bearing in mind that the ground floor was rarely inhabited by anyone. It was said that when Fustat was first built, a certain Muslim man by the name of Kharija ibn Hudhafa, who had been appointed as a representative of the Muslim commander 'Amr ibn al-'As, had built an attic room with a latticework enclosure, and that when news of this had reached the caliph, 'Umar ibn al-Khattab, he wrote to 'Amr ibn al-'As telling him that Kharija had only done this in order to spy on those around him and steal glances at their private parts, and commanding him to have the room razed immediately.

Moving through the city without anyone accosting or stopping us, we came to its public bath, known as the Farr Bath, which was small and unassuming by comparison with the ancient Roman baths. Thawna told me that the early Muslims had been pious and God-fearing and had preferred lives of asceticism and self-denial. He also told me that the city of Fustat had been built when Fort Babylon, which the Muslims had taken over when they first entered Egypt, could no longer accommodate all its inhabitants. The Muslim commander 'Amr had decided that it would not be fair to expel the native Copts from their homes around the fortress in order for the Muslims to displace them. Consequently, he left them where they were and built Fustat, which soon grew to be a major city and a governmental center in place of Alexandria.

We left Fustat behind along with most of the orchards that still belonged to the church and which, as Thawna had told me, had extended as far as the bank of the Nile before what was known as the Ahl al-Raya Mosque was built. We proceeded alongside the Habash Pond toward the river's edge in order to go down to Shubra, and from there to the areas that led to the marshlands. My eyes were glued to the place the entire way, awed as I was by the splendor of this huge pond in which the beauty of the Creator was manifested so clearly. Growing around it were lush shade trees of every shape and kind, some of which were crowned with blue, violet, and red blossoms in a way I had never seen before. I saw birds floating through its waters in a way that was distinct from what I had seen among the geese and ducks in Bashmourite territory. These birds' song—together with that of the birds in the trees—was exquisitely delightful, so heavenly, it took my heart captive.

Appearing to have noticed my enthrallment and my tardiness in urging the mule along, Thawna said, "We have to get past this place quickly. It will not do for us to stay here long, since around this pond there live people given to diversion and indecency, and we might even come upon a highway robber here or there. Besides, we have to be out of Fustat by sundown. Even so, we will stop for a while in the Shubra gardens to eat and catch our breath. Then we can continue on our way, enter the city of Atrib before dark and spend the night in its monastery. If we entered after dark, we might be waylaid by highway robbers or bands of hungry thieves that come out onto the roads from time to time in search of something to eat however they can come upon it."

Before we took leave of the lake and its magical landscape, Thawna sighed as he drank in its magnificent scenery with his eyes, then added, "Curses on the philosophers and rationalists. What a 'knower' is he who defines the already defined!"

I made no comment, since I had not understood what he meant, and we moved on at a good clip until we were about to enter the Shubra gardens, whereupon we saw some Muslim soldiers on horseback heading rapidly our way. As soon as we caught sight of them we got down off our mules, and they appeared to be God-fearing men, since they also dismounted out of courtesy and respect when they saw our clerical garb. They said some things to us, but I had not learned their language as I ought to have, so I only understood some of what they said. Meanwhile, Thawna hailed them and told them in their written language—which I was able to read and understand, "We are traveling under orders from our Father Joseph, head of the Church of the Virgin Mary at Qasr al-Sham', on a special mission to the marshlands."

As soon as Thawna uttered the word, "the marshlands," an angry look came over the face of their leader, who seemed to have become suspicious of us.

Thawna quickly added in clarification, "We have a letter from the administrator of Fustat to the effect that none of you should hinder us, since we are on a mission of concern to the governor."

Thereupon he reached into his saddlebag and produced a papyrus scroll which he handed to the military commander. When the latter opened it, it became apparent that it was written in both Arabic and Coptic, and he began reading it carefully. After he had checked to make certain that the seal was that of the emir in governance over us, he folded it up and returned it politely to Thawna, saying, "You must depart without delay, since some of the common folk have been agitating in Minyat al-Sirg, and I fear you may encounter some difficulties if they attack you on the way. Most of them are vagabonds and riffraff with no food or means of subsistence."

He then instructed two of his soldiers to escort us as far as the Shubra gardens. Upon our arrival at the gardens, we thanked the soldiers and bade them farewell as Thawna gave them some cakes and some high-quality Sakkuti dates which we had brought with us from the church, and which were the fruits of several old date palms that may well have been planted long before the church came into existence. Then we went into the gardens, which looked enormous and majestic to me with all their trees and varied greenery. One would have thought there was not a variety of plant or tree in the entire world that had not been planted on their soil. The Christ's thorn trees, the sycamores, the sant trees, the acacias, the blue gums, and the mulberry trees seemed even grander and huger than normal, since the waters that seeped from the river into the earth around them were rich and abundant, never leaving the trees in need of a drink, not to mention the plenteous amounts of alluvial mud which were brought in at the times of the Nile's rising.

Thawna, rich in knowledge, began mentioning to me the names of some trees that I had never seen before. Among them were the doom palm, the only part of which I had encountered before was its fruit, and which used to be brought to our Bashmourite territories by poor itinerant Sudanese who would sell them to us in the streets. The gardens extended all the way down to the edge of the Nile, where willow trees hung out over the bank with their tress-like branches and mingled with the waters of the river. The gardens were so full of people that we had to search for an empty spot under a tree where we could sit in the shade and have some of the food and drink we had brought. At last we found a lush, leafy mulberry tree, lay down on the orchard grass beneath it, prayed and gave thanks, then began to eat. As we were imbibing in some of our provisions, I asked Thawna a question that had been on my mind the whole way.

"Thawna dear," I said, "Perhaps you think that the Bashmourites will accept what our Father has to say and stop fighting the emir."

Thawna looked over at me briefly as he ate, not seeming to want me to bring up such a matter. For a few moments he hesitated to speak. However, he was about to say something when a woman approached us with two containers of syrup and some pancakes. As she presented them to us, she addressed Thawna, saying, "Would His Grace be so kind as to accept this small gift, and bless my children?"

She then pointed to a chufa tree where three young children were running and playing. When he gestured to her his agreement, she went and brought the children, all of whom were handsome little boys bursting with innocence. Thereupon Thawna blessed them, made the sign of the cross over them and recited verses of Scripture and prayers to protect them from harm, saying,

> For this reason I bow my knees before the Father, from whom every family in heaven and on earth is named, that according to the riches of His glory He may grant you to be strengthened with might through His Spirit in the inner man, and that Christ may dwell in your hearts through faith; that you, being rooted and grounded in love, may have power to comprehend with all the saints what is the breadth and length and height and depth, and to know the love of Christ which surpasses knowledge, that you may be filled with all the fullness of God. Now to Him who by the power at work within us is able to do far more abundantly than all that we ask or think, to Him be glory in the church and in Christ Jesus to all generations, for ever and ever. Amen.

After Thawna had finished blessing the children and reciting over them, he looked intently at the middle child, then inspected the pupils of his eyes. He did the same to his mouth after opening it with his hand. As he examined the boy's gums, he noticed that they were pale, with no sign of the redness of blood in them. The same thing was true of his pupils. Sensing the difficulty of the situation, Thawna asked the woman, "Does this boy eat a lot?"

"Oh, my, yes!" she exclaimed, "He eats more than both of his brothers combined, Reverend Sir. But I wish you would bless the younger one. He's afflicted with a demonic malady that has nearly been the death of me, too. I have done everything I know of to treat it, but to no avail. I have given up hope of his ever being healed."

She then lifted the boy's robe and part of the rough linen underpants that concealed his private parts until the top of his thigh was visible. There appeared on his flesh a badly festering abscess with redness all around its edges. The surrounding area of his thigh was also swollen.

Thawna groaned when he saw it.

Addressing the woman in a grave tone of voice, he said, "Cursed be Satan, my good woman. This boil is dangerous indeed, and could be the death of the boy if it remains as it is."

He then rose and headed for the place where our two mules stood. He took a small container out of his saddlebag, opened it quickly, and asked me to bring him a tender, but full-grown mulberry leaf. When I picked one and gave it to him, he placed some ointment from the container on top of it and said to the woman, "When you return home, wash the site of the abscess thoroughly with warm water, squeeze out the pus with a clean piece of linen, then apply some of this ointment to it. You must soak the piece of linen in a bowl filled with date root, then rub your hands and fingers well with the same in order to prevent your hands from being infected with what your son has on his leg. Do this once after your son wakes up in the morning, and once before he goes to sleep at night. You must also wrap the site of the disease with a clean cloth soaked in date root."

Then he continued, saying, "Your other son is afflicted with the satanic worm known as bund, which has taken over his body and settled in his gut. It is now eating everything he eats, and this is why he is so jaundiced and thin. Consequently, you must give him a drink made of resin from the Chinese cinnamon tree mixed with peppermint blossoms and sas, which in the Arabic language is called castor oil. It should be shaken well in a long-necked bottle, then given to him before he eats in the morning over a period of three days until the worm dies and comes out of his intestines along with whatever wastes are expelled. If he vomits, do not be alarmed, since this is one of the things that normally occur when this sort of a drink is taken. What it means is that the treacle has started to exterminate the worm, which is beginning to die and come out. Also, if he drinks boiled wormwood before going to sleep every night, this will bring faster results and deliver the boy from the state he is in."

The woman remained silent for a few moments, then said after some hesitation, "But sir, I tie an amulet onto him inside his clothes. Should I leave it in place, or should I remove it and just do the treatment?"

In amazement Thawna replied, "What amulet, woman?"

36

"A protective amulet," she said apprehensively. "It was made for me by a man who is famous for such things in our parts. In return for it I gave him a cup of wheat and two silver halves."

"Show it to me," said Thawna.

The woman reached inside the boy's robe and brought out a small bundle which she had fastened to a woolen rope and tied around his abdomen, causing the amulet to rest over his navel. Thawna took the bundle, which consisted of a piece of white linen with something written on it in red ink in the Coptic language. He then began reading it aloud to me:

I came out of the city of 'Ayn Shams with the priests of its great temple, the possessors of protection, and the kings of pre-eternity and prevention. I came out of the ancient city of San-al-Hajar with the mother deities who bestow their protection upon me and teach me incantations on the authority of the master of all things in the same number as there are doors leading out of them. This is in order for them to drive illness and the pains which issue from every worshiped entity out of this head of mine, this neck of mine, these two arms of mine, this flesh of mine, and these members of mine. It is in order for them to chastise the base rulers who have invaded my flesh with this illness and bewitched these bones of mine until the pain entered this flesh of mine, this head of mine, these two arms of mine, my body, and these members of mine. I adjure you by the compassion of Ra, who says, "I protect him from his enemies," and in the name of his guide Hermes, who communicates speech to him, composes books, and from whom scientists and physicians receive knowledge for the deciphering of every mystery. I am among those who are beloved to the Worshiped One and whom He causes to be alive. For the Worshiped One revives me and preserves my life. This is the book of healing for every illness. Hence, can Isis heal me as she healed Horus of every pain with which he was afflicted by Seth when he killed his father Osiris? O Isis, mighty sorceress, heal me and deliver me from everything which brings misery and suffering, from everything evil and satanic, from maladies borne of confusion and uncertainty, and from all the deadly and malignant diseases that afflict me, as you delivered and rescued your son Horus. Lo, I have come out of the water and entered the fire. So is it possible for me to avoid falling in the trap this day by saying, "I am young and worthy of compassion"? O Ra, you are the one over whose body I have recited this incantation. O Osiris, you are worshiped for your glory. Ra recites for the sake of his body and Osiris is worshiped for his glorification. I beg the two of you to deliver me from all that causes misery and suffering, everything that is evil and satanic, and all manner of malignant, deadly furies and passions.

Appearing to be lost in thought, Thawna said nothing for a while. Then he crossed himself and said, "Listen, my good woman. This is an old amulet which will do no good when it comes to healing someone of an illness. I advise you not to put it on your son, for the Lord is the One who preserves us and heals us of all manner of illness. When you get home, burn it or throw it far away somewhere, and have no more such charms made by wizards or anyone else."

However, no sooner had the woman risen and made ready to depart than he said to her, "On the other hand, if you make use of it as a means of healing your son, and if you think that it will do him some good, put it back on him in the place where it was before."

The woman was visibly overjoyed when Thawna said this, whereas prior to this her face had been clouded over by a look of distress and suspicion.

When she had gone, Thawna said, "I told her to keep the amulet for fear that she might not give her son the medicine. Common people without a solid grounding in faith, and women in particular, actually believe in such charms and amulets, which date back to the ancient times of paganism. The names in this little packet are nothing but the names of old gods which were worshiped at one time on this earth."

I had been wanting to find out what ointment he had given her to treat her other son. So, seizing the opportunity, I said to him, "May the Lord have mercy on them, Thawna, on these people who unintentionally mix paganism with the true religion because of a lack of knowledge and their vulnerability to the influence of heresies. But is the ointment you gave her not the same kind that I used to see so often in our Bashmourite region in the past?"

"No, Budayr," he replied. "It is not the whale oil that you are think-ing of, although it does resemble it. Rather, it is made from willow leaves, leaves from the common purslane, bittersweet sap, saffron, egg white, and a little opium. All the ingredients are crushed together into a powder, then some pure wine is added to the mixture and it is used in the way you heard me describing to the woman a little while ago."

Blurting out what was on my mind, I said, "But the boy was extremely weak, and might be suffering from some malady other than 'Satan's worm.' God knows. . . ."

I do not know why, but as I sat looking at the woman and her chil-dren, the thought had come to me that this little boy was destined to die. Then I started thinking about the deaths of young children and infants. I had been witness to such things many times when their families would bring them to the church for their bodies to be prayed over before they were buried. I would have to make preparations for the funeral, and I would be given wages for my labor.

The question of children's dying caused me no little consternation, so I asked him, "Do you think, Thawna, that God often takes children because of their parents' sins? Or is it for some other reason?"

Thawna replied, saying, "Do not think that, my boy. Rather, God looks upon the human race, most of whose members have done Satan's will based on misguided concern. And since Hell is full to the brim while Paradise is practically empty, He takes little children who still have no sin to Paradise, the place of mercy and compassion."

Then I asked him, "And why did God expel Satan from Heaven before He created the world and people?"

Eyeing a scarab beetle as it carted away a breadcrumb that had fallen as we ate, he said, "My boy, who am I, wretched, miserable crea-ture that I am, to be asked such a question?"

However, when I persisted, he said, "Saint Gregory the Theologian once said, 'From the time God created him, Satan began striving with his fellow angels to reach God. God, being patient with him, granted Satan a respite. Then, when God created a new heaven and a new earth and created man in His image and likeness—knowing from all eternity that Satan was a lover of vainglory—He commanded him to look upon Adam and his beautiful appearance. So, taking with him the host that

God had placed under his command, Satan went to where Adam was. When he beheld him, he was astounded at what he saw and said to his companions, "I want to set up a throne for myself on the clouds, and for the lofty mountains to be beneath me. I want to be like the Most High such that the entire world is in my grip and I am the one who reigns over it!" Satan then ascended to heaven again, and God—knowing what Satan concealed in his heart—said to him, "Were you impressed by what you saw, and are you pleased with the created world?" Then He added, "I have made you ruler over it." God said all of this to Satan lest he fall from the glory in which he found himself. All the while, however, Satan harbored evil in his heart and thought ill of God, and after pondering the matter further he said, "I want to know the nature of divinity so that, when I go down to earth, I will be as God and no longer have any need of Him." This, then, was his real concern: He wanted to behold divinity. He then went quickly into the midst of the angels, whereupon God commanded ten thousand of the heavenly host to cast him and all who were with him into the lowest depths of Hell, into the outer darkness.' This is what God revealed to Gregory the Theologian, who set it down in writing for us. Glory be to God, forever and ever."

Then we got up and led our mounts to the riverside to drink, letting them feed on fava beans and grass on the way, and when they had drunk their fill, we went back to the road, placing our trust in God, with the intention of entering Atrib before nightfall.

As we were about to enter the city of Atrib, I had the feeling I had seen the place before. It seemed to me that I had passed through it after running away from Tarnit and before I was found wandering aimlessly through the wilderness between Qasr al-Sham' and Helwan, and the ancient temple that rose up in the distance looked familiar to me. It had high walls and numerous gates, which came to twelve when I counted them, and we entered through the large one known as the Khalq Gate. Once inside, we found that it was a huge, populous city filled with market places. It contained a canal into which the waters of the Nile flowed, and which branched out into small ditches that carried water to people's houses. As for the houses themselves, they seemed exceptionally beautiful to me, especially those located on its main street, which ran perpendicular to the Nile. On this street there was a lovely promenade, and there was also a smaller road that intersected the main street and which ran the length of the city from south to north.

When we asked them, some good-hearted folks led us directly to the monastery, which had been named the Monastery of the Virgin Mary after our church at Qasr al-Sham', and we were amazed to find that its doors were still open even though it was approximately two degrees before sunset. When we entered, we saw many people, both men and women, buying and selling. Some of them were eating and drinking, and children were scampering gleefully about. Most of the people were peasants who had brought with them sweet drinks, julep, bowls of semolina, and chunks of leavened bread. The children, who were all decked out in new clothes, were waving palm-leaf noisemakers, jumping, shouting, and generally making a happy ruckus.

Taken by the unexpected scene, Thawna cried, "Lord have mercy on me, Budayr! Today is the annual Feast of the Virgin, which is celebrated on the twelfth of Paona. So then, we have arrived on the holiday."

"Yes," I replied. Meanwhile, I watched the holiday scenes in a daze, as they reminded me of scenes I had experienced so many times in my beloved village, Tarnit, even though the women's attire in Atrib was brighter and more attractive than the women's dresses in Tarnit. Most of the dresses were bright purple and saffron yellow, and rarely did one see any of them dyed with indigo the way one would have in Tarnit. I also noted that the fabrics of which these women's dresses were made were soft and delicate, flowing diaphanously over their bodies.

The monastery's caretaker took us to the bishop's headquarters, where we were received warmly and graciously. Thawna introduced us to the bishop and explained the reasons for our coming, whereupon he began asking us about conditions in Old Cairo and in our church.

Gradually shaking off his anxiety, Thawna said, "We are in constant distress. The governor oppresses us with the kharaj just as he does people everywhere, and he has his eye on the church's orchards and wine presses. From time to time he sends someone to calculate the number of people overseeing and working the land, and to tattoo everyone he finds there. Whoever is found not to bear the lion tattoo suffers grievous hardship. As you know, this policy was first applied for the purpose of tax assessment in the year AM 422 to farmers who had been forbidden by a governmental decree to leave their lands. However, these measures are now being applied to us in the churches and monasteries as well, and their application is stricter in Old Cairo than anywhere else in the land. The reason is that we now have both Copts and Muslims farming our orchards and operating our oil presses, so there is a need to distinguish one group from another. In Fustat, there are soldiers who mutiny from time to time because their wages have been cut off. We have taken pity on them, and some of them have begun working for us secretly in our orchards just to have something to eat. As we were on our way here to Atrib, we were told by the commander of a road patrol that people have come out demanding food in Minyat al-Sirg in the direction of Shubra."

The bishop murmured in affirmation of what Thawna had reported, then said, "May the Lord have mercy on us all. There are disturbances everywhere. And with every passing day I become more afraid for this monastery, especially now that a huge Arab tribe has taken up residence on the outskirts of the village in the direction of the desert. They are constantly launching raids on the crops and farmers. They loot the crops and ruin the land. In some cases they have gone so far as to kidnap girls and boys, and we are helpless to do a thing. We have asked the governor several times for protection against the raids, but to no avail. Our greatest fear now is that one of these days they will come in and plunder the monastery. And if the monastery is lost, the whole city will be lost with it, since most of its people work on its lands and in its factories, especially the linen and glass factories. The glass we make here rivals the best varieties produced in the factory in Wadi Habib near Maryut. I beseech the Lord not to let such a thing happen, especially in view of the fact that many families have left their homes and gone to the marshlands to join the Bashmourite as fighters in his army."

We all crossed ourselves, seeking the forgiveness of the All Merciful. Then the caretaker led us to an unoccupied monk's cell where we could rest for a while until evening.

We remained in the cell for some time, and before we knew it evening had fallen, so we got up and took part with the monks in the prayer, recited some theotokias, and concluded with a light Eucharistic supper. As we did so, the monastery courtyard was still filled with people, who had begun lighting lanterns and candles as night fell. Meanwhile, outside the monastery walls there was a huge din, as singing voices mingled with the beating of drums and the playing of the mizmar. Dancers began moving about freely in circles that included both men and women, all of whom appeared to be in a state of frenzied intoxication.

Thawna sighed irritably as he spoke to the bishop in protest against all this merrymaking inside the monastery's courtyard and beyond its walls, especially given the fact that it had not let up even during our chanting of the Psalms, our prayers, and our celebration of the Mass. As we sat with him after supper, the bishop said that he had tried on numerous occasions to prevent people from doing this, but without success, and that he was afraid of being too strict with them lest they be alienated from the religion and the monks, especially in view of the fact that most of them had been thorough-going pagans until quite recently, and had only recently entered the fold of faith. Afterwards, as we were heading toward our cell, Thawna told me that Father Shenouda, the abbot of the White Monastery who had been consecrated a long time before, had forbidden the common folk to take part in celebrations of saints' birthdays and other festivals and holidays, saying:

It is an admirable thing for one to go to the site of a martyr's tomb to pray, read, chant the Psalms, and purify oneself, and to partake of the sacred mysteries in the fear of Christ. As for those who go to talk, eat, drink, and amuse themselves—or, to be exact, to commit sexual immorality and crimes as a result of excessive drinking, corruption, and iniquity—such are infidels plain and simple. And while some inside the monastery are chanting the Psalms, reading and partaking of the sacred mysteries, there are others outside who fill the place with the sound of drums and reed pipes. "It is written: 'My house shall be called a house of prayer,' but you have made it a den of robbers!" You have made it a marketplace for selling honey, jewelry, and the like. You have made the celebration of martyrs' births into an opportunity to train your animals and race your donkeys and horses.

You have turned them into occasions to steal what is offered there for sale. After all, the honey vendor is lucky to find a few quarreling customers, and just barely ekes out some benefit for himself in return for his labors. Even the things that could not possibly happen to vendors in the public marketplaces happen to them at martyrs' birthday celebrations. What folly! What closed minds you have! If your daughters and mothers perfume their heads, adorn their eyes with kohl, and beautify themselves to deceive the people who look at them, and if your sons, your brothers, your friends, and your neighbors do this when they go to martyrs' tombs, then why have you built houses for them? There are many who go to martyrs' birthday celebrations to corrupt the temple of the Lord and to make the members of Christ into instruments of sin and iniquity rather than preserving them from all uncleanness. Allow me to tell you in utter frankness that many of you make excuses for yourselves, saying, "We have no wives," or "We have no husbands." However, do not make your visits to martyrs' tombs into an opportunity to destroy your bodies at the graves that surround them, in nearby buildings, or in their corners.

I replied, "So the Holy Father Shenouda was present among us, witnessing with his own eyes what was taking place here at this birthday celebration which, to my knowledge, is similar to what takes place at other such celebrations around the country. I remember from my days in Tarnit that the times when we went out for saints' birthday celebrations were the happiest, most festive times of all. We used to celebrate the birth of St. Stephen in Bashans every year and do the same things that these people here were doing at the Atrib Monastery. O God!"

I did not tell Thawna about the feelings that welled up inside me as I said this. Instead, the memory carried my spirit away with it, since it was at that lovely time of the spring that my passion for precious Amuna first began. She and I had been in the prime of our youth. The first time I ever saw her, she was going out with her sisters and her mother. She was wearing a dress made of wispy white linen embroidered with gold silk thread, and to me she looked more beautiful than a water lily in full bloom, more succulent than a glistening pomegranate blossom. I lost control over myself at the mere sight of her. My sinful heart lusted after her, and my spirit weakened under the force of my desire. I came up to her when the dancing began and began whispering amorous words in her ears until my spirit had infected hers. I took her and we distanced ourselves from the circles of dancers and the press of the people at the celebration, then we ran toward the fields and went into one of the mud shelters that the peasants had built in the fields to provide shade from the scorching heat. As we began exchanging whispers, I said to her, "O most beautiful of the lilies on the river's face, O loveliest rose in all the land, O pomegranate of the winter and orange of the summer. . . ." As for her, she whispered to me words of love no less wonderful. Her heart seemed to be overflowing like the banks of the Nile at flood time, and as though it had become like mine: a feather helpless to direct its own course as it is blown about by the breeze.

Lost to ourselves, we were overpowered by bodily attraction, possessed by the spirits of madness to the point where we swore to each other our undying love and affection, and I announced to her that I would ask my father to seek her hand for me in marriage once the harvest season was over. However, fate was swifter, and what was to be for the two of us was as it was.

I think I must have wandered far away with my thoughts as I recalled all that, since I did not hear anything but the end of what Thawna was saying as he concluded, "Then Father Shenouda died in the year 451 by the Byzantine calendar, after directing the monastery for sixty-six years. Yet even now there are many people who still have not given up early pagan habits. Lord, have mercy: Kyrie eleison."

I slept fitfully in the cell the entire night, since it was much hotter than it usually is at that time of the year, and the air was heavy with the vapor rising from the Nile despite the fact that we had yet to enter the month of Misra. The voices of those carousing and dancing outside the monastery along with the sounds of their drumming and piping left no room for drowsiness, still less slumber. And then there were the countryside vermin, such as mosquitoes and other flying creatures that feed off the green of the earth, and which had stayed awake all night buzzing and humming. As dawn approached, and as sleep took over one moment and wakefulness the next, I heard a commotion and the

45

sound of people shouting in the monastery. I left the cell hurriedly with Thawna—who had started with fright when he heard it—to see what the matter was. Following the voices through the darkness, we arrived at a row of monks' cells on the other side of the courtyard onto which our cell opened. A group of monks had gathered around one of their number and were beating and kicking him as he screamed and pleaded for help. Then they led him away roughly to the residence of Bishop Serapion, the monastery's abbot, with the two of us close on their heels. When they reached the abbot's quarters, he commanded them to stop beating the man so that he could clear up the matter.

Once the monks had calmed down a bit and had left the man in peace while the abbot clarified the situation, we were approached by a monk we had met during supper by the name of Narkisus, and who had with him some papyrus scrolls and papers that belonged to the monk being abused. In the meantime, some of the monks lit a lantern for everyone to see by. Narkisus said that when he opened up the papers, he had found them to contain heresies and teachings foreign to Jesus and the Church. After issuing instructions for more torches and candles to be brought, Father Serapion inquired as to how the monk had come into possession of these papers. Then he commanded him to read their contents aloud to all present, who were clad in nothing but flimsy night shirts. When the monk read aloud what the papers and scrolls contained, it became apparent that he had interpreted passages from the Hebrew scriptures in a way that did not reflect their true meaning, and that he had concealed what they contained by way of prophecies concerning Christ. For example, when he came to the passage about the bush in which the ram provided for the Prophet Abraham was caught by its horns, and which the church fathers had interpreted as a foreshadowing of the cross, he failed to mention this prophetic interpretation. It also became clear from his reading that he had misinterpreted many books, and that he was making claims that were at variance with orthodox teachings and which were bound to lead to serious schisms. He read, for example, the statement that Jesus Christ had been born of Mary and Joseph, thereby denying the miraculous virgin birth. He likewise denied that the Lord had been born without Mary going through the pain of labor. He said that Christ was both truly God and truly man, but that He was also one of two, thereby contradicting the true Gospel as testified to by Matthew as well as what he said about the church ("and the gates of hell will not prevail against it"). It became clear from his reading of the scrolls, which had been written in his own iniquitous hand, that he had read the books of the Sabeans and the Mu'tazilites. And as if this were not enough, he had been reading all of these things without apologizing or seeking pardon. As for us, we were all crossing ourselves and praying for forgiveness as we uttered the words, "God forbid!" Father Serapion endured the man and his blasphemous words with patience until he could get to the bottom of the matter once and for all. Then he asked Narkisus how the papers belonging to the accursed Fla'as—which was the man's name—had fallen into his hands, to which Narkisus replied that after his having argued with Fla'as that morning, the latter had given them to him to read after the night prayer. He reported that the monk had told him that he believed in the accursed teachings that had begun to spread in Arabia to the effect that the soul dies and decays with the body and is raised with it on the Day of Resurrection. Father Serapion said, "A council was held to discuss this teaching, after which it was denounced as fallacious by the Holy Church!" whereupon all the monks crossed themselves.

The man also believed that both the Son and the Holy Spirit were created. However, when he had reached this point in the reading, Father Serapion commanded him to be silent. He asked Fla'as about his belief in these heresies, but he neither replied nor asked for forgiveness. At this point, Father Serapion issued orders for the accursed monk to be dragged into a dark underground vault in the monastery, where he was to be denied food and given only two drinks of water a day until he had repented. He ordered the heretical documents burned and Fla'as's cell thoroughly searched and emptied, after which it was to be purged by means of a number of purifying rituals and agents in order to drive out whatever evil spirits had taken up residence there. And when all these procedures had been completed, the Psalms were to be read there the following morning.

The monks then took Fla'as and went on beating him until he bled and his clothing was in shreds. As a result, his flesh was exposed, and when they saw his private parts they found that his foreskin was still intact, thereby revealing the fact that he was uncircumcised. His scandal was thereby brought to completion and his uncleanness confirmed, and it thus became clear that he was not a true Christian after all.

All of us then returned to our cells to remain there until the time for the dawn prayer.

This was the first time since I joined the church that I had seen a heretic with my own eyes and heard him with my own ears. Consequently, I was highly distraught, and my distress was heightened further when I saw the way he was beaten and reviled. He did not have the strength even to raise his head or look at his accusers, so great was everyone's bitterness and hatred toward him.

When I came into our cell, I threw myself onto my pallet and asked Thawna politely for a drink of water from a jug that had been placed beside the window. After collecting myself a bit, I said to him distraughtly, "I can still hardly believe everything I saw. How in God's name can an infidel like this Fla'as dare to conceal what he is about and introduce false doctrine among his brethren in the monastery? What sort of clay is he made of, for God's sake? I swear, brother, I think he must be made of the clay of demons!"

Thawna sighed. Then, after taking the jug from me and drinking from it himself, he said, "Demons were not made from clay, Budayr. They were made from fire. And perhaps this Fla'as is a Melkite. He showed his true colors when it became apparent that he was not circumcised. Who knows? He may have been planted in the monastery for some reason. Maybe he came to spy out conditions in our monastic church. After all, he could not be a Jacobite as we are. We adhere to the system and law of the religion more than the Melkites do, and the issue of circumcision is one of the subsidiary points of disagreement between us and them. We Copts follow the example of our forefather Abraham, whom God Almighty spoke to with the words, 'Any uncircumcised male who is not circumcised in the flesh of his foreskin shall be cut off from his people.' Despite his advanced age, Abraham obeyed God and was circumcised. The Copts in our church in Old Cairo follow the law of God in this matter. And Jesus Christ, to Him be glory, the bringer of the new Law, was also circumcised. Otherwise, when he was crucified, the Jews would have discovered that he was uncircumcised, which would have been considered a blemish in his body. Moreover, if He had not emulated the Old Testament practice of circumcision, the Jews would not have recorded his name in the register of priests who served in the Temple. As we read in the Gospel of Luke, they handed him the Torah, and the passage which he read from it was, 'The Spirit of the Lord is upon me, because He has anointed me to preach good news to the poor. He has sent me to proclaim release to the captives and recovering of sight to the blind, to set at liberty those who are oppressed, to proclaim the acceptable year of the Lord.'"

"Yes," I said, then continued, "I used to think that the difference between the Copts and the Melkites was over one fundamental issue only, namely, that of the hypostatic union."

Interrupting me to clarify, Thawna said, "No, Budayr. We disagree on thirteen subsidiary questions in addition to the fundamental issue. We agree on the three hypostases with a single, united Essence. As followers of Jacobite teachings, we believe that Christ has a single nature and a single will and constitutes a single hypostasis. The reason for is that when the hypostasis of the only Son, the Logos, to Him be glory, willed to be united with human nature, he took from Mary's flesh full humanity with a rational soul and caused it to be one with His divinity 'without mingling, without confusion, and without alteration' as we declare in the Coptic divine liturgy. Through this union with the eternal Son before all ages—a union which is beyond human comprehension—the humanity derived from Mary's flesh, despite its 'density,' became one with divinity in its actions, including the healing of the sick, the raising of the dead, the cleansing of lepers, and opening the eyes of the blind."

"But what is the Melkites' relationship to the forbidden books?" I interjected. "Fla'as was accused of reading forbidden books."

With a sternness in his voice Thawna replied, "Budayr, let us just pray and call it a day. The forbidden books are those of the Sabeans and the Mu'tazilites, and there is no need to go into matters pertaining to them and this damned Fla'as. In other words, we had best mind our own business. It is nighttime, it is dark, and evil spirits are out and about. So let us not open a door through which they can come in and take over."

Then he began reciting: "But of that day or that hour no one knows, not even the angels in heaven, nor the Son, but only the Father. Take heed, watch; for you do not know when the time will come. It is like a man going on a journey, when he leaves home and puts his servants in charge, each with his work, and commands the doorkeeper to be on the watch. Watch therefore—for you do not know when the master of the house will come, in the evening, or at midnight, or at cockcrow, or in the morning—lest he come suddenly and find you asleep. And what I say to you I say to all: Watch."

Without waiting to find out what had became of the accursed Fla'as, we took leave of the monastery immediately after the morning prayer, the sun a radiant bride in her firmament. Then we left Atrib to continue on our way to the marshlands. The monks had supplied us with Atrib honey, which is famed for its high quality, its sweetness, and its ability to heal disease. Its healing powers, it seems, owe to the fact that the worker bees feed mainly on the blossoms of the black elder, which is said to have flourished in these parts for some time. They also gave us a small jar of clarified butter made from the finest buffalo cow milk. The buffalo cows in question, which are found in abundance in the villages surrounding the city, graze primarily on the succulent grasses that grow between the Nile and the wilderness area around Atrib. It was the villagers' custom in these parts—or so we had been told—to let the buffalo cows graze freely on the steppe grasses, after which they would be rounded up and brought in for milking at the end of the day. We had also been told that many of the lands in and around Atrib's villages belonged to its monastery, which meant that this monastery was among the largest and wealthiest in the country.

We saw the peasants on their way out to the fields, and whenever we passed by any of them, they would look up and greet us with reverence and respect, or ask us to bless them. Some of them also gave us sycamore fruit, mulberries, and other fruits that were being gathered at that time.

Thus we began passing through the villages until we reached the wilderness. Then we kept on going until we found ourselves before a lofty, imposing edifice that Thawna identified to me as Atrib's ancient temple ruin.

✠

I stood for some time in front of Atrib's ancient temple, taken by the grandeur of the sight. I could see its structures rising aloft atop gargantuan pillars of black Aswanite stone, which were crowned with capitals carved in the shape of lotus blossoms whose petals had yet to open. The capitals looked to me like the ones on the pillars of our church in Qasr al-Sham'. I asked Thawna if we could go in for a while to see the temple from the inside, since such grand old temples were a rarity in our Bashmourite lands, perhaps because of the water that covers so much of the area and the resultant frequent flooding, a reality which renders all structures, however magnificent they happen to be, vulnerable to destruction. I had a powerful urge to go in and investigate, perhaps because this was the first time in my life that I had had the chance to get a close-up look at a pagan temple like this. Thawna seemed a bit hesitant at first, but it was not long before he warmed to the idea, as though an inner voice had prompted him to do the same. We got off our mounts and ventured in, and once we had crossed the high stone thresholds, we found ourselves inside a wide, extended passageway, some parts of whose walls and pillars jutted out. As for the remaining parts, they were decorated with exquisite inscriptions more beautiful than anything I had ever seen in my life—drawings and geometric shapes that bespoke the finest taste and the most exacting symmetry. Thawna began crossing himself as he gazed at the inscriptions.

"God!" I said to him, "what a magnificent temple it is, Thawna! It seems to have been a place of great importance in its time. I wonder if it was built by one of the ancient Amalekite kings?"

Thawna made no reply, as he was engrossed in pondering the inscriptions and drawings engraved on what remained of the temple walls. Later he told me that they were writings that had been recorded in the ancient tongue.

I do not know why, but I imagined that Thawna was reading and understanding what was written on those walls. More than once during our tour of the place, I looked over at him and watched him furtively, and it seemed as though he was moving his lips the way one does when one is reading something. And every now and then he would cross himself.

In an attempt to bring him out of his reverie and engage him in some conversation, I said, "Do you see these magnificent pillars, Thawna? Do they not bear a close resemblance to the pillars in the congregational prayer hall in our venerable church at Qasr al-Sham'? It is as if whoever made those is the same person who designed the ones we are looking at right now!"

"Only those in our church?" he responded with a sigh. "We could say the same thing about churches and mosques everywhere. Have you not seen the pillars in the mosque in the Muslim capital city Fustat? Believe me, Budayr, neither the architecture of the Copts' churches nor that of the Muslims' mosques could be as magnificent and majestic as it is if it were not for these ancient temples. And the reason is that the huge pillars and the high-quality stones with which our churches and mosques were built, be they granite or basalt or whatever else, were brought from temples, particularly those in Memphis, 'Ayn Shams, and Atrib thanks to their proximity to Fort Babylon, Qasr al-Sham', and Fustat. In Upper Egypt, entire temple ruins have been transformed into churches and mosques. The only ones that have escaped such fates are those that are far enough away from villages and towns to be out of sight and out of reach. For some time these ancient temples served as refuges and dwellings for large numbers of Christian believers who were fleeing persecution by the Byzantines, the pagans, and their kings. In the Edfu temple ruin there is evidence of Christians having entered and taken shelter in its large halls, whose walls are covered with the soot from the candles, fires, and lanterns that were used for light by these God-fearing souls during their reading of the Psalms and their singing of the theotokias."

Thawna fell silent for a few minutes as he looked off into the distance. Then he continued, "However, this temple will not remain unharmed. It will not be long before it will vanish just like the temple of 'Ayn Shams vanished before it. 'Ayn Shams is the city that was known in ancient times as 'On,' and this temple was originally among a number of shrines to which people made pilgrimage from all over the world. It is said that these shrines were passed down to the Sabeans from Hermes I, who spoke of the sublime essences and stellar movements and who built the shrines and worshiped God in them."

Warming to his subject, Thawna went on, "It is said that in bygone eras, there were twelve shrines in this temple. The first five of these—the shrine to the First Cause, the shrine to Reason, the shrine to Politics, the shrine to Form, and the shrine to the Soul—were round in shape. The sixth shrine, namely, the shrine to Saturn, was hexagonal; the seventh shrine, that to Jupiter, was triangular; followed by the shrine to Mars, which was square; the shrine to the sun, which was also square; the shrine to Venus, which was an isosceles triangle; the shrine to Mercury, which was a triangle inside a rectangle; and the shrine to the moon, which was an octagon. The basis they gave for their worship of the shrines was that the Creator of the world is too exalted and holy to be characterized by the features of contingent beings. It follows from this that His servants—contingent beings that they are—are unable to realize or comprehend His majesty and, as a consequence, must draw near to Him by means of those beings nearest to Him, namely, the 'spiritual ones,' in order for them to make intercession for human beings and be intermediaries for them with the Creator. By 'the spiritual ones' they meant the angels, and they maintained that it is the angels who direct the seven planets in their orbits. These planets, according to their cosmology, were their shrines. In addition, they taught that each spiritual one must have a shrine, that every shrine must have an orbit, and that the spiritual one is to its shrine as the spirit is to the body.

"They held that in order to draw near to the Creator and receive blessing from Him, the servant must be able to see that which mediates between creatures and their Creator. Consequently, they sought refuge in the shrines, which are identified with the planets, and they ascertained their stations with respect to the celestial sphere, the times of their rising and setting, their conjunctions, the days, nights, hours, persons, images, and regions associated with them, as well as other things of relevance from the science of mathematics.

"They called these seven planets lords and gods, while they called the sun the god of gods and lord of lords, claiming that it is the sun that pours out its radiance in tongues of light through which it manifests its effects. Consequently, they would draw near to the shrines as a way of drawing near to the spiritual ones due to the latters' proximity to the Creator based on their belief that the shrines are the bodies of the spiritual ones, and that whoever draws physically near to someone has drawn near to his spirit as well.

"They would pray to a different planet every day, claiming that it was the lord of that day, and their prayers were performed at three times: the first at sunrise, the second when the sun reached its zenith in the celestial sphere, and the third at its setting. They would pray to Saturn on Saturday, to Jupiter on Sunday, and to Mars and the moon on Friday."

As we toured the ancient temple a bit longer, we came upon huge statues, meticulously crafted, that lay strewn here and there. Parts of them were shattered, and precious stones that had once covered parts of them, such as gold on their heads and precious jewels in the sites for their eyes, had been looted, while rocks had been thrown down carelessly all about. The statues were covered with superb, colorful drawings or engraved with the ancient pictorial language. I stood there gazing at it all admiringly. However, I never stopped stealing glances at Thawna from time to time, as I had begun to have doubts about him. I was convinced now that he could read the ancient script, and that he might know the meaning of these drawings and designs.

Appearing to sense what was going on in my mind, he said suddenly, "Let us be going, Budayr. We have to move quickly in order to arrive somewhere safe before night is upon us and we face unexpected problems on the road."

I nearly asked him whether he really had been reading what was inscribed on the stones, and whether he knew the ancient script that had now passed out of use. But when I remembered what had happened to the monk Fla'as, and especially given the fact that I had voiced my admiration for the idols to him—may the Lord forgive me for that—I was afraid he might be suspicious of me. So I kept my question to myself in spite of the fact that Thawna, as far as I could tell, was not stuffy or narrow-minded like some of the clerics I had met in our church. On the contrary, he was magnanimous and open-minded, learned, and a man of deep faith. However, it had been rumored of him in the church that in his earlier, pre-Christian life in his hometown Akhmim, he had first studied at the boys' school, then gone on to learn wisdom, medicine, and graphic arts at the hand of an elderly woman well-known in the town by the name of Dalluka. It was said that this woman had revered the religion of her sun-worshiping ancestors and clung to her pagan beliefs until her death, and that some Christian believers had nearly killed her more than once, as they had many other pagans.

In the end, after demanding that everyone avoid her, they left her alone, and in her old age she went to an ancient temple and took up residence there until, one morning, she was found dead by some nomadic herdsmen. There are those who say that Christian believers murdered Dalluka inside the temple, then razed it. But only God knows what really happened.

This type of information was grist for the mills of those who would whisper among themselves from time to time that Thawna dabbled in magic, chemistry, and alchemy. It was even said that Father Joseph once ordered an inspection of his cell. However, they found no damning evidence there. On the contrary, it was filled—as it continued to be from then on—with books on doctrine. All of this came up on account of a book on physiology that they had found him reading one day in the church courtyard. It was a book that contained myths, fanciful stories, and theological allusions, so they advised him to put it away and to devote himself to books on pure theology.

When we left the temple, which was quite extensive, we found what looked like a bunch of riffraff rummaging energetically through piles of rocks and potsherds near the parts of the temple that had been destroyed. I was alarmed by the sight of these people, who left their heads bare rather covering them with skullcaps or turbans as was the custom among both city and country dwellers. Their hair was dusty, unkempt, and wild looking, and they were clad in coarse, tattered cloaks. They looked to me as though they were among the irreligious barbarians who knew neither Coptic nor Arabic. Unsettled by their looks, I feared they might attack us and do us harm. I voiced my concerns to Thawna, proposing that we hide until they were gone. However, he began calming me down, then went over and greeted them, asking them how to get to where we were going. I knew, of course, that he knew the way as well as I did. However, it occurred to me that the question was simply his way of creating goodwill between us and them. And my intuition proved to be correct, since one of them came forward enthusiastically to give us directions. I looked over at the man inquisitively, only to find that he was holding a small idol made of black stone that was no larger than the palm of his hand. Then, to my amazement, he asked Thawna to take it and give him something in return for it.

Taking the idol from the scavenger's hand, Thawna began turning it over in his hand and scrutinizing it. Then he said, "No, I want something better than this. Do you have something made of gold, or that contains a jewel?"

After gesturing to Thawna to wait, the man disappeared for some time, then came back carrying a container about two hand spans' high which he presented to Thawna, eyeing him meaningfully all the while.

Thawna took the container, which at first glance looked worthless to me, then proceeded to lift its tightly closed, jackal-shaped lid. I tightened up a bit as Thawna did this, and when I looked with him to see what was inside the container, we found what appeared to be the remains of dried human entrails, though they smelled sweet. Thawna replaced the lid, deposited the container inside his saddlebag, and gave the scavenger half a silver piece, whereupon we departed as the man launched forth in profuse expressions of thanks and gratitude to Thawna.

"What on earth are you going to do with that, Thawna?" I asked reproachfully.

"Shush, Budayr," he replied calmly, "and you will see before long."

Then, before I could press him with more questions, he continued in explanation, "These people belong to the Hurbat, a group of non-religious people whose spirits have not been led to faith yet. Generation after generation they have made their living digging around in ancient temples and searching through their contents, and they are all over the country. They are called Hurbat after a god whose worship was widespread in ancient times by the name of Hur, and many of these temples were once devoted to his worship and glorification."

Whenever Thawna said things like this, I sensed that he possessed knowledge that he had not intended to divulge, but which would slip out from time to time. It also seemed to me, whenever he got on subjects like this, that there was something tormenting him, or that his spirit was not at peace and he had not arrived at inner certainty. At times like this I would almost ask him, "How do you know that, Thawna? Who passed on to you all this knowledge?"

But then I would think better of it and keep quiet. There was always something inside me that made me hold my tongue and prevented me from saying what was on my mind, perhaps because I was afraid he might tell me something that was contrary to my faith, and I would lose it, having been affected by the things that were said about him in the church. This may be why I was always doubtful of the soundness of his faith. However—and may God forgive me—I had never heard anything that would taint his reputation, and never once had he uttered anything but the purest, kindest words.

Hence, I kept quiet after Thawna had said what he did, though I was dying to see what would happen in connection with the container he had brought with us.

Having traversed some distance since leaving Atrib and its temple ruin behind us, we kept on going till nearly midday. After circling round the agricultural areas once again, we continued down a decline parallel to the river as we headed in the direction of our destination in the marshlands. We had now begun entering wooded, wilderness areas where, not long after we set out, the last of Atrib's villages disappeared from view. Such wilderness areas were not cultivated or farmed by anyone. Instead, they were covered for the most part by reeds, scrub, and numerous sorts of long grasses that grew up of their own accord. The path was rather difficult, since it would become so narrow in some places that we could only pass single file, and in other places, get so wide that we would get lost and not know which direction to go unless there appeared some sign to indicate where the path was, such as tracks left by a riding animal or a man's footprints. And sometimes, since there was so much water accumulated in the salt marshes, the edge of the river would disappear altogether and we would not be able to tell where the land left off and where the water began.

When we reached this point in the journey, I said to Thawna, "This is where the Bashmourites' territory begins. It extends all the way from the Mediterranean Sea in the north, but we still have a long way to go before we reach the towns and villages and the area where the war is being fought. This road is not very well traveled, since most people come and go on boats and canoes on the river when they want to go to Fort Babylon or Upper Egypt. And if they want to cross over to Alexandria or Maryut, they take boats on the Mediterranean Sea, which is not without its perils. An uncle of mine went to Alexandria once and on the way, a huge sea creature appeared near their boat. If it had not been for the Lord's protection, it would have capsized it and killed those on board. In the end, the boatmen managed to kill it with their spears and get the situation under control."

Suddenly the sun was concealed by clouds, and before we knew it, it had begun pouring down rain in a way we had never seen at this time of year before, since the month of Paona was among the hot months during which rainfall is scarce. We sought refuge from the unexpected downpour under a broad-leaved tree, where we stood waiting for the water to stop coming down. And in fact, it stopped as suddenly as it had begun. Before long, however, and as we were making ready to be on our way, the sky grew dark again as though we had been surrounded by the black of night, and despite the fact that it was only slightly after noon. We looked out at the horizon, and what should we see but a colossal army of locusts descending earthward. Some of them struck our faces and heads, while others landed on the mules. We began beating them off as we crossed ourselves and praised God, repeating the name of the Lord over and over as the mules brayed and bolted, terrified by these flying vermin that had descended from the heavens. I do not know how long we stood there with our eyes closed. However, when we opened them again and looked at the ground around us, we found that the green had turned to yellow, since the locusts had decimated every leafy green thing in their path. As far as the eye could see, nothing was left but bare stalks that looked like long spears thrust into the ground.

"Jesus our Savior," Thawna muttered solemnly, "this will be a catastrophe for the farmers and land owners in the towns and villages. These locusts will not spare any of their crops, most of which were just about to become ripe for harvest."

I made no reply, too busy thinking about the beasts and small creeping creatures of the earth that lay hidden among the stalks and grasses, and which were certain to have come out after the locusts' descent. What I feared, actually, was that such creatures would cause us harm, but when I expressed my fears to Thawna he said, "I do not think so, Budayr. On the contrary, most of these animals will be delighted over the locusts, which are a God-given banquet that has come to them straight from heaven. The Lord provides a cause for everything. As for us, we have work which we hope to accomplish in this place before we leave it."

As he spoke, he was looking around like someone in search of something. He walked along with me behind him until he stopped at a particular spot and began examining it with interest. It was a barren spot on which nothing grew, and as such, it was in sharp contrast to the soil around it. Noticing that the site was elevated slightly above the earth surrounding it, I asked in amazement, "How could this be, Thawna? How can the earth be rock-hard in this spot rather than being covered with mud like the ones around it?"

"First of all, Budayr, get down off your mule, then come with me so that we can accomplish our mission."

As he spoke, he took the stone container that he had gotten from the scavenger out of his saddle bag, then began walking somewhere with it as I followed. We came to a large opening in the ground, and before we went inside he said, "Tie the mules and come with me."

I led the two mules over to the tree under which we had taken refuge a little while earlier, and which was only a few steps away from the place where Thawna was waiting for me. When I returned, we went down a short distance into the hollow, then entered a dry, stony area. The place looked like the abode of some wild beast that lived in the region, and I was afraid to advance any further. However, Thawna lit a fire with the flint that he always carried with him in his pocket. When the place had become visible, I was astonished by what we saw, namely, colorful drawings of people and animals on the walls of the cave. And what amazed me even more was that we should have found it in this location. The pictures were of good quality and in fine condition, and their colors were as bright and fresh as if they had been drawn just the day before.

Holding his breath, Thawna murmured, "So, then, this person's 'companion soul' has led us to her mate, and the locusts were a sign that revealed the place to us."

He then proceeded to roll up his sleeves and began digging in the ground with his knife until he had made a hole large enough for him to place the container inside it. I trembled as I watched him, not comprehending a thing he had said. In fact, if the truth be told, I was a bit afraid of him at that moment, with him believing himself to be engaging in magical rites and mysteries. When he had placed the container securely in the hole and covered it with dirt again, he asked me to begin chanting a funeral mass with him. I hesitated a bit before doing so. But then I remembered Father Joseph's instructions to me, and that Thawna ranked among the deacons in the ecclesiastical hierarchy, whereas I was nothing but a sexton who came in on the bottom rung of the priestly ladder. Hence, without uttering a word of objection, I began chanting after him and crossing myself, taken captive by the words of the Lord:

> And as you wish that men would do to you, do so to them. If you love those who love you, what credit is that to you? For even sinners love those who love them. And if you do good to those who do good to you, what credit is that to you? For even sinners do the same. And if you lend to those from whom you hope to receive, what credit is that to you? Even sinners lend to sinners, to receive as much again. But love your enemies, and do good, and lend, expecting nothing in return; and your reward will be great, and you will be sons of the Most High; for he is kind to the ungrateful and the selfish. Be merciful, even as your Father is merciful. Judge not, and you will not be judged; condemn not, and you will not be condemned; forgive, and you will be forgiven; give, and it will be given to you: good measure, pressed down, shaken together, running over, will be put into your lap. For the measure you give will be the measure you get back.

When we had both finished, I cleared my throat, then asked him diffidently, "Pardon me, dear Thawna, but how can we pray and recite the words of the Lord over this object, which is the remains of a body that has not been baptized? Did our Lord Jesus Christ not say to people, 'Unless one is born of water and the Spirit, he cannot enter the Kingdom of God. That which is born of the flesh is flesh, and that which is born of the Spirit is spirit,' and by setting this condition, urge people to pursue the life of the soul? And is it not true, then, that whoever wants to resurrect his soul from its death must accept the conditions of immersion in the water of repentance, reliance on the Name of the Holy Trinity—Father, Son, and Holy Spirit—and obedience to all that our Lord Christ commanded?"

"You have spoken truly, good brother," Thawna replied, "and truly spoke the Lord in these words of His. However, this person whose remains we stumbled upon lived during the days of paganism, before our Lord, God's Messenger, had appeared. In fact, he may have lived more than a thousand years before that time. Consequently, he did not live during the era of faith. Even so, he was someone who, if he had lived among us now, may have believed and become like us, that is, people who seek to be conscious of God and follow the true religion. Through this prayer of ours, we make intercession for him and embrace him within the fold of believers. After all, all souls have been dead by virtue of Adam's sin since the beginning of time. When Adam sinned, God said to him on account of his sin, 'You shall die.' Hence, his soul died—he who had been alive through the Holy Spirit. And in fact, Adam prophesied concerning events which would lead up to his sin and death when he said of Eve, 'This at last is bone of my bones and flesh of my flesh; she shall be called Woman, because she was taken out of man.' Adam was stripped naked of God Almighty, who had been his garment, so to speak, and his soul died the true death, after which his body also died some 930 years later. And the souls of his descendents continued to be dead just as Adam's had been until the coming of our Lord Jesus Christ and His appearance in the world of nature.

"The viscera of the person whose remains rest here were removed and placed in this container in keeping with the customs of the people of ancient times, who believed, like us, that the spirit leaves the body at death. However, they—may the Lord forgive them—thought that this spirit would return to the body at the final judgment. This is why they took such great care to preserve it from decay, and embalmers would be paid large sums that varied according to people's means. And since viscera are the parts of the body most vulnerable to decay, they would skillfully remove them and place them with large amounts of natron salt in order to draw the water out of them, thereby causing them to wither and dry up. Then they would put them in containers such as the one that you saw, and mix them with myrrh, embalming spices, and costly cedarwood oil brought from Mount Lebanon. You have now seen one of these containers yourself, and all you found in it was some remains of the person's dried up intestines, a piece of the liver, and a petrified heart. It appears that some time in the distant past, grave robbers looted the tomb of this deceased person in search of what had been buried with him by way of gold, jewels, and other valuables for the time when he would be resurrected in the next life in accordance with ancient beliefs. It also appears that they carried this container off with them among the things they had stolen from the tomb, then threw it into the Atrib temple. It was then found by these new scavengers, one of whom sold it to me. However, the body's wandering spirit continued to drive the container—the preserver of its internal organs—to the site of the body. It thus led us to this place, and the locusts appeared to us as a sign so that we would stop and return it to its resting place. There may have been numerous other graves in this same area. However, they were obliterated along with the cities and villages of their inhabitants and were covered with alluvial mud and grasses, which have left nothing visible but this stony spot. Due to the fact that it has a higher elevation than the surrounding area, no mud or silt was deposited on it, as a result of which no vegetation has been able to grow up over it. Perhaps the entire site was originally stones, but was gradually covered by alluvial mud with the passing of the days and years. May God forgive the possessor of this spirit, and may He forgive us all, Budayr."

I do not know why, but for some reason I suddenly thought back on the depraved Fla'as and felt a terrible curiosity to know that would become of him. So I said, "Dear Thawna, what do you think will end up happening with Fla'as at the Atrib monastery?"

Thawna heaved a doleful sigh, then replied broodingly, "Let us pray that the Lord will guide him back into the community of the God-fearing, Budayr, and that he will acknowledge his fault, confess his sins, and repent of them. You know that what he said was a serious blasphemy. Consequently, if he wants to resurrect his soul from its death, he will have to confess all his sins to his spiritual father at the Atrib monastery. Specifically, he will have to acknowledge that he was a slave to Satan through his obedience to him in transgressing the Holy Scriptures and his reading of blasphemous heresies, as well as every other sin that he may have committed, whether by way of murder, fornication, theft, lying, bearing false witness, or any other sort of forbidden act. Once he has done that, the abbot will begin by putting him to a test to see whether he has really turned to God with all his heart, or whether this was just presumption on his part and a way of putting others to the test. The abbot will require him to fast, pray, and give alms out of what he possesses, and to prostrate as many times as he is able for a specified period of time. If it is confirmed through his response to this regimen that he sincerely and fervently longs for Christ Jesus and eternal life, the priest will subject him to suffering once again in an underground prison cell for another specified period of time, and if he confirms his desire for repentance, he will bring him to a wing of the monastery to attend a recitation of the Scriptures and of the Holy Gospel in particular. Then the priest will take him by the hand and lead him out lest he attend the celebration of the divine mysteries and his soul be sanctified by the Holy Spirit's descent upon him. All of this is a trial and a test of his patience and endurance to ascertain whether or not he has truly returned to faith and is able to remain firm in what is required of him. This is the way in which correction takes place through repentance and admonition.

"Then the priest will bring him into the church's western wing in the monastery and utter the prayer of the admonished over him. The absolution from the uncleanness of foreign nations will be recited over him and the priest will anoint him with unconsecrated oil while reciting over him a prayer that befits his new beginning. After this he will be instructed to raise his right hand and to confirm his renunciation of Satan and his hosts as well as the causes which proceed from him, lead to him, and operate through him, namely, murder, fornication, theft, lying, bearing false witness, injustice, bitterness, hatred and backbiting, laziness in prayer, pride—which is the root of all vices—the reading of heresies and forbidden books, blasphemy, and unbelief.

"When the admonished individual's renunciation of Satan has been verified through several repudiations in the presence of all the priests and monks, he is stripped naked as our Lord Jesus Christ, to Him be glory, was when he was crucified, and the priest puts him on public display as the body of our Lord Jesus was put on display when he was naked. He then affirms the orthodox faith, that is, he confesses, 'We believe in one God' and so forth, repeating after the priest with both of his hands raised. Then, once he has finished repeating the statement of faith after the priest, the priest asks him, 'Do you believe?' and the admonished individual—Fla'as in this case—says, 'I believe' three times in succession.

"Following this he is taken to the place of holy baptism and anointed with holy oil, after which the priest begins by praying over the baptismal water and asking God the Father, Ruler of all, in the name of the Only Son Jesus Christ Our Lord, to descend upon the Pentecostal water which, in the act of baptism, symbolizes His Holy Spirit, in order for the water to be consecrated. Then an entire Mass is celebrated over the water in honor of the occasion of the believing soul's rebirth through God, His only Son, and His Holy Spirit. Finally, in order for him to be completely purified, Fla'as will have to be circumcised. All of this applies if he truly returns and repents and if his soul is freed from the deception of Satan and his iniquitous hosts."

Thawna's gaze wandered for a few moments. Then suddenly he asked me, "How much farther do you think we have to go before we reach the Bashmourite's camp?"

I sat there calculating approximately which towns and villages we still had to pass through and how much time it would take to get there. Then I said, "We will be passing through several villages and towns, which may take the rest of the day, before we reach the area near the Harus Sea, and from there, God willing, we will make our way to the road that leads to the Bashmourite's camp."

Thawna thought for a while, then replied, "So then, we will have to spend the night somewhere close by, possibly in the first village we come to. And after that, if the Merciful One grants us life till then, we can continue on our way with the first morning light."

I went over to untie the two mounts, which were waiting for us under the tree where we had left them. However, after I brought them and we had mounted and started out again, the ground started to become extremely slippery and nearly impassable on account of the rainfall we had had. Locusts blanketed the path after having grown weary from their long journey and their gluttonous munching, and most of them had died and fallen to the ground. Shying and hemming at every step, the two mules appeared to have an aversion to walking over the locusts and the slippery path, and as a result we did not get very far. The sun was about to disappear from sight by this time, and we had grown weary and bored with our futilely slow progress.

So Thawna said, "Budayr, what do you say we spend the night here in this spot? Tomorrow is another day."

"Here, in this bleak, uninhabited wilderness?" I cried in dismay. "I do not think that would be wise or safe, Thawna."

Trying to persuade me, he said, "There has to be somewhere we can find shelter around here. Or we could sleep under a tree. Do you not remember the Virgin Mary's journey with the Lord Christ from Bethlehem to the land of Egypt and all her weariness and sufferings along the way? Yet she gave no thought to any of that. Did she not lean up against a tree trunk for rest and shade since there was not any shelter to protect her or any roof to shield her from the heat of the day and the cold of the night? The Lord is the One who protects us, Budayr, and we are on a mission for the glory of the Church. We have to preserve and protect Father Joseph's letter so that we can deliver it to the Bashmourite, since this is our mission. Consequently, we have to endure for its sake whatever difficulties come our way."

I fell silent after that, ashamed of myself for my outburst, and did not argue with what he had said, as he had restored to me the reassurance of faith. Meanwhile, he looked around in search of something we could take for shelter. We were near the river's edge, so he left me and went a short distance away to get a look at the place, and before long he called for me to follow him. When I got to where he was, he pointed with his hand to a place nearby on the lowest part of the riverbank.

"Do you see that?" he asked. "It looks like a hut that some fishermen built for shade. God never forgets His faithful servants, Budayr. Come on, now, let us go inside and let it be our shelter till tomorrow morning, God willing."

Thawna seemed overjoyed to have come upon this hut, and I for my part had begun to feel safer and more reassured from the moment I saw it. The fact was that Thawna, having never lived there, did not know the perils of the marshlands as I did. It is filled with wild animals and beasts that feed and live in its forests and thickets, and in most cases they are ferocious, deadly creatures that attack and kill riding animals and human beings. Perhaps the most dangerous among them is the wild boar, which prefers to hide and live in wooded areas and in any uninhabited wilderness. It is exceedingly treacherous, and everyone despises it for its uncleanness and its reckless assaults on crops. I got off my mule and pulled it along as I walked down with Thawna toward the edge of the riverbank. As I walked, I took hold of the edge of my ritually pure clerical robe to keep it from getting soiled with mud. Then we pushed the hut door open and stood in the entrance to get an idea of what was inside before night fell. As Thawna had suspected, we found indications that fishermen had been there. It contained a wood-burning brazier and some dry tree branches, as well as a mat of the sort made by fishermen that someone had rolled up and leaned against one of the hut's brick walls. We also found a jug with some water in it, some fishhooks, a disintegrating net, and various other sorts of fishing tackle.

We brought the two mules inside to keep them safe, then quickly rolled out the mat and began taking our provisions out of our saddlebags so that we could have something to eat and get some rest. As we were working, Thawna said, "What do you say we let the Lord provide some fish for our supper? I will catch a fish or two, we will roast them up, then we will eat before we go to sleep for the night."

He took a fishhook and went out toward the river while I stayed back to prepare a meal from what we had brought with us. The monks at Atrib had supplied us with some locally made loaves of bread whose dough had been kneaded together with lamb's rump, a delicacy for which Atrib was famed. I got up and put some tree branches in the brazier, lit the fire, and went out to gather some grasses to feed the mules before night was upon us and we could no longer leave the hut.

I crossed myself and prayed to the Lord in my heart for fear that the grasses might contain some poisonous plant that would kill our mounts, thereby delaying us on our journey. Father Joseph had offered to send a third mule with us, as is customary, so that if anything happened to one of the two we were riding, we would have another one to replace it with. However, Thawna preferred that we content ourselves with just two, since the third might be needed by the clergymen if they left Qasr al-Sham' to go somewhere in Fustat, or if they crossed over Giza on boats.

He said to Father Joseph, "Did the Lord ride anything but a single she-ass? God is the one who preserves us, sir."

Pleased with what Thawna had said, Father Joseph blessed him as he prayed for God to grant us success.

As I was cutting some grasses with the dagger that Thawna had given me before our departure from Qasr al-Sham', I heard a scream ring out from the direction in which Thawna had gone down to fish at the river's edge. I dropped what I was doing and went rushing to him, heading in the direction of his cry. I had the dagger in my hand so that I could fight off whoever or whatever had attacked him. However, when I reached him I found him squatting and doubled over. He was clutching his lower leg, which was bleeding profusely. The minute I saw him in this state, I started screaming myself.

"Calm down, Budayr," he said in an unruffled voice. "It was a snake. It bit me without my even feeling it. O God, its fangs were as sharp as a doctor's scalpel. Hurry now, Budayr, make an incision in the wound with the dagger before the poison spreads."

I hesitated before doing what he had asked of me, since the sight of blood turns my stomach to the point where I nearly vomit. Besides which, the thought of wounding Thawna with my dagger was painful for me. But I finally got hold of myself and gathered enough courage to start making an incision at the site of the wound, doing it in the name of the Cross, until most of the blood had come out. Then Thawna bent over his leg and started sucking the blood out and quickly spitting it out, after which he shed his clerical belt and tied it securely around the site of the wound. Last of all, he got up and, with him leaning on my shoulder, we made it back to the hut.

As soon as he had stretched out on the mat he said to me, "Go over to my saddlebag and you will find some small containers. Bring them to me quickly."

I reached into the saddlebag and took out several vials as he had requested. I was amazed, since this was the first time since we had left on our journey that I had known that Thawna was carrying all these things with him. Some of the vials were made of sant wood, amber, and ebony, while others were made of alabaster, amethyst, carnelian-like onyx, ivory, and jasper. He asked me to open the one made of ivory and let him swallow some of its contents.

I lifted the lid and removed some small brown grains the likes of which I had never seen before. They did not look like corn or fava beans, or any of the grains or legumes I was familiar with that are eaten or soaked. They looked more to me like peanuts, though they were smaller and, unlike peanuts, a dark brown color. I gave him the grains, which he crushed between his molar teeth before swallowing them.

"These are 'Arabs' grains,' Budayr," he explained. "The Arabs bring them from their faraway lands, and they will be of great benefit in keeping me awake. Do not dare let me doze off even for a moment, Budayr, even you have to slap me on the face or pour cold water over my head, because if I lose consciousness, the poison will spread easily through my blood until it reaches the seats of the nerves in the brain, and that will be the end of me."

"May God protect you from evil and heal you, Thawna," I murmured, crossing myself and feeling fearful and distraught. "I will do everything you tell me to. Do not worry about a thing. I am with you and the Lord will preserve you. I will stay awake by your side all night."

Then he asked me to give him the ebony vial, which was a tiny container, with the greatest of care. After taking it from me he opened it gently and cautiously, then took a small amount of the oil it contained, which looked to me like holy oil, then began rubbing it into the site of the wound where the snake had plunged its fangs. As he did so, he gritted his teeth, stoically enduring the pain without emitting a single moan or groan over the hardship that had afflicted him. When he had finished applying the oil, I took the vial and put it back in his saddlebag. Then I lit a fire with some dry corncobs for us to keep warm by. The flames blazed up, then died down, the cobs turning to red-hot embers, and I heated a bit of honey in one of three long-necked glass bottles that we had bought in Atrib and gave it to him to drink. When he had finished it, I sat down beside him and suggested that he eat something of what we had brought, or that we drink some wine. However, he refused, saying that wine is not helpful in cases of snakebite. I had thought that it would relieve the pain in his wound, but he explained to me that anything that could cause one to lose consciousness should be avoided in a case like his.

I cried out to God in my heart to save Thawna from the poison of that snake. It was a type my father had always warned me about, terribly dangerous, whose bite is difficult to recover from. I would get up from time to time and stoke the fire to keep it from going out, chanting the words, "But if Christ is in you, although your bodies are dead because of sin, your spirits are alive because of righteousness. If the spirit of Him who raised Jesus from the dead dwells in you, He who raised Christ Jesus from the dead will give life to your mortal bodies also through His spirit which dwells in you." I recited some of what I had memorized from the catechetical teachings, and I also recalled the words of John Golden Mouth, who said, "Every human being on the face of the earth must see what has been preordained for him."

At a little past midnight, Thawna began to lose consciousness as the fever took hold of him. His body started to tremble so badly that I put the woolen saddlebag over him despite the fact that he was already covered with the linen blanket that we had brought to keep us warm at night along the way. I closed the hut door and placed a rock in front of it, yet despite the intensity of the heat inside, Thawna kept shaking. The fever seemed to have gotten the better of him, and he had become frail and weak.

Struggling mightily to keep his eyes open, he said to me, "Listen, Budayr. If I lose consciousness, you have got to treat me with cold water. Bring it from the river in any pot you can find and keep my head wet the entire time, since that can be helpful. But if God takes me, do not despair. Do what's done for the dead and pray for God's mercy on me. However, you must get to the Bashmourite as fast as you can, since Father Joseph is awaiting his reply, and if he finds him pliant and willing to listen, he wants him to come and speak with him face to face. After all, this is our ecclesiastical mission, Budayr, my dear, good-hearted brother."

Then he began little by little to succumb to the fever, and this despite the fact that I had gotten up right away and brought cold water from the river. My cowl, which was shaped in the distinctive way that Copts' cowls are supposed to be, was useful for the way it remained saturated with water even after it had been wrung out and placed on his head. However, this did not stop the fever. On the contrary, it kept rising to the point where I was in utter despair, and I started weeping bitter tears over him. After all, Thawna was all I had left in this world. He was closer to my spirit and heart than anyone else on earth. As I thought back on my earlier life—Amuna, my mother, my father, my brothers and sisters, my friends and peers—I lost my composure and started bawling like a woman, since once Thawna was gone, I would not have anyone left in this world, God have mercy on me. Then suddenly, as I sat by his side, lost in spirit, heartsick and not knowing what I should do in the midst of this ordeal, he started to rave deliriously. He would mutter from time to time:

"Jesus the Savior, the Virgin Mary, our last supper, the snake, poison, the black elder. . . . Ah, the Divinity is greater than time, eternity, and all creation! He cannot be named, no eye can behold Him! We seek assistance in knowing Him through names and images. Gold, ivory, sandalwood . . . He is the Lord of all. Everyone knows Him in his own way. The Holy Trinity. The thrice-great Hermes, Tahouti, the Trinity of Mercies. Atrib the lost. Fla'as the blasphemer. The land is in agony. The gods have abandoned the earth and gone to heaven. Poverty and deprivation are everywhere. 'If you would be perfect, go, sell what you possess and give to the poor. . . . Nun, ya, fa', ya'. Ka, ba, ba', nun, waw, mim, alif. Imhotep, O Kyrios meta pandon imon, Imhotep, high priest, Eis anatolas vlepsete, the god of wisdom, Anastasis, sakamura, Thoxa Patri ke lo ke Ayjio Pnevmati, Ibnafmata haksbala. . . ."

As I listened to all the things Thawna was mumbling in his delirious rantings, I lost my composure entirely and my body started shuddering with fear just as his was shuddering with fever. I was convinced that Satan had taken over his spirit and had driven him to this kind of confused talk, which was mixed with everything pure and holy. I was gripped by a terrible fear that this mental and verbal disorder was a sign that my dear brother was on the verge of expiring, and that his death would be a destruction of both body and spirit. For these were demons—alas and alack—that were leading his spirit into the hellfire. I rushed to bring the scroll of the Bible that Father Joseph had given us to use against the dangers of our journey and the demons and evil spirits we might encounter along the way if we were not able to recall the verses we had memorized for such situations. Every verse in it had been recorded in both Akhmimite and Arabic, with a verse in Akhmimite on one side, and the same verse in Arabic on the other. I would read sometimes from one language and sometimes from the other, since Thawna—the virtuous and knowledgeable—had taught me a bit of the Akhmimite language, which I had not known at all before that. As for Arabic, I had learned some from a maternal uncle of mine in Tarnit who had been employed as a village mayor by the caliph-appointed administrator of the district in which his town was located—most such mayors being Copts due to the fact that they were most familiar with the villages' affairs and the conditions of their inhabitants.

During my halting reading, I suffered pangs of regret for not having learned the way I really should have. So may the Lord forgive me if I erred in forming His holy words with my tongue, and may my eye be struck blind if, in future, I do not go on to learn the language of His holy books by His will and grace.

At the same time, I made a vow that if, if God foreordained that Thawna should recover from his illness and we should return safely to Qasr al-Sham' after our mission to the Bashmourite, I would make an honest confession to Father Joseph of my first sin and truly repent of it. And I swore by the head of the Blessed Marcus ibn al-Qunburi—who said, "There is no forgiveness without confession"—to do it with an honest heart.

This was because I was sure now that what had happened to Thawna and the uncertainty and lostness I was feeling was all on account of the weakness of my own faith and my dishonesty toward Father Joseph in my confessions. May the Lord have mercy on me, I thought, and may the time come quickly when I can confess and be purified, that my bonds might be loosened through his word just as Abba Sawirus once absolved a deacon by his word. I promised myself that I would accept whatever verdict Father Joseph issued concerning me and submit to whatever ecclesiastical disciplines he prescribed for me. I would come before him in all humility as I ought to, my knees bent and my head bowed, then make three prostrations before the altar in the hope that he might consent in the end to pray the prayer of absolution over me so that, repentant and my spirit purged of all past iniquity, I might be granted the blessing of Holy Communion.

My tears would not stop flowing as I thought about all these things. In the meantime, my tongue kept busy reciting the Psalms and other verses from the scriptures. However, I was so distraught, I had stopped wetting him with water, fearing that if I put my hand on him or touched him, I might be possessed by Satan as he had been. The thought that it was Satan at work was confirmed to me when he uttered the forbidden name of Hermes, and from the way the things he said about Jesus and the Virgin were mixed with blasphemies that began emerging from somewhere deep within him. He had also uttered mysterious formulas that I knew nothing about. So, even though I considered Thawna to be my soul mate, my beloved friend, my companion, my spirit's twin, and my spiritual brother through baptism, I nevertheless had begun to doubt the soundness of his faith. This was especially so as I thought back on the things that used to be said about him in our church at Qasr al-Sham' and the stories some people used to tell about conversations they had had with him or situations they had experienced with him. For example, Deacon Stephanus had told me once about how he had wanted to leave his quarters one night to get some fresh air in the church's courtyard, but that when he got as far as Thawna's room, he found a huge mass of water that had been gradually rising and which, even as he stood there, reached the point where it was higher than a man is tall. He was so terrified he froze in place, unable to pass by lest he drown, so instead of going on to the courtyard as he had planned, he returned, trembling, to his own quarters. A sexton at the church by the name of Simeon had also related that around noon one day, he had found Thawna talking to a small hoopoe bird that had landed on his knee. He said that Thawna had been telling the bird something in a strange language that he had never heard before. However, after listening to stories like these, Father Joseph would counter their claims with verses from the Holy Scripture based on what he had seen of Thawna's good faith, his perfect obedience to church regulations, and his whole-hearted service.

I had the urge to open up all the deepest parts of him to find out what was there, and to search in his saddlebag, where I might find something that would satisfy my curiosity and reveal to me once and for all what the real state of affairs was. But I was afraid, too, since doing something like that might bring me harm, or bring me under some magic spell. So I stayed where I was, looking over at him and trembling with fright. The area around his wound had become swollen and puffy, and it had turned bright red as though it had been soaked in crimson dye. For a moment I nearly screamed with terror as he began crying, "Dalluka! O great mother! O you have been blessed by the Holy One, the mother of the gods, Isis, descendent of the first deities! Mistress of perfume and myrrh! O you who planted the sakamura tree and introduced it to the land of Egypt! O you who reign supreme over all lords, my schoolteacher! O you to whom I will be indebted all my life for my learning and knowledge! You who reign supreme over all those who are not known and whose names can never be uttered!

"Tahouti . . . yes . . . yes . . . I hold Kemet in my heart, whose supreme glory will never end. No, it will never end. The black elder. Yes, yes, yes, my mother, I will recite to you the lesson I memorized. Ah . . . it has diminished or ceased to exist, and is found only in al-Matariya and 'Ayn Shams. I know it is a location that is enclosed and preserved. I will say everything, my teacher. I beg you, give me just a little more time, a little more time. Do not punish me or allow me to get lost in the school's dark corridor, where Anubis will come out and tear my heart to pieces. My tongue is heavy. I will speak, but my tongue is heavy, and my body is plunging me into an abyss. Aah, its tree! It is about a cubit high, a cubit and maybe more. On it there are two layers of bark, the outer one red and light, and the inner one green and thick, and if it is chewed, its oiliness makes itself felt in the mouth. It has a pleasant, perfume-like aroma, and its leaves are similar to those of the rue plant. Ah, the harvest. I will speak about the harvest. Its oil is harvested at the rising of Sirius. Its branches are pounded until all of their leaves have been scraped off. As for the way in which they are pounded, it is done with a stone in such a way that the outer bark is cut through and the inner bark is split, but not all the way to the wood, since if it is split all the way to the wood, nothing will come out of it. However, if it is pounded in the manner we have described, its sap will be given time to flow onto the twig. After that, it is gathered with one's finger into a horn. Once the horn is full, the sap is poured into glass bottles, and this process is continued until the sap has run out. The more humid the atmosphere, the more abundant the sap will be, and conversely, in times of drought when there is little dew, the sap will be sparse. The bottles are then taken and buried at the height of the summer heat, after which they are dug up again and placed in the sun, and they are checked every day thereafter. At this point, the oil floats to the surface on top of a watery layer that has some sediment at the bottom, and the oil will be skimmed off the top. Then the bottles are put back in the sun. This process is repeated until no more oil is left to be skimmed off. The oil that has been collected will be taken and the sexton will cook it in secret, without allowing anyone to look on, then store it in cupboards. The amount of pure oil extracted from the sap after it has been filtered and clarified comes to about one-tenth of the original amount of sap.

"The consecrated oil in the baptismal waters. The black elder . . . .

"Have I memorized the lesson well, mother? I beg you to say to me, 'Bravo, bravo, my diligent, obedient student.' Grant me your blessing! Aah, my Lady the Virgin, O Mother of the Master, the holy oil has been placed in the baptismal water as the Lord has commanded. The Synaxarium I have memorized by heart, just as I have memorized the story without anything added or taken away. I say: I have memorized it. Yes, I will speak. I know it. So may the Lord Jesus preserve me for what you brought forth, O Sublime Virgin and with you, Joseph the carpenter from Jerusalem.

"The Satan Herod was king of the Jews, and you stopped at Basta, which was the first place you came to in the land of Egypt.

"Basta, al-Maqdis, Buways. The fourteenth of Bashans. Their people did not receive you, so you remained on the outskirts and stayed only a few days.

"Budayr . . . kind Budayr . . . the feudal peasant living in sin. Yes, you went to Samanud, crossing the Nile toward the West and on to the city of Ashmunein."

When I heard what he had said about me in his delirious ravings, I burst into tears.

"No! No, dear Thawna! I will never live in sin ever again! May the Lord have mercy on me. Get well, Thawna, and come back to me, and you will never find me anything but pure and repentant. I will confess to you, Thawna. I will confess to you my sin and my first transgression, which torments me and eats away at my spirit!"

His body began to tremble and shudder. However, he kept on ranting, his words coming faster and faster and more jumbled than ever:

"The slanderous mare standing on four pillars. The mare fell and broke to pieces when they looked at it and entered. To Him be glory, His sign in Ashmunein. Five laden camels pressed about you, O holy ones, as you passed through, but Jesus shouted at them, at them he shouted in Ashmunein, and the camels turned to stones. Faylas, Faylas . . . there for days, and from there to the city of 'Qis wa Qam,' Qawsiya, where Satan spoke from the bellies of the idols. And he said . . . he said . . . he said . . . ."

He kept repeating, "He said" till I was about to slap myself on the face. And I thought: He is in the throes of death for certain. O, how miserable and wretched am I! How could I have been afflicted thus with my bosom friend, my beloved Thawna?

However, I was astonished after this to hear him begin to speak as though he were repeating from memory some of the theotokias. He said, "Satan spoke out of the bellies of the idols that were there, and he said, 'A woman has come with her son and they want to destroy your abodes and places of worship.' One hundred men then emerged with their arms and drove you out of the city. Then you went in the direction of Mira to the west of Qawsiya and stayed at Muharraq Monastery, where you remained for six months and a number of days. Then Joseph the Carpenter was informed in a dream of Herod's death and instructed to bring the Lord back to Jerusalem.

"Hence, you all traveled back from Mira until you reached Qasr al-Sham'. You remained in the cave near the Church of Abu Sirga, then you departed for 'Ayn Shams and rested near some water, where the Virgin Mary washed the Lord Jesus's clothes. And in the place where you, O Holy Virgin, poured out the wash water, God caused the black elder to grow up. This was in Jordan. Thereafter it was no longer found there, but remained in this land.

"Aah . . . may you be pleased with me, great Dalluka, my teacher, the Virgin Mary, and the Lord, my Lord, Budayr's Lord, the Lord of Joseph, and the Lord of everyone on earth."

When I opened my eyes, which were nearly blinded from the daylight that was filtering down through the hut's reed roof, I did not find Thawna lying beside me on the mat. I jumped up in astonishment, gripped by the fear that had not left me since the day before. Then I rushed out after putting on my shoes, whose laces I had tied in a way that violated the orders that had been issued by Fustat's caliphal administrator. This was what Thawna had instructed me to do when we came into the marshlands' Halfa Wilderness so that the backs of our feet and our ankles would not be soiled by the mud, since in this place we could not be seen by any of the administrator's men. Even so, we had adhered throughout our journey thus far to the wearing of our saffron-yellow robes and the coarse linen belts around our waists, the use of wooden pommels on our saddlebows, as well as everything else that had been imposed on us as Copts in order to ensure that our appearance distinguished us from that of Muslims.

The moment I stepped out the door, I found Thawna standing before me.

"Good morning!" he said with a smile as though nothing had happened, and as though he had not been delirious with fever all the previous night.

Startled and overjoyed, I cried, "Thawna! Dear Thawna! My beloved brother, are you all right? How did you manage to get up and come out? Thank God you have recovered. This is a miracle from the Lord, Thawna. O God!"

I was so overwrought, the words came pouring out of my mouth in a torrent while tears gushed out of my eyes. I was like a lost child who has been found by his mother.

Thawna put his arms around me and patted me reassuringly as he said, "It seems you stayed up by my side for a long time last night, Budayr, and you tired yourself out. You did not even wake up for the morning prayer. In any case, I have performed mine, and I prayed for you, too. Thanks be to God, by whose bounty and grace I survived what happened to me. Black elder oil is one of the most effective oils for treating snake and scorpion bites, not to mention all sorts of other ailments, bites, and stings. The 'Arabs' grain' was also helpful in that it kept the loss of consciousness I suffered from having its full effect on the brain. Praise be to God. Now, then, let us have some breakfast. I have gathered some pomegranates. It seems that the owner of the hut planted them nearby, and I found them hanging down within reach, so I picked some. If we eat them, they will help to keep us from getting diarrhea from the green plants we pick and eat along the way."

We went inside to eat, and more than once I nearly brought up the things that he had said during his fever-induced delirium the night before. However, I held back every time, preferring to wait until I could come up with a tactful, delicate way to broach the topics I wanted to ask him about without causing him pain. So when he proposed that we prepare our food quickly and be on our way, I agreed to it immediately, and did not add a word.

From that point onward, we traveled for the most part alongside the river. The path would sometimes be cut off by the waters which, the deeper we went into the marshlands, became more and more ubiquitous. As a consequence, we would be obliged to veer outward and bypass the watery areas, then find our way back to the path again. Some fishermen would volunteer to take us in their boats for short distances near the riverbank, though they were afraid to go far from shore during that time of the year. Many of the towns and villages we passed through had gone to ruin, having been deserted entirely by their inhabitants, while many of their fields had likewise gone to ruin. We were informed by some of the fishermen that with their livelihoods cut off, not enough to eat from one day to the next, not to mention their fear of being tortured and beaten by those who controlled the villages and monitored the markets to ensure that people paid their taxes, many of the farmers who lived in the area had taken their wives and children and joined the Bashmourites, seeking protection among them and declaring their disobedience to the caliph and his governors. As we passed along, we saw large numbers of filthy, shabbily clad, miserable-looking young men and women wandering about aimlessly and begging in the roads. We were advised by the fishermen to avoid them as best we could, since hunger had driven them to such desperation that they might steal our mounts and rob us of everything we had with us.

An old man we met along the way informed us that most of these people were from the villages located along the edges of the wilderness in the direction of the desert inhabited by the Arab tribes, particularly those of al-Hawf al-Sharqi, who were not above attacking the villages, robbing their inhabitants of their property, and taking their children and sometimes their women. They had also destroyed crops to the point where most of these towns had gone to ruin and been abandoned by their residents. It was this same old man who told us about a miraculous incident that had taken place at the Convent of the Virgins, and which neither Thawna nor I had heard about before. In fact, I do not think anyone from our church knew anything about it prior to that time. All we knew was that Marwan, the caliph-appointed governor of the land, had sent men out against the Bashmourites, who had routed them and driven them back, and that when his men returned to him in defeat, he had authorized them to loot and kill in all the towns they happened to come to. Consequently, these men had gone to Upper Egypt and murdered a group of church leaders, after which they proceeded to loot their property, take their women and children into captivity, and burn down their monasteries and convents.

The old man told us that in the Convent of the Virgins there were thirty nuns who had consecrated themselves as brides of Christ. These nuns were captured by Marwan's soldiers, and among them was a teenage girl who had entered the convent when she was three years old. When they saw her, they were dazzled by her beauty.

"Never among human beings have we seen such beauty!" they declared. So they brought her out and consulted among themselves as to what they should do with her. Some of them said, "Let us cast lots for her," while others said, "Let us take her to the king." As they were thus engaged in debate, the girl said to them, "Where is your leader? I want to give him some information that is worth a sum of money. I call upon you to release me, since I am a servant of God and you have no right to spoil my worship. However, if I tell you about this thing which can bring you great wealth, will you let me return to my convent?" One of the men then came forward and said, "I am their leader." She said to him, "My forefathers, who were courageous, strong warriors, passed on to me an oil which they used to apply to their bodies when they went out to the battlefield with the result that iron could do nothing to them. Swords and spears that came against them would become like wax. Now, if you free me, I will give it you. And if you do not believe what I am saying, I will rub my neck with it while you look on. As for you, you are to bring forth the best sword found among your men, then let the strongest of them strike me, and it will not cut me. In this way you will know the truth of my words."

She had said this, however, because she preferred death by the sword to being defiled by iniquity and allowing her pristine body to be polluted. She then entered her living quarters and brought out a clay vessel containing some oil over which the saints had prayed and which she had kept with her. She applied it to her neck, her face and her entire body, after which she prayed on bended knee and stretched out her neck. The ignoramuses thought that she had told them the truth, not knowing what was in her heart. Then she said to them, "Whoever among you is strong and his sword sharp and cutting, let him demonstrate his strength in me, for you will see the glory of God in this oil." Thereupon a brave young man jumped up with a sword in which he took pride. Concealing her face with her nun's cape and full of serene confidence, she said to him, "Strike with all your might, and fear not."

So he struck the martyr saint and her head went flying. They then realized what she had done, and that she had deceived them. Full of remorse and terrible grief, great fear fell upon them. And from that day forward they never once looked lustfully at any of the virgin nuns. Instead, they left them in peace and went on their way glorifying God.

We, too, murmured praises to His glory after we had heard this. Thawna was so moved he had to fight back his tears, which kept falling despite his best efforts to contain them. Then we moved on, bidding the old man farewell and promising that if God granted us a safe journey, we

79

would tell Father Joseph about this martyr saint as soon as we returned to Qasr al-Sham'.

After we had gone some way, a village appeared in the distance, and Thawna proposed that we stop there so that we could wash up and change our clothes, the hems of which had become soiled with dirt and mud despite our assiduous efforts to keep them clean. I, too, was of a mind to stop so that we could cut our hair and shave. I was also thinking that this might provide me an opportunity to ask him about the things he had said during his illness. As we were riding along, I started thinking about everything that had happened to us, and when I got as far as our encounter with Fla'as the heretic, I recalled a story about a certain deacon who had been a sorcerer, and it seemed that it might provide the opening I needed to get Thawna into a conversation about the things I wanted to bring up.

"Thawna!" I exclaimed, "Do you remember the story about the deacon sorcerer that some of the patriarchs have told?"

When he heard my question, Thawna stopped in his tracks for a few moments until I had gotten several steps ahead of him in spite of myself.

"God have mercy!" he said, "Why are you remembering the story about that accursed fellow now, while we are on the road?"

I did not say anything for a while, then I continued, "I do not know why it occurred to me just now. I think the man practiced magic and killed a young boy, and was punished for it."

Warming to the subject, Thawna interjected, "No, no. He did not kill the boy. As the story has it, God had brought a terrible affliction on the land of Egypt. When 'Ubaydallah left the country, his son Qasim took power in the land, and the son turned out to be several times more evil than his father. As the Holy Gospel declares, 'every sound tree bears good fruit, but the bad tree bears evil fruit.' This man did evil before God and people in his kingdom and trod the path of iniquity. Solomon the Wise, son of David, once said, 'Woe to the inhabitants of that kingdom which is ruled by a boy.' Well, this Qasim was a mere boy, both in years and in actions, and he committed many transgressions. The beginning of the affliction was a terrible rise in prices. In the first year, the unirrigated lands were not reached by the Nile floods, as a result of which the fruits of the earth diminished, wheat disappeared altogether, and many people and animals died. In the second year, the land of Egypt was struck by an epidemic the likes of which it had never seen before. Even so, Qasim did nothing to turn from his evil ways. On the contrary, his wickedness increased. He raised the kharaj imposed on the people so many times that when one went to sleep at night, he would be afraid to see the light of day, and people would long for night to fall just to find relief from their sufferings. After the second deadly year, the third year saw another drought so bad that the Nile did not rise at all, and there was no relief in sight. On the contrary, the years kept alternating in this way by God's command: one year an epidemic, the next a drought, until the end of the seventh year, at which time the kingdom was taken from him. The epidemic would last every year from the beginning of Hator until the twenty-second of Paona, and most of it would hit Egypt on account of the many sins being committed there. Between the eighth day of Bashans and the first day of Paona, there were so many deaths that not all of them were recorded. One day two thousand would die, another day, one thousand two hundred, and another day, two thousand four hundred of the people living in Egypt and Giza, as well as foreign merchants, until they stopped digging graves and burying the dead, and a man would not be buried until the sultan had learned of his death and his name and his father's name had been recorded. This applied even to nursing infants. Then our ancestors, rich and poor alike, cried out to the Lord. They made entreaty to God with fasting, prayer, tears, and supplication until He had mercy on them and lifted the scourge.

"After this the merchants began selling wheat to the people again, since it was now available in abundance. In addition, some of them went to a deacon in the city of Memphis, which is the ancient Cairo, who happened to be a sorcerer. They paid him a large sum of money and asked him to cast a spell that would cause the price of wheat to go up. So he began committing deeds that incited God's wrath through his craft and his wicked sorcery. Now, this sorcerer had with him a young orphan boy who was his mother's only son. He had once said to her, 'You have nothing to eat and nothing to feed your son. So send him to me, and I promise to make him my own son and teach him my trade.' Hence, she handed her son over to him gladly. This infidel had gone to many sorcerers in various places who had taught him powerful magic, and he did what was required to make the price of wheat go up. He took the widow's son to a house and locked him inside, then hung him up by his hands and feet and did to him things that incited God's wrath. He would flay the skin on the boy's face and head every day until he had worked down to his shoulders. Wheat then disappeared from the market after having been sold at ten ardabs for a dinar and a bushel for a dinar. Around this same time, the school monitor went to the widow's house and said to her, 'Your son has not attended school for several days. Where is he?' So she went to that infidel and asked him about her son, to which he replied, 'I have not seen him myself for several days. He left to go back to you, and I have not heard any news of him.' When the woman heard what he had said, she went away in great sorrow. At this point, the boy had not died yet. However, he was still suspended in mid-air and a large area of his body had been flayed. Around the same time, the school monitor started to notice that his teacher—who was the sorcerer himself—would go repeatedly into a certain storage room, which was where he had the young orphan boy suspended. So the monitor thought to himself: Why does my teacher keep going in and out of that storage room these days? An astute boy, he quietly followed the teacher the next time he went into the storage room, and what should he find but the widow's son: crying and pleading and being shown no mercy. The orphan boy was saying things that would have broken your heart: 'Woe to you, my widowed, grief-stricken mother, for you know not what has befallen me! Woe to the womb that bore me and to the breasts that gave me suckle! Where are you, that you might look upon the torment of your orphan son? Would that I had died in your womb and that you had not brought me into this world to suffer such agony!' He went on and on this way as the monitor listened, until at last he rushed out, falling over himself with fright. When he reached the home of the orphan boy's mother he said to her, 'I have found your son,' whereupon she came in great haste after he had repeated in her hearing what he had heard from her son's mouth. She then went to the governor and lay her case before him. In response, the governor sent her with a number of trustworthy Muslims and a group of his subordinates to the infidel's house. They found him in the storage room with the boy, who was hanging in suspension, and whose neck and shoulders were badly flayed. They took the boy to the governor and, with him, the sorcerer, whose hands had been tied behind his back. The sorcerer's hands and feet were bound and his ears were cut off in the governor's presence, and he confessed to everything he had done. When the boy was brought in and they saw the condition he was in, they wrote immediately to Qasim, king of Egypt, who, when he read the letter, issued orders that the infidel should be stoned and his corpse burned."

After concluding the story of the 'sorcerer deacon,' Thawna turned to me earnestly and, looking me steadily in the eye, said, "Budayr, tell me honestly: Did I say anything improper when I was delirious with that fever?"

Not wanting to anger or embarrass him—since, after all, Thawna was like a teacher to me—I started evading the question. I told him he had said many things, including a hodgepodge of meanings and languages. I told him that he had spoken in Coptic part of the time and in Arabic part of the time, that he had used some Greek phrases, that he had uttered the name of Jesus the Word and the Virgin Mary, as well as other names and words in a language I did not recognize, although I thought it was the ancient tongue.

Looking over at me pointedly, he asked, "What strange names did I utter when I was delirious? For God's sake, tell me, Budayr, my good-hearted brother, the likeness of John Chrysostom—John with the golden mouth!"

When he continued pressing me I said, "I do not remember anymore, Thawna."

"Budayr, tell me the truth, by the Holy Cross."

At this point, sensing the depth of his anguish and pain, I said, "The fact is, and I tell you by the truth of the Cross, that you uttered the name of the one whose name it is not permissible to utter. You also mentioned the idols, Thawna."

I swallowed my saliva with difficulty as I told him this, and I did not dare look him in the eye for fear that he might accuse me of something or reveal to me some sin I had committed. After all, Satan is clever, and can deceive a person without his knowing it. What am I, I thought, but a lowly sexton that bakes the Eucharist bread and takes care of the church's mundane affairs? As for ecclesiastical work, I had no aptitude for it, nor did I have the right to delve into related questions, not to mention the fact that the worldly transgression into which I had fallen in Tarnit was still tormenting my spirit and polluting my thoughts.

With a sorrowful, despairing sigh Thawna said, "So then, my tongue was loosed when I was delirious, and it uttered things I have no desire to utter. It is true, Budayr, that I lived for a time in heresies before I was cleansed by the Church, and I immersed myself in scholastics and philosophy for long years. For a period of time I was a Christian Gnostic of the sort that claims to have true knowledge reserved for the elect, the kind that enables one to reach the First Cause and Source of all blessing through intuition and discovery of the soul. However, I was cleansed of all that filth by the grace of God, and I became a true, orthodox believer. This came about thanks to my diligence in faith and in reading true theology. But to be honest, Budayr, there are times when I have confused thoughts about this world we live in, and there are issues I do not understand in spite of my diligent study and my insight into people and their affairs. Tell me, please, Budayr: What's the meaning of all that is happening now? Our spiritual father at Qasr al-Sham' sends messengers to the Bashmourites, urging them to obey the authorities and the sultan and to pay the kharaj they owe. And now we are among those messengers he is sending, and my greatest fear is that the Bashmourites will react to us violently, or even kill us the way they murdered Isaac—the messenger Father Joseph sent to them last year—along with those with him. Besides, the Muslim Arabs are rising up against these governors, too, and refusing to pay the kharaj just as the Copts are doing. The fact is that the Muslims' religion commands the doing of what is good and prohibits the doing of what is evil and harmful, and it does not deny the Lord Jesus and the Virgin Mary. Most of the Arab Muslims are simple folk who are frugal and even austere in the way they live and dress, and their gathering places for prayer are devoid of gold or silver. Instead, they simply bow and prostrate themselves to God in reverence and humility. So then . . . tell me, I pray, dear Budayr: Why do these emirs and governors lord it over the people, acting like the emperors and kings of Byzantium in times of old? And why does our Father Joseph seek to mediate between them and the Bashmourites rather than supporting the Bashmourites against them? Why does he not command the governors to do what is good and forbid them to do what is evil so that they will be like the governors in the early days of Islam? According to what I have heard and read about them in books, they were pious and humble, fearing God and living lives of self-denial and austerity like monks in their cells. But look at those who are ruling us now. Look at this Marwan and the way he and his soldiers conduct themselves! They have turned into conceited bullies as though they were soldiers in the Byzantine army. I do not understand anything anymore, Budayr. I am afraid, brother, I swear to God. I do not know where the truth is anymore, or which way is up."

Amazed and bewildered, I crossed myself and said, "Is it you, dear Thawna, who is saying this? Is it you, with your vast learning and knowledge, who does not know where the truth is? No, I do not think so. But perhaps you do not know the Bashmourites the way I do, since they are my own people. They are boorish, coarse, brutal folks who do not know a thing about politics. All they know about is farming, hunting, and fishing. And it may be that Father Joseph knows what is best for them better than they themselves do. From his vantage point at Qasr al-Sham' in Old Cairo, he sees what they cannot see from their distant villages and hamlets, and he wants to spare them bloodshed. He is concerned to preserve their well-being and that of their women and children, and he wants to be a channel of blessing between them and the governor."

Thawna sighed wearily. What I had said did not seem to have impressed him. On the contrary, I detected what appeared to be a sardonic, condescending smile on his face as he nudged his mule to slow its pace a bit.

"How pure and innocent you are, my big-hearted Budayr," he said. "No, I do not think that is the only reason he does this, my dear. You see, what concerns Father Joseph first and foremost is our Jacobite

Church, its lands and its wealth, and the war he is waging is, first and foremost, against the heretical Melkites. In fact, he is hoping for the day when they are uprooted entirely from this land. The spread of Islam in the villages and hamlets does not worry him. On the contrary, he is keen to foster friendly ties with all Muslims, and particularly the emirs and governors, so that they can strengthen his hand against the Melkite Church. The reason for this is that, if the latter gains the upper hand in the country, this could allow the Byzantines to return and rule here again as they did in the past. Oh, Budayr, may the Lord have mercy on us. Our land is to be pitied, constantly in the throes of trial and affliction. It climbs out of a hole only to fall headlong into an abyss. Perhaps our tragedy lies in the fact that we earn most of our livelihood from planting and tilling, and the only way we know how to survive is by working the land. So maybe the best thing for us to do is to stick to the earth, seek peace, and spurn involvement in war and its affairs."

He was visibly pained as he spoke, and I recalled what he had said during his feverish rantings: "The land is in agony. The gods have abandoned the earth and gone to heaven. Poverty and deprivation are everywhere, O Jesus our Savior, O Virgin Mary."

I looked over at him with tender concern. He was looking distractedly into the distance, scanning the verdant horizon that stretched out before us. And as he urged his mount along the path again, he seemed to be hurting. Nay, more, he seemed to be in agony.

We entered the village, whose name, we had been told, was Ghayfa. It appeared at first sight not to have many people living in it, since the doors to most of its houses were shut, and when we first came down its streets, there were no children to receive us with shouting and noisy laughter even though it was the time of day when they would normally have been out playing and, the minute they saw us, would have announced to their families that there were strangers approaching.

When we reached its square—which was a spacious area used for threshing and winnowing wheat as one normally finds in towns and villages—all we saw was a single threshing machine off to one side.

A peasant woman with a gnarled, exceedingly wrinkled face appeared and began staring at us suspiciously from behind her half-open door. However, she seemed to decide after some time that we were trustworthy, having been reassured by the sight of our yellow attire and our braided belts, since this provided evidence of our belonging to the church. Thus reassured, she welcomed us heartily as though she had regained her youth, even though she was an elderly woman with only one front tooth remaining, in addition to an incisor tooth that became visible when she smiled. She apologized for her initial suspicion and her slowness to welcome us, explaining that she had a fear of strangers and poor vision owing to an eye disease with which she had been afflicted for some time. After we had hailed her reassuringly and begun making inquiries, she informed us that only a few peasants who worked the land were still living in the village. Most of them, she said, had abandoned the village, and it had become a way station for caravans of Muslim pilgrims on their way to Mecca. As a result, the majority of the villagers had converted to Islam owing to the advantages and benefits this afforded. They had come to prefer serving Muslim pilgrims over serving the land, given what the former brought them by way of dinars and silver, in return for the food and drink they served to the travelers. As a result, very few in the village retained an affiliation to the Church.

In response to further queries, the kindhearted mother informed us that this ancient village had been filled with people until very recently, and that those more elderly than she and whom she had seen before they died, used to say that the village dated back to the time when the king's goblet had been found missing in a city in Egypt, after which it was found in the camel-pack belonging to the brothers of the Prophet Joseph, who was said to be from this town of Ghayfa.

The old woman then received us warmly and had us sit in her guest area. She served us pickles, sardines, cactus fruit, and some of what she had cooked for her own lunch. She also gave us fenugreek tea sweetened with honey and served us what she had on hand by way of Fayyum grapes which—unlike the tiny yellow wine grapes that grew on our church's vines and which we called 'girl grapes' due to their lack of seeds—were large and pinkish red. When we had finished eating and drinking, we thanked her profusely and made ready to bid her farewell and be on our way. However, before we had had a chance to do so, she said she wanted to ask us a question, and that she had a problem which she hoped we could help her to solve.

As for the question, it was as follows: Most of the people who had remained in the village had embraced Islam, and of the small number of Christians remaining in the village, she had found no one suitable for her oldest daughter. Consequently, she had had no choice but to marry her to a man who had converted to Islam not long before. She had stipulated that he allow her daughter to remain a Christian if he wanted her to live with him under one roof, and in return she offered to let him have all of her money, assets, and land after she died and once her daughter had received her share of the inheritance. The man had agreed to her proposal and had allowed his wife to remain faithful to her own religion, which meant adhering to the rites of the Church just as she had done in her mother's house. However, she said, she was afraid she had disobeyed some command of God. All she had wanted was her daughter's happiness and to be assured that she was well taken care of before she died. However, she also wanted nothing more than for the Lord and Savior to be pleased with her, and to die with the assurance that she would receive grace in the Lord's kingdom.

When he first heard the woman's question, Thawna—who was the one authorized to speak in such a situation—was at a loss for words. As for me, I said nothing, since I had no right to issue judgments on matters I knew nothing about. For a while Thawna sat there without saying a word. Instead he just looked pensively at the woman, pondering the state of the world. However, at last he said, "These are difficult times, Mother, and there are questions which can only be answered on the Day of Judgment. May God forgive you, your daughter, her husband, and all of us. However, let me convey to you some of the luminous words written by the Apostle Paul to the people at Rome: 'I am carnal, sold under sin. I do not understand my own actions. For I do not do what I want, but I do the very thing I hate. Now if I do what I do not want, I agree that the law is good. So then it is no longer I that do it, but sin which dwells within me. For I know that nothing good dwells within me, that is, in my flesh. I can will what is right, but I cannot do it. For I do not do the good I want, but the evil I do not want is what I do. Now if I do what I do not want, it is no longer I that do it, but sin which dwells within me.'"

Thawna then began praying and making the sign of the cross while the old woman did the same. He explained to her that in order for God to preserve her and her daughter, she needed to get a copy of the book of God and keep it in her house. He added that this protection would be provided whether she actually read in it or not. He also advised her to go to church every Sunday for the communal prayers, to fast, and be diligent in adhering to orthodox Christian rites, and to urge her daughter to do the same. He explained to her that the Muslims' religion allows them to marry followers of the Jewish and Christian religions, given the fact that the followers of Islam acknowledge the prophets and messengers spoken of in the Jewish and Christian Scriptures. Then, at the woman's request, he proceeded to recite phrases and verses of protection over her.

Following this, the woman led us to the site of the problem she hoped we could help her to solve. It was a chicken coop that she had situated next to the place where she kept the animals that she raised in her backyard. Next to the coop there was a chick incubator. She said that she had followed the generally accepted rules relating to hatching, but that most of the eggs went bad and did not hatch. She then showed us the 'hatching house.' It was a rectangular structure: eight hand spans long, six hand spans wide, and approximately four hand spans high. It had a square door in the center that measured two hand spans, one inch by two hand spans, one inch. Over the door there was a small round window one hand span in diameter over which there was an awning consisting of four pieces of wood. Above the window was a barrier woven out of reeds on top of which there was some sasi, that is, the dried remains of the flax plant used as tinder. Above this there was a layer of mud, with the bricks arranged as is customary. The rest of the structure was covered with mud inside and out, top and bottom in order to prevent steam from escaping. In its roof there was the requisite window which was one hand span by one hand span, in which respect it resembled a chicken's breast. There were also two troughs made of clay mixed with flax straw. Each trough was six hand spans long and one and a half hand spans wide, with walls that were about one inch thick and about four finger-lengths high. This type of trough rested on a single slab, as it should, on a level floor, and was referred as to a tajin. The two troughs had been dried and mounted firmly on either edge of the ceiling, one of them over the door and the other across from it on the other side, having been stuck on securely with mud. These two troughs were meant to simulate the hen's wings. The 'house' was carpeted with a basketful of straw smoothed out, and over which a mat had been placed. The eggs had been neatly arranged on top of the mat in such a way that they were in contact with each other yet without being piled on top of one another in order for heat to pass among them. All of this had been put in place for the purpose of hatching the eggs.

The incubator door was sealed with a piece of wool tailor-made to fit it, while the small round window in the wall as well as the window in the roof were covered with flax straw. The structure was topped with dung to prevent any steam from escaping, and in the troughs there was about three whibas of dried cow's dung and a stove filled with live coals that had not yet burned down to ashes. The old woman said that she checked the eggs every hour by placing them on her eye in order to test their temperature, and that they did not burn her eye. She also said that she would turn the eggs over three times in three shifts, the purpose being to simulate the hen's turning of her eggs with her beak and her checking of them with her eye. This was what was called 'the first hearing.' She did not remove the dung that had turned to ashes, and she did not let it stop burning until midday. Instead, she would add more dung and light it again, then test the eggs with her eyes. When she did this, however, she found that they were so hot that they burned to the touch. Things had happened this way several times, and every time the eggs had gone bad. Consequently, she had gone to a priest who was known to practice magic in hopes that he could help make her egg incubation successful, and the priest had made her an amulet that brought no results. She then brought a parchment out of a hole that she had dug in the ground beside the incubator and showed it to us. Thawna opened it and we began reading it, as it was written in Arabic, Greek, and Coptic, all of which I was able to decipher easily. It said:

I adjure you, O Atrak, the great angel who stands to the right of the sun, and to whom all the powers of the sun owe allegiance: Go to the edge of the abyss. The silver, crush it. The steel, break it. The iron, melt it. The stone, shatter it. The waters of the sea, dry them up. The mountains, move them. Verily, I call upon you, the seven archangels: Michael, Gabriel, Oriel, Rakuel, Saruel, Anuel, and Saluel, to descend one and all—even Michael himself—to this place, and not to heed anything but what I say to you, that you might grant me my request and fulfill the desire that rages in my being and for which my soul longs. I will cross the seven rivers of fire, ascend to the seventh heaven where Lord Sabaoth is seated, and find Michael standing at the right hand of the Father. Make haste, make haste. I implore you, I adjure you, I beg you, O saints and witnesses! I, Theodora, the sinful old woman, place before you this accusation against everyone who spoils the eggs in my incubator, be they humans or evil spirits that disguise themselves as animals. May a curse descend upon everyone who spoils my eggs, may his kin be scattered, may he be stricken with adversity, and may the Invincible Arm and the Mighty Hand descend upon him at once. O ye martyrs and saints, make haste and carry out my request. Send your forces and your miracles!

Thawna gave the parchment back to Theodora, saying, "May God forgive us for all such things. Goodhearted Theodora, burn this nonsense in the fire the next time you bake your bread. As for your chicks and your incubator, the problem with them is that your lamp does not burn as it should because its wick is worn out and needs to be replaced."

The old woman had not realized this because of her poor eyesight.

Then, patting her on her shoulder, he said to her affectionately, "Mother, have you used anything that might help to strengthen your eyesight, and which would enable you to manage your daily life better?"

Replying in the Coptic-mixed-with-Arabic in which she had been speaking to us before, she said, "Every now and then I put drops in them made from powdered alum salt mixed with water from the Nile, which I store in bottles when it first comes down every year at the beginning of Bashans."

"No, no, Mother," Thawna rejoined quickly, "An alum solution is not enough by itself when there is opacity in the eye. Rather, you need to use the soft sap from the sycamore tree. And from time to time, especially in God's hot months, you should use drops made from a mixture of castor oil, blue vitriol, radish oil, and a small amount of pine resin, which should be mixed in equal proportions together with two parts of ritually pure water. These drops ward off the heat poisons that Satan casts into people's eyes."

Despite the hardship and weariness that attend such a journey, my expedition with Thawna to the marshlands was, for me, one of the most magnificent times I had ever experienced in my life. To be in the presence of an extraordinary man like him is, without a doubt, a sign of the bounteous blessings that God pours out on human beings. And if someone once said, *al-rafiq qabl al-tariq*, that is to say, "Who you are traveling with matters more than where you are going," then Thawna was not merely some new companion, nor just a pious deacon endowed with copious knowledge whom I was escorting on a necessary ecclesiastical mission. Rather, he was to me as the spirit is to the body, or as air is to breathing. He was a radiance that illumined my inward being and by whose light I made pilgrimage to holy places. By him I was guided to the shores of tranquility and certainty—I, the one who was ever and always stumbling about in the darkness of torment and despair, and for whom despondency was a constant companion. It was Thawna who led me to the truth that the veil over my being had its source in myself, that I myself was the cloud over the sun in my soul, and that I needed to recognize my soul's true nature and both its dark, sinister places and its supple, tender ones.

One time as we were sitting under a Christ's thorn tree for a bit of shade and rest, I began talking to him about what had been weighing so heavily on my heart, and I found myself confiding to him what I had never confided to anyone ever before, not even to Father Joseph. I told him my Amuna story, just exactly as it had happened, without embellishments or omissions.

When I had finished, he grasped my shoulder as he wiped my tears with his handkerchief and said, "You know, Budayr, the Lord is the

Cause of all Causes, and if it were not for this story of yours with Amuna, you would not have taken the direction you did in life, which means that you would not have come onto the path of the Lord in the Church and become a good Christian with sound faith. It may be that if you had remained a layman far from the life of service, you would never have become part of the clergy. The world carried you off to the shores of lostness and error, while your thoughts buffeted you this way and that without ever leading you to the path of certainty. Your story is not unique, dear brother. I, too, whenever I think back on my earlier life when I was living in heathenism and error, I am certain that the Lord placed me there in order for my feet to lead me in the end onto the path of truth and faith."

Burning with curiosity, I cried in astonishment, "Tell me, Thawna, I beg you, and do not hide a thing from me! Do you have a story like mine? Did you have experiences with women in your life before, Thawna? O God!"

Thawna smiled wanly, perhaps because I had spoken with such obvious enthusiasm, and with such a powerful desire to know about something that concerned him and which he had been concealing.

Patting me on the shoulder, he said, "And why would you think that I had never known women before, or be amazed to discover that I had experiences of my own with them once upon a time? Am I not a whole man standing before you, who was once an adolescent with a body that seeks what men seek?"

Then he began smiling again as he looked at me with tenderness and compassion. His response made me feel ashamed of myself. However, the fact is that I had seen Thawna as a kind of luminous being, as though he were a seraph in heaven rather than an ordinary, corporeal human being.

"No, no, I swear to God, Thawna, I did not mean to imply that you are not whole! It is just that I think of you as being above sins of the flesh, and it seems impossible that you could ever have fallen into them. After all, you are wise and levelheaded, a man deeply rooted in knowledge."

Interrupting me hurriedly, he said, "No, no, Budayr. That is only because you came to know me after I had been rightly guided. But in the past I lived in sin. The problem, though—let me be honest with you, Budayr, and may God forgive me—is that to this very moment, as I sit here talking to you, I have not come to feel that it was sinful. Rather, whenever memories go through my head and I see images from the past in my mind's eye—and it is as though these things had happened only yesterday—my spirit is energized, filled with joy, and I overflow with such bliss I can hardly bear it sometimes. I feel as though I want to jump up and down, fly, and soar to the highest clouds."

Bug-eyed with amazement, I stared at him in disbelief. When I looked into his eyes, they were gleaming with an intensity that made them all the more beautiful and radiant, and his face had become more handsome and regal looking.

Filled with curiosity and wonder over what he had said, I exclaimed, "God, Thawna! Are you really saying this? Are you saying that up to this very moment you still have no sense of sin?"

"That is right. That is right, Budayr. I do not feel sinful at all, and this causes me great distress, since I am supposed to feel sinful and repent to the Lord. I do not know why this happens to me, Budayr. Tell me: Why do not I feel regretful and repent? Nay, more than that: Why do I wish I could experience again what I experienced then, and which is called sin?"

I crossed myself hastily, and I got a sudden feeling that Thawna had begun having confused thoughts again.

I thought back once more to all the things that had been rumored about him in the past, as well as the things he had said when he was delirious with fever, and I thought it better to end the conversation, since there might be demons haunting the place that had begun to seize control over us, beginning with him.

Flustered, I said, "Thawna, let us pray the evening prayer. It is late afternoon now. Then let us get back quickly to what we were doing and be on our way."

However, as though he were addressing his own spirit in the mirror of a limpid spring, or as though some force were impelling him so irresistibly to speak that no one, no matter who he happened to be, could have stopped him, he replied without hesitation, "No, Budayr. We will not start moving again until you have heard my story. I want to tell you about my experience with Dalluka. I want you to know my beloved Dalluka, my teacher, my revered lady, my protectress and queen yesterday, today, tomorrow, and forevermore.

"How can I describe her to you, Budayr? Shall I describe to you her spirit? Or shall I sing the praises of her body? She was my first teacher. I learned wisdom under her tutelage, and from her I came to understand philosophy and mathematics. I gained experience in medical treatment, too. She was the last of the great women, and the centuries to come may well not produce anyone of her stature. She used to teach in the school at the temple in my town of Antionopolis. This temple was located at the edge of town in the foothills of a nearby mountain. Dalluka was a dignified woman, respected among the people, and famed for her knowledge and skill, which she was said to have inherited from her ancestors. At that time my father adhered to the pagan religion and would go to the ancient temples to worship, and it was he who sent me to study under Dalluka from the time I was ten years old. When I reached puberty, then adolescence, with the longings that belong to manhood, I fell madly in love with her. I was beside myself over her. Dalluka was a beautiful, captivating woman, like a winter sun on a cold day. Her erudition made her all the more magnificent, and her wisdom made her presence all the more enthralling. Her knowledge had even taken over her body, which had come to obey its every command.

"Perhaps you realize that the most marvelous body is one that serves as the vehicle for a great mind, as a result of which physical instincts are transformed into talents and character traits. In such cases, the individual concerned tames everything that is wild within him. And that is how Dalluka was. I did not know the secret that underlay my passionate love for her: Was it on account of her physique, which had been constructed with such masterful symmetry? Or did it owe to the spiritual abundance that she poured out on me in such an irresistible way, and which defied understanding and explanation? In any case, she came to control my spirit and mind until she had taken me utterly captive. As a result, I stopped eating and started drinking. She was the moon that ruled my nights and the sun that ruled my days. And she—knowledgeable and discerning woman that she was—seems to have sensed the state I was in, and was alarmed to think of what end I might come to. It happened that I had gone to see her one day at the temple to ask her about a matter relating to the performance of autopsies as taught by Galen. I had noticed in some cadavers that the mandible was a single bone, with no joint or seam, which was inconsistent with the view which Galen puts forward in his book to the effect that the mandible consists of two bones connected by means of a solid joint from the palate. In any case, she explained the matter in a helpful way. Then, after gazing intently into my eyes for some time, she said, 'Thawna, my beautiful beloved, follow me to where I can be alone with you.'

"Well, I followed her like one bewitched. And when she called me, 'my beautiful beloved,' it was as though, by the look in her eyes, she had cast a torch that set my body ablaze and stirred up a tempest in my soul. I do not know how I got to the end of the corridor: Did I walk, or did I fly? When we reached the open space at the end of the corridor, she took hold of me and began gradually to remove my robe. As she did so, she thrust her body, which by this time was naked like mine, toward me. It was not long before we had plunged into the wellspring of kisses, then we were raised aloft until we reached the paradises of transcendent ecstasy. This was the first time I had entered a woman's garden. And it was also the last, dear friend. It was not long after this that Dalluka was found dead. It was said at the time that a group of Christian believers had attacked the temple in broad daylight, then razed it after killing everyone inside. They had shattered the idols it contained, then destroyed everything on its walls by way of inscriptions in the ancient tongue.

"For some time after this, our family remained in hiding in the town, moving furtively from one place to another for fear of that same group until, finally, my father got me and the rest of our family out of the town altogether. May God have mercy on me and forgive me, Budayr, and may He gather me together with the repentant. But I tell you that Dalluka was the first and last woman in my life: Any woman I see, I see her only in Dalluka, who, to me, was all the women on earth. And this is why I am telling you—and may the Merciful One have mercy on me—that I will never forget her. She is hidden in the deepest recesses of my spirit, like a choice wine which, with the passing of the days, mellows and takes on the rarest of flavors. Her memory perfumes my spirit, and her fragrance is with me always. She helps me like a bright lamp on a dark night. For nothing in this world of ours can give a man certainty. Everything is in turmoil, Budayr, and the transformations take place so fast, they leave you nothing to pin your spirit to. What exists today is gone tomorrow, and what your eye beholds at this moment vanishes in the next.

"When I lived in my hometown, I thought I would never leave it. However, I left some years ago after Dalluka was killed. I lived for a time in paganism and atheism, but some time after that I entered the clergy. Then after I had gone to the monastery, I was brought to our church at Qasr al-Sham' and thought I would never leave there. And now here I am on my way to the marshlands, and only God knows whether we will return to Qasr al-Sham' again, or whether He has something else ordained for us."

It was only now that I was beginning to realize that Thawna was in turmoil just as I was. When he said this, he said it with firm faith and certain knowledge. However, it seemed that there were things happening around us that might drive one to confusion from time to time. It may have been that evil spirits were still more powerful than the good ones in directing many affairs.

I felt more tenderness and affection toward him than usual, and even a kind of pity. Wanting to console him, I said, "These are hard times, Thawna. But to everything there is an end, and God will never abandon us. He alone is able to grant rest and comfort to our spirits."

He sighed. Then suddenly he asked me, "You know? I am really looking forward to seeing the marshlands. I imagine them as islands in the sea, surrounded by water on all sides. But I do not understand how they can be 'marshy' as they are said to be, Budayr."

When he said this, I felt for the first time that I knew something he did not. And I think—and may God forgive me—this gave me a bit of satisfaction.

"Well," I hastened to respond, "it is difficult to describe them to you. In any case, though, you will be seeing them for yourself before very long. I can say, though, that they are land in which the waters from the Mediterranean Sea have mingled with the sweet waters of the Nile.

In these waters, sand from the sea has mixed with the alluvial mud and silt from the Nile. In some places there are thick, solid deposits of these materials, whereas in others the deposits are sparser and less solid. These latter areas have a liquid viscosity to them, as a result of which people's feet sink in them easily, and the slightest carelessness or inattention can cause one to go under and perish. The reason for this is that many of the more liquid, viscous spots have no solid bottom, and they can swallow a person up, enclosing him inside the mud just as if it were pure water. This is why strangers to the area need to have experienced guides with knowledge of the places where it is safe to travel. As for the people who grew up in the area, all of them being Bashmourites like me, they know it well, given their long experience with it from the time they were children. Consequently, they have built their villages and towns in the locations which they know to be on solid ground."

Thawna cleared his throat slightly, and seemed to be embarrassed to be asking me about something. He remained silent, perhaps because he was thinking about how to say what he wanted to in the most tactful, considerate way.

Then he said, "But—and please forgive me for this, Budayr—why are the Bashmourite people of the marshlands famed for being coarse, rude, and violent? I hope you will not take offense at my question, dear friend, since from the time I first met you, and in all my dealings with you at the church, you have been gentle and pleasant to be with, and never once have you said or done anything that would indicate harshness or rude manners."

I was at a loss as to how to answer him at first, for although I had heard this sort of thing about the Bashmourites during my peregrinations, I did not know the reason for it, and it caused me no little distress. In fact, I nearly beat up a man once because he had insulted me when he found out that I was a Bashmourite. He had said, *miyah maliha wa wujuh kaliha*, that is, 'briny waters and gloomy faces!'—a comment directed at me and my fellow Bashmourites. And I did not let loose of him until people around us had pried him out of my grip. The incident took place near a village I had happened to pass through and which looked miserable and a bit suspicious to me, with no crops in it or even anything green. Instead, its inhabitants were all outcast lepers who spent their time waiting for the Muslim pilgrims to pass through near the pool located on the edges of the desert so that they could beg them for something to eat.

I related the incident to Thawna, and then, in answer to his question, I said, "My father always used to say to us, 'We live like someone who lives in the water: We do not know where our territory starts and where it leaves off, and it is in a constant state of flux on account of the way the sea comes into it at times and recedes from it at others.' He also told me once that the reason we first came to live in these parts was the sea. Our distant ancestors had been seamen, but with the passing of time they started settling on land and grew accustomed to farming, which became a source of livelihood for them. At the same time, though, sailors' dispositions and morals continued to dominate their personalities, and these were passed down to us from one generation to another. In addition, our location near the sea meant that ours was the first territory to be crossed by any newcomers, strangers, or aggressors. Consequently, we have been invaded, plundered, and looted, especially by pirates who, if they land, will steal everything, even people. Hence, you will notice that people's facial features here are mixed, while they tend to have light complexions as though they were Byzantines or Syrians."

As I was telling him these things, I thought back on my father and the rest of my family, and feelings of longing for them welled up inside me. However, I made a determined effort not to let the tears fall. It seems that Thawna realized the state I was in, since he changed the subject, saying, "My Goodness, Budayr, did you really go to the lepers' village during your wanderings before you arrived at the church? That's amazing! Thank God you were not infected by them, since leprosy is a dread disease, my dear. May God have mercy on the physician Yuhanna ibn Masawiya—a learned, widely read man who wrote more than forty books, including a huge tome on the subject of leprosy. No one else had written on the subject before that time, not even Galen. It is said that the disease originates and spreads from a malady relating to a mordacious reptile, possibly a type of turtle, which some Arabs call fikrun."

I kept on moving along for some time without saying a word. Scenes from my visit to the lepers' outlandish village took on flesh before my eyes now that Thawna had succeeded in distancing me from

99

topics that stirred up memories of my family in Tarnit. It may well be that those lepers were the ugliest thing I had ever beheld in my entire life. They had gathered, women and men, in that place like creatures from some other planet. The noses of most of them had fallen off, and many of them hardly had any fingers left. They were unbelievably filthy, and perhaps the only evidence of their humanity was their eyes, which stared constantly at nothing. Despite my lostness during that time, I have never forgotten the sight of those people. In fact, they may have restored to me some of my lost awareness and feeling, since they served as a lesson to me to praise God for the situation I was in, and indeed, in all circumstances, at all times, and in all places.

Thus we went along, conspiring together against the long hours and minutes. And the deeper we went into conversation and mutual self-revelations, the more clearly I sensed that Thawna was my soul mate, my alter ego in pain and sorrow, my family and my people, the one who gives me certainty and helps me to accept my existence and my life.

We kept crossing one road after another until we came to a place called al-Hawf al-Sharqi. I had never seen it before, and neither had Thawna. When we entered the area, we discovered that most of its inhabitants were Arabs. However, we found that there were Copts among them as well, since the man who saw us approaching at the place where the fields began spoke to us in Coptic mingled with the tongue of the Arabs. He welcomed us warmly, then led us to a large, comely, well-built house which he said belonged to the town's mayor—known to the Arabs as the 'umda, and to the Copts as the mazut. He explained that anyone entering the town was required to meet the mayor so that he could inquire of the newcomer about the reason for his coming and grant him permission to stay if he so wished.

The man informed us that this town, like many others in al-Hawf al-Sharqi, was located along the path traveled by Muslim pilgrims on their way to and from the Muslims' holy land, and that many people had abandoned the tilling and planting of the earth and begun making their living serving the pilgrims because of the generous earnings this provided. When we went in to see the mayor, he received us so graciously you would have thought we were members of his own religion—he being a Muslim. He was pleasant and cheerful, yet not without the dignity proper to his station, and he expressed amazement at our having ventured to pass through their area at this particular time, since the entire region was in a state of uprising against the governors. When we informed him that we were carrying a message to the leader of the Bashmourites, he was even more astonished, since he had not been aware of the Bashmourites' rebellion.

He kept saying, "Subhan Allah!" over and over again and calling down blessings on his honored Prophet.

Then, insisting that we eat at his home, he got up and gave instructions for a lamb to be slaughtered. When the roasted lamb's meat—which had a delicious flavor—had been served to us along with the Arabs' tharid and the fruit of the season, we ate and gave thanks and praise to God. The man then began asking us about our religion and our rites and how we had first entered the religion of Christ. I kept quiet out of politeness while Thawna did the answering, and the man listened to him in all earnestness. The muezzin then issued the call to prayer in keeping with the Muslims' custom and the man got up, asking us to excuse him. He went in to relieve nature, and when he had returned, his servant boy brought him ritually pure water in a copper pail and began pouring it over his hands. He washed his hands up to his wrists, then rinsed out his mouth and washed his face and ears. He also washed his forearms and wiped his head. And lastly, he washed his feet. Having never seen such a thing before, I expressed my bewilderment to Thawna in a whisper, and he whispered back that the man was performing ablutions, that is, he was purifying himself by washing his body in the places which are especially prone to getting soiled so that he could come into the presence of his Lord clean and pure at the time for the ritual prayer. He told me that the Muslims do this five times every day, which amazed me every more. I had not realized that Muslims were conscientious about hygiene and ritual purity just the way we Copts are. It reminded me of the requirement that before ascending to the church's inner sanctuary, a priest must wash his feet in the copper vessel filled with ritually pure water and placed at the Holy Thursday ablution site. This is witnessed to also by the Torah, which tells us that in both the outer and inner sanctuaries there was a copper pail for cleansing the priests' feet before they entered the Holy of Holies in the tent of meeting.

The mayor found himself a spot in the corner of the room and began praying not far from where we were seated, without being embarrassed by our presence or finding anything to prevent him from practicing his faith despite the fact that, as could be discerned clearly from our words and appearance, we were people of the church.

Still more astonished now, I kept silent, as did Thawna, out of politeness and reverence as the man stood there praying in the presence of his Lord. When he had finished, he prayed for peace and blessings on his Prophet, then returned to where he had been sitting with us and began talking to us about the Arabs of the Yamaniya and Qaysiya tribes who had come to al-Hawf al-Sharqi. He told us that they had first started coming during the era of the first Muslim governors in Egypt and that they had settled in the area and begun farming for a living, but that the governors had oppressed them with the kharaj from time to time just as they had the Copts. He added that they did the same thing in connection with the calculation of the land area farmers were working, and that the people had finally raised a hue and cry. In the end, he said, they refused to pay the kharaj anymore, especially after the last surveyor came, at which point they began doing their own survey of the land under cultivation and deducting several isba's from every pole. The people had complained to the emir of the land, but he paid no attention to them. Consequently, they all took up arms and revolted."

As the man said these things he was very angry. He would stroke his beard nervously every now and then, praying down curses on the governors and calling upon God to send down retribution against them as a sign that would cause them to repent of the injustice they were inflicting on the people and return to the ways of righteousness. He kept saying that their conduct was not like that of the early Muslims, whom they ought to emulate in word and deed, and that the religion of Islam never enjoined injury or inequality. Rather, he said, if these governors and emirs persisted in their error, sowing evil, they were bound in the end to reap nothing but thorns and thistles.

The man kept speaking for a long time in his Arabic tongue, some of which I understood and some of which Thawna had to translate for me, though I did not hesitate to ask for his help. When we excused ourselves so as to be on our way, he came out to bid us farewell, then walked us all the way to the edge of town. We, too, remained on foot out of respect rather than mounting our mules. As we walked along, we saw people in the streets and alleyways, most of them clad in Arab attire. The women went about with their faces exposed and mixed with the men for the sake of buying, selling, and whatever other transactions they needed to complete, without any awkwardness or discomfort, whereas I had thought that Muslim women never left their houses for any reason or dealt with men under any circumstances.

After we had bade him a grateful farewell, the man parted with us, entrusting us into the care of the soldiers who were guarding the town's exits in a state of readiness and alert. Consequently, they let us pass without any harassment or difficulties and showed us the easiest way to get back to the river so that we could follow it into the Bashmourite territories. However, before we had gotten very far we were stopped by a kindly Coptic man who warned us not to travel alongside the river. He told us that there was a Coptic town known as Samanud where we might come to great harm on account of a disturbance that was taking place there. The reason, he said, was that some monks who had been sent there from a monastery which he did not name entered one of its churches, and when it was time for the divine Mass to be celebrated, added some words to the final confession, namely, "He who is resurrected is like a feature of the body of Christ. This is the resurrected body." In response, the celebrants and the people rushed at them in a fury and nearly murdered them. The man thus advised us to circle around the town, then come back to the river on the other side once we were past it.

We thanked him and continued on our way, but once we were by ourselves, Thawna said, "Have you seen the turmoil everywhere? Even some of the monks in monasteries have begun causing confusion and spreading heresies openly and without shame! People like this are still doing as was done in the past: coming up with fabricated, syncretistic creedal formulations based on their own whims, desires, and personal interests. They claim, for example, that Christ had a single will rather than a single nature! This is what was claimed once by the Byzantine tyrant Heraclius, who put forward the wicked monophysite heresy and tried to force us orthodox Copts to accept it. He even appointed a Nestorian patriarch over our church at that time. So what can I say? We have God, Budayr, and He is the One who preserves us all, from beginning to end."

On we went then. I led Thawna, bearer of Father Joseph's missive, with the greatest of ease, since I could distinguish without difficulty between the areas that were solid ground and which could thus be safely traveled over and the grainy, whitish areas that were bottomless pits of sodden earth and sand. We were now approaching the towns of the Bashmourite district, and after being interrogated by the soldiers that guarded its entrances, we soon passed through Arisiya. We explained to them why we were coming through these parts, and when they had granted us permission to pass, we headed for Nugum, which was the Bashmourite leader's campsite. When we saw it, we were awed by the same thing that had awed us in Arisiya, namely, that it was filled with peasants who had armed themselves with sticks, bows, rocks, slingshots, pieces of baked brick, pitch-covered reeds, quivers, and shields made from reed mats. On their heads they wore helmets made from palm leaves from the trees that grew up ubiquitously in their land's swamps and waterways, while some of them wore nothing but wraps around their waists, with small bells, red and yellow shells, ropes, and leather thongs taken from brooms and fly whisks around their necks, while the rest of their bodies were bare of anything but the wrap that concealed their private parts.

We asked some of them to lead us to a public bath where we could wash up and make ourselves presentable for a meeting with Mina ibn Baqira. Once there, we found it to be a lovely old bath. Commenting on it, Thawna said, "It may date back to the Byzantines' rule in the land." We were then led to a small room which we were told was the only one now being used for purposes of bathing and hygiene, since all of its other areas had been set aside for uses relating to the war. It had thus become a kind of arms depot and barracks for the Bashmourite's fighting men.

After we had finished cleaning up, we asked them politely if we might take a look at the place, and those who oversaw the bath agreed to our request, having sensed our kindness and our good intentions toward them and made certain that we were not spies for the governor of the land but, rather, clergymen who had nothing to do with ongoing war and who simply wanted to avoid bloodshed for all, be they Copts or Muslims.

When we went the rounds of the bath's various sections, we were astounded at all the arms and at the variety and number of fighting men, who included both Bashmourite peasants and some Arab Muslims who had joined in their revolt. Some of them were sitting around working on their weapons, while others stood practicing with bows and arrows, having turned the bath's main courtyard into an archery range. When they saw us they gathered around us, and I heard some of them calling us ugly names, referring to us as "spoiled Egyptian snobs," by which they meant people from Qasr al-Sham'. I did not translate that for Thawna so as not to anger or upset him. Instead, I simply urged him to move on quickly for fear that something not to our liking might transpire before we managed to meet with Mina ibn Baqira. We were also taken aback by the way women mixed with the men in that part of the bath: There were women shattering bricks, preparing stones and tiles, and making quivers. There were also elderly women busily engaged in cooking, cleaning, and the like. I saw a huge kettle over a blazing fire that had been kindled with reeds, in which they were boiling a kind of broth known as sakhin. The person who was giving us the tour of the bath told us that most of the fighters' food consisted of barley bread dipped in this type of broth.

As we were leaving the bath, one of the peasant soldiers approached us with a parchment. When Thawna opened it he found it to be written in clear Arabic. It said:

> There are no cactus fruits, no dalnis, no sardines.
> No baked bread, no nida, no tharid,
> So rise up against the governors, rise up,
> And woe to them if they pay no heed!

Thawna placed the parchment in the pocket of his robe without saying a word, and when we had left the bath to continue on our way again he said, "Have you noticed how unconcerned these soldiers are with matters of religion?"

"Yes, I have," I said, "and it really amazes me. But what amazes me the most is the presence of Arab Muslims among the Bashmourites. We never heard about that when we were at Qasr al-Sham'."

"And they are not just Arab Muslims," he replied. "Rather, they include Coptic Muslims as well. Did you not see the one that was scraping a cow's horns with a knife? It was obvious from the way he was dressed that he was a Coptic Muslim. He was wearing a turban, albeit a worn-out one. As for the woman he was talking to as she ladled out some broth for him, she was a Copt, too, since one of her shoes was black and the other was white. Discontent and anger have driven people to join the Bashmourite leader. Their reasons may vary, but the desire to disobey and revolt brings them all together. I heard when we were at Qasr al-Sham' that some of those who hold that the Muslims' holy book was created are being persecuted so relentlessly by the caliph that they have slipped out by stealth to Lower Egypt and joined the Bashmourites. It is an amazing thing to see these fighters' boundless energy and enthusiasm and the way they laugh and joke among themselves despite how obviously underfed they are. Did you see the one that was sitting there singing? You would have thought he was at a celebration, not in the middle of a war!"

While we were in the bath, some people approached us wanting us to join them in marriage, expressing the hope that we might stay for some time as there was no clergyman there to perform this function.

At the entrance to the Bashmourite's camp, we encountered men who were armed with clubs, swords, bludgeons, bows, and arrows. The minute they saw us approaching, they started shouting and aimed their weapons at us, and if it had not been for the mercy of God and my shouting at them to stop in a clear Bashmourite accent, they would have shot us through with their arrows. I explained to them that we were Copts with a message for Mina their leader from the head of the church of the Virgin Mary at Qasr al-Sham' in Old Cairo. In response, they held back briefly. Then, cautiously, they came up to us and started searching our clothes and our mules' saddlebags. They seemed crude and ill-mannered to me, lacking in good taste and courtesy. Even so, we bore with them patiently and Thawna was polite and friendly to them. Eventually, once they were satisfied that we had not been lying to them, Thawna showed them the letter complete with its official seals, and they led us to the Bashmourite's residence. On the way, they took us down the town's streets, guarding us with their weapons from all sides.

As we passed through the town, I wondered apprehensively whether somebody in the place might recognize me and expose me. I looked warily into the faces I happened to encounter without stopping to notice the houses and buildings as Thawna was doing. As for him, he seemed amazed at how humble peasants' houses were and, by contrast with the homes in Old Cairo and Fustat, how lacking in good construction. Despite my fears and apprehensions, part of me hoped that I would recognize someone I had known and befriended once upon a time, or that I would come upon someone from my family. However, I was ever so grateful to God that I did not actually meet up with anyone I had known in the past. And perhaps that was thanks to one of the virtues of time and its power, namely, that as it passes, it changes people's features. We are not aware of the change unless we stop to take a look at ourselves. Even so, the people you knew in childhood and adolescence, you may not recognize when they grow older. And in this, no doubt, there is a divine wisdom.

When we reached Mina ibn Baqira's home—a large, old house built from bricks as peasants' houses tended to be, and whose beauty and spaciousness suggested that it may at one time have been the residence of the mayor or town chief—Mina was not there. We were told that he had gone out to attend to some fortifications in a nearby town. Hence, we sat down to wait for him. In the meantime, we began talking with those of his followers who were staying with us, and who had seated us on a 'peasants' bench' of the sort that, in those parts, is generally made from sycamore wood. Devoid of any appearance of luxury, ease, or wealth, the place was furnished with nothing but braided mats and low round tables like those used by peasants. We had been told that Mina was a very self-effacing man with ascetic leanings who had never strived to hoard wealth at others' expense, that his sole fare was bread, when it was available, and that he fasted often. Among those we spoke to was one who loved him especially, and who told us that all Mina ibn Baqira indulged in by way of spirits was an occasional sip of red watermelon wine, and that he had even taken to eating field mice as the peasants had begun to do.

He was revered by all in this place, because he had abandoned his former life as a kharaj assessor who lived in the lap of luxury. At that time he had been accustomed to eating rich sweets such as squash and carrot pudding, desserts made from rose water and ginger, and round cakes made from lemon, aloes, and gum-mastic. One of them claimed that during Mina's glory days, he had seen him indulge in the fare of governors and kings. Then he went on to describe a particular dish that used to be prepared in his household. To prepare this dish, he said, they would take thirty ratls of flour and knead it together with five and a half ratls of sesame oil. The dough would be divided into two parts, one of which would be spread out in a copper baking tin. It would then be topped with three roast sheep which had been stuffed with ground meat fried in sesame oil with crushed pistachios, and aromatic, hot spices such as pepper, ginger, cinnamon, gum-mastic, coriander, cumin, cardamom, nutmeg, and the like. This whole thing would then be sprinkled with rosewater to which some musk had been added. Then, at last, the other portion of the dough would be placed over the sheep. The person who gave this description appeared to be hungry and craving food, and as he spoke, he looked like someone who was dreaming with his eyes open. Smiling gently, Thawna joined him in conversation so that we could make the time go by and ward off the boredom of our long wait.

Then Thawna began asking them questions and telling them theological riddles to strengthen their faith and teach them correct doctrine without their realizing that they were receiving instruction and exhortation. He would listen with patience and compassion to their incorrect answers no matter how outrageous, foolish, or ignorant they were, then guide them to the correct answer, taking them by the hand onto the path of faith. One of the questions he put to them was: "Why does God require that the body be punished along with the soul?" When they fumbled about unsuccessfully for an answer, he said to them, "The purpose for requiring that the body be punished along with the soul is to intimidate and discipline the body. If, for example, a dumb beast is beaten for doing something time after time, it will be disciplined and stop doing this thing for fear of being beaten. Similarly, if the body is punished along with the soul for committing sins, it will be disciplined just as the dumb beast is. If the body craves sin, the soul will threaten it with the discipline it received before, as a result of which it will be afraid and comply with the soul in abandoning the sin it craves. This is the case, at least, if the body is punished every time it sins without one's falling into laxness or neglect. But if one follows this practice even for a short time, punishing himself both spiritually and physically through the law and exposure before others, the fear of punishment will be established in his soul and his body."

Then suddenly the Bashmourite arrived. He came in accompanied by a contingent of his helpers, and when he saw us, he looked at us with suspicion and alarm. I heard him asking one of his assistants about us, and when he told him who we were he said, "So, they are sending us messengers and writing us letters again. Will they ever stop?" I translated what he had said for Thawna in a whisper, and took care to stay close by his side as much as I could so that I could tell him everything that was being said in Bashmourite or answer any questions he might have. Then Mina came up to us and greeted us. When I returned his greetings in his own language, his features softened, his ire abated, and he began asking me about my family and place of origin. Being careful what I told him for fear of giving myself away, I said I had learned the Bashmourite language from my mother, whose father had been from these parts but had moved to Old Cairo, and that both my parents had died young, as a result of which I did not know anything about my family anymore. I told him that after my father's death I had been adopted by a stonemason, who raised me till I was a teenager, and that it had been my God-given fortune to find work in the church.

He requested some watermelon wine for us, apologizing for the fact that he did not have anything else to serve us. Thawna thanked him earnestly, then began speaking to him in all politeness and respect, while I translated what he was saying from Akhmimite into Bashmourite. What he said was: "I come, goodhearted brother, bearing a message for you from the head of our church in Egypt, namely, the Church of the Virgin Mary at Qasr al-Sham'. As you know, he has sent a number of messages prior to this one, and I ask you to read them and give me your reply to them as soon as possible. Before this, however, allow me to bring you greetings of peace and to introduce myself. My name is Thawna, I serve as a deacon for the church, and I am a believing servant. It is an honor for me to meet you, and from the time I entered your camp I have been praying for God to preserve and protect you and your men. It is my hope that you will provide me with your answer without delay so that I can return to my superior in Cairo. For indeed, as His Eminence has told me, the matter will tolerate no delay, and every minute that passes carries potentially grave consequences for him."

The Bashmourite's men were scrutinizing us as he spoke, their eyes gleaming with defiance and hostility. Meanwhile, they looked over our clerical attire and our shoes, giving silent voice to their disapproval of our coming to them clad in this way when they hardly had the wherewithal to feed and clothe themselves.

Thawna reached out and handed the letter, which had been placed in an alligator skin bag, to the Bashmourite. The letter consisted of a parchment written in several languages and was accompanied by another parchment which Thawna said was a protective amulet that Father Joseph had made himself for Mina, and which he was to carry with him whenever he went.

After hurriedly breaking its seals, the Bashmourite began reading the letter with great care. When he raised his head after finishing it, he looked like a fierce, raging lion despite his noticeably handsome features. Then, squatting on the mat across from us, as were the rest of his men, he said, "So, you at Qasr al-Sham' are asking us again to surrender to the governor, put down our arms and obediently pay him the dummaz he has imposed on us every year. And you are asking us to appear personally before Father Joseph without delay so that he can hand us over to the governor and we can offer him the obedience that is his due?"

Then, turning to those around him, whose eyes were fixed intently on him, he said, "Brothers, I am going to read you the letter from beginning to end. However, I ask you to bear patiently with what it says and to restrain yourselves rather than doing something that would make me angry and force me to punish you the way some have done on previous occasions."

He then proceeded to read, saying:

As the Bible says in Psalm 77, that which we have heard and seen and of which our forefathers have told us; as was declared by the Prophet Moses, who recorded what had happened on earth from the days of the first Adam and up to his own day, then by the prophets who prophesied concerning this cause; as is set forth by the teachings of the church's founding fathers and the speech which builds up good faith and brotherhood among those who share in baptism and who are clothed in light: by the founding fathers who established the strong foundation and the firm support, and by our Lord and Savior Jesus Christ who delivered us and saved us from our sins through His incarnation by the immaculate and blessed Virgin by opening our hearts and minds to hear His Holy Scriptures; by Philo, Justin, and Josephus, all of them Jews, who first reported the destruction of Jerusalem and set down for us the story of the Holy Church, namely, Africanus, Eusebius, and Musanus, who showed us the bad, the good, and the afflictions which befell the saints and the pastors of Jesus Christ's flocks, the suffering that was endured by the church and the orthodox people at the hands of those entrusted with power over them in every time and place, and not only in the region of Egypt, but in Antioch, Rome, and Ephesus, the seat of the heresy of Nestorius, who deserves to have his tongue cut out, and the rest of the outlaws of that time whom God scattered like dust before a great wind; by the cub of the wise lion Kirillos, who cut him off along with other outlaws and whose writings spread among all the orthodox churches of the inhabited world; and just as this was revealed to us by the book that includes all their names up to the time of Dioscorus—confessor and champion of the truth—who excommunicated Leo, the ferocious predator of souls, the six hundred and thirty who gathered at Chalcedon, as well as King Marcian and wicked Queen Pulcheria and all those who followed Leo in excommunication, I say:

You, O Mina, of all people, will be most aware that those living in the land of Egypt are perishing from injustice, loss, and the kharaj, and that the companions of the Chalcedonian Theofelix will spare no effort to take over our orthodox churches without right. Our uncorrupted churches, moreover, are already suffering now from injustice, tyranny, and the kharaj they are obliged to pay. Meanwhile, the Chalcedonians come bearing gifts and bribes for those in authority in order to take illegal possession of our churches, saying, "In the beginning governance was ours, as were the churches and everything that belonged to them." The Muslims, by contrast, handed the churches over to the Copts when they won victory over the territories of Egypt. Therefore, my son, we are now living in our own native areas and our churches are under our control. For indeed, God is not unmindful of our suffering and will never fail to come to our aid. However, it is beyond our capacity to resist these Arabs. They are a people accustomed to attack and retreat in battle, whereas God ordained for us a life of tilling and sowing from time immemorial. We have not the strength to fight against them, and if we attempt to do so by harassing and besetting them, they will turn against us until they have defeated us. And when that happens, woeful consequences may be in store for us.

They might do harm to the Universal Church and uproot it from the land altogether, thereby leading us to perdition. For the church is the preserver of Egypt, and if it is lost, the land will be lost with it forever. Hence, my son, let us negotiate with them over the kharaj and reach a compromise on terms that are acceptable both to us and to them. In this way we will be able to protect our orthodox Coptic church from all evil and affliction.

You know, my son, that I am asking you to desist from fighting against the rulers although you are reluctant to do so. You also know that the fathers and priests of the church have suffered great affliction at their hands since the time they came to be among us. You may be aware of what was done by Abdul Malik with Marwan after he came against him with great armies. After untold bloodshed, Abdul Malik gathered the leaders of his army in Egypt and imprisoned them for seven days. He likewise imprisoned the state clerks and those appointed as trustees over lands and inheritances, demanding that they pay what they owed and do what was required of them. Then he brought Abba Michael to Egypt on account of the kharaj owed by the church, but when we came to see him, he asked more of us than we could give. Consequently, he issued orders for us to be arrested, for our legs to be bound to huge wooden planks, and for heavy iron rings to be placed around our necks. Abba Moises, Bishop of Usim was with us, as well as Abba Tadrus, Bishop of Egypt, and Abba Eliyas Paulus, Abba Moises's spiritual son. They placed us in a windowless storage area that had been hollowed out of a rock and which was completely devoid of sunlight. We languished in iron shackles from the eleventh of Tut to the twelfth of Baba, during which time we did not get even so much as a glimpse of the sun. Three hundred men had been imprisoned with us, and there were women being held as well, the women being in even greater distress than the men. There would be terrible sorrow, weeping, and anguish as the day came to an end and the prison warden locked the prison door and departed, not to return until the seventh hour of the next day. However, the sick and ailing, both Christians and Muslims, would come to us in the prison for us to bless them and to confide things in us. Even barbarians would come to us and confess their sins, as well as prisoners.

I tell you, my son: This is only a small part of the suffering we endured together with the orthodox priests from our church. And our churches are in danger. I urge you, therefore, to turn back from what you are doing, in order for us to preserve and protect our churches and in order for our land to be delivered from all harm. As I write you this epistle, I bless you in the name of the Lord, and I bless all the Bashmourites throughout Egypt.

When Mina ibn Baqira had finished reading Father Joseph's letter aloud to his associates, he quickly folded it up again and handed it back to Thawna. Then, grinding his teeth as though a demon were on his back, he addressed his brethren in a voice choked with rage, saying, "So, this is the message that has been sent to you, word for word, without additions or deletions. The folks in Old Cairo want us to retreat from what we are doing and surrender to the Muslims' commander now that we have sent his soldiers reeling and now that we are about to defeat those who have degraded and humiliated us, driven us to starvation, destroyed our homes, and squeezed us to the last drop of blood. They have milked the country dry, and our crops have wilted and died. Or as someone once said to his oppressor, 'I am like someone who holds his cow's horns so that someone else can milk it.' Is it not their intention to flay us with the kharaj rather than with a whip? After all, if our lives became easier and more comfortable, we would overwhelm and drive them out. Even in our current, straitened circumstances, we have routed one army after another in all the villages of Lower Egypt, and this is something that has not happened since the beginning of our uprising in the days of al-Hurr ibn Yusuf, who set himself up as lord and master over us during the reign of Hisham ibn Abdul Malik. The person in charge of the excrement they refer to as the kharaj at that time was Abdullah ibn al-Habhab, who added a carat to every dinar. As a result, there were uprisings in Tanu, Nami, Qirbit, Tarabiya and most of al-Hawf al-Sharqi. Al-Hurr sent out troops to fight against them and many of them were killed, after which the people of Lower Egypt rose up also.

"Have you forgotten, brethren, the massacre they inflicted upon us when the peasants took up arms in defense of what was theirs in the year 121 as dated from the migration of the Arabs' Prophet? In that year, Hanzala ibn Safwan, emir of Egypt, sent out troops who registered a victory over us and left no one alive, not even women and children.

"Do you remember when Bakhnas came out in Samanud and was killed along with his companions by Abdul Malik ibn Marwan? Do you remember the uprising and what happened between them and 'Uthman ibn Abi Qas'a, the envoy who had been sent out to them by Marwan ibn Muhammad al-Ja'di and at whose hands they suffered defeat?

"Do you remember the events of the year AH 150 which were recorded by the Muslims' own writers and historians as witnesses from among themselves? At that time, the people rose up against Yazid ibn Hatim ibn Qabisa ibn al-Muhallab ibn Abi Safra, the emir of Egypt in the Sakha region, and resisted his men and drove them out. They then went to Shubra Sunbat and were joined by our people here in Arisiya and Nugum. When news of these things reached Yazid ibn Hatim, he authorized Ibn Habib al-Muhallabi to command his men and the notables of Egypt, who came out against us. However, we fought against the soldiers until they set fire to our villages and withdrew in defeat."

As I looked at the Bashmourite, I could see that he was in the grip of a zealous fervor. He also seemed pained as he recounted all these momentous events. His hands trembled, his voice would break with sorrow at times, and at other times, grow harsh and shrill with rage. I was astounded at his thorough knowledge of all these dates, which he had stored with such precision in his memory. God knows I was deeply moved by what he said and my heart softened toward him to the point where tears welled up in my eyes and I had to get a firm hold of myself to keep them from escaping.

As he began to speak again, his men had their eyes glued to him, full of emotion and concern. No one looked away from him, nor was there so much as a whisper lest they miss a single word.

And he said, "I am telling you about all these events, brethren, in order to remind you of what our fathers suffered. I speak thus lest your determination flag or your zeal grow cold. And now: Our good fathers in Old Cairo want us to lay down our arms. They are God-fearing people of the church who have devoted their lives to the Lord's service. However, they are not among those who labor and toil on the land. Hence, they do not truly know what we are going through here in Lower Egypt and in the marshlands. These governors have beset us with the kharaj to the point where people have been forced to eat the grass and worms in the fields. Some have fled to the deserts and wilderness with their wives and children, while others have died. The hunger and the inability to find food are so merciless, many have even lost their minds and gone wandering aimlessly from place to place. Disease has spread, families have been torn apart, and people's psyches have been devastated. Some have thought it best to enter the new religion, as a result of which there might be, under a single roof, one brother who is a Muslim and the other a Christian. In fact, the father may be the only Christian left in his household. And I say: I will put an end to this situation by none other than the edge of the sword. I will not stop fighting until I breathe my last. Life has become as death. They are one and the same in the midst of the present horrors.

"I refuse to live as a slave on my own land, compelled to pay two dinars and three ardabs of wheat, two qists of oil, two qists of honey, and two qists of vinegar, and all of it from what I produced by the sweat of my brow. I refuse to clothe them with what I have made, be it a woolen outer garment, a burnoose, a turban, trousers, or a pair of shoes, simply because I have no other choice. No, by God, I will never live in peace with all these things. May God forgive me if I have violated the wishes of our Father in Old Cairo, and may the All-Forgiving One have mercy on me if I have unwittingly disobeyed any of his commands. But the Lord will not brook injustice, and He is our ruler and the One who determines when we live and when we die. May He embrace us in His providential care and His boundless mercy, and may He have His way with us. In the meantime, we are His obedient, grateful servants."

As Mina spoke, I translated everything he said for Thawna in a low voice. As soon as he had finished, a clamor went up as the peasants' words of support and approval mingled in the air. His followers—the majority of whom were peasants who, like most others, were forbidden to leave their land as a means of escaping the kharaj in accordance with laws that had been imposed on them since some time back—began cheering and reaffirming their loyalty to Mina, announcing their submission and allegiance to him and continued commitment to their shared cause. When I heard them, I knew for a certainty that this young Bashmourite leader, who could not possibly have been more than thirty years old, had a magical grip on the people under his command. At the same time, I sensed that he was possessed of a kind of urbanity and grace, as though he had a touch of city folks' refinement and sophistication, and this despite the fact that his appearance differed little from that of the peasants-turned-serfs to whom he gave leadership. Like theirs, his features were coarse and thick, albeit mingled with a rugged attractiveness. He was tall and slender, with skin the color of wheat and honey, and his head was crowned with kinky black hair that hung down loosely about his shoulders. Like all the peasants with him, he wore clothes made of printed calico and a saffron-yellow vest as was the custom in those parts. On him, however, this lowly attire looked more elegant somehow. Truly did he speak who said, "Tattered though one's garb may be, beauty shines through for all to see." During the time we spent in the public bath, Thawna and I had gotten into a conversation with a man who had been in the Bashmourite's service for some time. He told us a bit of his leader's life story and how, some years earlier—before he had been led to the true religion—he had studied in the schools of Alexandria. From the time he was a young boy his father had sent him there to learn the worldly sciences, and for some years he had delved into the study of mathematics, astronomy, history, and philosophy. He had read the books of the ancients on physiognomy and acquired knowledge of alchemy, chemistry, and other types of learning for which Alexandria's schools had been famous since ancient times and which had trickled down from one generation to the next. Certain individuals with a passion for secular knowledge had committed such disciplines to memory, then kept them under wraps. At the same time, however, they pretended to everyone else to adhere to the Christian religion lest they be put to death, since from time to time, Christians from among the common folk would murder pagans who declared their true religious beliefs.

According to this same man, the Bashmourite had remained in error for quite a long time, jumbling knowledge with religion, and had fallen into confusion more than once on account of the many books he had read. He said that for a period of time, the Bashmourite had believed in the views put forward by Origen, who had been banned by Father Demetrius on the charge of having written about sorcery, rejected the books of the saints, and blasphemed by saying that the Father created the Son and that the Son created the Holy Spirit rather than saying that the Father, the Son, and the Holy Spirit are one God and that there is nothing impossible for the Trinity, whose power is one and whose lordship is one. This same man—who was among the people who accompanied us later when we departed the homeland after all the things that were yet to happen—also told me that Mina had fallen for a period of time into the error of the infidel Paul of Samosata, who made false claims about God and showed himself ungrateful to Him. This was the one who had been expelled by Patriarch Maximus—who sat on the seat of Saint Mark in the city of Alexandria during the days of King Gallienus and Valerian. After having lived in poverty, this Paul of Samosata enriched himself with the church's property and would loot places of worship in the name of religion and take payments offered by the God-fearing in the hope that he would rule in their favor. Then, if their opponents offered him a more generous bribe, he would turn against them. Thus it was that he amassed empty riches for himself through all manner of injustice. He presented himself as a worshiper of God and associated with those of lower classes. At the same time, he would lord it over the weak and roam the streets, where he loved to be called 'Bishop,' and caused people concern due to the large crowds that came after him. He also had books and registers that he would read as though he were demanding the kharaj, thereby deluding people into thinking that he was an officer of the state since he had armed men escorting him both before and behind. He hated genuine spiritual teaching, preferring superficialities. He rejected strangers if they entered the church, seeking praise from those that occupied positions of power in the state and striving for vainglory of every kind through wiles and deception. He even set up a seat for himself on an elevated pulpit as though he were one of the twelve disciples of Christ when, in fact, he was alien to the church. In addition, he would allow readings by women on holiday nights and Good Friday instead of reciting from the Psalter and praises, though believers would put their hands over their ears when they heard the women read. Moreover, he accepted nothing from the Scriptures and did not say that Christ was the Son of God or that He had descended from heaven and was incarnated through the Virgin Mary. Instead, he would utter untold blasphemies.

In addition, Mina ibn Baqira had been led astray for a period of time by the teachings of the infidel Mani, worshiper of Satan. This Mani had committed evil deeds during the time of the Persian Emperor Bahram I, blaspheming against God the Ruler of all, against the only Son, and against the Holy Spirit who proceeds from the Father. He even had the audacity to declare that all three of these are the Paraclete. Now, it happened that a certain mighty sorcerer of the people of Palestine had sought refuge with a wealthy widow, after which he fell from a rooftop and died. The woman then bought a slave, who was Mani himself, and educated him. When he grew up she gave the sorcerer's books to the slave, who read them and learned sorcery from them, after which he went to Persia and sought out its sorcerers, soothsayers, and astrologers. When he had advanced in the science of iniquity, Satan appeared to him, strengthened him, and gave him a love for enmity against the church. As a consequence, he led many people astray with his magic, and great wealth began to come his way. He even had young boys and girls who would gratify his lewd desires because he had enslaved them through his magic. He deceived a number of people, telling them that he was the Paraclete which Jesus Christ had promised to send in the Gospel of John, and declaring that the teachers and fathers of the Church were in error, may God cut out his tongue, because they said that God—majestic is His name—had dwelt in a woman's womb. He claimed that the prophets had uttered things which where untrue about Christ, because the God of pre-eternity is evil and does not will that anything should be taken from him, whereas the God of time and the temporal is righteous and makes no objection if creatures take things from him. He said many things so blasphemous, it is shameful even to mention them. Indeed, Satan himself never uttered the likes of them.

Then the Bashmourite came to his senses and was guided back to the true religion, whereupon he confessed his sins to the priest in his town, Nugum. He then returned to the marshlands, the land of his fore-fathers, where he became God-fearing and wise and turned away from iniquity and vile deeds. His father, who was a well-to-do man, dedicated him as his oldest son to the pursuit of knowledge, whereas he dedicated his other sons to agriculture as has been the custom in these parts since long ago. So when Mina had been educated and proved himself a diligent, bright student, particularly in mathematics, he was employed by the kharaj collector in Lower Egypt to calculate the dummaz owed by the villages in certain areas, and to advise the tax collector concerning the best ways to squeeze out the best these lands had to offer. Mina remained in this position for some time. Eventually, however, his conscience rebelled and he repented and sought God's forgiveness. It is said that in the course of doing this work—when the oppressor-now-turned-rebel had been extracting the kharaj from the peasants' lands and villages—he witnessed firsthand the injustices being suffered by the ill-fated farmers who had become serfs and slaves on their own lands by order of the caliph-appointed administrator, with no right ever to leave their lands, neither they nor their families. The only stipulation in their favor was that they were never to be bought or sold as slaves. These people had so little to eat they had even had to give up baking the bread called btaw, which they made from corn flour and fenugreek. The following is an example of what he extracted in a single year: 3,810,239 ardabs, and an eighth, a half, a sixth, and two-thirds of a carat of grain; a fourth of an ardab of jujube; 2,403 and a half ardabs of dyers' leaves; ten and a quarter ardabs of cultivated woad; 470 ratls of madder; 235,300 heads of livestock (goats and sheep); 200,000 black buffalo cows of the sort that yield abundant milk; 313 quintals and 38 ratls of unripe dates; 541 quintals and one-sixth of a quintal of bees' honey; 32 jars plus a qadus of honeycomb; 2,996 matars and a sixth and an eighth of a matar of clarified butter; and 320 ratls of cheese of the finest sorts.

It is said that what led the Bashmourite to turn away from the work he had been doing for the governor is that when, after figuring and collecting the aforementioned taxes, he was on his way home one day—home being a large, sumptuous house filled with the finest of things as was customary for the well-to-do of these parts—he heard the faint moaning of a young girl coming from somewhere in the tall esparto grass that grows up everywhere in the swamps in Bashmourite territory. He could hear a man speaking to the girl in a cruel, callous tone of voice as she begged and pleaded for mercy. Hearing this, Mina got off his mount and headed in the direction of the sounds, thinking that the man was trying to ravish her. However, when he got to where they were, he stood aghast at what he saw. For the man was tearing into the little girl's flesh with his teeth, to wit, eating her alive. He had already mangled the flesh in the tender parts of her arms and thighs, and the little girl was begging him to stop hurting her and to leave her in peace. However, the man just went on mindlessly grabbing at her with his teeth without listening to her cries and pleas for mercy. When the Bashmourite saw this, his blood boiled. In a mad rage, he flung himself at the man and wrested the girl—who by this time was half-dead—from his grip. Then he did battle with the man who, so severe was his hunger and deprivation, had been reduced from a human state to that of the beasts. Thanks to the man's weakened state and the descent of God's blessing and strength upon him at that moment, Mina managed to finish him off without much difficulty.

From that time onward, this world became as nothing in his eyes, so appalled had he been at what he saw that day. He realized that because of his work in the kharaj collection, he was an accomplice to the crime that had been committed against this poor young girl. Hence, he left it and never returned to it again. Then he took the little girl, who had a beautiful face and a luminous spirit, into his home and brought physicians to treat her. He waited patiently until she had reached puberty. Then—out of compassion for her and as a way of affirming the goodness and hope that he found in her presence—he decided to make her his wife. For he had taken a lesson from her story and saw her as a sign through which God had led him to desist from the evil and injustice in which he had been engaged. Then, after expressing his remorse over the way he had once lived, he gathered around him the Bashmourites and the peasants who were forbidden to leave their land and distributed among them his land holdings and other possessions in keeping with the words of Jesus, "If you would be perfect, go, sell what you possess and give to the poor."

The man who related the Bashmourite's story to me as we were departing by boat from the great city of Tanis at a later time told me that he had attended the wedding ceremony that joined Mina ibn Baqira in marriage to the girl whose life he had saved, and who was now maimed. He said it was a scene so moving, he would never forget it as long as he lived. The most moving part, he said, was when the officiating priest led the groom from the front of the church to the place where the bride was waiting for him, then asked Mina to place on her the wedding ring attached to the crown. When the girl did not extend her hand to indicate her consent as custom requires—having lost it in the attack she had suffered—there was not a dry eye in the place, especially when Mina kneeled before her, placed his hand on the floor and lifted her gown so that she could touch his palm with the sole of her foot, after which he placed the ring on her toe. The priest bowed their heads toward each other until they touched, and Mina took his bride to the front of the sanctuary and had her stand on his right as is customary. The priest then covered the two of them with a while silk outer garment to symbol-ize their pure, hallowed union. Meanwhile, prayers were recited, tunes chanted, and incense released into the air about them.

The man said to me, "The wedding made everybody cry. Even some of the deacons that were serving cried, too, especially when the priest was blessing them and anointing them with a bottle of holy oil on their foreheads and wrists as custom dictates. He also blessed the two crowns and placed them on their heads. When it was the bride's turn and he found no forearm or wrist to anoint, he lost his composure.

Consequently, rather than being heard as a triumphant shout, his voice came out weak and unsteady when he said, "Crown them with glory and honor, O Father, bless them, O Son, and crown them, O Holy Spirit. Rest upon them and complete them!" At that point, the entire congregation broke down. The sound of weeping and loud wailing could be heard all over the church despite the fact that it was supposed to be a joyful occasion, not one for mourning as though somebody had died."

The man also told me, "Mina ibn Baqira kept after the peasants constantly to disobey and rise up in rebellion, and not to pay the kharaj to the governor. He would tell them, 'You have nothing to lose. After all, you are being killed by starvation. So fight against those who are stealing your means of subsistence until either you kill them or they kill you.' In this way he would keep building them up with words and inciting them to disobey the governor and those who calculated the taxes for him. He would tell them that in so doing, they would be acting with Jesus Christ's sanction and blessing, since he never accepted injustice. On the contrary, he cursed those who amass wealth, and he cursed the priests of Jerusalem for their love of money, as a result of which they turned against him. He said, 'Mark did not call upon us to pay the dummaz,' by which he meant Mark the Evangelist. In this way he pleaded his case with eloquent words until they gathered around him, having despaired of their miserable lives and lost hope of making things better for themselves and their families. They went out with him to fight after he had armed them with bows, arrows, and spears, which he was said to have brought in by boat along the Nile from the land of Nubia. The boats did not arouse any suspicion, since once the arms had been placed on them, they would be covered with piles of clay jars, jugs, and all sorts of other earthenware containers that were routinely brought north from Qina in Upper Egypt.

It is said that these bows and spears were among the best types made by a tribe known as al-Bagga, whose women, as well as those related to the tribe by marriage from the women's side, had become famous for this craft. Each subtribe had a ruling chief, and they acknowledged the Lord and drew near to Him through the sun, the moon, and the planets. There were those among them who worshiped fire and the sun, and others who worshiped whatever seemed good to them, be it a tree, a dumb beast, or whatever. In other words, many of them were still pagans. It is also said that they would pass on inheritances not to the deceased person's own son, but to his daughter's son or his sister's son. This is because, or so they say, the birth of one's sister's son and one's daughter's son is more verifiable, since whether the child is from her husband or from someone else, it is still her own son.

The spears with which the Bashmourite armed his fighting men were referred to as 'septenary spears' based on the fact that the blade, which was the same width as the blade of a sword, was three cubits long, while the handle was four cubits long. A distinguishing feature of these spears was that, thanks to a pommel at the end of the handle, they would only come out of their bearer's hands with the greatest of difficulty. These spears were the ones being carried by the Bashmourites when Thawna and I had first come in to where they were. It is also said that the women who produce these spears stay in a particular location in the district of al-Bagga in which no men are allowed to mix with them except those who have come to make a purchase. If one of them should bear a girl child from a man who has come into their midst, she allows her to live, whereas if she bears a boy child, she will kill him, since they say that men bring nothing but affliction and war.

The bows we had seen with the Bashmourites at that time were large and thick, made from a variety of Christ's thorn and fir, and they were used to shoot poisoned arrows. The poison they used was made from the roots of the ghalf tree, which would be cooked over a fire until they became like glue. Thawna, knowledgeable as he was about so many things, had told me about this when I asked him after we had come out of our meeting with the Bashmourite.

I did not know what prompted Thawna to remain silent after the Bashmourite's speech rather than coming back with a rejoinder of his own. I did not understand why he did not urge him to stop fighting and obey what our Father Joseph had said. And if the truth be told, this silence of his gave me a sneaking suspicion—may God forgive me for it—that Thawna had been influenced by what the Bashmourite said and that he actually agreed with him. I myself had felt with him and had been moved by all that he said. However, to be moved is one thing, and to go against what Father Joseph had said was another. Consequently, I nearly spoke up to remind Mina of what Father Joseph had said to him in his letter. However, Thawna nudged me with his foot to keep quiet, so I shut my mouth.

Noting Thawna's failure to respond, the Bashmourite went on talking and began finding fault with Father Joseph for seeking to dampen his zeal rather than strengthening him in his war and blessing him, and for advising him to stop fighting rather than urging him to continue. Then he said, "The head of our church is afraid of what the Muslims might do to his church if it supports the Bashmourites. His only concern is that the governor might become angry with the orthodox church and lend his support to the Melkite Church instead."

When the Bashmourite had reached this point in his speech, I could see that Thawna was furious. This was the first time since I had known him, including the years I had spent with him in the church and in the course of our journey, that I had seen him get this angry, and his ire impelled him to speak.

"You are not admitting to the truth!" he retorted. "Rather, you are afraid of facing it so that you can go on fighting without thinking about why! The lands that belong to the church belong to all of us Copts. And all of the church's property, including its furniture, its utensils, and what have you, will go to the heretical Melkites, most of whom are Byzantine foreigners. If the governor and his army become angry with our church and its orthodox fathers, what this means is that all of its possessions and lands, which we inherited from our fathers and grandfathers and which we have maintained since ages past, will go to the Greeks, the Byzantines, and all the foreigners who are followers of the Melkite teachings. Besides, have you ever stopped to ask yourself where the church's property came from? Have you? Tell me, for God's sake: Is it not true that many of these properties and lands belonged originally to a large number of the wealthy fathers who denied the world and its treasures and gave everything they had by way of fortune and fame to the monasteries and churches? Do I need to remind you that most of the lands and buildings belonging to the church came from gifts and donations, and that these are the possession of all of us Copts? Besides . . . ."

Thawna fell silent suddenly as guards led a man, a woman, and four children in to where we were sitting. The guards said that they had found them slipping into the village and had been suspicious of them, so they had beaten them and brought them here. The man, the woman, and all of the children were in a pitiful state, and their bodies were caked with mud from walking such a long distance barefoot. The children, half-naked, looked on blankly, numb from hunger, emaciation, and fatigue. When the Bashmourite asked the man about himself and those who were with him, he first requested a drink of water, then said that his name was Bakhnas and that he had fled from his hometown in Upper Egypt one night with his wife and children. He said that he had fled because he had nothing with which to pay the local kharaj collector, who was bent mercilessly on extracting what people owed. He said that as many others had done, he had gone seeking refuge with his wife and children to a town by the name of Kom Ashqaw. The governor's men had dubbed the fleeing peasants 'a colony of foreigners,' and he had heard it being said that the governor had written to the mayor of Kom Ashqaw instructing him to expel all the fugitives and send them back to their lands. This was why he had fled again with his family. They had traveled at times on the river, coming up the Nile stealthily in fishermen's boats, and at other times they had walked through the wilderness areas until they reached the outskirts of Nugum. They had slipped in without knowing anything about the war that was raging between the town's inhabitants and the governor's army.

The man prostrated himself before Mina ibn Baqira and tried to kiss his feet in a plea for mercy, begging him not to turn him over to those who would send him back to his land again. He continued to plead for mercy and compassion in such a heartrending way that it brought tears to my eyes. Reassuring the man, Mina took him by the hand and raised him up off the ground, then asked his helpers to get him and his family something to eat and drink and find them clothes to wear. Mina also invited the man to stay if he so desired and to join his fighting men.

When the man and his family were gone there was a brief silence. Then in a low voice the Bashmourite asked, "Do you see? This is just one small example of the things we see here every day. By God, I swear that if I thought for a single moment of turning away from the path I am on, the very next moment would bring me face to face with something to bring me back to reality. I am like someone who has his hand in a fire, who feels nothing of this world but its searing blaze and the way it consumes his flesh. I assure you, goodhearted fathers, that if you lived here with us for even a couple of days, you would do an about-face from the position you now defend. You would cease to believe in any truth or justice on earth, and in this trouble-ridden world."

When we heard this, we crossed ourselves and asked God's forgiveness.

As the Bashmourite spoke, I had been hurriedly translating every word he said for Thawna, who replied sternly, "Listen Mina, I could tell you about lots of situations like the one we witnessed just now. What you are talking about and what we just saw are commonplace events these days. However, to acknowledge them is one thing, and to do what you are doing is another. Your war on the Muslim governors cannot possibly last forever. Sooner or later they are going to defeat you with their superior arms and their more powerful armies. The Arabs are not farmers, but a people for whom attack and retreat are their daily bread. As for you, you will never be able to achieve independence on your land and with your people. You will never be able to determine your own affairs in isolation from those who are presently in control of Egypt. So give up your dreams and your illusions. It may be that I see what you do not, since I am more distant from the situation. In any case, I did not come here to debate with you, and I have no authorization to respond to what you have said. This is Father Joseph's message to you, and I am nothing but its bearer and deliverer. All I ask is that you give me a message to take back to him at Qasr al-Sham'. This is the sum of my purpose and my mission. Finally, though, let me remind you that these Muslims are closer to us than the Melkite Byzantines. For although some of their governors have behaved in an arbitrary, despotic way and lorded it over us, in the beginning they wanted nothing for us but our well-being and security, and their Prophet, who was a high-minded, munificent man, gave instructions that we should be treated with kindness and respect. When the Muslims first came to our country, their governors treated people well. And you know now that there are many Muslim Copts and Muslim Arabs who are against the governors and their tyranny. Nor should you forget that we are the ones who brought them here in times gone by and welcomed them so that they could strengthen our hand against the Byzantines. We were content to accept their rule as an alternative to that of these other foreigners. Mina, do you want the country to fall again into the hands of the Byzantines? Think about it, and fear God. We are living in difficult times. Everything is changing, being transformed and transmuted, and the wise, discerning man is the one who looks to the distant horizon rather than staring at what is under his feet. This revolution of yours could lead the country onto a path from which there is no return because if it falls back into the hands of the Melkites, our church will never find its feet again. Our property and our wealth will be lost forever. Perhaps you know that the goodhearted fathers are striving by every means possible to protect and preserve the church. They have Arabized the prayers as a way of preserving the religion and the divine liturgy, since they realize now that most of the people have begun using Arabic more and more in their daily lives, and that unless they do so, the majority of them will not even understand either the religion or the Coptic prayer anymore. And I say to you: If your uprising is defeated, the blood of these peasants will be on your head, because the force exerted by the caliph's army will not be an easy thing. You, of all people, know the meaning of the saying 'When the mighty fall, blood flows.' For no one will have mercy on you. As you judge, you will be judged. Also, dear sir—and this an aspect of the reality God created in His wisdom—people always side with the victor against the vanquished. I tell you all these things out of concern for you and those around you. I sense that you are a man of sound doctrine, with a character not unlike that of the saints, for you live a rugged, harsh life like these peasants who have been confined as serfs to their lands, and you seek neither glory nor fame. But think about the matter, and weigh it in the scale of reason and prudence. Do not be like the one of whom the proverb was coined: 'Beware lest you be requited with evil for the good you have done.' This is what I have to say to you. Take it as coming from a brother who wants nothing but your good, and who desires nothing for your people but security and peace."

For a long time the Bashmourite sat gazing distractedly at our clerical robes. Then, his voice hoarse with agitation yet without batting an eyelid, he said, "Respected Father, what you have heard and seen here in our midst is my message to our Reverend Father in Qasr al-Sham'. We are a people who have been driven to consume each other, and may God have mercy on the one who said, *al-faqr yuwallid al-kufr*, that is, 'poverty breeds unbelief.' But, so help me God, this will not continue forever, since we have determined to consume with our spears and bows those who have consumed our daily bread and forced us to sell our children and families. We will either be a fire that roasts their bodies, or a banquet for their swords and daggers. Let our flesh be their kharaj, and our dissevered heads their jizya.

"I also want you to make clear to our Father in Qasr al-Sham' that the harm that came to his former messengers to us was inflicted on them without my knowledge, and that those who were beaten or robbed or whose companions were kidnapped received such treatment at the hands of certain plebeian followers of mine on account of their own misbehavior, haughtiness, and self-righteous attitudes. One of them had vilified everyone here, including myself, accusing us of being infidels and turncoats, as a result of which one of my men lost his temper and killed him. Even so, I punished all those who attacked these messengers, and I executed the murderer myself to make him an example to those who refuse to learn. I say this with great sorrow and regret, since we are not highway robbers or criminal thieves. Rather, we are a people who have been forced into what we are doing. God alone knows how I detest war and the things of war. I am a man who never occupied himself with such things ever before, and never in my life did I imagine that the day would come when I would be forced to do what I am doing.

"You can be on your way now, respected deacon, if you wish, and if you would like to remain among us until tomorrow morning, you are welcome. It is actually better for you not to go yet, since it is nearly nightfall, and you would not want to meet with harm along the way."

I was afraid Thawna might agree to stay the night and something unpleasant might happen. However, he declined, saying we needed to get back quickly to Old Cairo, since he did not want to be tardy in delivering an answer to Father Joseph and apprising him of what was really happening here.

As we rose, the Bashmourite jumped to his feet and extended his hand in farewell. Then he said, "So, then . . . you are leaving now. As you wish. May you go in peace."

He instructed his followers to escort us as far as they could go outside the town's borders, though I noticed that as he bade us farewell, he contented himself with squeezing our hands rather than kissing them as believers usually do with members of the church and priests.

It was nearly sundown when we began our departure from Bashmourite territory, and the ground had become muddier than ever due to the sudden increase in the waters from the Nile. We had only gone a short distance away from the large barn in which we had met with the Bashmourite and begun heading for the town's main street in order to exit from there in the direction of the Nile when a number of men, women, and children came out of their houses and gathered around to get a look at us now that news of our presence in the encampment had spread. They seemed to be staring at us as though we were some novelty or wondrous thing the likes of which they had never encountered before. Our mounts had begun moving slowly and with difficulty over the increasingly slippery ground, and the boys and girls were helping them along. Then, taking advantage of the occasion, they started running their hands over our clerical robes and looking in amazement at our shoes as though they had never seen shoes before, or as though they were expensive or luxurious. Some of the young children were completely naked with nothing to cover their bodies, while others were just barely clothed in tattered rags.

As for the women, I noted that despite the aspects of their appearance that revealed their destitution, they were strikingly attractive, with lovely faces. As we rode along talking, Thawna drew my attention to the fact that if the Bashmourite was defeated by the governor's soldiers, the girls in this place could well suffer greatly on account of their

129

beauty, a beauty that no one could miss despite their emaciation and their shabby clothing. Thawna kept handing out our provisions to the children until we had run completely out of bread, cakes, clarified butter, and honey. Meanwhile, the women grabbed the food away from the children, so unbearable was their hunger and so great was their need for nourishment. As I was offering a young girl the honey I had left in a small cask, she gazed at me for a long time, her eyes overflowing with gratitude. I for my part could not help but look back at her, and I noticed that she was pretty, buxom, delicate, with a lovely form. Her body was nearly naked owing to the lack of sufficient clothing with which to cover herself. As a result, I found myself quite agitated, not knowing whether what I was feeling was compassion or lust or a mixture of the two. Alarmed at my condition and at this resurgence of bodily desire, not to mention the sudden way it had come over my spirit and soul, I began urging my mount to speed up unnecessarily.

I suspect that Thawna noticed my agitation, and as I went rushing off on my mule, his lips seemed to part in a smile as he said, "Whoa, there, dear brother, Budayr! The Master was right when he said, 'The eye is the lamp of the body.' Slow down, brother of mine in baptism, and bridle your body with verses from the Holy Scriptures and remembrance of the Truth. Consider always the words of sweet-tongued Paul in his first letter to the Corinthians: 'Do you not know that your body is a temple of the Holy Spirit within you, which you have from God? You are not your own; you were bought with a price. So glorify God in your body.'"

I swallowed my saliva with difficulty. Then, with heat surging through my entire body and a blazing fire that was about to consume my spirit, I shouted out in reply, "May the Lord have mercy on me, dear Thawna. May the Lord have mercy on me, and may He forgive me for the sin that came over me against my will. May the demon of the body leave me and go to hell!"

Before I knew it, tears were streaming down my face and I started wiping them off with the sleeve of my robe. Memories of Amuna came rushing into my imagination, welling up inside me like water gushing forth from the bottom of a deep spring. I started thinking back on my times of earthly bliss with her, and the misery and wretchedness that followed her parting. Then I began asking God's forgiveness over and over, reciting verses of repentance and remorse and trying to drive the image of the girl I had seen from my mind's eye. It would fade for a moment, but then the Satan of the body would keep playing tricks on me until her image had taken on flesh anew with force and clarity. Struggling mightily to calm myself and recover my stability and lost certainty, I steered the mule away from the girl, who still managed to follow me. Then, in a rapid, unexpected gesture, she reached out and touched the cross that hung from a long rope on my chest, and which I had made from strands of good-quality cow's hide. Beside myself, and having nothing left to give her, I took it off mechanically and placed it around her neck. As I did so, I avoided looking at her exposed flesh. As for her, she took my hand in both of hers and pressed it fervently to her bosom, then lowered her head and kissed it. At that point, fearful that I would not be able to keep my feelings in check, I withdrew my hand hurriedly and started pushing my mule as fast as it would go as though I wanted it to fly away with me, and I did not stop until Thawna shouted at me, saying, "Slow down! Have you forgotten that the ground is muddy and slippery and that it is dangerous to move over it too quickly?"

The Bashmourite guards who were escorting us to the outskirts of the town rebuked the people harshly for fighting among themselves over the food they had taken from us. As we went along, we were informed by one of the guards that the soldiers sent out by the governor had looted everything in the region during their successive raids, and that there was not a single church between Damietta and Rashid—that is to say, anywhere along the entire length of the Bashmourite coast—but that its most important furnishings had been looted and carried away, including even its chorus cymbals and the items of priestly service in the sanctuary. Consequently, no one attended communal prayers anymore. He also told me that graves had been pillaged and looted, if not by the soldiers, then by thieves, vagabonds, and those in search of anything they could find to eat or wear. One of those who had come out to guard us said that in a Jewish cemetery that had been looted near Samanud, the most amazing thing had been found, namely, bodies which had been preserved and wrapped in bandages as was the custom in ancient times, like those found periodically in the ruins of pagan temples.

The guards also told us that marriage contracts were now finalized in what remained of private homes and sometimes even in the streets since there were so few priests available to take on this task. Most of them, they said, had left the area and gone to Wadi Habib and the monasteries in Wadi Natrun after their churches had been destroyed and they had despaired of finding anyone to support them. As for the holy oil required for baptism, it was no longer available anywhere in the area, as a result of which there was no longer anything to baptize people with. It happened that some people had brought a priest by force—bound in chains—to a nearby village. People were heartened by the priest's coming. However, Thawna and I were shocked to hear that the man refused to baptize or perform the church rites because of the lack of holy oil. We were told that most of the schools had been destroyed, as a result of which the children were not attending school and most of them no longer knew how to read and write. And as if this were not enough, manufacturers and artisans had wearied of life here, as a result of which some of them had emigrated to other countries, while a group of them were said to have crossed over to the island of Cyprus on the land bridge that leads there from the cities of Farama and Arish.

One man told us that after reaching their wits' end, many Copts had become Muslims, having found life too difficult with Mina ibn Baqira. However, there were also Muslims who had joined his uprising, since the Bashmourite did nothing to prevent people from following the religion of their choosing. Every day, he said, there were people who stole away to the governor's military encampments, as well as Arab Muslims who came to join the Bashmourites. Consequently, he said, things were highly unpredictable, being in constant flux and subject to change from one day to the next.

When we heard all these things, we were touched to the quick, and Thawna's eyes welled up visibly with tears. He spoke of how sorry he was that he had not brought food and clothing with him for these unfortunate people, or ointments and medicines to give to the women and children. He said he had noticed the many diseases they were suffering from, which manifested themselves in the form of ulcerous sores, pustules, and bloating in various parts of their bodies, particularly their stomachs. What this indicated, he said, was the spread of a disease known as chlorosis, which results from anemia and poor nutrition.

He said, "This illness, despite the danger it poses if it goes on for some time, can be cured easily with a mixture made from figs (in a ratio of one part to thirty-two), sea salt (one part to eight), freshly baked bread (one part to eight), and sweet fuqqaʻ (one part to three). The mixture is cooked all together, then strained and taken all in one day. It is a very old recipe that has been passed down over many generations. If I had known how widespread this malady is here, I would have prepared a large quantity myself and brought it with me to distribute it among people."

Then he added, "There are some diseases that can be cured with readings from the Holy Scriptures, and others that can be cured through medical treatment. Most stomach ailments that result from hunger can be treated with medicaments that compensate the body for the good food it has not received. Given the fact that these peasants have had poor diets for a long time now, they are suffering from severe emaciation, jaundice, and bloating of the intestines, but all of this can be overcome. As for the mosquitoes and other pests that are found in such abundance here on account of the large amounts of stagnant water and the ubiquitous salt bogs, this is the real tragedy, since this is what brings on fevers and blood diseases whenever more bites occur."

What Thawna had just said reminded me of something that had happened in my long-lost childhood, when a large number of people in my village died in an epidemic. It was said at the time to have been caused by an infernal fly that had come to the town from the wilderness areas and begun causing people to get sick. But the cause was not discovered until it had wiped out entire families. When I mentioned this to Thawna, he said, "An epidemic will descend on districts and towns and wipe out most of their populations when a curse from God comes upon them because of sins they have committed. God may strike them with an earthquake or a lightning bolt, or unleash devastating floods. At other times He might afflict them with pests such as mosquitoes and the like which are indwelt by evil spirits that cause them to assault people's bodies, thereby causing illness and pain, weakening their bones, sucking their blood, and bringing about emaciation and, ultimately, death. The attending physicians need to look for the cause of the curse so that they can eliminate it. They also need to ascertain the true nature of the evil spirits that have come to reside in the insects, something which is done through repeated recitation of incantations and scripture readings. Following this they should treat the people with plants and minerals and prescribe the substances suitable for curing the diseases brought by the epidemic."

As we rode along talking, people followed us on foot down the narrow lanes and gathered about us on all sides for us to bless them until we were about to head out into the wilderness. When we reached the road that had led us into the town, they stopped and left us to move on by ourselves after bidding us a fervent, poignant farewell.

Though we were moving on, the scenes I had witnessed in the Bashmourite's encampment refused to leave me: the wasted little children in their rags, the ravenous women snatching food out of the children's hands, the tumble-down houses, and the Bashmourite's men clad in their peculiar attire and carrying weapons that looked as though they belonged to thieves and hooligans. My feelings vacillated from one moment to the next between compassion for these people in their unspeakable misery, and aversion for their rebellion and their refusal to obey what Father Joseph was saying. As I left the scenes behind, my heart was gripped by nostalgic longing, and I wondered: If I had stayed in my hometown, in the place where I grew up with my family, and if my life had taken the course it was supposed to rather than my being propelled by fate into the situation I am in now, would I have been one of these folks? Would I have become one of the Bashmourite's followers: obeying his every command, going about with nothing but a wrap around my waist, wearing a palm-leaf helmet and armed with a spear? I felt lost, sorrowful, as though my heart had been ripped right out of me, and as though my questions had no answers. However, of one thing I was certain: that one's homeland carries with it a feel, a scent, and a set of concrete images that stand out in full relief and never leave your soul or your senses no matter how much time passes and no matter what distance separates you from it.

Noticing my long silence and picking up on my despondency, Thawna said, "So then, here we are on our way back to where we came from. Like they say, *Titi titi, zay ma ruhti zay ma jiti!* Father Joseph, who is waiting for us at Qasr al-Sham', is going to be sorely distressed when we come back without the Bashmourite and without even so much as a promise that he will stop fighting. After all, this is going to make it appear in the eyes of the governor as though he has no influence over the followers of his own church, and that his word has no authority. And the Melkites are going to take full advantage of the situation. They will play a sweet tune in the governor's ear and insinuate in that diabolical way of theirs that Father Joseph does not really want to quell the Bashmourites' uprising, that he is in cahoots with them, and that he wants to cause disturbances in the country. These are just the sorts of lies they are always feeding him in the hope that one day they will have the control and influence that our church has now. Their ambition is to take over our churches, our monasteries, and all our property. In any case, you saw your hometown again, and without any unwelcome events along the way. You are happy about that, are you not?"

Still preoccupied with the other things he had just been telling me, I murmured hastily, "Of course, of course. And thank God nobody I used to know saw me or recognized me."

Following my steps precisely and exercising the greatest of care not to ride over a spot that was not solid ground, Thawna continued, "But I fear, Budayr, that this Bashmourite is going to meet an unhappy, regrettable end. Perhaps I have told you about what was being rumored secretly in the church before we came out, to the effect that if the Bashmourites do not settle down, stop waging war on the governor's soldiers, and agree to pay the kharaj required of them, the Muslims' caliph is going to come and settle the matter himself. I thought it best not to tell Mina about this for fear that he might lose his temper and defy me, thinking that I had just come to bring an ultimatum from Father Joseph, in which case he might have subjected us to harsh treatment that would have led to no good. But to be honest with you, I nearly weakened for a moment there, especially when he got more and more adamant and heated up. I nearly shouted in his face, 'You fool, do you not know that the caliph is going to come personally to put an end to this whole thing if you do not learn your lesson and turn back from the path you are on? And do you realize what that means? They are going to annihilate you, that is what it means. And when that happens, you will be the one who has committed the crime against your people and yourself, since the man will have no mercy on either them or you. This is someone who has done battle with the army of Byzantium, so by comparison, fighting you will be mere child's play, or like some afternoon equestrian tournament.'"

"No, no," I said, "thank God you did not say that to him, since as you have seen, he is not the type to take advice and stop what he is doing. Besides, Father Joseph did not ask you to speak to him about that. But what I cannot understand, brother, is why some of the Arab Muslims have joined up with the Bashmourite. How on earth could that be?"

Thawna remained silent for a few moments, then said, "The Muslims are divided into factions and sects just the way we are in Christianity: Jacobites, Melkites, and so forth. And there are differences of opinion among these groups having to do with various points of the religion. Do you remember when you were washing up in the public bath and I was waiting for you outside? While I was standing there, a man approached me looking this way and that. When he had reassured himself that the coast was clear, he gave me a note which he asked me to read, then hurriedly withdrew. When I went in to wash up after you, I read it, and I discovered that he was asking me to find his wife, children, and extended family, who are living near Mount Yashkur overlooking the Nile and Birkat al-Fil. He joined the Bashmourite in secret after fleeing from the governor's harassment of him and the group he belongs to, which is referred to as the Carmatians. The caliph himself has been oppressing them not only in Iraq, but in all the regions of his caliphate. He said that many of his comrades had been imprisoned and tortured for declaring their disobedience to the caliph, who had made the sheikhs and other representatives of the religion accuse them of being infidels and atheists. He was asking me to reassure his family of his well-being and offer them whatever assistance I can, since he has nothing to support them with."

Continuing, he said, "I have heard of another group of Muslims called the Alawites, who have also broken with the caliph. You have seen with your own eyes now what is taking place in al-Hawf al-Sharqi.

The struggles never end, and there is chaos and turmoil everywhere. All this troubles me deeply, Budayr, and I feel that the disturbances in the world around me shake me up on the inside. In spite of my faith and the genuineness of my belief, I will tell you honestly: I am afraid, really afraid, as though I were a sailor lost on a terrible dark sea. And I am afraid for our church. I do not know what will happen to it if the Bashmourite is victorious, but at the same time I am afraid for these poor unfortunate people if they are defeated. I wonder how the land will be governed and which of the Muslim factions will triumph. My only hope, Budayr, is that never again will our country fall into the hands of those despicable Byzantine Melkites."

Hardly had Thawna finished what he was saying before a thick, dark band of something appeared on the horizon. It extended to infinity, like a swath of ink that separated the blueness of the heavenly expanse above us from the greenness of the earth that stretched as far as the eye could see. The disk of the sun blazed like a red inferno as it vanished little by little, announcing its final departure and preparing the way for a rapidly approaching darkness. Meanwhile, the dark band crept gradually in our direction. Startled and bewildered, we froze in place. Then, getting hold of himself again, Thawna began urging me to flee, saying, "It must be the caliph's horsemen, dressed in black. Get off your mule and run before they catch up with us and their horses trample us underfoot."

No sooner had I done as he said than they reached the spot where we had just been. They were advancing gradually, but without difficulty, since they had with them a Coptic guide who was showing them the places where it was safe to proceed. By this time they had become clearly visible, and were easily distinguished by their honey-colored robes.

After jumping hurriedly off my mule and leaving it where it was, I hid myself in a spot not far away in the tall esparto grass and reeds. However, I was so flustered and afraid, I did not notice what Thawna had done. I had been taken totally by surprise, never having foreseen what was happening to us now.

I was so terrified, my heart nearly stopped beating when I saw one of them draw the two mules along with him, then pause slightly as though he wanted to go looking for their owners. However, the person behind him urged him to keep going lest he hinder the movement of those following him. Then I started crawling ever so slowly, being careful to keep myself well concealed among the reeds lest I be noticed by someone passing by. Darkness had fallen, and I started calling out to Thawna in a low voice in an attempt to locate him. I was terribly frightened this whole time, praying to God that I would not be bitten by a snake like the one that had bitten Thawna, and that no wild animal would come out at me and mangle my flesh or otherwise do me harm.

I had not been hiding long when the army halted its advance, and its rear guard stopped somewhere nearby along the narrow path. I realized this despite the surrounding darkness from the shrill sound of their horses' neighing and whinnying. They seemed to be shying quite a bit due to the unfamiliarity of the place and the unaccustomed amount of water to be found there. I suspected that the soldiers had surrounded the area and blocked the roads leading to the Bashmourite's encampment, and my suspicion proved correct, since it was not long before they began lighting torches and throwing them in the direction of the encampment. Nor was the response long in coming from the Bashmourite's fighting men, who in turn began hurling fire at the caliph's army. I started crawling again in hopes of saving my skin. At the same time, I was afraid of being pulled by the muddy waters into areas of danger, so I tied some long, supple, firmly rooted grasses around myself. In the process, my robe and most of my body had gotten dirty, and even my face was covered with mud and filth. As the battle raged, I prayed that no evil would befall me, as the Bashmourites had started shooting the caliph's soldiers with slingshots and throwing rocks and pieces of brick in their direction. As for the Muslim soldiers, they fought primarily with spears and arrows, though they focused on the use of flaming fireballs. Hence, it seemed they intended to set the encampment on fire before entering it.

Feeling desperate and exhausted, I began crossing myself over and over and reciting verses from Scripture so that the Lord would help me through the situation I was in. Feeling as though I was about to get drowsy, I took off my clerical belt and tied myself more securely with the grasses. And before long I fell fast asleep.

The next morning I woke up to the twittering of a bird that had lit nearby. When I opened my eyes and looked at it, I found a huge flamingo digging about in search of one of the fish that generally come swimming into these parts from salt water areas—perhaps a brown fish, a Nile carp, a salmon, or a shilba. When I saw it I took it as a hopeful sign with which to greet the new day, especially now that it had begun blithely singing its morning songs to the Lord. I started to get up to take a look at it myself, but whenever I tried to move any of my limbs I met with great difficulty. Even so, I forced myself up, determined to get going no matter how much pain I happened to be in. After all, I had to look for dear Thawna and find out what had happened with him. In the process, I discovered that my clothes were soiled and wet from the greenish mud on which I had slept. I looked around for some running water in which I could wash my clerical robe. However, the only thing visible was a vast expanse of green. I uttered the divine name and made the sign of the cross, then said to myself: Let me walk around a bit, then, and I am sure to find some water somewhere or other.

I dragged myself along with difficulty like a baby taking its first steps. Taking care to distinguish the water from the solid ground lest I be pulled under in some slick area and drown, at last I reached a narrow stream in which there was running water. Standing at its edge, I took off my clerical robe, thereby exposing my arms, as all I had on now was my peasant's waistcoat and the trousers I always wore under my robe. I began dipping the robe into the water, repeating the name of God and crossing myself and reciting verses of ritual purification, then wrung it and shook it out so as to get rid of as much excess water as I could. Finally, I spread it out on top of the grass in the hope that I could rest for an hour while I waited for the sun to dry it, then put it back on. As I was thus occupied, I started thinking about how I was going to get back to Old Cairo under these difficult circumstances. I wanted to find out how the Bashmourites had fared in their battle with the caliph's army the night before, so I thought: As soon as I have my robe on again, I will head back to the Bashmourite's camp to check things out. And perhaps I will find Thawna, who may have withdrawn there during last night's battle in order to seek refuge with the Bashmourite's people if he did not manage to flee back to our church in Old Cairo.

Then suddenly I remembered that Thawna had come to me in a dream the night before, so I started recalling the dream in my mind's eye. Thawna had been dressed in the sort of rags worn by mystics and ascetics and he was leaning on a sycamore wood staff like those who go wandering through the wilderness. Standing atop a high hill, he gestured to me with his hand and said, "Follow me, dear Budayr, to Wadi Habib." As he spoke these words, he looked serene and content, his face luminous like that of a saint. I looked around me in search of a place where I could walk toward him. However, I found myself surrounded on all sides by wild beasts that prevented me from approaching him. I raised my hands, crying out from the depths of my being, "Thawna! Thawna with the abundant knowledge and understanding! Come help me! I cannot!" I kept calling out to him, but he began withdrawing from me little by little until he had disappeared from sight as I crossed myself and bewailed my ill-fortune. As Thawna faded into the ether, he blessed me with his raised hand while I stretched out my hands toward him, hoping for deliverance.

Once I had recalled the dream, my spirit recoiled inside me and I was gripped by a sense of foreboding. The flamingo suddenly let out a cry and flew away, and when I looked up at the sky above me, what should I see but a frightful-looking desert-dwelling eagle hovering over the spot where I sat waiting for my robe to dry. Based on my own knowledge and experience, eagles were not generally seen in Bashmourite territory. Rather, most of its birds were of the types that migrate from the direction of the Mediterranean Sea such as quail, partridges, pheasants, storks, and the white ibis, which is well-known in the entire region.

For a while I sat there thinking, trying to figure the situation out. I was so agitated and afraid, my throat had gone dry. And I thought to myself: Maybe it wants to hunt a bird that has landed nearby, or some animal that has come venturing out of its underground burrow. I had begun to get thirstier and thirstier, and I began praying, encouraging myself to be patient. I did not dare scoop water out of the stream with my hand, since some desert dwellers had warned me against drinking from the salt marshes and their small streams even if they appeared to be running water. These people, who had come to the church in fulfillment of some vow they had made, had told me that in the area where they live there is a type of leech that enters the palate along with the water one has drunk, after which it attaches itself to the muscles that control the swallowing reflex and feeds off its host's blood until he gives up the ghost.

Then before I knew it, the eagle that had been hovering overhead swooped down and grabbed my clerical robe, then flew back up into the sky. Beside myself, I tried to run after it, but I did not get very far on account of the weakness in my legs and body and my fear of slipping and falling. Exasperated and enraged as I watched the eagle make off with my robe, I was at a total loss to explain why it would have behaved in such a fashion. After all, what on earth was a bird going to do with a piece of clothing like that? I called down curses on it as I remembered the words someone once spoke: *Ma tara tayrun wartafaʻa illa kama tara waqaʻ*—or, "What goes up, must come down."

I stayed where I was for a while, dazed and motionless, contemplating the state I was in with nothing on but my drawers and my linen waistcoat. Not having the slightest idea what to do, and feeling completely naked, I thought: Let me get up and walk a short distance, since the eagle may have dropped the robe on the ground somewhere nearby, in which case I can pick it up and put it on again even if it is covered with mud. Then maybe I will come by some kindhearted folks who would be willing to lend me a robe, whatever it happens to look like, for me to wear back to Old Cairo. Even so, I was in an extraordinary state of hopelessness and dismay. I continued to feel perplexed, unable to think of any explanation for what had happened to me. I said to myself: Maybe the Lord will be gracious to me and show me a miracle now, by producing some clothes out of thin air and consoling my forlorn spirit. Shoring myself up to endure my situation patiently, I murmured the words of the Apostle Paul to the church at Rome: "Therefore, since we are justified by faith, we have peace with God through our Lord Jesus Christ. Through him we have obtained access to this grace in which we stand, and we rejoice in our hope of sharing the glory of God. More than that, we rejoice in our sufferings, knowing that suffering produces endurance, and endurance produces character, and character produces hope. And hope does not disappoint us, because God's love has been poured into our hearts through the Holy Spirit which has been given to us."

I also recited what I could remember of the words of the Lord recorded in scripture, praying and crossing myself over and over as I thought about the lives of the saints, the martyrs, and the church fathers and patriarchs. I said to myself: Let them be an example to me, and let my dependence be upon the Lord alone as I wander, lonely and a stranger, in this bleak wilderness like a baby fish in a gargantuan fisherman's net. Let me be a witness to my time and to the state of this alien world. Then I began thinking back on the time when I had gone wandering aimlessly in the wilderness after leaving Tarnit and how I had encountered wild beasts and spent long nights sleeping on the ground without so much as a bite of bread or a sip of water. Even so, the Lord on high had willed for me to survive and recover. Hence, if He, the Invincible Master, had tested me in my early youth through the trials of physical desire and passionate love, it had only been for the purpose of ushering me into the realm of spiritual desire and a passionate love for Christ in the days of my manhood and maturity. After all, thanks to God's kindness and bounty, I had become a man of the church, happy, contented, and praising Him for all things. He was no doubt looking upon me now just as He had been before. And perhaps He was going to subject me to a test by means of which I could attain His grace and favor.

I remained this way for an hour, or maybe it was more than an hour, since the shadows of the grasses around me were changing and had nearly disappeared from view, which meant that the sun had reached its zenith. It was noon, then, and I was lying on the ground. So I said to myself: What are you waiting for, boy? Time is getting away from you while you sit around just thinking. Get up and walk so that you can find a way out of this situation and get yourself something to wear in place of your kidnapped robe. You also want to look for Thawna and make sure he is all right. However, no sooner had I started to stand up and get going than I heard the stomping of hooves approaching. I looked up, thinking that my longed-for relief had arrived, only to find myself surrounded like a bird in a trap. Over my head there stood a contingent of black-clad men decked out for battle. Afraid, I stepped back slightly as they shouted to each other and pointed at me, saying in their language, "It is a Bashmourite who is under the ban, and who is hiding here. Get over here right away!" Thereupon other soldiers joined them and dragged me from where I was standing as I screamed in Arabic so that they would understand what I was saying. I was so utterly terrified, I nearly wet myself, having lost all control over the loci of feeling in my body and limbs.

"No, no!" I screamed, "I am not a Bashmourite! I am not one of those farmers who are forbidden to leave their land! I am Budayr, the sexton at the church of the Virgin Mary at Qasr al-Sham' in Old Cairo!"

Then the world started to spin about me and, so great were my fright and shock, I fell unconscious.

When I came to after my swoon, I found myself in the Bashmourite's encampment again, and in the same house in which we had met with the Bashmourites' leader, Mina ibn Baqira. I started looking around me to make out what had happened, and confirmed to myself that it was, indeed, the very same place where Thawna and I had sat among the Bashmourite's men the day before. However, most of the walls had been demolished by the fighting and shooting, and what was left of them was covered with soot and various other aftereffects of the conflagration. I began crying out to myself: Thawna! Where are you, my precious Thawna! Did you escape, or were you killed? Or have they taken you captive the way they have me? Trembling, and my senses dissipated by an all-encompassing gloom, I said to myself, "Glory be to the One who can cause everything to change from one moment to the next. . . ." Then, in a faint, despondent voice I said, "May I be comforted by 'the Father of mercies and the God of all comfort, who comforts us in all our affliction, so that we may be able to comfort those who are in any affliction, with the comfort with which we ourselves are comforted by God.'" As I kept on repeating these sweet words of the Apostle Paul, I found myself surrounded by a group of soldiers and bound with iron shackles. And such also was the state of a large number of women, men, and children, some of whom had begun to weep and wail, while others just looked about them, grave faced and speechless, perhaps from the severity of the shock, and perhaps from sheer exhaustion and bewilderment. I tried to explain to the soldiers who I really was, but before I could begin to speak, their commander laughed, saying, "So, you still insist that you are a cleric from the church at Qasr al-Sham' in Old Cairo?"

I took heart from what he had said, thinking that he finally understood and believed what I had told him earlier.

"Yes, sir," I said. "I am Budayr, the sexton for the Church of the Virgin Mary at Qasr al-Sham'."

All the soldiers laughed, while one of them remarked, "A priest without a beard? Has any of you ever seen such a thing?"

I ran my hand over my chin in spite of myself, feeling upset that I was beardless. There was not a single hair under my temples or on my chin. But then I remembered how dear Thawna used to tell me, "You look just like John Golden Mouth." At that point I lost my composure entirely. My emotions were so stirred up at the thought of him and I longed for him so badly, I started to sob. I felt totally helpless and did not know what to say anymore. After all, they were not going to believe me no matter what I told them. They were gathered around me the way wild animals gather around a prey they have felled and begin tearing at its flesh. So then, I thought, come what may, let me ask them about Thawna.

Pleadingly I asked, "By the truth of your religion and the One you worship, sirs, have you seen my coworker and companion, Deacon Thawna?"

They all laughed at what I had said, and it seemed they were determined not to believe me.

However, one of them said seriously, "What did you say, man? Did you have a companion with you from the clergy? I think I saw him."

Crying out like someone who was dead and whose spirit has been restored to him, I said, "Is he alive? Tell me, for God's sake, and may you be richly rewarded in this life and the next!"

Looking puzzled, he said, "It seems to me I saw a man dressed like a priest, and who looked a bit befuddled. He was passing me quickly as I entered the town and shrieking, 'So, then, there is no hope or refuge but the wilderness! Long live our wilderness—the sacred wilderness of Habib! Let us take refuge there the way we did before!'"

Then he turned to his fellow soldiers and said, "I think this man is telling the truth, and that he really is a member of the clergy. So I suspect we ought to leave him alone and let him go his way."

"Telling the truth? Did you say, 'Telling the truth'?" retorted the commander furiously as he shoved his colleague out from in front of me. As he did so, he took hold of my forearm and began waving it in their faces as he asked me sarcastically, "So what is this on your forearm, you double-dealing, despicable farmer? Is that not the lion tattoo? Does it lie, too?"

I almost defended myself by telling him that I had been given this tattoo when I was a little boy, long before I entered the church. Later, the governor had issued a decree requiring that even monks in the monasteries be tattooed just like the peasants and all other Copts who were obliged to pay the jizya. This was after the Muslim governors had gone to excess in oppressing the Copts and after many Copts had entered Islam as a way of escaping the jizya. Others had entered monasteries in order not to have pay this unjust tax based on the fact that in the early days of Islam—in the days of the first caliphs—monks had not been required to pay the jizya. I wanted him to give me just a little time to prove to him who I really was and the reason for my presence in the Bashmourite's encampment. But he was a malevolent, violent man—may God shame him and burn him in the hellfire—who neither listened to me nor gave me time to say what I wanted to. Instead, he raised his gross, heavy hand and gave me a slap on the face so forceful and excruciating, it sent me reeling. After that, I did not know a thing anymore, and I fainted. Weary, hopeless, miserable, and spent, the only thing I could see in this world was ruin and perdition, and I had lost all hope of these people's believing me no matter what I said and no matter how I might try to convince them.

I think I was transferred to a large barn which may have been used to store wheat during the days when the peasants were still farming the land, since when I came to again, night had fallen, and I found myself sprawled on the floor among a large number of others, some of whom I had been with before. I could see their miserable-looking features in the light of the torches being held by the guards who hemmed us in from all sides. The sight of the women would have brought tears to anyone's eyes no matter how stoic he might try to be. The majority of them were actually young girls, and most of them may well have been unmarried virgins, since the soldiers had not taken any notice of the older women. After all, what would they have had to offer them? There was a large number of young children with the women who were crying out to them for food. As for the men, both the mature ones and the teenagers, they were broken, wounded, and in a generally pitiful state. Ignominy was now their lot one and all, and they were overcome with bewilderment and despair.

Several hours later they brought a basket of bread and a clay jug of water. They gave us each a small round loaf of bread and began passing the jug around so that we could wet our pallets. Yet, no sooner would one of us lift it to his mouth to take a quick sip than the soldier would snatch it away from him again, sometimes even before it had reached his lips, and give it to someone else. Consequently, most of the people got nothing to drink and the children kept up their screaming, while some of them may even have died on that account. Then one of the soldiers informed us in a commanding tone that we would have to get ready to leave. He said we would be going to Tanis an hour after daybreak and that as soon as we heard the horn being blown, we should be ready to line up and move out. We were to line up two by two, the women with other women and the children, and the men with the men. The minute everyone heard this, weeping and wailing rang out. In fact, some of the men began slapping their cheeks and screaming like the women. They realized fully now that they were captives, with no release in sight and none to reverse their ill-fortune. It was as though they had already died and their fate had been sealed, especially when the soldier added that from Tanis we would be traveling on ships and boats to the seat of the Muslim caliphate in Baghdad.

I had begun munching on my loaf of bread before the announcement came. But the moment it reached my ears, I stopped. I just sat there frozen, speechless, staring into space. The whole thing, from the time we had left the church at Qasr al-Sham' and up to that moment, seemed like some sort of diabolical nightmare, the kind that descends upon you sometimes if you have gone to sleep without having been sincere in your prayers and cleansed your heart of the day's sins. There

146

were moments when I felt as though I had fallen under some sort of alchemic or magic spell. For no matter how wild I might have let my imagination run concerning the perils and difficulties that Thawna had talked to me about at such length, never in my life could I have conceived of the fate that was going to be mine as of the following morning. Was it conceivable that I would be leaving my country and homeland against my will, taken away as a captive who might be sold in the slave markets of Baghdad—I, Budayr ibn Bushay, the Bashmourite Egyptian, who had been born and lived my entire life on this land, the land on which my fathers and grandfathers had lived from time immemorial? That I would end up a captive of the caliph, among those being shipped away to Baghdad? I did not know whether to cry or laugh. It was—as Thawna used to always say about anything that was serious and comical at the same time—a ludicrous joke, like the ones told by the heretic and infidel Paul of Samosata. I pictured myself being put on an auctioneer's block, being gawked at by those coming and going as the slave trader bargained over my price as though I were some chattel or dumb beast. This was all so difficult for me, I felt myself on the brink of madness, and I started recalling everything I had suffered in my entire lifetime and all the torments I had ever been through. Then, heaving a sigh in spite of myself, I whispered imploringly, "Osanna . . . Osanna, merciful Jesus," as beloved Thawna used to always say whenever he was distraught or faced with a difficulty.

I began crossing myself with a trembling hand, sensing that nothing short of a miracle from Heaven would be able to extricate me from my predicament. Noticing my dazed stupor and my lack of interest in the food, the man lying next to me asked me to give him my loaf if I did not plan to eat it myself. So I handed it over to him gladly, having no desire for either food or drink. On the contrary, I wished I could die. I wished the Lord would gather me into His Kingdom before I had to part with my country and homeland, to suffer ignominy and humiliation in strange lands of which I knew nothing and on which I had never so much as set foot.

Then, bolstering myself up again and affirming my faith and trust in God, I said to myself: There must be some way out of the situation I am in, and the Lord is bound to reveal a sign sooner or later that will make clear to these dictatorial, idiotic soldiers that they have made a mistake in what they have done to me. Father Joseph might even have sent someone out from Qasr al-Sham' to help me and dear Thawna, bringing with him an order from the governor or the caliph to release me and bring Thawna back so that we could return to where we had come from. Thinking about such things revived my spirit, and I started to feel so hopeful that I no longer noticed my physical pain or the terrible thirst that was searing my throat. Even so, I gulped down the water they had brought us in buckets, then decided to start reciting the night prayers and go to sleep until daybreak. By that time, I thought to myself, the Lord will have looked upon me with the eye of compassion and embraced me in His boundless mercy.

I slept for maybe an hour or two, then woke up in a panic. Sensing that there was someone running his hands over my body, I sat up with a start. Then before long, in the dim light of the sole lamp that the guards had left lit in the corner of the barn, who should I see sitting beside me but the pretty young girl that I had encountered in the road the day before as Thawna and I were leaving after our meeting with the Bashmourite. I started with fright, then began edging away from her, as I could feel a fire spreading through my body and setting my spirit ablaze. I was distraught, as well as amazed to find her in the spot next to me, since they had put the men and boys on one side of the barn and the women, girls, and infants on the other. I started looking around me, at a loss as to what to do. I was fearful that someone might wake up and suspect me of something, or that one of the guards keeping watch at the barn door might notice her presence next to me and become suspicious of us, an eventuality that was bound to lead to unwanted outcomes. My face must have revealed what was going through my mind, since the girl whispered to me imploringly to keep quiet. And in fact, I had been on the verge of scolding her aloud so that she would get away from me. Then she took my hand in both of hers as she said in a whisper, "I ask you please to listen to me, goodhearted Father. I saw you yesterday with your companion, the other priest, as the two of you were leaving our encampment together, and you gave me your cross. I am one of the women your companion blessed. So, I ask you please to help me find a way to keep these soldiers from taking me away with them. I want you to spare me what will happen if they take possession of me and I am alone among them, since I am unmarried and a virgin. All my family has been killed, and I will surely lose my mind if one of those criminals lays a hand on me."

Then the girl began weeping bitterly, though I did not know what to do for her. Then suddenly she stopped crying and gazed at me intently as she drew up close to me and her body brushed against mine.

"Marry me, young Father," she said. "My name is Suwayla. Marry lost Suwayla, now. Now, and quickly. Maybe something will happen to spoil their hopes. If I get pregnant, I can only be sold in the slave market for a paltry price. So if I tell them I am pregnant, maybe one of them will take me to someone's house as a domestic servant. This way, I can preserve myself and find some inward stability, since I will be far away from people like them. I have thought about killing myself, Father, but I am afraid, and I do not have the strength to do it."

Then suddenly she flung herself on my chest and began embracing me and kissing me on my face and my mouth with a violent passion. My own passions aroused, I lost hold of myself. I forgot the world, lost all sense of time or place, and began drawing her into my arms and kissing her back. "Suwayla, Suwayla!" I cried out to her in a whisper, running my hands over every part of her tender, soft body. And when my lips and fingertips began stroking her breasts' succulent fruit, things spun out of control and I was like someone gone mad. I flung her down and crouched over her. Then, gathering the life force that had gone surging through my body, I gave it to her. It was as if, in that act, I was defying weakness, despair, and annihilation. At the same time, I was being swept along by an overwhelming, fiendish pleasure that I had no power to resist.

When we had finished—Suwayla having received my response to her with a response even more vehement—I found myself flooded with a sense of unbounded relief. It was as though all the aches and pains in my body had never been, and I was swathed in an unspeakable serenity the likes of which my spirit had not known since my long-past union with my Amuna-who-was-no-more. For some time I lay there pressing the girl's hand to my heart, patting it at times and kissing it at others. And I said to her, "I will never leave you. I will put you in the pupil of my eye. My eyelashes will protect you, and I will never leave you as long as I live! From this moment onward, you are my wife, my beloved, my most intimate, and thus will you remain till the Day of Judgment."

Then, thanking me and uttering fervent praises to God, Suwayla gathered herself together, stood up, and withdrew quietly and circumspectly without anyone noticing her. As for me, I did not know what to say or do. For despite the pledge I had made to her, a pledge in which I had been utterly sincere, a terrible sense of remorse came over me, as I realized I had fallen into sin. I knew that Satan had gotten the better of me and taken control over my spirit and body with his uncleanness, and that I had weakened and surrendered to him without making any attempt to stand firm in the face of his wicked deception.

It was during those moments that I first came to know the real meaning of sin and guilt. I also realized that the advice I had received from the fathers in our church at Qasr al-Sham' had made perfect sense. How many times had they encouraged me to marry lest I fall into sin? And more than once they had pointed out to me an upstanding girl with the thought that we might be joined in holy matrimony. However, I had rejected the idea out of hand, because from the time I lost my precious Amuna I had lost all desire for women. As for this girl, I could not for the life of me understand why I had taken to her the way I did. Yet the truth is—although I regretted what I had done with her—I had desired her from the moment I first laid eyes on her, and I felt deeply agitated when I noticed her looking at me for such a long time when we were on the road.

So I began praying for God's forgiveness and bringing to mind some of Paul's first letter to the Corinthians, which Thawna had always encouraged me to memorize and hold in my heart so that it would preserve me from sin and harm whenever I recalled it and recited it aloud: "Do you not know that he who joins himself to a prostitute becomes one body with her? For as it is written, 'The two shall become one.' But he who is united to the Lord becomes one spirit with him. Shun immorality. Every other sin that a man commits is outside the body; but the immoral man sins against his own body. Do you not know that your body is a temple of the Holy Spirit within you, which you have from God? You are not your own; you were bought with a price. So glorify God in your body."

Then I wept bitterly, wishing I could castrate myself the way Saint Origen had done long before, despite the Pope's displeasure with him on this account, since the sufferings caused by desire and the struggle to overcome it are one of the consequences of choosing a life of sincere faith.

I wished a miracle would happen, and that I could close my eyes and open them again to find myself back at the church at Qasr al-Sham', standing before Father Joseph to confess all my sins to him: the one I had fallen into just now and the one I had committed long ago with Amuna. In fact, I wished I could be exposed not only before Father Joseph, but before everyone. I wanted to suffer whatever punishment Father Joseph thought most fitting, since I had not had genuine faith that the Host presented to us in the paten and chalice is the body of the Savior and the Judge. I promised myself that I would not punish my body with fasting, sleepless nights, or anything else until I had confessed and accepted the discipline of public penance. I also decided that if it was not in God's plan for me to return to our church at Qasr al-Sham', I would confess in the first church I came to after I had gotten out of this place, even if it happened to be in Baghdad.

If you were to put all the troubles and horrors I have met with in my entire life in one balance, and in the other, the time I spent between our departure from the Bashmourite's encampment and our arrival in Tanis, the former would not outweigh the latter by an iota. The journey we made in that single day seemed, to me, to last ages on end. In the early morning they brought us out lined up in rows, after which they led us onward on foot, surrounded on all sides by guards and soldiers and preceded by the military commander together with a contingent of his horsemen. Streets which, up to the time of the battle, had been teeming with people and their noisy bustle, now looked more like the streets of Sodom and Gomorrah after the curse had descended upon them: Corpses lay strewn here and there and the stench of death and charred remains hung heavily in the air, mingling with the odor of soil from the demolition of the towns' wretched mud dwellings. Appalled at these despots' mindless cruelty, I thought to myself: Why all this devastation and destruction for the sake of a few simple houses which would have collapsed in no time if they had done nothing but throw a few stones at them?

Our exodus in this most miserable of states followed by our march through the streets of these ruined cities was almost beyond description. We walked on, just barely able to drag our feet along and suffering the agonies of thirst and hunger, aches and pains, since there was not a single one among us but that he was either bruised, broken, or injured. As for the women who followed us in the rear, their conditions were the worst and their suffering the most severe, and by the time we reached Tanis that day, many children had been lost.

Throughout this time I was saying to myself: Everything I have suffered thus far and what I am going to suffer in the days to come is nothing but the fruit of the iniquity I sowed in my early days with Amuna, as well as the more recent sin that Satan caused me to fall into inside the barn. I felt as though I had been made for nothing but iniquity and transgression, and that this was bound to be my fate no matter how much time passed. Was not my rapid surrender to Suwayla simply a confirmation of this? It was as though my spirit could never live or thrive on anything but the torments of sin and remorse. And what made my torment even worse during this journey of captivity was not knowing what had become of Thawna and his not being at my side. Had he escaped after the soldier saw him? And was the soldier's statement to the effect that he had gone to Wadi Habib correct? Or had he gone back to Father Joseph at Qasr al-Sham'? My worse fear was that he might have been killed or suffered harm. If only he were by my side right here, I thought, to console me and support me with his immaculate spirit and his abundant knowledge! Besides, if he were here, he might have prevented me from doing what I did with Suwayla and brought me back to the right path. Yet, despite my terrible sense of guilt, I felt compassion for Suwayla, this unfortunate girl who, as far as I could tell, was going to meet with the worst possible fate in her future life now that she had lost her family and loved ones and everyone who cared about her on this earth. Looking around at all the other people departing with me, I kept thinking about their unknown fate, which was my fate as well.

As I imagined what state we would all be in after we had been put on display in the slave market to be gawked at and sized up by those coming and going, I recalled a scene I had witnessed during my wanderings between my departure from Tarnit and my arrival at Qasr al-Sham'. It may have been in the city of Memphis, possibly at 'Ayn al-Sira or Helwan—I have forgotten exactly where I was, since I was not familiar with any of the towns of Egypt at that time, and they all looked alike to me. In any case, I will never forget how the slave trader had set up his tent at the edge of an orchard. He stood several boys up on his platform and started auctioning them off as the people stood around sizing them up like livestock. As the auctioneer was thus occupied, he was approached by an old man and a gray-haired woman who were dragging an attractive teenage girl behind them. The man was shouting angrily and saying that the slave trader had cheated him, because he had sold him the slave girl based on the claim that she was a half-breed from Qandahar with a golden complexion, on the basis of which he had taken twenty dinars for her. However, after the man took her home, the slave trader's fraud had become apparent, since once she had taken a bath, her golden complexion disappeared. She explained it by telling them that on the day before she was sold, the slave trader had put her in a tub filled with a caraway solution for four hours, and the man discovered that she was actually Sudanese with a coarse, unsightly body.

Fuming with rage, the man said that he had bought her with the understanding that she was a virgin, but had determined later that she was not. The old woman who accompanied him testified that she had examined the girl and that when she looked inside, she had found sour pomegranate pearls and green gallnuts that had been kneaded together with cow's bile. She said, "The real disaster for the buyer" (who was apparently a relative of hers) "is that the girl is pregnant." She said she had put ambergris incense under her and prevented it from coming out through her sleeves or the openings in her clothing, and that the scent of the incense had not come out through the girl's mouth. She added that she was certain—though only God knows all things—that the slave girl was pregnant with a girl, based on the fact that after the golden hue from the caraway had faded from her skin, her complexion had become dull and lackluster. She said she had measured the girl with a thread from the center of the navel to the center of her back from one side. She had then marked the place with ink and extended the thread around to the other side. When she did this, the thread reached farther than it had from the other side, which meant that the girl was pregnant with a female.

Upon hearing this, the crowd lit into the slave trader and beat him and his boys to a pulp. They forced him to return the twenty dinars to their owner and take back the 'tainted' slave girl, then led him to the police inspector at his headquarters. When I remembered this and imagined something similar happening to poor Suwayla, I got terrible pains in my abdomen. I prayed to God that nothing bad would happen to her and that by some miracle, she would not remain captive or be sold as a slave.

As for the destruction of my homeland and having to leave it behind, it ate away at my heart as the waves of the sea eat away at the shore. Captivity and having to part with one's homeland are like being reduced to nothingness in the midst of life's fullness. And this was the sign of the affliction that I had been destined to suffer for the rest of my days. I thought about the person who would buy me. For although I was able-bodied and in good health, I was not—may abundant thanks and praise be to God—the sort of young man that men seek out for physical pleasure. Nor was I strong or muscular enough to tempt anyone to buy me for purposes of backbreaking labor. I began trying to conjure up the kind of person who would buy me—his physical features, his character, his personality, his profession, and the type of work I would do for him. I wondered how he would treat me, and whether he would believe me if I told him that I had been the sexton at the Church of the Virgin Mary at Qasr al-Sham' in Old Cairo.

As I thought about these things, I prayed for God to inspire me with some way to escape from this captivity of mine, to save my skin, and to return to Old Cairo again rather than having to leave my home-land. Then I began racking my brain in search of a way out of my predicament. In the process, I recalled a story I had heard once, and struggled to remember its every detail so as to weave a yarn similar to it that might be of use to me. Once, when I had sought refuge by night in some ruin during my wanderings after running away from Tarnit, I met a thief. When he saw the state of poverty and degradation I was in and realized that there was no hope of getting anything out of me, he took pity on me and befriended me. He told me that one time he had scaled the wall around the house of a wealthy Jew. However, the Jew had found him out and, with help from his servants, managed to trap him inside the house. Then he turned him over to the police inspec-tor, who gave orders for him to be confined in a room with high walls inside the prison. Outside this room there was a warden who guarded him and who would talk to him and hand him food from under the door. One day Za'bal—which was the thief's name—told the guard that his fingernails had gotten too long and that he needed a pair of scissors, so the guard brought him one.

Then he said to the guard, "There are mice in here that bite me if they come too close. Bring me a palm branch that I can use to shoo them away." So he did. Over a period of several days, he would strike things with the branch and let the guard hear the sound of it. Then he peeled the leaves off the branch, cut off pieces of the size that might be gnawed off by a mouse and gathered them together. He also cut into pieces the wool mat that he used to sleep on and braided the pieces together into a rope which he used to climb to the top of the cell wall. Then, during the final hours of the night, he let himself out through its small, high window without anyone's taking any notice.

During this departure of ours, I wished that somewhere along the way, wild animals would come out and devour us, thereby delivering us from our ordeal, or that the Lord would send a violent tempest to overturn the boat that was to take us to the Palestinian shore on our way to the seat of the caliphate in Baghdad. My hands were in terrible pain from the shackles they had bound me with—in which respect all the other captives were suffering likewise—and the black-clad soldiers kept goading us to move faster so that we could reach Tanis by nightfall.

When we took leave of the Bashmourite's encampment, the sound of wailing and lamentation rang out again. Everyone was aware now that their separation from motherland, family, and loved ones was an inevitability, and that it was drawing nigh like death with its heartbreaking loss. Feeling as though I were losing my life and that I had reached the depths of despair, I started to weep myself. I beseeched the Lord to have mercy on me and to lift me up to His kingdom where I could find relief and solace. However, it was not long before I remembered something Thawna used to always tell me about the Lord's journeys with his Blessed Mother, and about the sufferings of the church patriarchs and all the free saints. As I pondered these things, I took heart and my spirit began to grow still. I thought to myself: It may be that the Lord willed to place me on this journey with these unfortunate, suffering people in order for me to encourage them, strengthen their faith, and urge them to endure their ordeal with patience. Hence, I resolved to speak to them about the martyred saints and about the sufferings of Father Dionysius during the days of the infidel emperor Valerian, whose representatives arrested Father Dionysius on Valerian's orders and murdered untold numbers of martyrs. They would split open children's bellies, take out their intestines and wrap them around reed cylinders, then cast them to the demons.

Yet, although they punished the Patriarch Dionysius and demanded that he worship their idols, he said to them, "You worship what you love, but we worship God Almighty. Our prostration is to Jesus Christ, Creator of the heavens and the earth, whom we love." In response, the prefect said to him, "You do not yet know how patient the kings have been with you. But if you bow down to their gods, we will honor you." After speaking with Father Dionysius at great length, the prefect took a group of those who were with him and issued orders for them to be killed. He then took Dionysius out and exiled him to a place called Colluthion, which means 'veil.' The people of this place, however, were kind to him and to all those who were with him who had not bowed down to idols. After this, the prefect's men brought him back to be sentenced to death. The prefect said to him, "News has reached us to the effect that you seclude yourself with your companions and celebrate the Mass." To this he replied, "We abandon our prayers neither by day nor by night," and he spoke many other words to him as well. When the prefect had left, the patriarch turned to those who were with him and said, "Go everywhere, pray and celebrate the Mass. For though I am absent from you in the body, I am with you in spirit." The patriarch was then taken back to his place of exile. Those who had been with him were grieved by his parting, but they said, "We know that the Lord Jesus Christ is with him in all his ways." During those days untold numbers were martyred in the name of the Lord Jesus Christ for their refusal to bow down to idols.

As we advanced toward Tanis, I saw the ruins and devastation that the soldiers had left in their wake: We did not pass through a single encampment, town, or village but that its crops had been burned, its houses and dwellings razed, and its streets and lanes left devoid of everything but dogs, cats, and vermin.

As I walked along, I made friends with a young Bashmourite man by the name of Bakhnas ibn Ayyoub, who said to me, "The soldiers destroyed all the Bashmourites' positions in Samanud, Saha, Shubra, Sunbat, Arisiya, and Nugum. They set fire to them all and did not leave one stone upon another. Even domestic animals and birds that were being kept in shelters such as geese, young chicks, and rabbits were running through the streets screaming and hopping with their feathers and skin on fire. He said that what had happened in our area—by which he meant the Bashrud region as it was referred to by these soldiers in their own tongue—was not an isolated event. At the same time, he said, they had launched more attacks on it since they knew that the Bashmourites' leader, Mina ibn Baqira, was entrenched there and was using it as the headquarters for his campaign to drive them out of the land.

As we continued on our way, the young man told me that Mina had gone on shooting at the caliph's army until his ammunition ran out. It became apparent that most of his shooting and that of his men had done no good, since the soldiers were outside in the darkness, and the Bashmourites' torches would go out immediately on account of all the water in the places where the soldiers were standing. As for the ones that fell on the Bashmourite's encampment, there were so many of them, they turned the night into day, making everything visible as though it were in bright sunlight. When the soldiers had overcome Mina sufficiently to make their way into the encampment, they brought out their swords against him and his helpers, including Bakhnas himself, until most of them were killed. However, the Bashmourite went on fighting them off, having brought out a cutting sword that had been brought to him from Byzantium by one of his close associates. He continued defending himself until he had dizzied and humiliated the soldiers. When word of this reached their commander, Afshin, who was also the one leading our procession now, he came and joined issue with him personally. The match between them went on for an hour until, at last, Afshin delivered the coups de grace. After he had fallen, Mina went on cursing and vilifying his enemies until he breathed his last, calling upon God to mete out vengeance upon them, cause their fortunes to turn against them, and bring them to ruin.

The young man wept bitterly over his leader, Mina ibn Baqira, saying to me, "The poor girl that he had rescued and who later became his wife, came and wept over his body for some time. But when the soldiers saw what condition she was in on account of what had happened to her, they left her alone and did not take her captive with the other women, since after all, she would have been useless to them."

Suwayla was walking behind us with the women captives. I took care to avoid looking at her for fear that our eyes might meet, in which case I would weaken and my heart would soften, or the memory of our physical encounter would be stirred up again. If that happened, I was bound to incline toward her again and lose hold of myself. However, when they had us stop to rest for a while and drink some water, I stole a glance at her in spite of myself, and when I did, I found her in a dreadful state. Overcome with weakness and exhaustion, her face was covered with dust, and her pretty hair was matted and disheveled. I could not help but feel pity for her, and my heart grew tender. So I made a pledge to myself to do everything in my power to protect her. To this end, I prayed to the Lord and recited passages from the Scriptures, though without crossing myself as I longed to do on account of my shackled hands.

When we entered the city of Tanis about an hour before midday, the caliph's soldiers had made ready for our arrival and come out to meet us. The local riffraff gathered around to get a look at us and to shame and humiliate us as was their custom whenever this or that side vanquished the other. They started shouting in our faces, labeling us renegade infidels, while their children pelted us with garbage and clods of dirt. Meanwhile, the soldiers drove them away with whips lest they attack and murder us. When we entered the city's main street, whence we were to head seaward and board the ships that would carry us away from the land of Egypt, I found Bakhnas ibn Ayyoub in a pained, sorrowful state. I offered him words of consolation and encouraged him to be patient and strong. I also tried to engage him in conversation so as to help him forget his sorrows. He told me that what was making him cry was that his mother was originally from Tanis. He had spent part of his childhood in the city, since he would go there with his mother to visit his maternal grandfather for the holidays. He said he had a great love for Tanis, and that this was what was grieving him so sorely, since it was from this very city that he would be departing Egypt. He went on to tell me that he had gone to school and that, despite his being a peasant, he had a passion for learning the histories of earlier peoples, because his maternal grandfather had been a copyist for the school who worked also on recording histories. In some books his grandfather had left behind from the school, Bakhnas had read that despite its being surrounded by water, Tanis had once been one of the greatest cities in the inhabited world. A bay city with villages surrounding it and the site of winepresses and unparalleled culture and architecture, it had once been flooded by the sea. However, many years later it was rebuilt and repopulated, complete with gardens, vineyards, date palms, and other trees, farms, and raised aqueducts. This well-informed young man—whom I was urging to talk so that we could get our minds off our situation and forget about the crowds' harassment—told me that the water still came down into the aqueducts all year round, and that once people had taken the water they needed from them, they emptied into the sea. He said it was a day's journey from Tanis to the sea, and that between Arish, where we were likely to disembark from the boats, and an island in the sea called Cyprus, there had once been a strip of land on which one could cross over on riding animals until the water level rose and covered it up.

Two hundred and fifty-one years after the reign of Diocletian, water from the sea had encroached on the location referred to today as Tanis Lake, and submerged it. The amount of water continued to increase every year, with the result that the low-lying villages in the area were submerged entirely. Of those located at a higher elevation, there remained Touna, Bour, and others which were now surrounded by water. The people of the villages, located in what was now a lake, would take their dead to Tanis, where they had been dug up one after another. The process by which all this land was submerged had come to completion a hundred years before the Muslims took over Egypt.

Bakhnas went on to say that one of the kings whose residences were at Farama had fought wars with one of the chief magistrates of Ballina and the land immediately adjacent to it. In these wars, trenches and canals were dug that extended from the Nile to the sea, their purpose being to make each side inaccessible to the other. However, these events had contributed to the process by which the waters of the Nile branched out into tiny tributaries and took over the surrounding land.

He had also read somewhere that this city had a wall which in the past had had a hundred gates. The people of the city had been famous for their carousing and indecency and every year—according to some reports—one hundred effeminate men were born. It was also said that the people of the city were lovers of cleanliness, gentility, singing, and pleasure, and that most of them would go to bed inebriated. Once, the city had been struck by a disease known as 'the Tanisian death-rattle' that afflicted its people for thirty years. As we walked down the broad street, Bakhnas noticed my amazement at the city's beautiful architecture, its grand houses, and its many tailors, most of whom were advanced in years, sitting at the doors of their shops and sewing ornately embroidered robes. Every now and then they would look up from what they were doing and eye us indifferently, as if they had grown accustomed to the sight of captives being escorted by soldiers from their city to the ships on the seaward side of town. Bakhnas told me that most of the city's tailors were completely taken up by their work and did not like to meddle in other people's affairs, since they made a generous living making sumptuous, elegant robes the likes of which are not produced anywhere else in the world, and that the caliph's robe itself—known as a badana—had been made here in these shops. What distinguished this robe was the fact that only two uqiyas of spun thread went into the robe's warp and woof, whereas the rest was woven with gold in a masterful way that required neither tailoring nor sewing. One robe alone was worth a thousand dinars, and there was not a linen robe in the world—of the plain type without gold thread—that would fetch a price of a hundred dinars cash other than the ones made in Tanis, and possibly Damietta. This is what had made Tanis one of the most regal cities in all of Egypt, for although fine garments were made in Shata, Defu, Dummayra, Touna, and on the nearby islands, none could hold a candle to those that came out of Tanis.

I was also told by Bakhnas that some years earlier in Tanis, a she-goat had given birth to a kid that had several horns and whose head was attached to its chest. The front half of its body was covered with white wool and its rear half with black hair, and its tail was like that of a ewe. And just the year before that, a whale had been caught in Ashtum that was twenty-eight and a half cubits long, of which nine cubits were the length of its head. It had a girth of fifteen cubits, its mouth opening was twenty-nine hand spans, its tail was five and half cubits wide, and it had two large fins, each of which was three cubits long. It was smooth and dark-colored, with thick skin and black and white stripes on its stomach. Its red tongue was about a cubit long with a rough, hairy surface that resembled feathers and from which rakes were made, and it had eyes like a cow's. The emir of Tanis had issued orders for the whale's stomach to be split open and for it to be cured with one hundred ardabs of salt. Its upper jaw was raised with a long wooden stick, and a man could carry large baskets of salt into its belly while standing erect rather than having to bend over. News of this great whale had spread all over the Bashmourite territories and people had begun making pilgrimage to it, as it had been left lying where it was so that people could see it with their own eyes.

I crossed myself in awe at the power of the Almighty Creator. Then he said to me, "In Tanis there are so many extraordinary things, it would take hours and days to tell about them all. Just to give one example: Some time ago, the water in its lake became sweet both summer and winter, then in the following year it went back to being salty all year round. In general, it is sweet for six months, then salty for six months."

When we arrived at the bay on which the city was located—by which time, despite my severe physical pain and exhaustion, I was feeling much more serene and patient thanks to Bakhnas's stories about Tanis—they had us sit down briefly to rest as they had done along the way in order to give us some bread and a drink of water. But no sooner had we sat down than the sky began raging with thunder and lightning, a powerful wind blew up, and the atmosphere was infused with a thick darkness. Together with the guards, we went on watching the storm for about two hours. Then there appeared in the firmament a pillar of fire that turned the sky red, and the earth even redder. At the same time we were surrounded by dust and smoke that took people's breath away, and which lingered until after midnight. The guards kept us in our places, so we spent the night where we were on the beach, and did not get on the boats until shortly before sundown of the following day. So difficult was it for all of us to part with the homeland that, when we boarded at last, we did so filled with trepidation, taking one step forward and one step back. Never as long as I live will I forget the weeping and lamentation that went up from all the captives on that day, men and women alike.

Nor will I forget the sight of the tears that streamed down everyone's faces, as though we were in a wake mourning the loss of someone dearly beloved. We went on this way for some time until the sailors began loosening the sails and unfurling them in the face of the wind. At that point all of our hearts sank, since we realized that we really were bidding farewell to the homeland and that this was the destiny that had been preordained for us. Bakhnas buried his face in my chest and began sobbing like a woman. Then suddenly, we heard a sweet, heartrending voice being lifted up in song. At that most difficult of moments, the voice was especially captivating and profound. Like everyone else, I turned toward the sound, and what should we see but a Sufi majdhub standing opposite us on the shore, his body completely naked except for a rag with which he concealed his private parts.

And he said:

Must every year bring exodus to a strange land?
Is there no reprieve? To separation, is there no end?

The vast expanse has jaded my mounts,
If only to perdition this expanse would descend!

The dove's lament robbed me of sleep in Riyy,
So I, too, lamented in my sorrow and fear.
But though my lament brings a flock of tears in its wake,
The dove laments without shedding a tear!

When I heard his words, I broke into sobs along with everyone else. Then I remembered the story of Archiledes and Siniskaltiki, and I began recalling part of what I had read of it in the Synaxarium that dear Thawna had given me once to read, and which was written on a gazelle parchment in gilded Coptic script. And I began whispering to myself, "Behold, I am in search of someone immortal to whom I can confide my sorrows and who, when I die, will pray for me." And again there came to mind the words of John Golden Mouth, "Every human being on the face of the earth must see what has been written on his brow, that is, what has been preordained for him."

I looked over at Suwayla, and wanting to console her, I said in a voice audible to everyone, "Be still, little one, and remember what was written in the Synaxarium, 'Friendship is not food and drink. Rather, true friendship is this: If your friend should fall into sin, you must do everything in your power to deliver him. Christ was a friend to Adam, for no sooner had Adam fallen into disobedience than he offered His body and blood for his sake, thereby restoring him to the position he had occupied before.'"

Then the rowers commenced their rowing, and the boats began moving away from the shore and making for the high seas. As Egypt's terra firma began gradually to disappear from view, I kept my eyes fixed upon it, not letting it out of my sight for a single moment. And as its image shrank and receded before me, it was etched within me so vividly and indelibly, it would remain with me as long as I lived.

PART II

I had never traveled the sea before, nor experienced its presence. Moreover, I was in a desperate, broken state: feeling helpless and dejected on account of all that had happened and the inevitability of parting with my homeland. Hence, when I came face to face with the ocean, it was as though my heart had split in two and my blood had turned to ether. I barely managed to lift one foot after the other and put it back down again as I boarded the huge nautical edifice, which I heard the soldiers referring to as 'the steamer.' It was a seagoing vessel fitted out with cannons from which enemies at sea could be fired upon, and it looked like a huge, fearsome eagle, all of which served to intensify the dread in my heart and the loathing in my soul.

They began sorting the captives, of which there were many, with some estimating our number at three thousand and others at less than that. The women and children were placed back at the rear of the ship, while the men of various ages were divided up according to the various uses to which they could put us. My fate was to be placed with the furnace crew in the belly of the ship.

The steamer they had put me on was not the only one leaving Egypt. Rather, the captives had been distributed among a number of ships as well as three galleys. This, at any rate, was what I was told later by Binyamin Suri, who was the finest person I came to know during my work at the furnaces. Galleys are smaller than steamships, with three sails each. That is what I was told by Binyamin, who was endowed with abundant knowledge and expertise in this area thanks to his many years of working at sea. The galleys, or sallourahs, which had been named after a type of swift-flying bird due to their exceptional speed, were fitted out with forty oars each. Each of them had been loaded with everything the caliph had brought from the land of Egypt, including both things which he had received as offerings and gifts and those that had been taken by force, as was the case with all of the papyrus produced by the inhabitants of the Bashmourite territories, as well as the goods they made use of in commerce and in otherwise earning their keep.

Our steamer had been loaded prior to our boarding with everything the sailors would need by way of provisions and supplies, including bread, water, all sorts of fruits, various food staples, quince, watermelon, chestnuts, dried chickpeas, broad beans, onions, garlic, white cheese, white Yemeni alum to be carried to the most distant horizons, as well as various and sundry other things too numerous to mention. Some time after this, Binyamin told me that the grain storage bins referred to as 'the blessed granaries' were what supplied the daily rations for the fleet's crews, as well as those given to the Sudanese slaves who worked on them.

When Bakhnas was taken up to serve on deck, where he was to work the masts and sails, I missed him terribly and felt quite miserable to have had to part with him. They seem to have perceived his fortitude and stamina based on his huge frame and powerful muscles, and my heart ached over his loss despite the brevity of the time we had known each other and enjoyed each other's company. However, God had willed for our spirits to be swifter than time through the impulse that had brought us together and the honesty, sincerity, and purity of intent that had grown up between us. After all, when someone loves, the crystal of his spirit continues to spin without ceasing until it encounters another of love's crystals that is likewise spinning about in search of companionship and affection. When the two crystals collide with the speed and force of their rotation, love's light is generated, and it pours forth with a brightness and power unequaled by the light of time despite its grandeur.

As for Bakhnas, one of the reasons I had come to love him so much may have been what he had told me about Suwayla. He told me that she had lost all of her family several years earlier in the last epidemic to strike the Bashmourite territories prior to the most recent war. The epidemic had wiped out untold numbers of people and animals. Only ten years old at the time, Suwayla had gone out wandering aimlessly in the marshlands until a kind man had taken pity on her, brought her to live with him and his family and raised her as one of his own. However, a devilish malady began afflicting her from time to time. Oblivious to the world around her, she would scream and fall to the floor, her body stiff as a corpse. She would remain this way for a while, rolling her eyes and drooling until the Lord looked upon her in His mercy, at which point she would come to her senses again. A gentleman of substantial wealth who worked as a manufacturer of writing paper made from the leaves of the papyrus plant found in such great abundance in the Bashmourite territories, her adoptive father begrudged her nothing. Concerned to find a cure for her illness, he had taken her to be blessed by many priests from our Sacred Church, who had anointed her repeatedly with holy oil and recited verses from Holy Scripture over her, but to no avail. At his wits' end, he would sometimes take her the rounds of the Melkite churches, and other times, to the pagan priests, yet without finding a way for her out of her dilemma.

Down in the ship's hold, I worked at the furnace with the men whose job it was to stoke the fire. As for me, my job was to be on watch, paying constant, tireless attention to the coals to make sure they were glowing and hot while the ship's engines turned. The ship was also propelled by rowers, a gang of strapping, intrepid men who were the roughest human beings I had chanced to meet in my entire life. Wearing nothing but what barely sufficed to conceal their private parts, most of them were Sudanese slaves whose coal-black skin would glisten like polished ebony when they perspired. At their heads there stood the caliph's soldiers, who would sear their backs with whips if they slowed down in their labor or if they dared entertain thoughts of slacking or being lazy. As for those who worked with me at the furnace, most of them were ruffians or worse, who would speak to me in Arabic colored by a heavy accent not lacking in a certain charm. Among themselves, however, they spoke a strange language I had never heard the likes of before. When I asked Binyamin—who was thoroughly versed in matters pertaining to navigation and life on the sea since the men of his family had been working at sea for generations—to tell me more about them, he told me that most of these men belonged to a class of slaves referred to as 'untouchables' who were brought from India and Sind, after which they were sold on the slave market for next to nothing on account of their ignorance, rudeness, and inability to learn to read, write, or practice a profession. He told me that in their countries of origin no one approached them or talked with them. As a consequence, they lived as despised, accursed outcasts. He even said that those belonging to their countries' noble castes would punish them by pouring molten lead into their ears if they dared so much as to raise their voices when speaking in the presence of a noble Hindu.

Witty and cheerful, Binyamin Suri was a joy to be around. He had compassion on me and treated me with warmth and affection. He would speak to me in a bit of Coptic now and then, and at other times in Arabic. He also had the ability to communicate with the untouchables, and would say things to them in their own language. Binyamin was in charge of the fuel depots. Hence, his job was to oversee everything that went from the fuel depots into the furnace, which was located where we were down inside the steamer, and to regulate it in such a way that its firebrands stayed red hot at all times.

When I commented once on Binyamin's linguistic talent and his ability to babble away in whatever language he pleased, he just laughed and said, "That is true of everyone who works on the sea. A seaman's constant comings and goings cast him onto many a shore and into the midst of all sorts of folks. Consequently, he gets to know their languages, their customs, their likes, and their dislikes."

We kept working all day. After leaving Ashtum on Lake Tanis, our goal was to reach the shore near the city of Farama. However, due to the fact that the wind was against us and wreaking havoc with the current at Ashtum, we were delayed in moving out onto the Mediterranean Sea proper, and before we knew it, night was upon us. We were then approached by some guards who instructed some of us to come with them. We soon found ourselves in another section of the ship's hold, where they made us carry a large container filled with water in which natron salt had been dissolved. We set it down somewhere out of the wind, after which they brought an iron basket shaped like a cross, which they had fixed onto a sant-wood ring. They cast these into the container and they floated on top of the water. After this the skippers came and brought out a strange stone which was the size of a fist, or a bit smaller. They started bringing the stone near the surface of the water in a circular, counterclockwise motion until its 'sign' appeared, its 'sign' being that the basket rotated on the surface of the water in the same direction as the rock. If the person holding the rock withdrew his hand quickly, the basket would stop moving and one side of it would settle toward the south and the other toward the north. And in this way they would determine which direction the ship should move.

We reached the city of Farama two days later at dawn. As soon as some of its features became visible on the horizon, the deck crew rushed to gather in the sails and prepared to anchor the steamer on shore. Making use of massive iron weights for anchors, the sailors started letting out the ropes to which the anchors were fastened and thrusting them into the sea. When the steamer and the galleys had come to a complete halt, we were approached by a rush of porters who worked for the caliph's army, owners of riding animals, and people who must have received news of our advent by carrier pigeon while we were still en route, since otherwise they would not have been waiting for us at that early hour of the day. They began transferring some of the boats' cargo on camel back while instructing us captives to carry things along with them. No one was exempted from this task but the women and children, and it caused us no little hardship given the tremendous effort we had expended already during the previous day and night.

Then suddenly the dawn drew back its curtains to reveal a peerless, youthful sun that sparkled over the vast blue expanse of water and sky. Filled with joy at the sight of it, I began praying furtively, thanking God for everything and praising Him for His grace revealed in the dawning of a new day. Then before long, who should I see approaching but Bakhnas ibn Ayyoub. They had loaded him down just as they had the rest of us, but the minute he saw me, he lay his burden down and came charging at me with his arms spread wide, overcome with a longing equaled by none but my own for him. It was the time for rations to be distributed, so we sat down on the sand to eat what they had brought us by way of bread, onions, and dried dates. Bakhnas informed me that many people had fallen ill, especially among the women and children. In fact, he said, some of them were about to give up the ghost, and given the large numbers of sick who still required attention, the nurses and physicians at work on the ships' decks were in a state of exhaustion. Consequently, they had begun giving people nothing but laurel water and sniffs of ammonia to wake up those who had fainted from seasickness. He also told me that one of the captives had nearly gotten himself killed by advising them to give people sips of wine to relieve their anguish, since Muslims forbid the drinking of alcohol under any and all circumstances, even to ward off illness or to treat this or that malady.

When I put my arms around Bakhnas I noticed that he reeked of vinegar, which alarmed me and put me off. When I finally got so curious I could not contain myself any longer, I asked him about it, and he told me that, like the other deck hands that worked the sails, he had been instructed to drink some sea water, then vomit it up so as to prevent seasickness and its devastating effects on both body and soul, including dizziness and nausea. They had also been told to daub their faces with vinegar for the same reason.

Bakhnas and I went on talking. Meanwhile, the more intensely the sun shined, the more clearly Farama's features came into view. When I looked at it more closely, I discovered that it was the site of a fortress overlooking the sea. Judging from the looks of the porters and those with riding animals, who included Bedouins, Arabs, and Copts, it also appeared to be inhabited by a mix of people. Bakhnas told me he had read somewhere that at one time Farama had been connected to the island of Cyprus by a land bridge that was eventually submerged by the sea. It is said that among the places that went underwater was a site for cutting piebald marble. He also told me that someone had once started razing stone gates on the fortress's eastern side in order to extract lime from them. However, by the time he managed to remove a stone or two, the people of Farama had come out against him with weapons and forced him to stop. These are the gates concerning which God spoke through Jacob, saying, "They may not be destroyed."

Never in all my life will I forget the way Bakhnas looked as he sat there in the sand speaking to me about Farama, with the blue expanse beyond us bounded by nothing but the sorrow in his coal-black eyes. A cloud of unspeakable melancholy descended upon his features, including his broad forehead and his upturned nose, beneath which there was etched a dark mustache and a beard as coarse as the hair on his head. And after that day I never had the good fortune to see Bakhnas again. I asked about him repeatedly of everyone who might have happened to see him, but to no avail. People offered conflicting accounts of his whereabouts and his fate. Hence, someone once told me that he had fallen off a mast and been swallowed up by the sea, while someone else claimed to have seen him being led away with a group of captives bound for Damascus. Hence, Bakhnas's disappearance is a mystery that haunts and troubles me to this very day.

I had thought at first that they would take us directly to the seat of the caliphate in Baghdad. However, not long before we parted in Farama, Bakhnas told me that we would be going to Antioch, and that most of those who had taken up arms against the caliph would be transported to Damascus. He said he had heard someone saying that the caliph had issued orders for all the offending villages and towns in the Bashmourite territories, as well as the areas surrounding them, to be razed to the ground and plowed under, and for everyone remaining there to be taken away on ships. The caliph had come to Egypt in order to quell the uprising among the Arabs who had settled in the west in the vicinity of Alexandria and Lubia, and he feared that what had happened before might repeat itself following his return to Baghdad, in which case strife would be stirred up anew and the rebel Arabs would join forces with the Copts once again. The caliph had given the chiefs of the towns who had surrendered a choice among several different places of exile within the territories under his rule, and they had chosen to be taken to the great city of Antioch, which was the site of the largest church in all of the caliphal territories. They chose Antioch in particular because of the similarity between the Jacobite Church and the Church of Antioch, and because there were only minor points of disagreement between it and the Coptic Church in matters of principle and doctrine.

Before we reboarded, they brought hides and pieces of wool that had been soaked in a mixture of vinegar, water, alum, and natron and attached them to the outside of the ships in order to prevent them from being damaged by naphtha if sea brigands or Byzantine sailors decided to attack, since this latter group was constantly roaming the sea, especially at night. Another precaution they had taken was to apply mud mixed with leaves, natron, and marsh mallow kneaded together with vinegar, since all these things are resistant to the effect of naphtha fires. In addition, they kept a close watch on the goods being loaded onto the ships, some of which they would not allow on board. A certain man leaving Farama, for example, had wanted to bring with him some roosters in cages, since they brought him a good income from the cockfights he staged in the marketplaces. However, the soldiers insisted that he leave them behind, since there was a possibility that they would crow along the way and reveal the ship's location to enemies who wanted to attack at night. In the end, the man decided not to make the journey after all and stayed home with his birds, which he said were priceless to him.

After this they took us in the direction of the city of Arish to meet up with some spice merchants who had come there from the lands of China and India. Upon our arrival in Arish, they took some of the merchants on board with them. This, at least, is what I heard from Binyamin Suri, who said that they had come on board laden with expensive merchandise such as silk, perfumes, spices, paper from Samarqand renowned for its high quality, as well as other precious items that had been brought from the lands of the Far East and which they were taking to Antioch, and from there, to Constantinople and the Republic of Venice.

From the time we set out from Arish, the ships plied the seas night and day. During that time the only sleep I got was in the form of catnaps. My overseer would periodically allow me a brief slumber during which someone else would stand in for me at my job. And thus it was that overnight, I found myself traveling the seas and traversing cities and countries—something I could never have imagined myself doing even in my wildest dreams. I had become like someone who was living a fantasy. I noticed that when I went to sleep, I would have bizarre dreams and night-visions in which eras that had once been, merged with eras yet to come, a phenomenon that convinced me of a certainty that my spirit was lost and had fallen headlong into an abyss of hopelessness and confusion.

Not long before our arrival in Antioch and after finishing my work shift, I fell fast asleep right before dawn. In the dream's tumultuous wave, I saw Thawna, Amuna, Suwayla, and another young woman with a fair complexion, a lithe, willowy physique, and hair that cascaded down like a black curtain over her back. They were all standing on the shoreline of a choppy, tempestuous sea and beckoning to me to come to where they stood. Trying to reach them, I began swimming as fast as I could through the stormy waters. However, every time I tried to approach them, my strength would give out on me and the waves would wash me farther out to sea. I kept trying over and over to no avail until I gave up in exhaustion and broke into bitter tears. Then, while I was in this state of despair and misery, water began surging forth out of the sea's shimmering depths. And what should I find but the girl I had seen with the others on the shore, emerging from the depths of the sea: ethereal, luminous, and translucent like a seraph from the heavenly realms. Then she began nudging me ever so gently through the water until she had brought me to shore, yet without so much as touching my body or letting me feel her fingertips on my skin.

My longing to see Suwayla intensified as we made our way further out to sea in the direction of Antioch. After all, the sea's clamorous, thunderous, raving, roaring, howling, stormy litany is one that will awaken dormant sorrows and send hearts reeling. I was praying to God that I might see her again, if only just once. Then, let come what may. I missed her so badly, sometimes my tears would flow in spite of me. Everyone around me thought I was crying over my situation, or because my eyes could not endure the intensity and heat of the flames. In any case, as my shift was about to end one night, one of the guards came in to where we were working in the fuel depots and announced that a Coptic priest was needed immediately. Since I had never been anything more than a lowly sexton once upon a time, I did not answer. Instead, I just went on working busily as before. But then the man nudged me with his foot, saying, "Hey, you. Did you not say you had been a man of the church in Old Cairo? Why do you not answer, then? Why do you act dumb and ignore orders as though you were deaf, or as though it were of no concern to you?" I thought to myself: Thank God they finally believe I am a man of the gospel and the cloth, and not of the sword and the spear. But before I had had a chance to rejoice, affirming what he had said with a hearty, "Yes, sir! I am coming!" he ordered me to stand up and follow him without delay. I walked behind him up to the deck of the ship, whereupon we came to the place where the women and children were being kept. And there I found Suwayla, flat on the floor and surrounded by some of the younger and older women, who were weeping, sobbing and uttering well-known Coptic formulas of lament. Her eyes remained closed, as she was in the throes of death. Beside myself to see her this way, I rushed toward her, taking her head in my hands and crying out sorrowfully, "Suwayla! Suwayla!" I kept calling out to her over and over like someone who has gone mad and cannot bear to endure or remain silent any longer. Her only response was to open her eyes slightly and, with difficulty, gesture with her head in the direction of her chest. When I looked at it in the light of the torches, whose flames flickered and danced to and fro in response to the sea's raging wind, I found my cross hanging from her neck and resting on her bosom. When my eyes fell upon it, I could contain myself no longer, and I let out an agonized groan that was heard by all. Then I began sobbing in spite of myself. However, she repeated the gesture in such a way that I understood her to be saying, "Take it." I grasped her hand and stroked her cheek, my tongue murmuring the words of the Lord, "Do not love the world or the things in the world. If anyone loves the world, love for the Father is not in him. For all that is in the world, the lust of the flesh and the lust of the eyes and the pride of life, is not of the Father, but of the world. And the world passes away and the lust of it. But he who does the will of God abides forever."

Filled with sadness, I continued reciting and praying as I thought back on the time of Amuna's death, and the way she lay there before me just as Suwayla lay before me now. Then I came to God's glorious words, "Behold, we call those happy who were steadfast. You have heard of the steadfastness of Job, and you have seen the purpose of the Lord, how the Lord is compassionate and merciful."

For some moments I went on repeating in a low voice, "Behold, the Judge is standing at the doors. Behold, the Judge is standing at the doors." I found Suwayla parting her lips in a feeble, but contented smile. Then, staring outward in a pensive, melancholy gaze, she tilted her head in the direction of the horizon from which we had departed from the land of Egypt, and I realized that the angel of death had descended and would be taking her away. As the tears in my eyes froze up and I began to return to my senses, I gently lowered her eyelids with the palm of my hand, then continued with my recitations of scripture as I rested her head on the floor. It was not long before the guards told me to finish quickly in order to return to my work, so I removed the cross from her neck, held it in my hand and kissed it. Then I stood up, asking them to join with me in the rites of her passage into eternity so that we might be the ones to bid her farewell during her last moments. The guards' treatment of me had softened somewhat, and I sensed that they were convinced now that I really was a man of the church.

When dawn began to appear on the horizon, they brought several other corpses from various places on the ship. I counted up a total of twenty-one bodies, one of which belonged to a teenage girl and thirteen others to young children whose corpses had been lined up next to each other on the floor. They then asked me to recite the funeral prayer over them, so I kneeled reverently and began reciting what I could remember of the relevant Scripture verses and prayers for forgiveness, making the sign of the cross over them one by one. As I did so—and may God forgive me for this—I anointed them with my hand in place of holy oil, asking God to grant unbounded mercy and forgiveness to these righteous souls.

As I was earnestly absorbed in all these things, the sound of a muezzin rang out, tenderly and movingly issuing the Muslim call to prayer. He then issued a call for a prayer to be performed over a group of Muslims who had likewise bidden farewell to this world, and who had been placed along the other side of the ship. When I had completed my prayers, I waited until people had finished praying for the deceased Muslims as well. There then began the process of casting the dead into the water. I counted the total number of throws that were made from both sides of the boat, and they came to sixty-three. Every time a body was cast into the deep and a human being's remains hit the surface of the water, it produced an awesome, horrific clap like the report of a cannon. Never—till my time has come and my body is covered with the soil of the earth—will I forget that somber, thunderous sound, nor the sight of the breathtaking horizon as it drew back the curtains of the darkness to reveal a mournful sun rising little by little into the vast expanse. All these things were etched into my memory, recorded with the pen of a terrible sorrow in the depths of my awareness.

The guards, as well as everyone else on deck, stood there in speechless, humble reverence, looking on sorrowfully as though they were contemplating the power of death and the cheapness and insignificance of life in the face of death's majesty and ineffable mystery. Some seagulls happened to fly overhead, and an ache welled up in the depths of my soul. Before long, tears were streaming down my face again, the gulls' cries a lament that reminded me of an old hymn my mother would sing whenever she felt troubled or sad. It said:

> *Sorrow over my loved ones has made me ill*
> *For no other cause that I can tell.*
>
> *So heavy are my grief and lamentation,*
> *My faith nearly bids me farewell.*
>
> *An age passes by, precious one, but the longing*
> *For my beloved is a burden beyond portrayal.*

After an enervating voyage that had taken nearly ten days, Antioch became visible to us in the distance. The steamships and galleys had stopped from time to time at various Syrian frontier outposts subject to the caliphate's jurisdiction to stock up on supplies and fuel. The sea had been against us part of the time, churning and raging so violently that had it not been for God's providence and care, one of the galleys would have capsized. At other times it had been so smooth and calm that the ships had flowed along without difficulty or dread of anything except an occasional sea monster of the sort that would appear from time to time, such as a small whale that had appeared to us once and which the sailors had hastened to harpoon. They were overjoyed with their catch. For in addition to the benefit they hoped to obtain from the whale's meat, some of which could be eaten, it offered other benefits as well. They began cooking up the better part of it in kettles, causing its flesh to turn to liquid fat that could be used to caulk the ships and plug up holes in its wooden planks. This is what I was told by Binyamin Suri, who added that this was done for ships that traveled the Red Sea, which was teeming with coral reefs.

Once the ships started making their entrance into the Antioch Sea, we were assured safe passage from that point onward, there being no more cause to fear raids by the Byzantine navy or sea brigands. The black flags and banners that served as the caliphal emblem were then raised to full mast and everyone—despite their weariness, grief, and pain—experienced the thrill occasioned by our safe arrival. Hence, we all set about with a fresh burst of energy to complete the tasks before us as best we could before we dropped anchor and disembarked.

When they let us off the ship on Antioch's soil, Binyamin said it was two o'clock in the afternoon. I was amazed at this, since the sun was not visible from the city. As we approached it, I surmised that the reason for this was the presence of its towering fortress, which had been constructed on a lofty promontory. Then I caught a glimpse of the city's wall, and I can say without exaggeration that it was the highest, hugest wall I had ever seen. Once I had settled in Antioch, I learned that it had three hundred sixty towers manned by four thousand guards. One contingent of four thousand would guard it for a year, then be replaced the following year by another contingent. The wall had been built on both the plain and the mountain, which made it a wonder of wonders.

A large crowd of people had gathered to see us at the time of our arrival, and it was said that they had anticipated our coming, since what was known as 'the Syrian telegraph' had preceded us, informing them of our approach to the city after what had happened in the Bashmourite territories and the marshlands. As we entered the city, the people began cheering our arrival, though I did not know at the time whether they were cheering on account of the Muslim caliph's victory or because, like us, they were followers of the Christian religion and on the path of righteousness in the love of Christ. Later I learned that the Patriarch of Antioch welcomed the advent of the Bashmourites to this great city of faith. They then took us away to a large church in the city which I heard them referring to as the Qasyan Church, so that they could count us and sort us anew with the purpose of sending some of us to Baghdad, keeping some of us in Antioch, and sending others to be sold in the large slave markets in Damascus.

The church was stately, with huge walls surrounding it. Its towering gate led into two courtyards, one of which was used in the nighttime hours and the other in the daytime. Each of them was used for twelve hours, as I came to know later. When I entered it—that is, the gate—I came upon untold numbers of servants and others seeking their livelihood in one way or another. Then, out of a chancellery at one end of the church there emerged a contingent of clerks, who brought their paper and pens and, once we had been counted, started recording each person's particulars. However, this process did not include the women and children, whose numbers were recorded without regard for their distinguishing features or identities. In the case of the men, those who were known to have been combatants were put on one side, while those who had simply been farmers or artisans were placed on the other. They continued sorting us until no one—be he elderly, young, or a beardless teenager—was left unaccounted for. Once this task had been completed, they distributed rations to everyone, so we sat down to eat, after which they let us wash up in the public baths, a facility next to the church wall for use by wayfarers, common folk, and the indigent. When I entered the bath, I found that its water was sweet, as though it had just flowed out of the ground, and that the fuel used there was good-quality laurel wood. Hence, I cleansed myself and praised God heartily for everything.

Those responsible for sorting the captives hesitated for quite some time over how to classify me and got into a debate among themselves over who I really was. There were those who said I was an imposter who was making a false claim of being associated with the church so as to avoid being sold on the slave market or being cast together with the peasants. Others, however, were of the opinion that I was truly a representative of the church, and they did not want to be held accountable by God on the Day of Resurrection for having treated me badly. After all, the Muslims' Qur'an instructs them to treat the People of the Book, that is, Christians and Jews, with kindness and respect. Those who held the latter view were among the God-fearing Muslims, upon whom I will call down God's blessings and care all the days of my life. And it was this group whose opinion won out in the end. Hence, it was suggested that I would need to appear before the fathers of the church so that they themselves could test me to determine what knowledge I had of the religion. So, soon after I had eaten and bathed along with everyone else, they brought me before a number of fathers and those whom the Arabs refer to as qasawisa, or priests, a term they used to describe anyone who wore clerical garb.

When I came in to see the clergy, I launched into an angry diatribe concerning what had happened to me. However, it soon became apparent that they did not understand a word I was saying, since they were speaking a strange language that differed from that of the Arabs. I had been speaking Coptic mixed with Arabic to the extent that I was able, and among them there was an elderly man who asked me prudently and calmly to say what was on my mind. However, there were soldiers standing beside me, and in their presence I was filled with such a burning anxiety, I could not think clearly. Be that as it may, the elderly priest began asking me questions about the situation of the churches in Egypt and inquiring about the conditions of the Christian religion and the Copts there. I courteously and respectfully answered his questions, which to my amazement were phrased in Coptic, though I detected a slight foreign accent. So, too curious to restrain myself, I asked him, and may God forgive me, "Are you a Copt, sir?"

The man had a kindly bearing and seemed congenial and devout, an impression which was confirmed when he replied gently, "We are all servants of God, son. My maternal grandmother was a Copt."

Then he delved with me into questions about prayer, fasting, matters of doctrine, the Sabbath, and what is permissible on the Sabbath. I said to him, "'The Sabbath was made for man, not man for the Sabbath; so the Son of Man is lord even of the Sabbath.' This is what the Savior said." I then told him the story associated with these words as it is related by the Apostle Mark, which I knew by heart as it had been told to me by my dearly beloved Thawna:

> One Sabbath he was going through the grain fields; and as they made their way his disciples began to pluck ears of grain. And the Pharisees said to him, "Look, why are they doing what is not lawful on the Sabbath?" And he said to them, "Have you never read what David did when he was in need and was hungry, he and those who were with him: how he entered the house of God when Abiathar was high priest and ate the bread of the Presence, which it is not lawful for any but the priests to eat, and also gave it to those who were with him?"

When he heard me say these things, I thought I saw a flicker of a smile as he nodded his head in agreement. He then spoke to the soldiers in their Arabic tongue, telling them to leave me, since he would accept me into the church. He then spoke to the other priests in their strange tongue—strange to me, that is. The soldiers thus left me in the priest's residence and went on their way.

I worked for some time as a sexton at the Qasyan Church in the service of Father Thomas, where I was in charge of his affairs in his private residence in one of the church's towers. It was the custom for the priests' quarters to be located in the church's numerous towers and for their respective servants to live downstairs. Through my work there I became familiar with many things in the Antioch church, which, although it was one of God's greatest churches in the world, differed in numerous ways from our Coptic church. Unlike those in our church in Egypt, the fathers of this church and all the other clerics as well, lived lives of ease and luxury. The system of service in Antioch likewise differed in many ways from that in Egypt. The statement of faith was recited on the morning of Holy Thursday before the bishop or priest, and the penitents who had previously been Arians, Macedonians, Novatianists, and Appolonarists were accepted into the church after being anointed with holy oil on the forehead, eyes, nostrils, mouth, and ears. As for the Paulinists and the Monarchianists, they were baptized with a single immersion, while the Montanists and the Sabellians, who believe that the Father and the Son are a single hypostasis, were received into the church as though they had been pagans. That is, from the first day they were considered to be Christians, on the second day, catechumens, and on the third day, they were asked to make a sworn profession of faith as the priest breathed into their faces and ears three times. They then received exhortation and were kept in the church for a period of time listening to the Scriptures. The same applied to the Manicheans. As for the Nestorians, they were required to confess the faith in writing or to deny their fealty to both Nestorius and Eutyches. The bread of the Eucharist was to be received with one's right hand placed over the left in the form of a cross, while the wine was to be taken from the chalice.

The Mass would begin with the acceptance of the people's approach and with the preparation and presentation of the Host on the table of oblation, or prothesis. This would be followed by a reading of the names of bishops and popes, both living and deceased, and of all priests and deacons, followed by mention of emperors and the people, for all of whom prayers would be offered. The candle would precede the Holy Gospel and the words, "Come, let us worship and bow down" would be chanted. After this, the bishop would ascend the pulpit to the east of the altar and bless the people, after which the Epistles would be read as a sign that Christ had sent his disciples to preach the good news of the Gospel. The Gospel would then be chanted, offerings would be received, and the deacon would call upon the catechumens to leave. At this point, the priest would unfold the indimansi, which serves as a substitute for the table of oblation, and commence the major procession of the Mass in which the elements would be brought to the table of oblation before having been consecrated. As I understood from Father Thomas's explanation, the major Mass procession represents the transfer of the body of Jesus from Golgotha, symbolized by the altar, to the tomb, symbolized by the prothesis. This was when the Cherubikon, or the Cherubic Hymn, was chanted in celebration of the entry of the angels, the Holy Spirit, and the saints with Christ the King. I would always be deeply moved when it was sung:

O ye who mystically represent the cherubim
and who sing the three-fold praises to the life-giving Trinity:
Let us now lay aside every earthly care,
for we are about to receive the King of all,
preserved in invisible form through the angelic stations.
Hallelujah!

Fans would be working ceaselessly throughout this time since, in addition to the fact that they prevented flying insects from falling onto the service utensils, they served as a symbol of the wings of the six seraphim. After the priests' entry into the sanctuary on the evening of the Sabbath, it was forbidden in the Qasyan Church for anyone to bend his knees until Sunday evening. The reason for this was that the night that follows the Sabbath is taken as a harbinger of the resurrection of the Savior, in celebration of which spiritual hymns are sung and the holy day is observed in the transition from darkness to light.

Father Thomas was one of the most tenderhearted human beings I had ever known in my life. A magnanimous, compassionate, godly man, he had made the rounds of numerous churches and monasteries in Egypt, Palestine, Beirut, Crete, and Cyprus. I learned that he had spent considerable time in the land of Egypt, where he had learned the Coptic language. However, what most endeared him to me was his passion for ecclesiastical chants set to music. He had memorized the chants of the ancients—as he himself once told me—such as those composed by the renowned cantor Romanus, Safruniyus of Jerusalem, and Andrawus al-Aqriti, who was born in Damascus and served for a period of time in the Church of the Holy Sepulchre. This man had strayed into Monothelite teachings for some time, then repented. Father Thomas had a passion for recording tunes in special notebooks by the use of signs and symbols. As he worked on a project of this nature, I would stand for hours, holding candles or getting things he requested. In general, he would be so engrossed in what he was doing, I did not dare say a word. One time, however, too curious to keep quiet, I got up the courage to speak, and I asked him about the meaning of the signs he was recording.

"Are you not familiar with these?" he asked in astonishment. "Did you never see anyone recording church tunes in your church at Qasr al-Sham'?"

When I replied that I had not seen anything like them before, he was amazed, and asked me, "Then how do you preserve the theotokias and the glorious chants?"

"We have the triangle and the mizhar," I replied quickly. "Perhaps you saw them during your stay in Egypt. However, we do not use things like this," by which I meant the musical instrument that he used in the church at Antioch, which had several strings and was referred to as a lyre.

However, it was not primarily the tunes or the order of service that differed in the church at Antioch from our church in Egypt, since the Qasyan Church, which Father Thomas had told me was named after King Qasyan, whose son had been brought back to life by the Apostle Peter, the chief of Jesus's disciples, was frequently the site of ecclesiastical tribunals due to the widespread nature of heresy in the city and its environs. In addition, theological councils were frequently held there, since it was the supreme church of the East, with a jurisdiction encompassing Georgian Cilicia as well as the lands between the Tigris and Euphrates.

One day, after the clergy had finished celebrating the special Mass that is celebrated every day of the sacred forty-day fast with the exception of Saturdays, Sundays, and the Feast of the Annunciation, a huge commotion broke out at the church's Eastern entrance. A group of believers rushed in, driving a number of men and women before them. They had subjected them to a brutal beating, and blood was flowing from their heads, their noses, and their bodies, as well as off the animal skins which they had been using to disguise themselves. When I came out with others in the church to see what was going on, I learned that these people had been found engaging in ancient pagan rites that had been forbidden by the Church and which included rites in honor of Kronos, the god of time. In celebration of a holiday devoted to an ancient god by the name of Bacchus, they had dedicated the three weeks between the twenty-fourth of November and the seventeenth of December—which are the names of the months used in Antioch—to drinking wine, exchanging clothes, dancing, and other practices that were common in pagan times. No sooner had they reached the church courtyard than the priests and monks rushed over and started taking part with the believers in vilifying and abusing these riffraff. In fact, they beat and kicked them so mercilessly, most of them fell to the ground exhausted and on the verge of death. Then before I knew it, they had led them away to the church prison pending their trial on charges of violating the prohibitions that had been issued by the popes, especially given the fact that they had also been involved in certain pagan rites of spring. They would keep fires lit on the first of the lunar month, for example, and the women and men would exchange clothing on the occasion of the Feast of the Harvest, all of which was forbidden under church law.

After the crowd had dispersed and I was alone that night after finishing my duties, memories of dear Thawna welled up within me. I remembered the way he was in his dealings with people, urging them ever so compassionately and gently to arrive at the wellspring of all faith. He would never rebuke them or speak harshly to them, and never once had I seen him abuse or persecute any godless, ignorant person who had yet to discover the truth of the religion. He was always patient and persevering in responding to such people's questions no matter how naive, silly, or even ill-mannered they happened to be. As I peered out of my cell's narrow window into a furious-looking, overcast night sky, I suddenly began talking to myself. I ached with such a longing for Egypt and its cloudless, star-studded sky, tears began to flow as I repeated some lines that I had learned by heart from Binyamin Suri, who would always sing them while we were working at the boiler in the belly of the steamship. I sang,

> Bear patiently an age that has done you harm,
> For thus have all ages passed.
> Joy comes and, after it, sorrow,
> But neither joy nor sorrow will last.

I was disconsolate over the scenes of torment that I had witnessed the previous day. And my agitation grew even worse when I remembered the misery I had seen as we departed from the Bashmourite territories in the land of Egypt: the corpses strewn everywhere after the battle with no one to bury them; the wounded and burned screaming in pain; others pleading for a drink of water, yet with no one to hear their cry; women and children who could hardly walk, yet with no one to perceive their torment and take compassion on them. Then there was what had happened to Amuna and Suwayla and the disappearance of Thawna, whose unknown fate was eating me alive. I was lost in a strange land in which I had never expected even so much as to set foot. And last but not least, there was the church of Antioch, whose spirit, to me, seemed alien somehow to that of our own church, and whose rituals I had yet to grow accustomed to. Thus, for example, when they celebrated the mystery of baptism, the catechumens would come to the church clad in white garments. Then, after reaffirming their confession of faith and affirming that they had nothing more to do with the worship of the idols and evil spirits that they had worshiped before, they would be immersed three times in a deep basin of water in the name of the Father of Lights, His Son, and the Holy Spirit. As for those who were unable to speak—that is, young children—they would be raised and instructed in the principles of the Gospel by virtuous individuals known as sponsors or trustees, and at the time of baptism these sponsors would stand in for the children by confessing Christ and renouncing evil spirits.

Days went by, during which preparations were made for the rite of confession for those who had been imprisoned after being tortured into declaring their repentance and remorse. They were brought in the morning to the church courtyard looking pitifully weak and emaciated. Then they were divided into four groups. The first group consisted of the weepers, who stood at the church entrance imploring the believers coming in to pray on their behalf. The second group consisted of those they termed the hearers, who were allowed to come into the church since it had been demonstrated that their sins were less serious than those of the first group. Those in the second group were placed in a location designated for hearing the recitation of the holy books and the prayer. Then there was the group referred to as the kneelers, who were required to remain kneeling for the duration of the prayer time. These were followed by the participants, who were allowed to stand inside the sanctuary and take part in the prayer with the believers, but without partaking of the sacred mysteries. I later learned from Father Thomas, when I asked him about the matter, that these people had declared that they would make payments of gold to the church in return for a lightened verdict. I also learned that all of them, before being brought to the church and divided into groups, had officially declared their remorse before a number of priests who would later offer testimony to the holiness and purity of their conduct, and that this would be presented to the church by respected individuals.

Yet, astonished as I was at all of this, and unable as I was to swallow much of what went on in the Qasyan Church, little did I know that what I had seen thus far was nothing compared to what lay in store for me.

Then one spring night, a little over a year after I had come to the Church at Antioch, and after a period during which it had rained heavily most days of the month—specifically, the month of April, or Nisan in the Syriac language—the sky was unusually charged with lightning and thunder, producing all manner of terrifying noises that would have unsettled even the most placid of souls. Directly after this, a lightning bolt struck a conch shell embedded within the church's altar. As a result, a piece resembling something that had been chipped off with an ax or a pickax was split off the face of the eagles sculpted into the front of the altar. An iron cross that had been erected above the shell fell, a tiny piece was chipped off the shell and the lightning bolt went down through the opening, two finger-widths across, through which there descended a thick silver chain on which the qandil was suspended. The chain was broken into countless pieces, some of which were smelted together, and those pieces that had been smelted together were cast to the floor. A silver crown that had been suspended in front of the altar table had fallen as well.

We all went rushing to the service area of the church in an attempt to salvage whatever we could of the priestly utensils. We found that two of the three square wooden seats on the western side of the church, which were located on an elevated platform, had fallen, while the large, silver, gold-inlaid crosses that had been mounted on them had been wrenched out of place. The two outer seats had been shattered and the splinters had gone flying both inside and outside the altar. However, it was not apparent that they had been burned as was the case with the silver chain. As for the middle seat and the cross mounted upon it, they were unharmed. The four marble pillars that supported the silver dome over the altar table, each of which was covered with a piece of brocade, had been broken to pieces both small and large. However, these pieces looked more like something that had rotten and fallen apart than like something that had gone through a fire. As for the table and its brocaded coverings, they showed no signs of damage.

Among the disasters that took place that day was that some of the marble that went to make up the altar, along with the lime beneath it, had brokèn off as though it had been beaten with an ax. Among the pieces that broke off was a huge slab that leapt out of its place and landed, shattered, on top of the square base of the dome that covered the table. Meanwhile, what remained of the marble went flying onto various locations nearby. As Father Thomas was trying to rescue a set of small glass lamps, a marble splinter collided with one of the lamps, causing it to break. The flame from the lamp caught hold of his light silken nightshirt, which within moments had been transformed into a robe of fire. I had been busy rescuing an old Gospel stand made of ebony wood and inlaid with silver and ivory, but the minute I saw what had happened, I dropped what I had in my hands and went running toward him along with everyone else who had seen the flames taking hold of him. In an attempt to put out the blaze, we grabbed a wool rug that had been spread on the church floor to prevent drafts and threw it on top of him, as well as a wet shawl. Then we carried him hurriedly into the church's courtyard and placed him in the pouring rain. Soon thereafter, some of his servants brought a pail full of urine and, once we had brought him out of the rain again, quickly dowsed him with it from head to toe. I was shocked that they would resort to the use of such an unclean substance. However, once things had quieted down, I learned that this was a tried and true method of treating burns.

For several days thereafter Father Thomas did battle with death. Most of his skin and flesh had been burned, as well as his head; the fire had penetrated into some of his internal organs, and he had lost his eyes. The fathers of the church, who were well known for their wisdom and skill in medical treatment, had exhausted all their knowledge in an attempt to save him, including the use of specially prepared ointments and drugs. As for the deacons and the priests, they kept vigil at his head, reciting passages from the Gospel and prayers for healing inspired by the Scriptures. It appeared for a while that he was improving and that death's specter had begun to retreat. Even so—may God forgive me—I did not expect him to fare well. For none of them had made him a protective amulet or done recitations that would benefit his condition. Hence, when his illness dragged on, I suggested to them ever so humbly and courteously that we do for him what we had done once in Egypt for those who had been burned on the ferryboats when certain ill winds had blown in. What had happened was that these winds, which were more violent and laden with dust than they had generally been in previous years, had caused fires to break out in the cabins of some ferryboat owners along the Nile, as a result of which many people were burned. I had gone to help them with Thawna and others from the church at Qasr al-Sham', and Thawna had treated them with sap from the black 'am'at, burnt, well-fermented goat's dung, carob poultices, and an incantation which was to be recited over the site of the burn and which I knew by heart from having heard it repeated so many times before. It goes like this: "O Horus, son of the Sun, fire is in the land. But whether there is water or not, water is in your mouth and the Nile is in your feet when you come to put out the flames."

This incantation would also be recited over the milk of a woman who had given birth to a son, over a loaf of bread, and over a ram's wool. In any case, the items mentioned above would be placed over burns as a poultice and would bring great benefit. However, everyone at the Church of Antioch rejected such practices. In fact, there were those who mocked them. It caused me no little sorrow that they failed to appreciate tried and true remedies that had been used from time immemorial, and that they refused to believe what I said about them. Following this, Father Thomas's health continued to deteriorate and, little by little, he began to slip away. Not long after this the city was struck by an earthquake that lasted for an entire hour, and which was accompanied by a frightening sound out of the firmament. Edifices that had been built by Emperor Justinian came tumbling down, and many people, who were said to number 4,870, died under the rubble. Most of the city's residents who survived the catastrophe fled elsewhere. Ships at sea sank as a result of the huge waves set up by the quake, livestock perished, and the wheat that was sent to the city every year by the Byzantine Emperor—and which came to eighteen thousand bushels—went bad. Following the earthquake the city was overrun by mice, and in particular by a certain gargantuan variety that I have never seen anywhere but in Antioch. Much of what remained of the crops was destroyed after the quake. As for the people who remained in the city, they were afraid, crying out to God not to afflict them with a plague like those that invariably descend in such circumstances.

Immediately after Father Thomas died, they placed me in the service of Father Michael, whom I had come to know superficially before that time. An elderly man with constantly shifting eyes and a deep scar on his forehead, he would look at me in a friendly way whenever I saw him passing through the church corridors or crossing its courtyard for one reason or another. He would usually just smile and greet me as he made the sign of the cross in blessing. Then one time he stopped me and said, "I have an old Coptic parchment, and I was wondering if you might drop by for an hour or so to read it to me after you've finished your duties."

Delighted to have found something that reminded me of my homeland there in Antioch, I replied with obvious enthusiasm, "I am at your service, sir. I will come to see you after sundown, when I have finished doing the things Father Thomas needs of me and he has given me permission to leave for my residence."

Looking me over from head to toe with evident pleasure, he shot me a smile that I will never forget as long as I live.

Then he added, "Come, and I will treat you to some halawa hamra the likes of which you may never have tasted before."

I do not know why, but I felt uneasy at that point, despite my longing to eat halawat sadd al-hanak, which they referred to here in Antioch as halawa hamra. I started thinking back to the way my mother used to make it for us on the night before Epiphany. My brothers and sisters and I would gather around her as she browned the flour in the fat from a sheep's rump. She would gradually add the syrup until it was browned and slightly burned as its sumptuous, dearly loved aroma wafted into our noses. Then we would eat it while it was still piping hot in Toba's bitter cold. During the moments of that brief encounter, Father Michael's glances burned something inside me, and I walked away feeling as though I had been stung. I crossed the church courtyard, rushing to Father Thomas's quarters as fast as my legs would carry me. When I got there, I related to him what had transpired between Father Michael and me, requesting his permission to go see him after I had finished my duties. In response, he fixed his eyes on me in a long, cold, questioning stare as though there were something he was not telling me.

Then, in an indignant tone that I had never heard him use before, he said, "You are going to be busy with me after sundown. The entire clergy will be meeting in preparation for trials that are to be held tomorrow."

Then he added firmly, "Make certain you do not miss it."

Before I was transferred to his service, I had thought of Father Michael as a gentle, serene man despite the discomfort I felt around him. However, when I got closer to him and lived in his company, he showed himself to be an enigmatic, eccentric creature, and little by little, I became convinced that he was, in truth, a devil who was corrupt through and through. Before he went to bed at night he would rub his face and hands with a paste made from butter and honey, and he would perfume himself with fragrant oils like those used by women. On hot nights, he was in the habit of sleeping in a sleeveless nightshirt, and one day after dismissing me early, he remained in the company of one of the boys whose job was to bring wood from the forests southwest of the city. Not long after I began working for him, I started noticing that many of the deacons and monks avoided him, and would refrain from lining up beside him during prayer or sitting next to him at dinner.

On one occasion a group of people were put on trial for seeking out magicians and sorcerers, as was a man who had been putting bears and other animals up for display and selling their fur and wool as amulets and good luck charms. There were so many offenders, the trial went on for quite some time. One man, for example, had been absent from the Sunday prayers for three weeks in a row, and he was put on trial despite the fact that he was a layman rather than a member of the clergy. Others on trial included two women who had been chatting during the Easter Sunday prayers and a group of perfume merchants who had destroyed some holy books in order to make paper cones out of them. Because evening was approaching, the remainder of the trial was postponed until the following morning. At the time when the trial was set to resume, a woman and man were brought forward. The woman, who was a mere teenager and dazzlingly beautiful, had been condemned along with the man for cohabiting out of wedlock and for making their living by producing and selling pornographic drawings. The woman was like-wise condemned for arranging the hair on her head in an eye-catching, seductive fashion. I had never heard of anyone being condemned for such things before. In any case, when the verdict was issued against her, I noticed that Father Michael remained silent and motionless. In fact, unlike all the other clergy present, he remained this way through-out the entire trial. A huge uproar ensued when the woman and the man refused to express remorse and confess to their sin. On the contrary, they vilified the church, saying that it forbade what God had declared lawful. They went on to say that the Lord had created women and men to enjoy life and its pleasures and that if He had not wanted women to enjoy men and men to enjoy women, He would have created everyone alike. They said other similar things, all of them so heretical and sac-rilegious, it would have turned babes' hair gray. Upon hearing these things, everyone there was fuming with rage. These two devils denied Christ's ascension to Heaven and said that the Virgin Mary had not been a virgin but, rather, gave birth after committing fornication with Joseph the Carpenter. At this point some of the fathers, unable to endure any longer, began slapping their faces, pulling out their beards in rage and wailing like women. A number of the believers in attendance would have killed the man and the woman then and there if the guards had not prevented them. Yet throughout the entire frenzied commotion, Father Michael sat there silent and stony-faced as though the matter were of no concern to him.

The longer I spent in Father Michael's service, the more uneasy I began to feel. One reason for my unease was that he would insist that I give him a massage every night before he went to sleep, his stated reason being that he had aches and pains that got worse during the night and which nothing but a massage could get rid of. Despite the fact that I detested the job, I would grudgingly agree to it, since I had grown accustomed to obeying the fathers in the church and resisted going against them in anything. Then one night, I noticed that Father Michael was speaking to me in a particularly kind way. He invited me to drink a glass of grape arrack, which he himself was in the habit of drinking every night before he went to bed. When I declined, he told me he had only invited me because he had noticed me looking careworn and miserable. He was correct in his observation, since on that particular day I had been feeling troubled and despondent, assailed by worries and in a generally difficult state. When he said what he did, I felt a bit put on the spot. So I took the glass from him out of courtesy and started sipping it slowly as he poured more out of the flask before him, gulping down one glass after another until he appeared to be drunk. Then, after rising with difficulty and getting into bed, he asked me to give him a massage. So I began massaging him, but with difficulty, since I was dulled and weakened on account of the arrack I had drunk. As I massaged him, he began moaning and groaning in an exaggerated, affected sort of way. Then he turned over on his back, exposing his private parts, and asked me to massage his hips. Taken aback by his request, I declined. But before I knew it, he had grabbed my hands with his and begun compelling me to touch him and to do what I had no desire to do. When things got to this point, I pushed him away and went running out of his quarters, down the tower and back to my own room. Then, with my head spinning, my insides churning and my whole being gripped by a terrible nausea, I vomited up everything in my gut.

From that night onward, I did not sleep a wink. I began recalling all the things I had heard about Father Michael from others in the church, and the things I myself had experienced with him since the time I had begun working in his service. I had noticed that without my knowing why, some people would look at me pityingly whenever I said I had begun working for this man. On one occasion, as we were helping with the baptism of a group of young children, a young sexton I knew whispered to me that I should beware of Father Michael. Unsettled by his enigmatic warning, I begged him to tell me what he meant. So, he fearfully informed me that most of the people who had served with this priest had come to mysterious ends. One of them had disappeared and had never been found, while another had died suddenly. He said that the man's personal history in the church at Antioch had been tainted with evil. However, so profound was the man's wickedness and depravity and so rigorous were the precautions he took to cover his tracks, no one had ever been able to pin anything on him. Then I recalled something that had happened on a journey we had taken together to Constantinople. I had been instructed to go with him as his assistant together with a group of other priests. I had never attended church councils before. In fact, I had never even heard of such things in our church in Egypt. However, the reason for this solemn ecclesiastical gathering, I had been told, was that a schism had reared its ugly head between the Orthodox Christians and those who adhere to the doctrine of the single nature of Christ. Meanwhile, the Paulinists and the Manicheans had been stirring up trouble as well. Heated discussions led to the passing of laws prohibiting residences from being turned into monasteries without the bishops' approval, and requiring anyone who wished to live a life of asceticism and piety to give up all his personal possessions before entering the monastic life. Such laws stipulated that no patriarch could come from the plebeian class or have formerly been a monk unless he had received progressive training on the various levels of the priesthood and completed the legal period of time at each level.

Now, since the council, which was being convened in the Church of Hagia Sophia, was discussing the issue of icons, a large number of iconoclasts gathered outside, assaulted the guards, and forced their way into the church. Once inside, they rushed in to where the forum was being held, bellowing, shrieking, and causing turmoil and confusion. It was not long before an all-out mêlée had erupted, complete with kicking and fist fights, and those who had stormed the meeting suspended the sessions by force. In short, it was something I had never seen or heard the likes of in all my life. As we pushed our way inside, trying to seek refuge from what was happening, Father Michael started nudging me in the direction of a darkened corridor that led to the church's con-fessionals. It was a long corridor, and I kept running behind him until I found myself before a door that led into a part of the patriarchal man-sion next to the church. The second passageway we entered was even darker than the first, since it was slightly past dusk and the Constanti-nople sun, as it had been ever since our arrival there, was sparing and niggardly. No sooner had he opened the door leading into the second corridor than he began hugging and patting me as though he wanted to calm me and assuage my fears. However, his patting was overdone in a way that was not to my liking, especially after he started putting his arms around me, and I felt that what he was doing went beyond what was fitting for someone of his dignity and rank. Besides, I thought, this was not the way to calm me or set my mind at rest. So I gently disen-gaged myself from his grip. At that time, however, I still didn't suspect that he was this wicked or depraved.

After that night in Antioch, Father Michael began treating me harshly. He also began making demands of me that he had not made before. One time, for example, he asked me to go to a swampy area in the northwestern quarter of the city to bring him some reeds of the sort that he liked to sharpen for use in writing and recording. It was an uninhabited area filled with dangerous wild creatures and, as everyone knew, going there was a hardship. Hence, if it had not been for God's protection and my knowledge of how to survive in such a place—given the similarity between it and the Bashmourite territories—I would surely have perished. On another occasion he asked me to bring him wild herbs for him to treat himself with from the graveyard north of the Dawq Gate outside the city wall. This, too, was a wilderness area teeming with scorpions, spiders, and other creatures that bite and sting. One of them grabbed hold of the skin on the back of my neck, and if it had not been for my quickness to sense its presence, it would have poured its poison into my blood and I would have been a goner for certain.

Thus it was that I began to sense the danger that this evil man posed to me. I was sure he wanted to get rid of me as soon as he could, since he suspected that I might reveal his secret and expose him among the people of the city as the wicked, depraved Sodomite that he was.

Yet, it was not even this that impelled me to take the step I eventually took. For Father Michael had begun embroiling me in a predicament from which it seemed that nothing but death could deliver me, and I feared that he would charge me with a crime that could only be committed by those whose lives hold out no hope and who can be reformed by nothing but the purifying fire.

One evening after I had finished my duties for the day, he said to me in an authoritative tone of voice, "After midnight, when the church is quiet and everyone is asleep, you are going to slip out unnoticed and make your way through the city until you reach the St. George Gate. Someone will meet you there, and you will give this to him. Then you are to come back the way you went, without making a sound. All you will say to him is, 'The black carnation sends you greetings.' If he gives you something, bring it back. However, make certain that you do not try to discover what it contains."

He handed me a rolled-up parchment that had been sealed and stamped, and as I reached out to take it from him, I was gripped with terror. He eyed me with a cold, threatening look that warned me of the dire consequences that awaited me if I chose to disobey him. I did not know my way around the city very well, since I spent most of my time within the church walls, and was not allowed to go roaming about outside or leave for any reason. I had been to the St. George Gate once or twice when Father Thomas was still alive. We had gone there for Father Thomas to bless a woman who had given birth to male quadruplets that died shortly thereafter, and on another occasion I had gone there to fetch a group of people whom Father Thomas said had violated some of the "One Hundred and One Laws" that had been promulgated at a synod held in AD 692, and who raised livestock, drank wine, and took meals inside a church located there. I began turning all these things over in my mind, fearful that even if I made it to the place where he wanted to me to go in the dead of night, I might not be able to find my way back. I was also afraid I might be accosted by thieves or highway robbers.

"But sir," I said to him imploringly, "I do not know how to get to the St. George Gate. Besides, I might not be able to recognize the person to whom Your Grace wants to send. . . ."

Looking as though he were about to ravish me as a lion ravishes its prey, he retorted hurriedly, "You will go out through the church's south door, and from there you will keep walking in the same direction. Stay on the same street until you come to the St. George Gate. Before you reach it you will see a landmark you cannot miss, namely, al-bimaristan, that is, the hospital. When you come to it, continue walking alongside it, and at the St. George Gate you will meet a reverend father who will greet you in Arabic. Return his greeting, and bring with you whatever he gives you if he instructs you to take anything."

Trying to think of something that would relieve me from having to go, I asked, "And the door, sir?"

"You will find someone there to open it for you, idiot!" he shouted with his raspy, choking voice.

Then, after a slight hesitation, he smiled wickedly and said, "If you happen to meet anyone on the way there or back, just say you've been to see Bint Yuhanna!"

I was aghast at what he had just said. In fact, I was thunderstruck: How could I possibly say such a thing if I happened to meet up with someone on the way? Bint Yuhanna was a well-known singer in the city who would give herself to anyone who came her way, and if someone in the church wanted to insult or deride someone else, he would say to him, "I wish I had a daughter who could take your place, even if she were Bint Yuhanna!"

As I slipped stealthily out of the church after midnight, I was amazed to find that, in fact, the door was ajar without there being anyone there to let me out. In the grip of a terrible fear, I began walking with hasty steps. The mountain peaks visible in the distance looked like fearsome demons that were peering down at me from their lofty heights in the light of the pale moon, which was concealed by dark clouds from time to time. Soon I found myself walking alongside the hospital wall, just as Father Michael had told me I would. Feeling apprehensive, I began calling down God's mercy on Father Thomas, who used to bring the ill to the hospital. In fact, once a year he would bring lepers into his own bath and wash their hair with his own hands, a task in which he was assisted by the deacons and sextons.

Shortly thereafter I reached the St. George Gate, which leads out of the city. At that particular moment it seemed very close to the shore, since the fragrance of the sea breeze was making its way into my nostrils, while the violent pounding of the waves shattered all silence.

When I came up to the gate, filled with such fear I wondered if I could bear any more, I found a man standing before me, his priestly vestments visible in the sparse moonlight. As soon as he saw me, he came up to me. In a trembling, rushed voice I said to him, "The black carnation sends you greetings, sir." Then, in a harsh voice that sounded familiar to me somehow, he said, "And I, too, send him my greetings." After handing me a velvet bag which I thrust inside my clothes, he went his way, and I went mine. As he departed, his steady, forceful steps struck the ground so loudly, one would have thought he was on horseback.

I began replaying his voice in my mind. His Arabic was peculiar, and it seemed to me that he had pronounced the *d* sound as a *t*. Dying with curiosity to know who the man was, I could not stop thinking about it. I took the bag out and ran my hand over it. It seemed to contain a rolled up parchment, and as I wondered what was written on it, my apprehension was heightened. Then suddenly, as I approached the door of the church, I realized who the voice might belong to, and for several moments I froze in my tracks, stunned by the revelation. I also realized how serious the matter would prove to be if my hunch was confirmed.

Not long before Father Thomas's death, the Qasyan Church had been visited by a Byzantine priest who met with a number of the clergymen there, including Father Michael. I was present at the meeting, pouring the plum drink that was being served to the guest, who spoke Arabic with a strange accent. He spoke at length about the Saracens, and Father Thomas, who was furious and in complete disagreement with the man, was arguing with him heatedly and refuting his claims. Later that evening, I asked Father Thomas about the meaning of the word 'Saracens,' which I had never heard before. He said that the man had been referring to the Ishmaelites, or the Muslims, who were descendents of Ishmael son of Hajar, and who were thus descendents of the Prophet Abraham. He said the man had been sent by a high-ranking church official, his purpose being to urge the followers of Jesus in the Qasyan Church to help the Byzantine Church and the Byzantine Army to wrest the holy places from the hands of these Saracens.

So, then: Here he was corresponding with those people again. O God! I thought to myself in near disbelief, my steps slowing down as I neared the church door. All fear of the road and its dangers had left me now. However, a fear of another sort had begun to come over me.

Father Thomas had said at the time that what the Byzantine priest had said was an example of "a word of truth spoken in the interests of falsehood." After all, he explained, the Byzantines only wanted to protect their own interests, and did not have the least concern for the Christian holy places. Father Thomas had responded to the man saying, "These sacred places are safe in the Muslims' hands, and all Christians make pilgrimage to them without any hindrance."

"Besides," he added, "The Muslims are Arabs just as are all Syrians even if they happen to have a different religion, and tolerance has been the hallmark of their rule ever since they took over the country's affairs."

I now knew for a certainty that I was doomed to perdition as long as I stayed with Father Michael. As far as this man was concerned, there was not room for the two of us. Hence, once I was back at the church that night, I did not sleep a wink. After examining the matter from all angles, I concluded that whenever I managed to climb out of a hole, I ended up falling into a bigger one. I was afraid to tell a soul what I was thinking lest things turn against me, because from the time I had lost Father Thomas, who had cherished me and treated me with kindness and compassion, I had not found anyone I could really trust. Then quite unexpectedly, God led me to confide my concern to Deaconess Rasfa.

One of the things I had noticed in particular about the church at Antioch was the practice of allowing women to serve as deaconesses. I had learned that this had been an accepted practice in this church since its earliest centuries. As Paul wrote in his first letter to Timothy, "Let no one be enrolled as a widow who is under sixty years of age, or has been married more than once. And she must be attested for her good deeds, as one who has brought up children, shown hospitality, washed the feet of the saints, relieved the afflicted, and devoted herself to doing good in every way." Rasfa was one of the deaconesses whose task was to assist the priests in baptizing women, instructing female catechumens and overseeing women believers during the Divine Mass. She was also assigned the task of visiting the sick and wounded. As Rasfa herself had once told me, she was among those included under the Justinian Code. Hence, the Lord had had mercy on her and she had been accepted as a deaconess—even though she was not even fifty years old yet—based on her commitment, as was stipulated by the Code, to the preservation of dignity and upright conduct. Rasfa was both a widow and a bereaved mother, having lost four of her children in a single stroke of fate when they went out to sea one day to fish, only to have the water swallow up their boat, after which the waves spit them out on the shore, one corpse after another.

Rasfa had been tender and solicitous toward me as though I were her own son ever since the day when I saved her life. What happened was this: We had been celebrating the annual Feast of St. Barbara, which takes place on the fourth of December. It was a day of gladness and rejoicing and people were in high spirits. They had come out sporting their finest attire, and many of them were riding colts and she-mules. Then, as was the custom at this celebration, the crowds—together with the governor, the patriarch, and the heads of state—began making their way toward the saint's shrine. I was walking with the clergy behind the deaconesses when, all of a sudden, people started making a rush for the church, because someone had shouted out that the saint's icon was shedding tears. Everyone had come running in hopes of verifying the miracle with their own eyes and receiving its blessing. With everyone trying to get there before everyone else, a group of people fell down, including Deaconess Rasfa. When I saw what had happened, I rushed to lift her up again and shield her from the stampeding crowds, which could easily have trampled her underfoot.

From that day onward, our mutual affection was sealed, and I knew that she was a pure, earnest believer. In fact, she was like a saint. She began telling me many things about this church, and she did so in eloquent Arabic, the reason being that her father, as she herself told me, had been from a group of tribes of Yemeni origin known as the Ghassanids, while her mother was a Syrian from Antioch. Seeing that she was someone I could trust, I decided to go see her at the first opportunity that opened up the following morning in order to seek her advice and counsel. I went to see her because I was suffering from a headache and I wanted her to give me something to relieve the pain. This is what I told Father Michael, at least. Once I was with her, I related to her quickly what had happened to me the night before.

Looking to her right, then to her left, she said to me in a whisper, "Do not breathe a word to anyone about what you just told me. Listen. If you stay in this church, your fate is sealed. He's bound to get rid of you sooner or later. There is only one thing left for you to do."

"And what is that, Blessed Mother?" I said anxiously. "Help me, may the Lord have mercy on you. I have worn myself out thinking!"

Then, still in a whisper, she proposed something that never would have occurred to me in a million years.

All day long I kept thinking about what Mother Deaconess Rasfa had said to me, turning it over and over in my mind. And I concluded in the end that I had no choice but to do as she had advised me. With my heart thus set, I went the following day at noon to see Father Dionysius, the head of the church. Once in his presence, I did a prostration. Then, with my head bowed, I mustered all the courage I had and said, "I want to confess to you, sir, that I have lied. May the Lord forgive me. I had said that I was from the church at Qasr al-Sham' in Old Cairo. But that is not true, Father. I am nothing but a poverty-stricken peasant from the Bashmourite marshlands."

I then proceeded to roll up my sleeve and show him the lion tattoo on my forearm as evidence that I was, in fact, nothing but a wretched servant, a poor farmer who had been forbidden to leave his land for any reason.

Father Dionysius listened to me dispassionately, like someone for whom such things were a daily occurrence. Eyeing my face searchingly, he thought the matter over for a while. Then, gesturing to his attendants he said frigidly, "Take him to the jail until we have looked into his case."

The price I was obliged to pay for my lie was one of bitterness and pain in the subterranean vaults of the Qasyan Church prison. In that place, one wishes for one thing only: death. A mere one and a half yards in size, my place of confinement was something on the order of a hole that had been carved out of rock underground. It was just barely large enough to turn around in, and with just barely enough air to breathe. If one was among the more fortunate, he would be left alone in the cell without anyone else to share its air, which only came in through narrow, widely spaced openings. After closing the prison's iron door, the guards would remain far away at the other end of the long, darkened, narrow, tortuous passageway that led outside. When they brought me into the place that had been reserved for me, they left me some water, dry bread, and salt mixed with the bitter cores of apricot pits. I learned later that they added these to the salt in order to ward off scabies.

The things I went through in the Qasyan Church prison were the worst I've ever experienced in my entire life. The place is a present horror, a crushing ordeal, and the source of frightful damage to both body and soul. Throughout the time I was there I asked God to help me do one single thing, namely, to keep my sanity. For madness will most surely be the fate of anyone who is confined there for any length of time. Consequently, I would talk to myself frequently and recite various passages from the Scriptures and the liturgy. I would recall some of the canticles and theotokias that we used to sing regularly in our church at Qasr al-Sham'. I would also invent games to play with myself. For example, in the dim light that filtered in through the small basement window I would make funny-looking shapes of animals and birds with my fingers, then look at their shadows on the stone walls that hemmed me in. I would recall scenes from my distant childhood and my village in the Bashmourite territories, especially from the beginning of the hot summer months when the sweet flood waters would mix in such quantities with the salty sea water that the rivers and canals were filled with birds, fish, and all sorts of other beautiful creatures that had made such waters their abode from time immemorial. When this happened, the place would turn into a veritable paradise, a place of beatitude and tranquility unequaled anywhere on earth. This was the time of year when the white lotus would be in full bloom, water lilies would display their lavender blossoms far and wide, and the papyrus plants with their long stalks and dark flowers would appear here and there. My eyes never wearied of beholding such wonders, nor did my ears ever tire of hearing the chorus of birds as they chanted, warbled, and chirped with the most magical and exquisite of voices.

I would close my eyes and let my spirit fly far away from the Antioch prison. I would alight in my homeland, my place of birth, walk down its narrow, somber lanes, then take hold of my mother's dress and breathe in its fragrance. I would watch my father as he sowed the fields, the sleeves of his white linen tunic rolled up to reveal his powerful forearms. I would look over at all my siblings: There was my older sister Mariya, who sailed away one day with a Melkite sailor to the land of the Greeks, never to be heard from again, and whose parting my mother bewailed from that day onward as though she had departed for the land of the dead. Then there was my younger sister, Basant, who, of all my brothers and sisters, was the closest to my heart. Never in all my life could I possibly miss any of them as much as I have missed her. Three years younger than I, she was graced with a beauty and tenderness that were beyond description, and which no spirit could ever forget. The last time I saw her was when Amuna died, and the image of her from that day will be forever imprinted in my imagination: Stunned beyond words, her eyes open wide like a couple of large chunks of ambergris hardened with shock and sorrow.

I would spend long hours summoning up all the scenes I had ever witnessed back home. Sometimes my spirit would be grieved, and at other times, refreshed. I would long for Time's wheel to turn back and take me with it to the things my spirit yearned for and that still caused such tender feelings to well up inside me. And at other times I would rejoice: Remembering that life contains enough of the Lord's delights to lift His servants up to heights of joy and tranquility, I would praise Him for the good things with which He graces his servants on this earth, and my spirit would be revived with hope. Then I would open my eyes to find the prison's stone walls before me, but without fearing them, and I would go back to reciting my spiritual litanies or utter prayers of thanksgiving and praise. I would pray often for God to grant His forgiveness to those whom I had known and who had died, and to all the loved ones who had ascended to the Kingdom of Heaven. I often recited the Psalms, which I knew by heart, to strengthen myself and keep my faith firm. I will never forget how many times I repeated the words:

Yea, though I walk through the valley of the shadow of death,
I will fear no evil,
For Thou art with me.
Thy rod and Thy staff, they comfort me.
Thou preparest a table before me in the presence of mine enemies,
Thou anointest my head with oil,
My cup-runneth over.

I would also pass the time trying to recall the various kinds of birds and fish in our Bashmourite territories. I would name them one by one, trying to remember everything about their colors and shapes. The birds I recalled were: the quail, the nastafir, the starling, the falcon, the golden oriole, the dibsi, the nightingale, the pelican, the turtledove, the ringdove, the blue jay, the hawni, the crow, the hoopoe, the hussayni, the jaradi, the piebald, the 'monk,' the hassaf, the barin, the 'chain' fish, the dardari, the 'deacon,' the basis, the green fish, robin redbreast, the sparrow, the 'negro,' the atrush, ibn al-Samman, ibn al-Mar'a, the bat, the spoonbill, the finch, and the partridge. On one particular night, I managed to list nearly one hundred types of birds that I knew, including those that cry, sing, coo, twitter, warble, caw, shriek, cheep, chirp, whistle, and peep. As for the fish, I went on consoling myself with them one time till I had counted up seventy-seven types, namely: the whiting, the balmu, the baru, the goldfish, the balas, the saksa, the aran, the shumus, the nasa, the tubar, the baqsamar, the ahnash, the eel, the ma'iya, the brownfish, the ablil, the fuways, the dunis, the martanus, the asqalamus, the nafat, the jibal, the trout, the hajaf, the qallariya, the rukhs, the 'ibar, the tuna, the latt, the qajjah, the qurus, the grayfish, the firakh, the qarqah, the zulayh, the laj, the aklat, the madi, the jalla, the salla, the sadd, the balak, the tilapia, the qafa, the sur, the whale, the hajar, the bashin, the sharbut, the nassas, the torpedo fish, the shu'ur, the cuttlefish, the labas, the sutur, the rasi, the rayfan, the labis, the bream, the abunis, the labba, the 'blindfish,' the garfish, the qalamidus, the halabuwa, the 'dancer,' the qurundus, the jatr, the hubakarah, the mujazza' dalisi, the ahshabala, the white bassal, the ruquq, Umm 'Ubayd, the balu, Umm al-Insan, and the insariya, along with crocodiles and turtles.

I do not know how much time went by. I could no longer distinguish sunrise from sundown, since my nights were no different from my days. Instead, time ran together for me in an amorphous stream. No longer able to leave my place, I joined the ranks of the living dead, or the dead who still exist, but who have no right to assert their existence. I began going into trances which might have been fever, and might have been sleep: I really could not tell which. I would only come out of them long enough to take a drink of water or swallow a piece of dry bread. Then it happened one morning that the guards came and brought me out. I walked with difficulty as they shoved me roughly ahead of them. Not having been able to walk or move about for so long had stiffened my joints, and I was little better than a hemiplegic. At the same time, having been deprived of sunlight for such a long time, my eyes could not bear the sun's brightness. I crossed the church courtyard to the bath, where they left me to wash up. May God forgive Father Dionysius, since by this time I stunk to high heaven after having gone so long without a chance to attend to matters of hygiene.

It was finally decided that I should be taken to Baghdad, the seat of the caliphate. After all, I was the caliph's captive, and given that I was not a member of the clergy as everyone had thought me to be at the Qasyan Church, they would have to hand me over once again to the caliph's soldiers so that I could be taken to Baghdad and my case could be disposed of there as they saw fit.

I committed my way to God. Whatever was yet to be, it would not be like that which had been, and whatever was to come to pass thereafter could not possibly match what had come to pass before it. The following morning, after gathering up my meager belongings by way of clothes and other things which were of no value apart from the fact that they happened to be mine, I found myself departing from the Qasyan Church, a place where I had endured things the likes of which I had never endured before.

I left Antioch at sundown. During my final days there, they had issued a legal ruling against a young deaconess in the church by the name of Bersise, who had been caught committing fornication with a chandler who supplied the church with candles. Hence, she had broken her vow and strayed from the path of righteousness. I was part of a group of people under light guard. They took us to another town in Syria by the name of Aleppo, which was on our way to Baghdad. It took a day and a night to get there. The road that led from Antioch to Aleppo was teeming with life, and we encountered no ruined, abandoned areas the entire way. Most of the surrounding land had been planted in various sorts of grains and other crops, and as we traveled on from Aleppo, we would stop for a while in some of the villages that we came to. Most of these villages contained springs and flower gardens, and the guards would leave us to eat something as they fed and watered the horses. We had just sat down to rest on the edge of a patch of arable land which was somewhere around a feddan in size when some peasants came rushing out toward us. As soon as they had seen us and recognized the caliph's soldiers, they came to advise us to move on quickly. The area where we were staying was near a mountain known as Likam, which was the site of an ancient fortress overlooking a lake that a group of Byzantines had made into their headquarters. The members of this group had vowed to make war on the Muslims, the peasants informed us, and had sworn not to marry. Something on the order of monks and knights at the same time, they were known as the Dawiya. When they heard this news, the soldiers quickly gathered us together and we proceeded on our way back to Aleppo.

We soon arrived back in Aleppo, which was surrounded by a massive black stone wall with a citadel atop it in the direction facing Antioch. Aleppo also had a huge trench that had been dug as far as the sea, and in the center of which there were tanks for storing potable water.

Some of the soldiers had left us and gone to the city police in order to receive people who had rebelled against the caliph. Meanwhile, someone came to us saying that a dragon had appeared in the city some time earlier. Broad as a lighthouse and terribly long, it would crawl about the earth swallowing up every animal in its path. Out of its mouth it spewed fire that would incinerate everything it came upon, including trees and plants, and it would pass over houses that it had burned to the ground. People fled from it right and left until it had covered approximately twelve parasangs, at which time God Almighty came to people's rescue with a cloud that descended upon it and carried it away. As the cloud carried it along, it wrapped its tail around a dog and lifted it up in the air as the dog yelped. Then, as people looked on, it disappeared from sight. The person who told the story concluded his report, saying, "I saw the place where the dragon had crawled along, and it was wide as a riverbed!"

When the soldiers returned, they brought with them a group of people who, like me, were being exiled to the seat of the caliphate. The city mayor had issued orders for them to be sent away because some of them, who were from a village by the name of Huta, had taken up arms against a group from another village by the name of 'Ayn Jara. Between the two villages there lay a stone that had been set up as a boundary mark. The people of Huta had taken the stone down and cast it aside, after which all the women of 'Ayn Jara came out dolled up, dressed to the hilt, and looking for a wild time. However, they had no sense of the indecency of what they were about or how their passions had gotten the better of them. When the men came out to put the stone back in place, the women went back home again, at which time they woke up to the indecency of the way they had conducted themselves. The mayor then issued orders for the stone to be removed and for some people of Huta to be arrested on charges of theft. In fact, he asked the caliph never to allow them to return, since they had frequently put the stone to use for their own benefit and brought shame on the people of 'Ayn Jara.

Then we continued on our way through the city in the direction of the Iraq Gate. As we did so, I discovered that it contained a river called Quwayq. When we passed alongside it, we paused briefly because one of the soldiers wanted to catch one of the turtles that were so ubiquitous there. He wanted to get some of its blood for his mother in Iraq, since he had been told that sprinkling oneself with this tortoise's blood could help to relieve joint pain. As we lingered there, a fisherman's melodious voice rang out from the other bank of the river. He sang:

If only love remained and there were no parting
With the beloved or what I long for!
Quwayq is a torrent of blessing that comes, then goes.
It drifts in, then drifts out once more.

I noted the people in the streets and those who had stopped briefly to look at us, and I found them to be eminently handsome both in their features and their physiques. Their skin color, for the most part, ranged from milky to reddish to brown, and their eyes were black. I was amazed at how many quarters the city contained, as well as the number of houses, gardens, and baths. I was likewise impressed with the sedate beauty of its stone buildings and the diversity of its markets with their displays of vegetables, fruits, oils, soaps, fabrics, and furs that were hung up on shop doors in such a way that they revealed the original shapes of the animals from which they had been taken: sables, lynxes, fennecs, squirrels, foxes, and other animals whose hides are considered of value. In the slave market we passed through, I saw Circassians, Turks, Byzantines, and Abyssinians. Then we were brought out through the Iraq Gate and set out for Baghdad, the city of the caliphate.

Never once in the entire journey was my mind at rest. I was in a constant state of cogitation and reflection. And I realized that travel is simply the distance between here and there, or, rather, that it is the 'here' which, no sooner have you taken hold of it than it escapes from you to 'there.' As a result, you are in a never-ending state of in-between-ness that summons history and spurns all maps. Consequently, the spirit goes roaming through its past, and takes hold of the universe in singular peregrinations of reflection and discernment. From the journey's beginning to its end, whenever I had a moment alone I would think about the things that had happened to me in the land of Egypt, then in Antioch. Then I would place them under the penetrating light of the luminous meteor, the bright star of meditation. And after a bit of thought and examination, I concluded that what I had once believed with perfect certainty was nothing but a type of doubt that could never satisfy a person's innermost longings, that axioms are nothing but beginnings, and that true doctrine only manifests itself through action, not through words and honeyed humbug. After all, there are people who take doctrine captive: They exploit it as a means to the gratification of their own passions and the fulfillment of their worldly ends. In other words, not everyone who recites the words of the Lord puts them into practice. There are those who, as they chant sacred words, are hoarding piles of filthy lucre. Rather, words of faith have to be joined with compassionate action. Otherwise, they are nothing more than a deceit, an untruth, a sham, and an attempt to swindle and manipulate people with Scriptures in which people put their trust and rites they hold sacred.

As I entered that in-between-place of questioning, I ceased to believe—may God forgive me—in a certain thing, and I came to doubt what I had thought to be indubitable. I began to place question marks where they had not been before, though I am not sure whether this was a result of my growing sense of pain and misery, my helplessness and the hardship of the journey, or whether it was a kind of divine munificence and inward unveiling. I could not seem to stop asking the question: Could the Creator of the rain, the trees, the clouds, the fruits of plant and field, the multitudinous varieties of birds and animals, not to mention human beings and everything on land and under the sea, possibly be in need of all the ephemeral trivialities that human beings come up with on His account by way of crowns, vestments, gilded this, silver plated that, and lofty edifices in order to demonstrate His power and greatness? Surely, I thought, even the smallest mountain of His creation remains unequaled by even the most magnificent edifice or church building. After all, the Lord is full of majesty and highly exalted above all such things in His works and in the signs of His power and bounty. Surely He is too great to stand in need of something that has been crafted by human hands.

Red earth, yellow earth, green earth, and black earth: All these I had been destined to traverse with wonder and awe as I passed through the villages, towns, and deserts on my way to the circular city known as Baghdad. This was the city that had remained for so long in my mind's eye, like a dream constructed from the mists of imagination and the embellishments born of conjecture and hearsay. I had etched it in my mind based on the detailed mosaic of places and worlds I had already seen and experienced. And despite the hardship entailed by my departure and subsequent journey and the bitterness and humiliation of captivity, my longing for Baghdad grew with every step we took and with every successive road we trod. What a lovely thing it is to long to see a city, and—once you have constructed it within your mind and soul, brick upon brick, out of fantasies derived from cities and towns incessantly ablaze with cruelty, violence, and conflict—to dream that you are going to behold it with your own eyes and enter it on your own two feet.

Many things had happened to us since we set out on our journey. However, they paled one and all by comparison with what we saw when we passed through one of the desert areas surrounding a certain village, and which merchants and their caravans were obliged to traverse on their way to or from Baghdad. As we proceeded through the area, an unbearable stench reached our nostrils. We thought in the beginning that it must be coming from the remains of the prey felled by some wild beast and which had begun to rot in the blazing sun. However, as we muttered in complaint over the revolting odor, what should we hear but an agonized, heartrending moan. Rushing toward the source of the sound, we were appalled by what our eyes beheld. There on the ground lay a man in fetters, who was groaning in unbearable pain. He was bug-eyed, and his tongue, which was blackened, swollen, cracked, and dry, was lolling out. Meanwhile, thousands of worms swarmed over him, so thick they were like a robe that covered his entire body. When one of us plucked up enough courage to come nearer, he found that the man had been wrapped in the fatty rumps of several sheep, which had been fastened securely to his body with ropes and strips of wool. The unfortunate man appeared to have been in the hot sun for some time, as the sheep's fat had turned into a mass of worms that had begun eating him alive. This, at any rate, is what we were told by one of the guards. Upon hearing this, I started sobbing uncontrollably and ran to vomit up everything in my gut. Then a bout of pain so acute came over me that I was helpless to do anything or even to move. My pain and paralysis were made all the worse when one of the guards rushed over to untie the man, but was prevented from doing so by the chief guard, who said it was hopeless. The worms had reached more than one place on the man's flesh, he said, and he was about to give up the ghost. The chief guard also expressed the fear that if we came closer to the man or tried to help him, we might be infected with some disease. Consequently, he took us hurriedly past the man, and we left the wretched creature to his miserable fate. When we had gone one or two parasangs, we happened upon some people who asked us about the whereabouts of a man who had been shackled and left in the desert. They said they had been looking for him for several days, but to no avail. The chief guard showed them the place where we had just stopped near the man, and asked them about the man's story. They replied that he was a merchant who was said to have betrayed and robbed some of the people who were with him in the same caravan. His victims, in turn, had inflicted on him a punishment used by the Elchanites, a cruel, loutish people who had devised the most ingenious ways of tormenting their foes and other victims. They went on to say that these same people had split one of the merchant's sons in two in revenge for what he had done, without a thought for mercy or compassion.

After that incident, I was afflicted the entire rest of the way with a kind of apathy and numbness. I was sickened by all this cruelty, violence, and thirst for revenge. For a moment I wished I could die, since it seemed to me that death was the only possible refuge left to me after my extended sojourn in the barren, trackless wilderness of this earthly life. This sense of mine persisted and intensified every time they urged us to move faster so that we could traverse the distance to the city of the caliphate in the shortest time possible.

Some time later, we glimpsed domes and buildings that were so perfectly formed, they looked as though they had been shaped in molds. Some of the soldiers began shouting and raising a happy din over our near arrival at the gates of the cupolaed city. In the midst of it there appeared a magnificent green dome that bore the statue of a horseman with a spear in his hand. As we approached, my attention was drawn to the spear when one of the soldiers said, "Look! The horseman's spear is pointing toward the East. So perhaps those who have rebelled against the caliph will exit from that direction, as it has been said that they will."

Laughing derisively, another soldier commented, "Do you really believe such tales? The idea that a rebel against the caliph will come out in the direction the spear points is just a myth. Keep on moving, and keep your mouth shut. Let us just get there and complete this mission of ours in good form."

As we drew nearer, the city wall appeared gargantuan to me. It was more extensive than any I had ever seen before, whether in Egypt or in the lands I had lived in as a stranger, and it encircled the entire city. I would guess it was more than thirty-five cubits high, its towers looked to be around five cubits thick, and it had battlements along the top. When we came close enough to take a careful look at it, I noticed that it contained many gates. They had us stop at a gate known as the First Syria Gate, which consisted of two entrances. It looked as though the first entrance led only into the area separating the inner and outer walls, while the second led into the city, and between the two entrances there was an antechamber and a walkway. After being granted permission to enter by the guards, we entered an arched vestibule of baked brick and gypsum in which there was a seating area with a staircase that led up to the wall. The seating area was covered by a towering, ornate dome that may have been as much as fifty cubits across. There were other domes on the wall as well, and it was these which had been visible to us from a distance before our entrance into the city.

We were then led down the city streets to the caliph's palace. I was a bit alarmed to find the general populace gathered in huge numbers in the markets, in the streets, and on people's rooftops. The soldiers who had brought me into the city along with a number of other captives were, like me, astonished at the thick crowds we were encountering even in the local shops and on the balconies. When they stopped to inquire about the matter, they were told that the caliph had granted the Byzantine emissaries permission to appear before him, and that everyone was waiting for their procession to pass by on its way from a house known as Dar Saʻid, where they had stayed for two entire months without being granted an audience with the caliph. The person who informed the soldiers of these things said that everyone who owned a shop or a room overlooking the spot where the envoys were expected to pass by on their way to the caliph's palace had rented out what he had for a good number of dirhams, and that along the Tigris River, kites had been launched and a variety of small boats had come out in their finest array.

After this they marched us through successive markets, baths, and neighborhoods until we reached the caliph's palace, which was adjacent to a beautiful mosque. Before they took us inside we were met by an inspector of sorts, who may have been the chief of the caliphal court, and who disputed with them about my status just as I had been disputed over every time I had been turned over to a new set of overseers. However, after a lengthy exchange, it was decided to place me in the oven room of the caliph's kitchen.

I may have been blessed with such good fortune because I had happened to reach the caliph's palace at the time when everyone was busy preparing to receive the Byzantine emissaries, as a result of which they decided forthwith to place me in the oven room rather than selling me or relegating me to a prison cell somewhere. Or perhaps they made the decision they did because of the experience I had gained with ovens and boilers during my journey from Egypt to Antioch and because, given my frail constitution and fragile health, they had nothing to gain from selling me. Whatever the case may be, God had destined me for a particular fate. As they brought me across the palace courtyard, everyone was busy covering the floors with beautiful carpets and decorating the place with impressive implements and machines. The chamberlains and other members of the courtly retinue were lining up according to their respective ranks at the doors and in the anterooms, corridors, passageways, courtyards, and sitting rooms. The soldiers were arrayed in a double row in handsome attire and with reins in their hands, the mounts beneath them decked out in headgear of gold and silver. The soldiers, who were displaying their varied weaponry and implements encased in ornate fabrics, were followed by squires, as well as other servants that worked inside and outside the palace clad in exquisite uniforms, with swords in their hands and beautifully adorned belts about their waists.

Together with one of the soldiers, I was ushered out through a far door that led from the main courtyard to the caliph's kitchen. Try as I might, I could never do justice in words to the things I laid eyes on there: As soon as I came through the door, I found myself in a spacious courtyard surrounded by rooms on all sides, with baby peacocks, ducks, geese, and turkeys running about here and there. We then entered a large, spacious side room that opened onto still another room. When I looked in through the door of the second room, I saw piles of wood and coal arranged in neat, orderly fashion. As for the first room, it was the oven room, which contained ten ovens lined up next to one another. There were men and boys working the ovens with energy and enthusiasm, and the room's high walls were black with soot. The soldier under whose command I had been placed called out to someone whom he referred to as 'Rayyis Husayn,' and before long there appeared a massive man with a sharpness and force to his gaze that took one's breath away.

The man hailed the military chief, who said, "This is a captive of the caliph's. He is an Egyptian Copt, and he will be your charge from here on out. He will take his orders from you in the fuel depot, and you will be responsible for everything that concerns him."

"Yes, sir," Rayyis Husayn replied evenly.

He then escorted me to a spot in the fuel depot, which seemed more like a spacious inn than a single room.

He said, "This is where you will live and sleep after your work shift ends every day. In the beginning you will work with me during the night shift, then sleep a few hours after daybreak, after which you will start making preparations for sunset. Make sure you do not disobey me in anything. Now, might you tell me your name?"

"Budayr . . . Budayr, sir," I replied with a gulp, and with a bitterness rising to my throat.

As I was answering his question, one of the palace servants came in and shouted, "Hurry, Husayn! Bring the incense burners, and come oversee them yourself. You will be the one to carry the large censer during the Byzantine emissaries' tour of the palace, so get cleaned up right away. Here is a new uniform for you to wear."

"All right, all right, right away," Husayn replied.

If I were ever asked who I am most grateful to in this world next to God Almighty, I would reply without hesitation: First, to my precious, beloved Thawna. And second, to my master and benefactor Husayn ibn Falih al-Maraghi, who had come to Baghdad from a city within the caliph's jurisdiction by the name of Maragha and whom I will never forget as long as I live. Thawna is the one who had compassion on my soul, who showered me with love and mercy, and who showed me so much that I had once been ignorant of. He was like a father and family to me, my companion and friend, the helper who bore patiently with the torments of my soul and who stayed by my side during my times of gloom and despair. He was the one who established me firmly in faith and graced me with friendship and affection. As for Husayn ibn Falih al-Maraghi, the gratitude I feel toward him is like the gratitude of someone who had been sinking into a deep abyss toward the one who brought him out to live once again. It was he who helped the blind to see, the dumb to speak, and the deaf to hear.

Whenever I began drawing comparisons and contrasts between the two men, I would wonder at myself. After all, what they had in common on the outward plane was little and hard to discern, while what separated them was plentiful and plain to see. However, what I realized in the end is that they had the same essence, albeit camouflaged by externals and formalities. I realized that this essence was what had drawn me to both of them, and it was this which had caused me to be brought into their orbits as planets are drawn into the orbit of the sun. These two men had within them something that transcended this earthly life; they were in the world, but not of it. They both had a disdain for glossy outward appearances, being concerned instead for the inward and the hidden. Both of them perceived the vanity of life on earth and the futility of existence. They were neither concerned about this world's disapproval, nor deceived by the presumptuous power of its thrones. They both found themselves in positions of worldly preoccupation in which their attention was engrossed by matters temporal and ephemeral: one in a church, and the other in a caliph's palace. Nevertheless, neither the former nor the latter vied for the things that are vied for by those who generally occupy such positions.

We stokers lived and spent our nights in the fuel depot, and our job in front of the ovens and stoves was never-ending, since the work in the kitchen went on day and night. There was always something savory, salty, rich, sweet, sour, bitter, or spicy in the process of being prepared. Most of those employed as stokers were either, like me, captives who held out no hope of being sold or of providing physical pleasure, or criminals who had been sentenced for one reason or another to long prison terms. As a result, they were put to work in the fuel depots as part of their punishment, and because their physical labor provided a means of supporting their upkeep.

As for Husayn ibn Falih, it was his own personal fate that had led him to work in the fuel depot. He was neither a captive nor a criminal as all the rest of us were. Rather, he had been born and raised in the caliph's kitchen, which was the only home or motherland he had ever known in this world. He had lived most of his life in this very place, and it was said that he had never known his father. His mother had emigrated with Husayn from her distant hometown to the city of the caliphate when he was an infant, and she had made her living for some time by selling tannour bread in the city's marketplaces. She became so well known for the bread she made that the common folks dubbed her "the Tannour Lady," and owing to her fame, she was brought to work in the caliph's kitchen. It was said that the current caliph's father had come to the point where he refused to eat any bread but hers, and that every day she used to make bread for him from no less than a bushel of wheat, which is quite a huge quantity.

Husayn had spent his childhood running and playing at the feet of the caliph's chefs and stokers, as well as all the servants and slaves who worked in the kitchen. He lived happily and comfortably until, one day, his mother died of a fatal illness that had spread like an epidemic one year, claiming untold lives. With Husayn now an orphan, the folks who worked in the kitchen took pity on him and kept him among them, treating him like one of their own children and giving him all the care and guidance he needed until he became a young man, at which point he went to work in the fuel depot and oven room. For some reason known to no one, it fascinated him to look at fire and play with it. In fact, he was so skilled in dealing with fire and everything related thereto that he became the chief specialist in this connection. In the beginning I used to be amazed that Husayn would be called "Mu'allim," that is,

"Teacher," which I took to be something of an overstatement of his abilities. However, with the passage of time, and after I had experienced firsthand what it is like to work in the kitchen's oven room, I realized that it is a task that requires skill, intelligence, acuity, taste, a high degree of discernment, and the ability to estimate and assess. After all, he was able to determine how hot and intense the flames were and, as a consequence, how suitable they were for each type of food, whereas an inexperienced person might have mastered one type of dish but ruined another.

The temperature that suits khashkananj, for example, which is made from semolina flour, sugar, and ground almonds, then sprinkled with camphor and rosewater, might not be appropriate for safidhabaja, and the temperature required by shish kebab might be of no use for faludhaj. The variety and number of foods that were cooked every day required careful attention and extreme vigilance on the part of those who worked in the oven room. Every day the chefs would be asked to prepare dishes that they had not prepared the day before. When I happened to do a count one day of the large kettles on the fire, which contained meats marinated in vinegar, puddings, and boiled meats and vegetables, they came to twenty earthenware pots, not including the medium-sized ones, the copper kettles, and the frying pans in which Persian dishes were being prepared. On that same day, we had prepared beef jellies, fried cuttlefish, ma'muniya, and jawadhib dajaj, which was a chicken dish made sometimes with rice and bread, and other times with sugar, rice, and red meat. The sweet dishes included one made from thickened sugar syrup, rice cooked with milk, clarified butter, and honey, in addition to various sorts of breads, such as a European bread referred to as afla'amuni, flat bread, qinnawi bread, mawi bread, and toasted bread.

As time went on I found myself drawn more and more powerfully to Husayn ibn Falih, and this despite the fact that when I began working with him, I had not taken to him, and had even felt distrustful of him. He was forceful and seemed a bit of a tyrant, barking out orders right and left in a manner that I found boorish and rude. Consequently, when he came back on the evening of the day when the Byzantine emperor's emissaries had been received and related to us what he had seen as he carried the censer in the procession, I did not say a word. I preferred to remain silent, savoring the delicacies we had been served from the leftovers of the huge feast and gazing at the ornately decorated table-cloth that had been spread for the Byzantine emissaries. Husayn had told us things that were beyond belief about the procession that had come out to receive the envoys and the efforts that had been expended in the palace in order to show off the greatness and mighty power of the Muslims' caliph.

He said, "The caliph issued instructions for the Byzantine emperor's two emissaries—a young man and an elderly man—to be taken on a tour of the entire palace after all the soldiers had been sent out. The only people allowed to be present inside the palace during the tour were the servants, the chamberlains, and the Sudanese servant boys. The servants allowed to be present numbered seven thousand, including four thousand white servants and three thousand black ones. And there were more than seven hundred chamberlains."

He went on, saying, "The caliph's vaults were opened up for the two visitors, their contents displayed in orderly fashion the way a bride's trousseau is opened up for viewing by her well-wishers. Curtains had been hung and the caliph's jewels were arranged in compartments on top of graduated tiers covered with black silk brocade. However, when the envoys stepped into the 'tree house,' they were more astounded than ever. On a silver tree that must have weighed more than five-hundred thousand dirhams, there were silver birds that whistled and chirped like wind-up toys.

"There were thousands of silk brocade curtains with bowls, elephants, horses, partridges, lions, and other beasts embroidered on them in gold thread, as well as huge curtains from Yemen, Armenia, and Bahans, some bearing inscriptions and others plain, and embroidered ones from Dubayq. There were rugs and oblong carpets from Dawraqa and of the Jahramiya and Darbujarradiya varieties which the leaders walked on along with the Byzantine emissaries in the hallways and courtyards, while other varieties displayed in booths, including those from Tabaran and Dubayq, could be looked at but not walked on."

Now, despite the fact that at that time I still had my reservations about Husayn ibn Falih, I sensed a compassion and simplicity in the way he related to his servant boys and those who had less experience than he did in the oven room. He did not get angry with them even when, as he was describing how dazzled the Byzantine emperor's two emissaries had been at everything they saw, one of them claimed that he was exaggerating and even making things up. According to Husayn ibn Falih, the envoys had been especially impressed when they were brought inside a building known as Khan al-Khayl which, according to Husayn ibn Falih's description, consisted primarily of porticos with marble columns. On its right side there were five hundred mares bearing five hundred gold and silver chests without lids, and on the left side there were five hundred more mares, each of which was covered with a silk brocade cloth that extended down to its ankles. And each horse was being led by a servant clad in a beautiful uniform. Following this they were escorted into a building which was connected by means of various corridors and passageways to enclosures where wild animals were kept. This building housed varieties of wild animals which had been brought into it from the enclosures and which, according to Husayn ibn Falih, would come up to people, sniff them, and eat from their hands. From there, he said, they were led to a building where there were one hundred lions: fifty on the right and fifty on the left. Each lion was being held by a lion trainer and had iron chains about its head and neck.

After being around Husayn for such long hours during our work together on the night shifts, I gradually found myself feeling drawn to him. I had not understood at first why he went on laboring all night long despite the fact that he was the chief stoker from whom everyone else took their orders, and without whose permission not a single piece of coal or firewood would enter the oven. However, after some time had passed I realized that the caliph would generally stay up all night, at which time songstresses and dancers would be brought to him, he would engage in conversation with distinguished men of learning and raconteurs, and fine-looking male and female slaves would entertain him with song. During such evening sessions, the caliph would be served the finest beverages and the most delectable cuisine and be presented with rarities that had been brought from all parts of the caliphal realm. As a consequence, Husayn would remain wakeful and attentive to whatever food needed to be heated or cooked for the caliph's dining table.

One night after our fellow workers had gone to sleep and Husayn and I were sitting alone in front of the ovens, the man whom I had thought to be so unemotional suddenly began humming and singing in a tender, heartrending voice. I found the man whom I had thought to be coarse and tyrannical moving gently and mellifluously from one song to another as though he were a practiced singer. And when he came to the place where he sang:

Like a fist tightened over a firebrand,
Many a worry has caused slumber to flee.
I turn my face toward my envier
In feigned merriment for him to see.
Longing like spear blades pierces the heart,
Yet tears hold back in obedience to me.

I was so shaken by the words and their meanings and so transported by the melody that, past the point of being able to put on a show of serenity and self-control, I began weeping and sobbing till I had poured out all the pain and bitterness that had been locked up in the depths of my soul.

Husayn had been watching a dish known as 'akika that the caliph had been craving and had requested in particular on that night. But when he noticed the state I was in, he hurriedly left what he was doing, came over to me and began patting me on the shoulder with a worried look on his face. My sobbing had taken him by surprise, and he seemed bewildered. Then out of his pocket he produced a small package from which he removed a dull green pill and told me to swallow it. When I held back, asking what it contained and unwilling to try something I knew nothing about, he said earnestly, "Just swallow it and do not be afraid. It will relieve you of the state you are in. It is what we call 'poor man's hashish,' son. And little do you know what 'poor man's hashish' can do for you!" Then he crooned:

Leave off drinking and imbibe in the 'wine of Haydar,'
Aged and green as a fertile land.
A virgin who's never been wed to rainwater

Nor pressed with foot or hand.

Nary a priest has grasped her cup,
Nor to its flask has the unbeliever drawn near.
Abu Hanifa never declared it unclean
So partake of it with good cheer.

It tells stories that wine could never tell,
So let its naysayers have no say.
The days will reveal to you what you knew not
And those who know not will show you the way.

When I heard what he had said, of which I understood only part given the limitations of my Arabic at that time, I hesitated even more. I was still so despondent, my spirit had lost all passion for life, and I was about as low as one can get. However, he fixed his gaze tenaciously on mine till I reached out and took what he was offering me, hoping in my heart of hearts that it would turn out to be a poison that would put an end to me and allow me to rest from the torments of this earthly existence. Then I swallowed the pill, downing it with some hot water as he had instructed me to do. He looked over at me expectantly, and it was not long before I found that my spirit had grown calmer and my perceptions of things had softened. In fact, I was enveloped in a blissful tranquility, and as the flame surrounding the hot coals grew redder and redder, my eyes perceived their sweetness and beauty. When Husayn saw me in this state, he chuckled and began patting me on the shoulder again. Then he sang:

Indeed, wine is no match for its magic
As it leaps through one's soul, then comes to rest.
It kindles a rapturous blaze inside
And, though a mere plant, shows you life's best!

Interrupting him, I said calmly, "May God forgive me for my outburst, and may you forgive me too, sir. Sometimes I suffer from fits of despair. And when that happens, I do not know why I should have to go on living and enduring any more pain and misery."

Then I said many more things in the same vein, as though I wanted to confide all my thoughts to him in hopes of finding some relief. With his head bowed, Husayn listened as I poured out my heart, telling him my story and relating all the things I had suffered. When I had finished, there was a kind of numbness running through my limbs and joints, causing them gradually to grow limp.

Husayn looked up and said, "Listen, boy. What you need is some amusement. You need to be distracted by something. If you go on this way, you are going to explode and die."

Then, gulping slightly with a twinkle in his eye, he grinned mischievously and asked, "Do you know about women? I will take you to the brothel. You are bound to find some relief there."

Bewildered, I asked, "What is this brothel you speak of, sir?"

He laughed uproariously, his oversized Adam's apple quivering madly, as though I had said something amusing.

"It is a house like a basket of delectable fruits," he replied. "You examine them from all angles, then choose the type that suits your taste. There are white ones, yellow ones, black ones, and red ones. Then you satisfy your desire until your anxiety and tension are a thing of the past."

Despite my numbed, weakened state, I was so enraged, I forgot he was my boss in the oven room.

"Damn it all," I retorted angrily. "What do you think I am, anyway? Did I not tell you I used to be a sexton at the Qasr al-Sham' Church in Old Cairo? Do you think I have sunk that low?"

Then, feeling lost and overwhelmed, I started to cry again.

At a loss for words, the man seemed to feel even sorrier for me now.

"By God," he whispered affectionately, "you are more of a Hanbalite than Ibn Hanbal himself! Listen, you goodhearted boy, you. Why do you not learn to read and write Arabic, then? That would be a good thing for you to distract yourself with. It would improve the way you talk and help you get rid of your Coptic accent. Maybe that way you would stop saying *iddini, waddini, al-bata', al-batu'*!"

Then he started to chuckle again as he mimicked the way I spoke. At the same time, the idea struck a chord with me. I stopped crying and started thinking about what he had said. I fell silent for a while, then asked, "But why should I learn Arabic if I am a Copt? I can communicate in it now, and I do not have any problem speaking with the people around me here. Everyone understands what I say, and I understand what they say."

Looking at me attentively, Husayn replied, "I do not know, really. I am just trying to find a way to get you out of the state of mind you are in. I am trying to find a way for you to distract yourself from your worries and sorrows. I could teach you a bit every night while we are waiting for the ovens to get hot and for the food to get done."

Just then he jumped up quickly and took the 'akika out of the oven. I was startled at the sight of it, as I had ever laid eyes on such a dish before in all my life. When he saw me staring at it so intently and sensed my astonishment, especially when a servant came and took it to the kitchen to dish it into bowls, he said, "Do not be amazed. With every day that passes there are more wonders to behold. Here in the caliph's kitchen they cook up delicacies from all over the globe. The 'akika you just saw is a rare dish that is prepared nowhere but here. There are even lots of elite folks who are not familiar with it. I made it just now the way I saw them make it in the kitchen one time. What you do is this: You take the tender rump, then you cut it up, sauté it, and remove the melted fat. Then you take the rich meat, chop it into small pieces, toss them on top of the sautéed rump, and stir the mixture till it is browned. Then you pour water over it with a bit of salt and let it cook until it is completely done and the water has evaporated. After this you top it with finely ground dried coriander and cumin, Ceylonese cinnamon, ground pepper, and gum mastic, then stir it. After this you take some Persian milk as needed with some crushed garlic in it, then pour it in the kettle. You leave this until it comes to a boil, after which you lower the heat under the kettle the way I did a little while ago, and leave it on a low flame until the milk coagulates and its fat rises to the top. After this you sprinkle it with a pinch of finely ground cinnamon, wipe the sides of the kettle with a clean white cloth and remove it from the heat."

Then he started humming again until he was overcome with drowsiness, turned over on his back and went to sleep right where he was on the floor. As for me, I stayed awake thinking about all the things he had said and staring into the live embers as their flames danced merrily before me.

As the days passed, I ventured deeper and deeper into Husayn ibn Falih's soul and revealed to him the depths of my own. He had started teaching me the Arabic language, which I had begun learning earlier at the hands of my beloved Thawna in Egypt. This had been a cause of great thanksgiving to God, since what I had learned of the language helped me through the ordeal I suffered in Antioch, and the expressions I had mastered were my aid toward understanding those I met there.

Even so, it was under the tutelage of Husayn ibn Falih that I made truly great strides in Arabic. He was patient and persistent with me from the very beginning as he taught me to form the letters in a lovely, measured script. He brought me an inkwell and ink that he had made himself by mixing the soot that accumulated inside the oven room with high-quality Hadramawt resin. We would stay up late together every night. Sometimes we would talk together, then he would teach me something as we imbibed in hashish of the variety referred to as kayf. Thus it was that I began progressing little by little, and in so doing, I entered the world of Husayn ibn Falih. It was a world that dazzled me, leaving me like a bewitched person ascending a staircase that has no end and who, with every step he ascends, finds himself drawn in spite of himself toward the next step above. From time to time he would unveil to me another of the many faces that had heretofore remained hidden behind that dry, coarse mask that overlay his features, and the crude, uncouth manner that was seen by everyone he worked with.

With the passing of the days I realized that inside my teacher there was a chronic discontent that sabotaged any happiness he might hope for and any pleasure he might enjoy. Every now and then he would allow me to get a glimpse of the inner torments he suffered due to his never having known his father or learned who or where he was. It seemed to me he had never forgiven his mother, not because he had never known his father, but because of the premature demise which had caused her to betray him and leave him alone in this world. How he wished she had stayed by his side, even if it had meant giving him a thousand brothers or sisters by way of iniquity and the forbidden. Husayn's dream was to be able to leave Baghdad one day for his native Maragha in search of his unknown father, thereby to douse the flames of his torment. As it was, however, he seemed never to leave the palace for anything but to visit the brothel in Baghdad, where he could abandon himself to wanton songstresses of every color and race, then return with his spirit calmer and his soul at peace, albeit only for a time.

One day when both of us were calm and mellow thanks to our 'poor man's hashish,' I asked Husayn why he did not marry someone and stop flitting from one woman to another of this particular variety. The question slipped off my lips spontaneously, without planning or forethought. Hence, the minute I had uttered it I felt embarrassed, and wished I could take it back. I felt as though I had crossed a line of sorts, or as though I were sticking my nose where it did not belong. Husayn put me at ease with his response. At the same time, however, he plunged me into a new spiritual dilemma. For although I loved and revered him in some respects, I could not disregard his failings or the dark, mysterious side of his spirit. This latter aspect of his character was a kind of paganism or primitive barbarism that had remained unchanged rather than evolving upward into the human and the sublime.

Husayn let out a long laugh as though I had said something funny. When he finally settled down again, he hawked and said, "Marry? I never want to get married, Budayr. The fact is, I have something inside me that causes me to want all the women in the world. One would not be enough for me. Nor would two, three, or four. Sometimes I think to myself: It must be on account of my mother. Maybe I am trying to get back at her through my constant scurrying from one woman to another. Then at other times I think I am looking for a woman just like her, but never find her. I do not know. But I do not suppose I will ever marry no matter how long I live in this world."

As Husayn said this, he seemed like an outright infidel to me, or like someone who constantly totters on the brink between faith and unbelief, or between vice and virtue. I gazed intently into his eyes in the hope of finding something there that would satisfy my curiosity and enable me to see who he really was. Instead, however, he caught me off guard with a distressing question of his own.

"And how about you, smarty pants?" he asked. "Why do you not get married? Maybe that way you would stop pining over Amuna and Suwayla. Believe me, if I took you with me even just once to the brothel, it would possess you just as you are possessed by poor man's hashish right now. Or do you not have urges the way other men do? Do you not feel any need for women? Were you born impotent? Are you hopeless on that score?"

Furious with him, I said, "You have no right to speak to me that way! I do not want to go into such things."

I sorely regretted the question I had asked him, which had opened the door for him to breach the limits between us this way. When he realized how distraught I was, he patted me on the shoulder and apologized in an attempt to smooth my ruffled feathers.

Then he said, "Come on, let me teach you something new tonight."

If the truth be told, I was afraid to reveal my real thoughts on the question he had asked me before I had found the answer to it myself. I was still tormented by my desire for women. For in spite of everything—my bitterness and difficult experiences with women, my agonizing grief over Amuna and Suwayla, and the vow I had made to myself never to have anything to do with another woman in this world—my desire for them would still come upon me from time to time. I would meet Amuna and Suwayla in my dreams, and what happens to men in such situations would happen to me. Then I would wake up realizing that Satan had seduced me and ensnared me anew in uncleanness. As a consequence, I would become dejected and spend the entire day perplexed and anxious until, when evening rolled around, I could immerse myself anew in my work. Then Husayn would bring me a roll of hashish that would make me forget the state I had been in. If the truth be told, I had started to get used to this pernicious habit and would sometimes be miserable on account of it, though I had not yet realized that such things are forbidden. I began depending on it regularly since it brought me such relief, ushering me into gardens of paradise that had been prepared just for me.

In fact, it was as though these gardens were Eden itself, which I was seeing with my own eyes and touching with my own hands. I could even smell it and taste the things in it. I would remain in this state for hours at a time, strutting about in contentment and bliss until I was sober again.

Writing Arabic had caused countless veils to fall from my eyes. As I pondered my own affairs, I began pondering the affairs of the world as well. And the more I did this, the more my questions multiplied. I wanted to know about creation and the world. I do not know how it happened exactly, but Husayn ibn Falih would push me to ask one question after another. His teaching of me was a door which, when I opened it and walked through, led me to still other doors. And as I went through these doors, too, I came to understand many things, some of which had to do with Husayn himself. I had once thought that the only reason he ever left the palace was to visit the brothel, or to sniff out news about his father and try to locate him through those who had known his mother during the days she worked in the marketplaces. However, I eventually came to understand that the man had other affairs to attend to in the city as well. He belonged to a group of people whose aim, as he put it, was to establish justice on earth. I did not know anything about the group. However, Husayn would talk to me at length about the conditions of people in the City of the Caliphate, and about the thousands of hungry folks who could not find enough to eat from one day to the next while here in the palace, foods were distributed in obscene abundance among a tiny number of courtiers, servants, and slaves belonging to the caliph, who was immersed in earthly pleasures and lived as the foreign rulers had in the days of paganism. He would tell me that Islam was a religion of justice and equality in which neither blackness, whiteness, wealth, poverty, race, nor nationality justified discrimination among people or allowing one group to tyrannize another. He would talk to me about Muhammad, the Muslims' Prophet, and about his cousin, the Imam Ali. He would tell me how God-fearing, otherworldly and just they had both been, and how they had established fairness and equality among people. In their day, he said, Muslims' only criterion for distinguishing one person from another was the degree of this or that person's piety, uprightness, and fear of God.

When I found myself alone before going to sleep or when I went out on some errand relating to the oven room, I would reflect on all these things. I would compare Islam with my own religion and reflect on the points of similarity and contrast between them. And in the end I concluded that God is the Lord of all human beings everywhere, and that the essence of every religion is simply to guide people and motivate them to follow the path of peace and tranquility. The purpose of every religion is to elevate people's primitive, barbaric ways of perceiving things to more sublime human levels.

The time came when Husayn felt it was necessary to teach me the Qur'an so that I could truly master Arabic and take hold of it with confidence. After informing me that it was permissible for non-Muslims to read and recite the Qur'an provided they were living pure lives, he began helping me memorize some of its verses. And thus it was that I began making my entry into the gardens of the True Criterion, as Muslims refer to the Qur'an. As I became familiar with its verses and their meanings, I found them to be a source of well-being and wisdom. My heart began opening up to Islam ever so gradually, to the point where I started wishing I could be a Muslim. If the truth be told, I remained hesitant and skeptical for some time. My spirit was in a state of confusion and torment as I asked myself questions and as I imagined my beloved Thawna before me, answering them all. There were many times when I thought to myself: If Thawna were in my place, he would surely believe in what I've come to believe in, and he would surely embrace Islam as I myself would like to.

Then late one night as I was sitting alone in front of the ovens, thinking and staring into the flames, I remembered something Thawna had said to me once to the effect that when he was at a monastery in the Qalzam Desert, he had read in a certain ancient gospel—one of the gospels that were now rejected by the Church—that Jesus Christ had told his disciples that the 'son of the promise' had not been Isaac, but Ishmael, and that he himself had come to prepare the way for the awaited Messiah. In fact, he affirmed that he was not worthy to untie the thong of his sandals, and that this Messiah was Muhammad, the Prophet of the Muslims. He had also said that one of the signs of the Messiah's coming would be the fall of idol worship and the settling of a white cloud over him when he departed from one place to another. Thawna told me that the Church had rejected this gospel, known as the Gospel of Barnabus, which contains the message of this Barnabus as well as some of the words found in the Shepherd of Hermas and some things found in the other authentic gospels.

My thoughts had become confused when I remembered these things. For some time I did not move a muscle, so lost was I in thought about what Thawna's words might mean. And as I sat there in this state, I felt a hand touch my shoulder with gentle affection. I turned to see who it was, as I knew that everyone around me was asleep, including even my teacher, Husayn ibn Falih, and I was startled to find no one there. However, I heard Thawna whispering in my ear and saying to me forcefully and clearly, "What are you afraid of, for Heaven's sake? Do it, and leave everything in God's hands."

I do not know whether this was the moment when I announced to myself that I would enter Islam, or whether it was successive events thereafter that compelled me to do so. Decisive moments in life are always the most difficult ones, and the least certain. They are like gleams of light in which essence takes precedence over appearance, and in which the unchanging and the constant mingles with the new and the variable. In those moments answers get lost along with the questions: When? How? Why did this happen? They are the isthmus that both separates and links what one was and what one has become.

Be that as it may, by the end of that night I had done what I had never thought I would do, and had never intended to do. It was simply a destiny that had been preordained for me, a path I had no choice but to follow.

Shortly thereafter I dozed off, having made up my mind that as soon as I woke up, I would announce to Husayn ibn Falih my desire to declare myself a Muslim. We had taken some poor man's hashish together before he went to sleep, and I do not know how long I slept or how the time had passed while I was asleep. All I know is that I woke up in a fright, with Husayn shaking me violently and the crowing of the palace's roosters piercing my ears.

"Get up right away, Budayr! They are asking for a new brazier for the caliph. The firebrands in his chamber have nearly all gone out."

I jumped up in a rush and fetched the brazier, then began placing the hot coals in it with copper tongs that were shaped like a lion's jaw. Just as I was about to finish what I was doing and put on my sandals to be on my way, I heard him saying in a firm, commanding voice, "Be prepared, and do not be afraid."

I did not understand what he meant by what he had said, as I was still only half-awake. In any case, I proceeded quickly behind the guard who had come to request the coals, carrying the brazier with the greatest of care and attention. I followed him down one corridor after another, guided by the light of the torch in his hand. Then we began passing downward through a number of courtyards and anterooms, after which I followed him up a staircase until at last we reached a breathtaking door whose silver and gold trimmings glinted in the light of the guard's torch. The two sentries standing watch would not allow us to approach the door. Instead, one of them went up and knocked on it timidly several times, then took several steps back and gestured for me to come forward. As I began to step up to the door, it opened, and from beyond it there emanated the sounds of singing and merrymaking. A songstress's captivating, coquettish voice rang out, saying:

O night, tarry with me! I desire not the morning.
My daylight is the one in whose embrace I rest,
His face my full moon, his saliva my wine,
And his cheek, of all fruits, the best!

Then, in a flash, there appeared from behind the half-open door a slave girl as beautiful as any woman I had ever beheld. Standing before me clad in nothing but a diaphanous gown embroidered with gold and silver thread, she extended her hand, as delicately crafted as a silver decanter, to take the brazier from me.

Never as long as I live will I know for certain whether what I experienced in the moment that followed was real, or whether I was in a garden of bliss. Was it the poor man's hashish that had prepared me for what was to be, or would appear to be, or was it the Truth manifesting itself in visible form to everyone who had eyes to see? The slave girl appeared to me in a luminous, ethereal form, and for a moment, it seemed to me that I had seen her before. I froze in my tracks for an instant in disbelief, searching my mind for some elusive memory that had been sparked by the young woman before me. Then suddenly I remembered the dream I had had on the steamship as I was being exiled from Egypt. As I recalled the dream, I nearly swooned, since I realized that this slave girl was none other than the young woman who had pushed me through the water to dry land. Pitch-black night came flowing waterfall-like down to her hips, over the whiteness of her body as seen through the lovely gown. Meanwhile, her mouth, sweet as hyacinth, parted to reveal the lustrous teeth I had seen in my dream. Her eyes were the fire that had burned my senses when, as she gazed at me, I saw them glistening with a lustrous greenness. I felt the earth spinning beneath me and a volcano erupting in my blood, while tempestuous winds caused an upheaval in my chest. However, rather than falling to the floor with what I held in my hand—shaken as I was by a violent internal upheaval and on the verge of grabbing her breasts and pulling her toward me—I found myself reaching slowly and mechanically for the hot coals. Frozen in place with my gaze fixed on the luminous full moon shining before me, I started grabbing handfuls of the red-hot coals and squeezing them with all my might as firebrands far hotter and more intense smoldered inside me. Like someone with a touch of madness or demonic inspiration, I did not feel the slightest pain, and not a scream or moan escaped from my mouth. On the contrary, it was as though what I held between my palms and fingers was nothing but a handful of wind or cool water.

The slave girl looked at me in stupefaction, as did everyone else around me. By this time my hand had started to cook, and it was not long before the girl let out a scream so bloodcurdling, one would have thought the blast of God's final judgment had come upon her. Then she fell to the floor unconscious in front of everyone. I do not know how long I went on in that state. All I was aware of after this was that a man wearing a gold-embroidered cloak appeared, surrounded by an attentive entourage. As soon as the two sentries and the guard saw him, they prostrated themselves, and thus I realized that he was the caliph. Even so, I remained unfazed, indifferent to everything around me and unable to feel the searing heat of the fire as it consumed my skin and flesh. Upon seeing me in this state, and the slave girl lying on the floor, the man exclaimed in a tremulous voice, "Well done!"

Then, still shaken by the force of the surprise, he said with gravity and dignity, "May God have mercy on you and forgive us, you unfortunate young man. Go now. You are free. And the slave girl is yours."

Then he left us and went back in to where he had come from.

I left the caliph's palace the next morning with the slave girl in tow and my few belongings stuffed into a knapsack. All I had to my name was a few pennies they had given me, telling me that they were the caliph's gift to me along with the slave girl. I had also been given a signed and sealed note as proof that the slave girl was my possession and that I had the right to dispose of her however I chose: I could keep her, sell her, or give her away.

Upon my arrival back at the oven room the night before, my teacher Husayn ibn Falih had rushed to treat my wound with egg white and an aloe ointment and by sprinkling it with some flour. Despite the pain in my hand, which was still quite intense, I was nevertheless happy to have my freedom back. At the same time, though, a feeling of desolation came over me at the thought of having to leave Husayn ibn Falih. Besides this, I had the worry of being a foreigner in this land, where Husayn was the only person I knew. So here I was, obliged to part with him from that time onwards, and truthfully speaking, I was afraid I might end up miserable and lost, wandering aimlessly once again the way I had been in my younger years before I was taken in by the Church at Qasr al-Sham'.

However, Husayn ibn Falih, may God be his help always, had arranged everything for me. For as he escorted me out to the palace gate, he gave me a letter addressed to some of his friends, advising me to make my way to them in a certain part of the city. He said they would be loyal brothers to me and help me in every way they could.

Bearing a guarantee of safe passage from the caliph lest I be stopped or questioned by guards, city authorities, or anyone else, I proceeded out the gate with a trembling heart that was barely my own, and with the slave girl walking behind me. I was full of confusion and uncertainty, not knowing even whether to go left or right. At first I did not dare turn my head to look at the girl as she walked along wordlessly behind me. However, when we were out of sight of the caliph's palace, I looked her way. By this time I had given her situation a good deal of thought and, after mustering my courage and the strength needed to speak, I said to her, "You can leave me here. You are free from now on, and I have no need of you."

Upon hearing what I had said, her jaw dropped in disbelief and she stopped in her tracks. "And where will I go?" she asked. "I know no one in this city. I have lived in the caliph's palace ever since I was a young girl. So tell me, sir, for God's sake: What will I do? I beg you to keep me with you. I will be your bondmaid, wherever you go, forever!"

At a loss for words, I sensed the dilemma I had gotten myself into. When I came back to the oven room after what had happened to me at the entrance to the caliph's chamber, I had been stricken with a kind of disorientation and loss of feeling, and this despite Husayn ibn Falih's consolation, his attempts to reassure me, and the jokes he cracked about my having won a slave girl the likes of whom other men would not dare to dream, not to mention the fact that she had belonged to the caliph himself. I had lost all desire for anything in this world, and particularly for women. After everything that had transpired the previous night, I had come to see just how weak the soul is in the face of the desires of the flesh. I had seen how, within a matter of moments, bodily lusts can cause a person to plunge from the heights of his humanity to the depths of his animality. Not wanting myself to be this weak and depraved, I promised God never to let this happen with the charge He had just placed in my care. I promised never again to degrade and abase my spirit. Consequently, I found myself in a bad way, truly not knowing what I was to do with this slave girl.

At the same time I felt compassion for her.

"So, then," I said, "Come with me to where I am going. However, from this time forward you will be like a sister to me, like the daughter of my father and mother. No matter what happens, I will never lay a hand on you. And now, may God foreordain all good for you, and may He give me strength to endure myself and whatever the coming days bring."

As we walked on after that talking, I learned that her name was Rita, though this was not her original name. She had been called Tamara by her mother, whom she remembered well and still pined for from time to time. She had been kidnapped as a young girl in a raid by thieves on the place where her nomadic family had been staying, and from the time she had been sold to a slave trader in Baghdad, she had lost track of her family entirely. From that time on, she said, she had been passed from one master to another until the last man who had owned her presented her as a gift to the caliph. The caliph had then given her a place in his social gatherings due to her skill at playing musical instruments and her beautiful singing voice.

Following the map Husayn al-Maraghi had drawn for me with such meticulous care, I went down streets and winding alleyways, sometimes to the right, sometimes to the left. Then I crossed bridges over the river until at last my slave girl and I found ourselves in an area of the city known as Khan Abi Ziyad. Once there, I inquired about the person I was seeking, namely, Shihab al-Hallaj, or Shihab the cotton ginner. When we arrived at our destination, the day was quite far advanced, bathed in the light of a potent, obdurate sun that knew no mercy. People pointed me in the direction of a place where I found a man ginning cotton in his shop together with a young boy. When he saw me standing at his door, he rose to receive me and I came forward and introduced myself, telling him about my situation. Then I gave him a note that Husayn ibn Falih had written to him. Upon reading the note, he gestured to one of his boys to take me to a nearby area where his home was located. As we drew nearer to the house, I noted that it was spacious and distinguished-looking by comparison with those adjacent to it. At the same time, it was plain and symmetrical, its walls spattered with red clay. As we followed the boy in, we came upon low-ceilinged rooms built of rough-hewn wood. As for the top floor, it contained rooms along whose walls there ran raised benches on legs made of unbaked brick and stone covered haphazardly with clay.

The boy then called from outside the door to the residents of the household. In response we heard the voice of a woman who appeared to be Shihab al-Hallaj's wife, since he said to her, "Your husband sends his greetings, and has sent you this man and his slave girl. Please make them feel at home."

Before long there emerged a woman of whom nothing was visible but two large, almond-shaped eyes. She greeted us and asked the boy to take us up to one of the house's upper rooms so that we could get settled and rest a bit. Once we were in the room, the boy disappeared briefly and went to consult with the woman who had received us, after which he returned with a bowl of quince and apples and a drink made from rosewater that was the most delicious I've ever tasted in my life.

In the meantime I was still thinking about the slave girl, concerning whom I had become of two minds, and uncertain whether to let her go or keep her. When Shihab returned home near nightfall after finishing work in his shop, he sat with me and I spoke to him frankly of what I was thinking in connection with the girl, and how I wanted to part with her in a way that would cause her no harm.

After thinking the matter over a bit, Shihab advised me to let the question rest for a few days so that God's will concerning the girl could become apparent. Then he got up and took her to be with his wife, who could be a sister to her of sorts. At the same time, he told me that once my hand had healed and I was able to work again, he would find me employment in the marketplace so that I could earn my living and face whatever the coming days would bring.

During my stay in Shihab's house, I would occasionally get a whiff of some sweet fragrance, and I was amazed that such a location could receive such a sweet-smelling breeze. So, when my relationship with the cotton ginner had become closer thanks to the time he spent with me every evening after finishing his day's work and the ease that had developed between us, I said to him, "Your house has a pleasant fragrance that never goes away. It makes me feel as though I am in a rose garden or a meadow of flowers. You and your family are so lucky to live in a place like this, which may be the only one of its kind on earth!"

"Is that what you think?" Shihab replied with a chuckle. "The fact is, son, that my wife manufactures perfume and fragrant oils here in the house, then sells her wares to hawkers and women who come to buy from her."

He then promised to show me the place where she worked in the house. The next morning, Shihab accompanied me to a lower room near the front of the house's courtyard, where I found untold numbers of bottles, small and large: some copper, others silver, others glass, and all of them filled with perfumes. There were also containers filled with flower essences. Shihab would have me sniff some of them, after which he would tell me something about them: One was taken from violets, another from nenuphar, that is, European white water lily, or from the narcissus, the kardah, the iris, and so forth. There was a collection of beautiful wooden containers carved in the shapes of birds, and which were filled, he told me, with extracts from lilies, myrtle, marjoram, sweet basil, and bitter orange. I was astonished at all this, and at the fact that his wife did this type of work. I held him in some awe as a result of it, as I did her, since it was apparent to me that he respected his wife and appreciated the work she did.

Shihab al-Hallaj sent me to work for a friend of his by the name of Afif al-Warraq, whose surname means 'the manuscript copyist and paper manufacturer.' This man's occupation was book production. Hence, people would give him things they had written, and he would make handwritten copies of them and bind them with paper and inks that he produced himself. The end product was always something beautifully and masterfully done, which preserved for posterity what their authors had penned.

The way this came about was both providential and entirely coincidental: One night as I was writing down some lessons that Husayn ibn Falih had taught me, Shihab came into my room and saw what I had written. It was a lovely Qur'anic verse from the chapter entitled, al-'Asr, which reads, "Consider the flight of time! Verily, man is bound to lose himself. . . ." Delighted with my script, the man said, "My Heavens, you have beautiful handwriting! By God, I think your problems are over. Tomorrow I will send you to see Afif al-Warraq, and you will make him a very happy man."

Afif's shop was located in the Tuesday Market near Ivory Lane in the Door of the Arch area. I had been taken by the Tuesday Market from the first time I ever set foot in it on account of its spaciousness and its numerous lanes. There was a lane for oil vendors, a lane for cobblers, a watermelon market, and a soap market. I learned later that one year on the night before 'Id al-Fitr, which is the holiday that falls at the end of Ramadan, these merchants had sold 502,000 ratls of soap based on the calculation that each person needs a ratl of soap on the night before this holiday. As for the oil vendors, they sold 1,108.5 jars of oil, with each jar being the equivalent of sixty ratls.

Afif was a calm, taciturn man whom I rarely saw with a happy look on his face. On the contrary, he looked to me as though he was in a constant state of worry and preoccupation. His hair was grayed and his face full of wrinkles despite the fact that he still had a long way to go before approaching middle age. He had a constant habit of grinding his molars, like someone who is bearing up under misery and hardship or suppressing a never-ending rage. In the beginning I used to think his reticence and long-suffering were part of his God-given nature. However, after I had gained some experience in the arts of his craft, I came to realize that his profession may well be one that requires such qualities. After all, refined sensitivity, seriousness, and patience are necessary prerequisites for anyone who pursues the work of the stationer, the calligrapher, the scribe, the illuminer, or the bookbinder. For all such tasks call for a kind of creativity that only emerges through the use of one's imagination and the art of properly arranging and focusing one's thoughts.

A place of pilgrimage for everyone who occupied himself with writing literature and recording the sciences, Afif's shop ushered me into a world that I had never known before, namely, the world of study and research. Those who needed things to be copied would meet there frequently, whereupon long exchanges would ensue and debates would heat up over their varied and sometimes conflicting ideas. I would listen to all this as I worked on whatever tasks my teacher had assigned me, and thus it was that in that small place, I witnessed with my ears things I had never seen with my eyes. I came to understand the ideas and beliefs of peoples I had never so much as caught a glimpse of. I became familiar with scholars and personalities of note who, through what they had written, had become veritable suns and moons in their various sciences and disciplines. I would make the rounds of Baghdad while sitting at my desk, recording the fruits of its thought and the distillations of its intellect. And in this way I became convinced that she was the greatest metropolis in this entire earthly realm: She was at once a mosque and a pub; a Qur'an reciter and a reed pipe player; a pious devotee who awaits the dawn after spending the night in prayer, and someone having a morning draught in a public garden; one man who's spent his night in worship and devotion, and another in singing and merrymaking; the surfeit of wealth and the desolation of poverty; religious doubts and the certainty of faith.

When I first started out in Afif's employ, I was set to work macerating cotton, which was sometimes derived from the remains of Shihab al-Hallaj's ginning operation and sometimes from other ginners at the marketplace. My job was to mix the remains of the cotton with old rags and water until they had been properly macerated and kneaded, at which point they were fit to be spread out to dry. The apprentices and other assistants who worked for Afif were not allowed to observe the process of spreading out the paper mixture, how the exact thinness or thickness of the paper was determined or what went into making it suitable for writing and copying. This caused me some consternation in the beginning. However, I later came to understand that this was common practice among stationers. After all, it would not be proper for anyone but them to be privy to the secrets of the craft. Hence, such secrets remained in their possession in such a way that they alone could master the art and practice it as they themselves saw fit.

There was a particular type of paper that was aged. Sweet, pure water would be placed in suitable copper containers. To this would be added high quality corn flour and the mixture would be boiled down. A small amount of saffron was added for coloring, then it was poured into large bowls or pots, after which the paper was dipped gently into the mixture. Then it was spread out to dry in such a way that the edges of the paper would not stick to each other. Whenever it had dried a bit, it would be turned over lest it stick to the surface on which it rested, and in this way the paper would be brought to a state of perfect readiness for use in writing.

One day as we were busily engaged in our work at the shop, we heard loud shouting and wailing. We all jumped up to see what the matter was, and what should we find but that a huge fire had broken out in the pearl and bead artisans' market. People were rushing to put it out as water carriers ran back and forth with pails. When, several hours later, things had settled down and it became apparent that what had burned extended from the front of the market to the Harrani Arch, it was said that what had caused the fire to break out was that a camel bearing a load of reeds had been passing through the pearl and bead market. As the camel passed by, a man had been making a hole in a pearl and had some fire in his hand. The ends of the reeds on the camel's back came in contact with the fire and burst into flames, and it was only a matter of moments before the flames were making their way toward the camel. When it felt the heat of the flames, it bolted. Sparks went flying right and left, and everything in its path started to burn. The camel kept running until it met its end, many people in the houses and buildings that went up in flames died as well, and a great deal of property and wealth was lost.

In the beginning, Afif would not allow me to copy manuscripts. After all, I was still ignorant and inexperienced in this great art, which requires skill and dexterity. Instead, he assigned this task to two assistants who helped him with the innumerable books he was asked to copy by seekers of knowledge, businessmen, and anyone else who needed this or that manuscript copied for whatever reason. The best paper was snow-white, flexible, glossy, perfectly proportioned, and durable. The highest quality type of paper I saw was the Baghdad variety, which was thick but flexible with delicate, evenly proportioned edges and of the recognized, standard size. In general, nothing was copied onto this type of paper but the Holy Qur'an, though it may also have been used by those responsible for recording government correspondences. The next best type of paper was the Syrian variety, which was divided into two categories, Damascene and Hamawite, and which was inferior to the Baghdad variety. Next in order of quality was Egyptian paper, which was rarely glossy on both sides, while the type that had both a glossy front and a glossy back was referred to as masluh. Then there was the fawa paper, which was cut to a small size, as well as being thick, rough, and stiff. This type was not used for writing, but rather, for wrapping sweets, perfumes, and the like. As for the most inferior type of all, it was the paper made by the Byzantines and the Europeans, which wears out quickly. I happened to see some once when a man passed by to see Afif in his shop. He was a spice merchant who traveled far and wide and would sometimes go to the Republic of Venice. He showed Afif some of this paper, which was in the form of a document written in Latin script related to some aspect of his business.

Little by little Afif began to teach me the secrets of ink manufacturing. As a result, I came to know which type of ink is appropriate for each type of paper. The type he taught me to make is referred to as tobacco ink, and in order to prepare it, one takes a ratl of Syrian oak apples and crushes them coarsely. These are soaked for one week in six ratls of water with a small amount of myrtle. This mixture is then boiled down to two-thirds or one-half of its original volume, after which it is strained through a cloth and left for three days, then strained once again. Finally, one uqiya each of Arabic gum and Cyprian vitriol is added to each ratl of the resulting liquid. Enough of this 'tobacco ink' is added for the degree of blackness desired. In addition, one must add some aloe and honey to it, since aloe prevents flies from falling into it, while honey preserves it for long periods of time. One-third of an uqiya of the 'tobacco' is needed for each ratl of ink after the tobacco has been crushed thoroughly with the heel of the hand together with crystallized sugar, saffron fibers, and verdigris. However, it must not be crushed in a mortar lest it lose its superior quality.

After this he began gradually to let me take part in the actual copying of manuscripts. I had begun exhibiting the qualities he prized in connection with this craft, namely, attention to detail, perseverance in drawing and writing, skill in sharpening the pencils used in the craft, an understanding of which letters were to be formed with which edge of the pen and how to repair the nib of the pen in the proper manner. I had also mastered, at least to a certain degree, the shape and design of the various Arabic letters and how to gauge their correctness. The alif, for example, is a compound shape consisting of a line which stands up perfectly straight, leaning neither to the left nor to the right. As for its height, it comes to eight points with the pen with which the letters are written, while its width is to be one-eight of its height. And thus I discovered that the shape and design of each letter has its own secret and cause. The first thing I ever copied in the measured style of the calligrapher was a type of protective incantation or formula, sometimes referred to as an amulet. I had thought at one time that such things were only written in the ancient pagan language, the way pagan priests had done in Egypt, and as I had observed more than once with my beloved Thawna. Afif informed me that amulets were the concern of some Muslim sheikhs and that it was preferable for lay people not to occupy themselves with them. However, people would frequently come to him and request that he copy amulets for them. The strangest thing I ever wrote of this nature was an amulet that had been brought to us by a man who wanted to be able to fly in the air. I copied the formula from a parchment according to which it was among the works of 'the seven words' known as the qirashiya, which is guaranteed to bring its intended result provided that it be used only in seeking God's favor, and not for any purpose that would occasion God's displeasure. I was told that after the recitation of the names, it had to be perfumed with the smoke produced by burning aloe. This is what I wrote:

47265 hah qirash hah hitza khurash gah mundhu iqshatasna hah. 'Antalantahasna hah 'ada naqasha hah dina naqashna hah kataltaysan tal'ud latasna hah. By the right of some of you over some others, by the right of the seven planets, and by the right of Him whose name and obedience to Whom is incumbent upon you: You must fulfill my request and come to my aid. I have sworn to you by the Yellow King, by the right of the Red King, and by your right over each other, that you must fulfill my request and come to my aid. Come to my aid! I have sworn to you by Yagog and Magog, by Harut and Marut that you must fulfill my request!

The best thing that ever happened to me in Afif's shop was my getting to know a young man my age by the name of Yashkuri. One of the most handsome men I had ever laid eyes on, he had an endearing appearance and a moonlike face fit for a king or a prince. However, I had noticed that he rarely spoke with anyone, and he did not gather with us at lunchtime despite the fact that Afif had established the custom of having his workers eat together after the noon prayer, with him in their midst. Instead, Yashkuri would go on busily with his work in the area of the shop where books were embellished and gilded. He was one of the most skilled hands Afif had in these particular crafts. Once day I came in to his work area after the mid-afternoon prayer and found him having his lunch off to one side of the room. Startled, I assumed he refrained from eating with us out of pride and disdain.

"So," I said jokingly, "do you think we are going to keep tabs on how much you eat if you come sit with us? Or that we are going to steal your food? Do you not know about the table manners Afif imposes on us? We eat politely, with just three fingers, and we only dip into the food that is right in front of us. We do not go after the best morsels or dip out of the center of the tray. We lick our fingers before we wipe them on the cloth, and we take three separate drinks from the tin mug rather than gulping everything down at once. Before we sit down to eat, we wash our hands with potash, and we do the same after we have finished. And we wipe our mouths, too."

Clearly dismayed at my suggestion that his abstention from eating with us was due to pride or contempt, his eyes welled up with tears. The reason he did not eat with other people, he explained, was that most of them were repulsed by those with an illness like his. Then, apologizing for what he was about to do, he rolled up his sleeves for me, allowing me to see the leprosy that had afflicted his arms and the luminous appearance it gave his skin. Beginning at his wrists, it extended up his forearms in haphazard, map-like patterns. He told me that most people refused to have anything to do with him on this account, and that if it were not for his deftness and skill in the areas of embellishment and gilding, which were his specialties, Afif would not have let him continue working with him after he was afflicted with the disease. On hearing this, I was deeply pained. I sensed clearly that I had been unfair to him and that by saying what I had said, had stirred up feelings of bitterness on his part. I thought back on my beloved Thawna, who used to mix with lepers and go down to the places where they lived in the deserts on the Feast of Jonah. He would gather them together himself, clothe them, and speak words of comfort to them. I, too, got tears in my eyes as the memories stirred up my own sorrows.

From that day onward, touched by his sorrow and his self-imposed isolation, I was Yashkuri the leper's constant companion. He, for his part, softened toward me and came to trust me to the point where he opened his heart and began pouring out his woes to me. He slept in an attic room over the shop, and so thorough was his personal exile, he would only go out for absolute necessities, especially in view of the fact that he had emigrated from Kufa some time earlier and had no family in Baghdad. Instead, his primary occupation outside the shop was attending gatherings of mystic ascetics and their spiritual mentors, whose conversation brought peace to the soul, solace to those who had little in this world, and a means of rising above the trials of this earthly existence.

Sometimes, after we had finished our work in Afif's shop, the two of us would go out at sunset and walk for exercise along the Moses Beach, which runs directly past the caliph's palace. We would go on walking and talking for an hour or two until we came to the place where the water branched into two forks, one of which led to the market for riding animals then flowed in the direction of the provender vendors, and one of which led to Dar Banuqa, where it came to an end. When Yashkuri's mood had grown mellow from the sight of the water and the verdure around us, his heart would open and he would confide in me some of what he was thinking and feeling. I thus learned that there was a woman he had loved with a passion and, after considerable effort, had managed to win her hand. However, she had divorced him when he was afflicted with his disease. As a result, he had grown even more dejected and had cursed Fate for having withheld from him what it had granted to others by way of the affection of those he had loved and cherished. For a time he had been in such anguish that he thought of taking his own life. However, during that same period of time, he had come to work in Afif's shop, where he came to realize things he had not realized before. For in this place, he said, he had discovered that Baghdad was not merely a city — rather, it was cities and countries. In fact, the marketplaces for words and ideas in Baghdad outnumbered those for grains and other basic provisions. It was worlds interlinked, ideas in conflict, and inspired, authoritative texts along with their human interpretations. All this, he told me, had opened his eyes to meanings he had not perceived before. As a result, he had begun to lay aside his worries and occupy himself instead with scholastic theology and theologians. Then one day there fell into his hands a book he had been asked to gild, entitled *The Book of Doubts*, which had impressed him deeply. When I asked him what had impressed him about the book, he told me that it had caused him to doubt things in the past to the point where he imagined that they had not taken place, and to doubt things that had never been to the point where he imagined that they had actually happened. He had even begun to doubt whether his wife had actually left him and begun living as though she had not, even though she really had. He also doubted having read *The Book of Doubts*!

He had believed in the necessity of knowing and giving thanks to the Giver of Blessings, knowing the difference between good and evil, and pursuing the former and avoiding the latter. He had also believed that before the descent of revealed scriptures, people had been able to depend on their human reason but that in spite of this, people are veiled by their minds from the truth, both those who have been told about the Apostle and those who have not. He had believed in many things of this sort. However, he had then become aware of more and more questions and issues. He observed the way people make war on each other with arguments and proofs, and he had seen the appalling conditions in which the common folk were living. The scholastic theologians were in one world, and the ordinary populace in another. While people lived in penury and deprivation, scholastic theology offered them nothing to meet their needs or ward off their hunger. Consequently, they had fallen prey to vagabonds, scoundrels, and villains, who made sport of their hunger and used them as firewood to fuel their wars against the caliph, his army, and others in positions of authority. He had vacillated and his thoughts had been scattered for a time until, in the end, he had decided to turn away from scholastic theology and its proponents. Instead he had chosen to follow the path of the knowers of God, the wayfarers who seek the pure divine love. He had divorced and forsaken this earthly existence and, in so doing, had won the love of God and the true knowledge of religion.

My admiration for Yashkuri grew with every passing day, and his influence on me became gradually clearer. I had become certain that my own problem was nearly identical to his, and that our respective ordeals in this world were near mirror images of one another. Similarly, I was certain that the way in which our fates had become intertwined was none other than a blessing of Divine Providence, a sign of God's loving, watchful eye upon me. Hence, I began sticking closer and closer to him. He had struck me with the idea of rising above everything outward and apparent, and I realized that the pain and sorrow in my own soul were companions of sorts to the pain and sorrow in his. I saw that our common perception of the futility of existence and the fragility of everything visible and perceptible to the senses, everything embodied and concrete, owed to the confluence of our respective circumstances, and that my desire to renounce the world and distance myself from people was similar to his, and this despite the fact that, unlike Yashkuri, I suffered no illness or defect that would drive people away from me or cause me to avoid them and keep to myself.

One day a man came to Afif, handed him a book, and offered to pay him two hundred dirhams to copy it for him. Afif leafed through the book briefly, then hit the ceiling. I had never seen him so angry in all the time I had known him. He gave the book back to the man abruptly, saying, "No, by God, I will not do it. In fact, I would not do it for all the riches of Qarun!"

After the man had left and we had all gathered around Afif thinking that something terrible had happened, he sat there muttering in indignation, and in an obvious state of pain and distress. Afif felt comfortable with me and treated me kindly. He had affectionately dubbed me "the Egyptian," and would kid me for the way I pronounced the letter jim like the French letter *j* the way the Persians do. So, later, when all the other workers had gone their separate ways and I was alone with him, I begged him to tell me what was in the book. He replied that the man who had come to him was a relative of his who followed a religion that Afif himself had followed before he became a Muslim. Known as Kiyumarthism, it was a religion that had spread in ancient times, and which some people still followed. He said that the man had given him an ancient book on this religion that he wanted him to copy for him in secret. However, it was a book that promoted unbelief and falsehood, as it contained the arguments that had been put forward by followers of Kiyumarth, the religion's founder, to the effect that there are two first principles in the universe known as Yazdan and Ahrumun. According to the followers of Kiyumarth, Yazdan had existed from all eternity, whereas Ahrumun was created and temporal. What had led to the creation of Ahrumun was that Yazdan once wondered to himself: If I had a competitor, what would he be like? Now, this was a bad thought which ill-befit the nature of Light. As a result, darkness came into being, and this darkness was called Ahrumun. Ahrumun was evil by nature, predisposed to dissension, corruption, iniquity, treachery, and mischief. Hence, it rebelled against the Light and opposed it both in nature and in deed. War then broke out between the hosts of Light and the hosts of Darkness. Eventually, the angels mediated a truce between the two forces in which it was stipulated that the lower world would be under the sole jurisdiction of Ahrumun for seven thousand years, after which he would depart from the world and hand it over to the Light. They also said that those who had been in the world before the truce had been exterminated. The book contained all sorts of other vain prattle as well.

Afif said, "The man wanted to take advantage of the fact that I am a relative of his mother's and that we have known each other since childhood. However, I became a Muslim, thanks be to God, whereas he still follows the religion of our ancestors. He even has children with names that are sacred according to his religion, such as Ribas, Misha, and Mishana, the latter two being the mother and father of mankind according to their traditions."

As Afif was telling me this, I suddenly thought back on what had happened when Thawna and I were at the Atrib Monastery.

"So then," I interrupted enthusiastically, "They are Sabeans! How amazing!"

"No," he corrected me. "They are entirely different from the Sabeans. The Kiyumarthites are Zoroastrians, whereas the Sabeans are one of two sects that date back to the time of the Prophet Abraham, upon him be peace. The followers of the other of these two sects are known as the 'hanifs,' or followers of the true, monotheistic religion. As for the Sabeans, they said, 'In order to know God Almighty and obey His commands, we need a mediator. However, given the intelligence and purity of spiritual beings and their nearness to the Lord of lords, this mediator has to be a spiritual being, not a material one, since a physical being will be a human being like us, who eats what we eat and drinks what we drink, and who resembles us in both substance and form.' They said, just as it is written in our wise holy book, "'And indeed, if you pay heed to a mortal like yourselves, you will surely be the losers!" Given the fact that the Prophet Abraham was assigned the task of wiping out false teaching and establishing the pristine way of the hanifs, the idol-worshipers protested both in word and deed. Abraham then said to his father Azar, "O my father! Why dost thou worship something that neither hears nor sees and can be of no avail whatever to thee?" "And then he broke those idols to pieces, all save the biggest of them." In so doing, he was issuing a binding command through action just as, by breaking the idols, he silenced his opponents. At last he completed his task, as God tells us in the words, "And this was Our argument which We vouchsafed unto Abraham against his people: for We do raise by degrees whom We will. Verily, thy Sustainer is Wise, All-knowing."'"

Yashkuri had informed me that Afif al-Warraq was of Persian origin and that he was a former Zoroastrian who had embraced Islam. He had also told me that some of Afif's family still practiced Zoroastrianism. However, despite the fact that Afif was a Muslim and a believer in the oneness of God, it was apparent to me that he was a follower of this or that sect. For although he was a partisan of Imam Ali, there was a particular group that he met with periodically. I picked up on this fact over time, having observed members of this group coming to visit him now and then. When they met, they would converse freely with each other about all manner of things, and I realized that they were among those who opposed the caliph and bore resentment against him because of people's miserable conditions and his way of managing affairs. On more than one occasion I had heard them cracking jokes about the caliphate's pomp and obscene extravagance when the Byzantine emissaries had been received, saying that the lavish display of wealth on that day had exceeded even what the Khosraus, emperors, and pharaohs had been known for in their day. They said that in Baghdad and elsewhere in the lands under the caliph's rule, there were untold numbers of people who went to bed every night on an empty stomach. The common people, they said, could not tolerate any more and had begun rising up everywhere against this foolishness, a fact that was bound to lead to unrest, tribulation, ruin, and the displacement of many who lived on the land. As a consequence, people like Abu Muslim al-Khurasani, Sunpadh, Ishaq al-Turk, and Ustadh Sis might give leadership to revolts if things went on this way. In fact, consequences far more dire and bitter might be in the offing.

As I progressed in copying and writing, Afif would give me increasingly important and refined manuscripts to work on until, eventually, he began letting me work on the critical translations that were being done by fine scholars and masters of knowledge and wisdom from Greek, Syriac, Persian, Sanskrit, and Coptic in every branch of the sciences and arts. Whenever I finished copying one book and was about to begin another, I felt as though I were leaving one paradise and entering another. There was a man who was constantly bringing Afif works that he had translated or written. He seemed to have a superhuman mind and a capacity for work and research that surpassed that of the jinns themselves. I was so dazzled by his work that I held him in utter awe. On one occasion, Afif gave me a treatise that this man had written on matters relating to women and childbirth. It happened some time after this that Yashkuri told me of a twin sister of his—his only sibling—who had married a well-to-do merchant from Kufa who was going to take her with him to Andalusia and settle with her there in a city known as Tulaytila. Kawaʻib—which was his sister's name—was pregnant with her first child, and Yashkuri was afraid she might go into labor on the way there. Given the circumstances, he wanted to be able to do something for her. Consequently, I decided to make him a copy of this venerable man's treatise in the hope that she might benefit from it if she did, in fact, go into labor while she was traveling.

The treatise, which has to do with pregnancy from its earliest stages, tells us that when a woman first determines that she is pregnant, she should rest and leave off strenuous activity, including anything that might disturb the fetus by way of hopping, shouting, carrying heavy objects, coming down from an elevated spot or coming up from a low one. The writer advises the pregnant woman to minimize her intake of refreshments so that her nerves will be taut, and to go easy on things that she craves, since taking in too much spicy or sour food can weaken the fetus, while clay will cause it to grow cold. At the same time, she should take large amounts of sekanjabin in order to relieve the burning, since the cravings experienced by a pregnant woman involve a process of burning up what remains of the woman's menstrual blood. From the fifth month onward, hair begins to grow on the fetus's head, at which point the pregnant mother should take in large amounts of those things that generate blood so long as there is nothing to indicate that they can be done without, such as the continuation of the woman's menses during pregnancy. The woman is to carry on in this manner until her due date approaches. If she suffers from 'hot illnesses,' she is to limit herself to cold beverages, which include, for example, sekanjabin with honey. If there is a dire need for a laxative, this should be achieved with cucumber or manna, which is an exudate of the flowering ash, since medicines with a laxative effect either cause miscarriages or weaken the fetus due to the fact that they dissolve the mother's waste products into the fetus's source of nourishment. When it comes time to give birth, the mother should take in large amounts of things that cause the digestive and reproductive tracts to become 'slippery' and massage the lower abdomen with oils such as almond oil and violet oil. She should also bathe frequently and apply hot compresses made with cooked saltwort and fenugreek, which ease childbirth. When she feels the approach of labor, which involves sharp contractions and the descent of water and blood, she should sit on an elevated spot with her legs spread far apart, and she should depend on a midwife to deliver the baby. If the process is easy, it is as it should be. Otherwise, the midwife should palpate her back and her upper abdomen and give her a sniff of cucumber peels with saffron, then tie a clean silk rag spread with butter around her left thigh. If the baby's head appears, it means it will be a normal delivery. Otherwise, it will be a difficult one. If it is born in the winter months, it should be received in some soft cotton or silk and be kept away from the cold. Then the mother should wrap herself up well and drink things that will help to dissolve the afterbirth, such as infusions of aniseed, dill, fenugreek, and raisins with honey. In the winter, she should be rubbed with oil in which garlic and labdanum have been heated.

As for the newborn, its umbilical cord should be cut off to a length of about four finger-widths, then tied with a light woolen cord and dressed with a rag moistened with oil in which cumin, thyme, and a bit of salt and myrrh have been cooked. The infant's body should be rubbed with salt, shadhina—also known as 'blood stone'—myrtle, myrrh, and costus, either mixed together or separately, which makes its body stronger and protects it from yeast infections and lice. If the stub of the umbilical cord falls off within three or four days, it should be dressed with a stocking and oil, sea shell ashes or lead sulfide, dragon's blood, turmeric and moss in order to dry it out. The baby is rubbed with salt in order to protect it from dirt and lice; however, the nose is not rubbed with salt due to its inability to tolerate it. The baby's eyes are washed by placing drops of oil in them, after which it is wiped with something soft, while its members are immersed in the desired manner and its bladder massaged in order for it to release urine as it ought to. The anus is opened up with one's little finger and the same is done to the nose after the baby's fingernails and toenails have been trimmed to prevent them from causing it injury. The baby is then swaddled, neither too loosely nor too tightly, bearing in mind that a female infant should be swaddled more loosely around the middle lest she be unable to conceive later in life. The baby's lower abdomen and the folds in its skin should be daubed with powdered myrtle and oil for fear of its getting diaper rash, and it should be washed with tepid water every three days except in the winter time, and with the exception of infants that have a tendency to get a fever, which should be washed every seven days. And of course, one must take care to be gentle when pouring the water, handling the baby's joints, undressing and dressing it, and in drying and massaging it with oil.

It happened once that the man stopped coming around for a period of time. It surprised me, and I wondered what might have caused him to grow lax after coming to us so regularly for so long given his great need for our services. However, Afif informed me that he had died of psilosis, and that two months before his demise he had begun translating a book by Galen on the principles of medicine production. He also told me that until the time he fell ill he had been in fine health and pursuing his riding habit. However, it was well known concerning him that after going riding every day, he would go into the bath and water would be poured over him. Then he would come out wrapped in a plush robe, have a glass of wine and some cake and recline until his perspiration had dried. Then he might go to sleep, get up again and perfume himself with incense, at which time he would be served his food, which consisted of a large, fatted pullet that had been cooked zirbaj-style along with a loaf of bread that weighed one hundred dirhams. He would sip on the broth, eat the chicken and bread, and go to sleep. When he woke up, he would drink four ratls of aged wine, and if he had a craving for succulent fruit, he would eat Syrian apples and quince. And this had been his custom until he died.

Despite Afif's wariness of speaking with me about certain things, he would periodically give me a book that I was to deliver to this or that location in the 'City of Peace' after nightfall. He would warn me not to allow anyone to see me, especially a spy or a policeman, and he would give me a thorough, precise description of the location or house to which I was to deliver the writings. At first I thought they concerned people he dealt with in relation to manuscript reproduction or paper manufacturing. However, one time, after he had warned me with a special urgency of the need for circumspection, I succumbed—may God forgive me—to a wicked impulse to peek at the document I had been entrusted with. When I opened and read the book he had given me, I discovered that it was a hand-drawn map that I was to deliver to a friend of his in the neighborhood known as Rayd al-Zuhayriya. When I saw it, my heart skipped a beat. As I speculated concerning what it might mean and the purpose for which it was being sent to this man, I concluded that something momentous must lie behind it.

It looked like this:

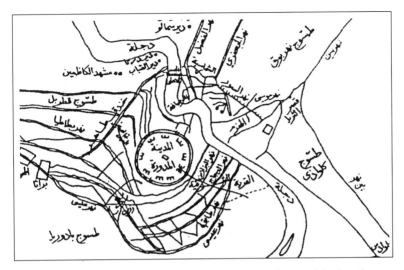

When I was back at the shop the next morning and had a chance
to take my friend Yashkuri aside, I told him what had happened to me
in connection with the map. He remained silent for a few moments,
then told me that I should keep quiet about it and not let on to Afif
that I had any interest in the matter. Even so, I begged him to let me
in on what it meant, and at last he said, "Afif is an adherent of a sect
known as the Nazzamiya, which mixes the ideas of philosophers with
those of another sect by the name of the Mu'tazila." He told me that
the Nazzamiya followed the confused ideas set forth by its founder,
Ibrahim al-Nazzam, who said, "The Creator cannot truly be described
as having a will. For although He is described legitimately in connection with His actions as being possessed of a will, what such statements
really mean is that He is their Creator. If God is described as willing
or desiring the actions of His creatures, what is meant by this is that
He commands them and prohibits them." He also said, "The actions of
creatures are nothing but movements. Stillness or silence is a movement of dependence, while knowledge and desire are movements of
the soul." However, in speaking of a movement, he was not referring
simply to a shift from one place to another. Rather, the term 'movement' as he used it refers to the beginning of some change, as when
the philosophers affirm 'movements' in manner, quantity, situation,
place, and time. This Nazzam ibn Sayyar had put forward a number of
confused notions of this sort, and of which Afif was quite enamored.

He also said, for example, that "Man is, in reality, soul and spirit, of which the body is the instrument and mold." He thus had a predilection for naturalistic philosophers' views of human nature according to which the spirit is a subtle body which is interwoven with the physical body and inseparable from the heart and its parts just as 'wateriness' is inseparable from a rose, 'oiliness' is inseparable from sesame seeds, and 'fatness' from milk. It is the spirit, he said, that has power, ability, life, and will. Moreover, it possesses such capacity within itself, whereas capacity is prior to action.

When I realized these things and saw what Afif was really about, I kept this knowledge to myself as Yashkuri had advised me to, and I stopped asking Afif about anything unrelated to my work and livelihood.

Yashkuri was attached to a sheikh who had renounced the things of this world, an attachment with which I was soon infected myself. According to Yashkuri, the man had lived for a period of time in a city by the name of Harran. Some of the inhabitants of this city retained the intellectual disciplines, philosophy, and religions of the Greeks, such as Pythagoreanism, Neoplatonism, the science of chemistry, and the science of the cosmos as based on the wisdom of Hermes. Such people had retained vestiges of these sciences despite the influences of later trends. Yashkuri's sheikh had studied these sciences until God guided him to Islam. Then, grafting this onto that, his tongue overflowed with truth and wisdom, as a result of which Yashkuri was drawn to him just as I myself was being drawn to him now. Our sheikh used to hold his sessions after the mid-afternoon prayer in a zawiya where we would meet to take in his morsels of wisdom and the fruits of his thoughts. Among the things I came to perceive through this was the world of sovereign lights, as well as the two perceptible worlds, namely, the earthly and the heavenly realms, and the realms of darkness and light. The sheikh based his knowledge on the guidance found in the Qur'anic verse that reads:

God is the Light of the heavens and the earth;
the likeness of His Light is as a niche
wherein is a lamp
(the lamp in a glass,
the glass as it were a glittering star)

kindled from a Blessed Tree,
an olive that is neither of the East nor of the West
whose oil wellnigh would shine, even if no fire touched it;
Light upon Light.

Little by little I entered upon my new spiritual discipline and the passage from the West, which is the realm of the material and the body, to the East, which is the abode of the stations of light. This required that I traverse fourteen arks, which embody the force that attracts, holds, digests, propels, invades, generates, shapes, and grows, as well as that which arises from rage, lust, and the humors of the body. I also had to traverse the ten tombs of the outward and inward senses. The purpose of all this was for me to be able to transcend the heavenly bodies and ascend by means of the Active Intellect, passing through all intelligences until I reached the portals of the Light of Lights, where my soul could find contentment through its liberation from the prison of material existence and its entry into the stations of illumination.

According to our sheikh, walking was my way toward achieving some of this. Hence, when I was still in the station of the seekers, which is the first of the five stations of renunciation, I would go walking with my friend Yashkuri whenever I could, and we would keep on going until we were so exhausted that our bodies were about to give out.

However, as the days passed it became clear to me that, contrary to what Yashkuri had thought, Afif was not an adherent of the Nazzamiya sect after all. The way it happened was that a man who lived in the direction of the Anbar Road by the name of Daryush called upon his neighbors, his household, and those living in the same quarter of the city to work with him for the sake of commanding what is good and prohibiting what is evil. People responded positively to his call on account of the fact that tricksters and wanton folks from among the state's soldiers and guards had done the people of the city great harm. They had behaved in flagrantly immoral ways, engaged in highway robbery, and taken young boys and women openly off the roads. After one of their gatherings, they would come to a man and take his son away from him and he would be helpless to resist. They would approach a man and demand that he give them something or lend them money without his being able to object. In fact, many people were so afraid for their children and women that they forbade them to go out to the marketplaces. These villains would gather together and come to a village. Then, outnumbering the village's inhabitants, they would take whatever money, objects, or anything else they could carry away with them. There was no authority to prevent them, since they were the sultan's entourage and he took pride in them. Consequently, he was in no position to prevent them from doing the wicked things they did. They would levy fines on passersby on the roads, in the holds of ships and on their decks. They would demand 'protection money' from orchard proprietors and commit highway robbery, but no one would try to stop or punish them. In short, people were suffering greatly on their account. The last thing they had done was to go out to the village of Qutrabbul and loot it while everyone looked on, taking merchandise, household goods, gold, silver, sheep, goats, cattle, donkeys, and other things and carting them off to Baghdad where they put them up for sale. The people to whom the property belonged came and complained to the caliph. However, he was unable to lend them any support, and he restored to them nothing of what had been taken from them.

When Daryush and the people saw all this: the way people's possessions had been sold in the marketplaces, the corruption that had spread in the land, the injustice, the outrages, the highway robbery, and the sultan's lack of concern for their welfare, they went about to upright people everywhere and said, "Along the road there might be one or two rogues, and possibly as many as ten, and they have gotten the better of you even though you outnumber them. But if you joined forces with each other, you would vanquish them, and they would stop practicing such iniquity among you." In response, the people they had spoken to began pressing hard against the wrongdoers and tricksters in their midst. However, when Daryush tried to prevent them from doing what they were doing, they resisted him and prepared to fight him. In response, Daryush came out against them with greater numbers of those who, like him, wanted to establish justice and prohibit wrongdoing, and they were victorious. Among those who took part in the battle was a military man by the name of Sahl ibn Salama of Khurasan. Sahl ibn Salama had called upon people to establish justice and righteousness and to live by the book of God and the example of His Prophet, upon him be blessings and peace. He hung a copy of the Holy Qur'an around his neck and urged all people everywhere, both the high-born and the lowly, to answer his call. He established an official registry in which he recorded the names of everyone who came to him, then went the rounds of Baghdad looking for people who were demanding protection money from those they claimed to watch over and levying fines on passersby and those who frequented particular locations. "There is no such practice in Islam!" he cried. There was a man who would come to certain orchard proprietors and say, "Your orchard is under my protection. I will ward off anyone who wishes to do it harm, and in return, you owe me such-and-such an amount every month," whereupon the owner of the orchard would have to pay his 'protector' whether he wanted to or not. The man engaged in this practice grew very powerful. However, Daryush opposed him.

It had become apparent that Afif was one of Sahl's followers and had been exchanging letters with him. This, at any rate, is what I learned later from Shihab al-Hallaj. When the caliph did away with Sahl for saying, "I will make war on anyone who violates the Holy Qur'an and the Sunnah, be he the sultan or anyone else. Justice is required of all people regardless of who they happen to be!" Afif fled at once to the city of Basra, spiriting his family away in the dead of night and abandoning his shop and his wealth. Nearly a month passed after that, during which time I lay low in Shihab al-Hallaj's house, not daring to leave. This is what Shihab had advised me to do for fear that I might be caught in the crossfire, as it were, and held accountable for the crimes with which Afif and his ilk were bound to be charged.

As these events were swirling about us, I expressed my amazement that Afif—this quiet man whose craft required the utmost in kindness and gentleness—would have become involved in such affairs.

Shihab told me, "What drove Afif to what he did is this: He had an only son by a woman other than the one he's married to now. The boy was with his mother in the marketplace one day when, out of the blue, some corrupt military men came along and raided the market, wrought havoc in the place, and kidnapped the boy along with some other people. When Afif learned of what had happened, he was beside himself. He went out searching high and low until finally, some people tipped him off to the fact that the boy might be with a man who had become known for castrating young boys who were brought to him either through kidnapping or slavery. Afif raided the place together with a group of his brothers and found the boy with his penis carved off, his scrotum split open and his testicles removed. In his urethra they had placed a lead shaft to prevent it from healing over, and which they would remove when he urinated. Afif gathered up his son, who by this time was half dead and half alive, and would have murdered the castrater if he had not been prevented by the man's cronies. He brought the boy home, but he died not long thereafter, and he grieved over him bitterly. It was not long before the boy's mother followed him, so insufferable was her anguish and sorrow. It was then that Afif vowed to take revenge on his son's kidnappers and murderers. He joined the group known as 'the Army of Righteousness,' until what happened to Sahl, the group's leader, and to Afif himself."

Afif had sent to Shihab with the message that I should follow him to Basra if I wished. I hesitated a great deal at first since, despite the fact that Afif had sent me what I needed to take care of my affairs and had given the relevant people instructions to help me get there safely, I was still dejected and troubled. After all, here I was, once again, being forced to relocate against my will. I had warmed to the idea of settling in Baghdad. But what worried me most of all was Rita. For although I had freed her from bondage, I still felt responsible for her somehow. And although she had remained in Shihab al-Hallaj's household, where she was helping Shihab's wife with her business and other affairs, I was afraid to leave her to an unknown fate.

After things settled down, I began leaving Shihab's house from time to time. One day as we were walking to one of our sheikh's lessons, Yashkuri said to me, "Do you remember the jeweler who came to Afif's shop one time and asked him to copy a treatise on jewels and stones for him?"

"No, I am afraid I do not," I replied.

"How could you not remember?" he asked. "Have you forgotten what happened that day? Afif brought the man a drawer of rocks and asked him to test them in the proper way so that he could remove the ones that were genuine and get rid of the rest. The man brought some snakes and asked for some chickens, then started feeding them scrapings from the rocks, of which there were thirty or more. Fewer than ten of the stones passed the test, and the rest of them were fakes."

"Ah," I said, as the incident started to come back to me. "That was some time after the fire in the marketplace. Now I remember."

"Right. Well, I saw the man by chance today, and he told me he wanted to gild and embellish a book on rocks that he had had copied for him in Damascus. Then he told me that he could get me work with a friend of his who is a copyist there if I wanted. I have decided to go. I have no work here, and I hate living in Baghdad, so I want to leave. Will you come with me?"

Soldiers had raided and looted Afif's shop after his departure, and both Yashkuri and I were out of work.

After a bit of reflection, I said to him, "No. I have other plans in mind. I want to go back to Egypt."

And I was speaking the truth. I had come to miss my country more and more, and I wanted to look for Thawna. I had promised God to do so, and had vowed to myself that if I found him, I would renounce the world and devote the rest of my life to worship.

"So be it," Yashkuri replied. "As for me, I will go to Damascus to improve my situation, and from there I will go west. I would like to go to the furthest reaches of the Muslim lands. God may guide me, and I in turn might guide others who have no faith. I might join study circles held by the leading scholars there. After all, Andalusia is full of them and brimming with their great knowledge. However, before that I will make the major pilgrimage to Mecca, God willing, and go to the Aqsa Mosque to visit the tombs of the prophets in Jerusalem."

✠

I, too, longed to make the pilgrimage and to visit the beloved's tomb. However, I feared it would take so long, were I to undertake such a journey right away, that by the time I made it back to Egypt I would not find Thawna, or he would have died.

I felt terribly ambivalent. Even so, I said, "I have made a vow, and I have promised God that if a certain thing comes to pass, I will make the pilgrimage to His house seven times."

In my heart of hearts—and I speak the truth—what I wanted was to tell Thawna about my decision to embrace Islam and to invite him to do the same. This was my most cherished hope. The question of what would become of Rita was worrying me as well, so I confided in Yashkuri about it and told him about her situation. I was undecided. On the one hand, I had no desire for her. It was as though what had happened to me after I saw her on the night when I took the hot coals in my hand had marked the end of my feeling for women. Or as if Rita had been nothing but the cause that would bring about my final renunciation of the opposite sex. On the other hand, I was certain of my responsibility for her. After all, I had changed her life irreversibly. It was because of me that she had left her life of ease and privilege in the caliph's palace.

After relating all this to Yashkuri and begging him to give me some advice, he said, "Give her a choice between staying in Shihab's household and going back to Egypt with you."

"No, no," I interjected quickly, "I do not want her to go with me. I have no desire for women's company."

I returned to Shihab's house, and during dinner that evening I told him of my decision to go back to Egypt. Then, when I came to the part having to do with Rita, he smiled happily and said something that left me tongue-tied, namely, that his wife Rawayihiya had decided to marry him to Rita! She said that she had first consulted Rita about the idea, and that she had no objections.

Shihab al-Hallaj insisted that I not leave Baghdad until after the wedding. Hence, I postponed my departure until after the big night. On the day of the occasion we went to a public bath in Suq Yahya, which was one of the few public baths in the city. When we went inside, I noticed that its inner walls were covered with the finest varieties of colored marble. As for the bathtub, it was square, and its walls were inlaid with stained glass bowls that allowed light to come in. There was a warm room next to the bathtub in which there were no stoves, nor could one detect the odor of smoke anywhere. Rather, the hot water flowed in through a pipe that made the place warm and pleasant, and there was another place where cold water came in as well. Clad in wraps that covered us from the waist down, we came out of the bathing area to a place where there were marble-covered benches. After a brief rest, we got ready for our second bath, then headed into the sauna, where the water was at its hottest. We let Shihab get a work over by the masseur, who rubbed him down and washed him with hot water from the tub. In the meantime, we cracked jokes and kidded with him, and I was amazed at the frank conversation Shihab exchanged with his buddies, without the slightest shyness or embarrassment, about marriage, physical desire, the various methods of lovemaking, and the state he was going to be in with Rita when he consummated their union.

Shihab had never had any children by his wife Rawayihiya. Hence, after having lived with her for years following the death of his first wife, and this during the days when the bubonic plague was sweeping through the city, he feared being either sterile or impotent. I was amazed at the bath attendant who, as he removed the hair from certain parts of Shihab's body, joined in the conversation and starting issuing advice. He told Shihab to eat moderately before having intercourse, since coitus on a full stomach causes joint pain, numbness, varicose veins, hernias, and malignant tumors, while coitus on an empty stomach weakens one's vision, exhausts the body, and causes heart palpitations, jaundice, tuberculosis, and hectic fever. As for intercourse after eating fish or yogurt, he went on, it causes hemiplegia, and after eating acidic foods, it weakens the nerves and causes tremors. The best time for it, he said, was the latter half of the night, when one's food has been digested and the inside of the womb is hot.

"Shihab is lucky," he said, "since he will be consummating his marriage when the moon is in conjunction with Venus, and the pleasure will be intense. The reason is that this is the time of the 'air signs' and the time of Libra, and it is not permissible to have coitus when the moon is in its 'earthlike' station, its state of 'combustion,' nor when it is about to depart from the sun or in conjunction with Saturn and Mars."

One of the people present with us was a friend of Shihab's by the name of Khalil al-Nassaj, who brought up a subject that I found peculiar. He noted the fact that he often engaged in coitus interruptus with his wife, and he said he was afraid that something bad might happen to him on account of it. He added that he had been obliged to start doing it since he had so many children and did not want to exhaust himself making enough money to feed them all or be tempted to bring in income in ways that were not legitimate. Just then the hairdresser came in to do his part for Shihab, and heard what Khalil was saying.

"Scholars hold different opinions on the issue," said the hairdresser. "In fact, opinions range from the view that it is forbidden entirely to the view that it is permissible in all situations. There are some who say it is permissible if the woman agrees to it and forbidden if she does not agree, and others who say that it is permissible with a slave woman but not with a free one. However, the best practice is to avoid coitus interruptus and, instead, to send one's seed only to the arable land, as it were, that is, to the woman's womb."

The hairdresser added that he had heard his sheikh say some things on the subject, for example, that a child is formed by virtue of the sperm's falling into the womb due to four successive causes, namely: marriage, coitus, waiting patiently for the man's ejaculation, and waiting for the semen to flow into the womb. Some of these causes are more immediate than others. However, abstention from the fourth is like abstention from the third, while abstention from the third is like abstention from the second, and so on. At the same time, they are not like abortion and burying infants alive, since these are crimes against an existing, living entity. There are also differing levels of such existence. The first level of existence is for the sperm to enter the womb and be mixed with the woman's secretions so that it is prepared to receive life. Destroying this is a crime. However, once it becomes a zygote and an embryo, the crime of destroying it is more serious. Once spirit has been breathed into it and the fetus takes on human form, the crime becomes even more heinous. And the most heinous crime of all is to destroy the child after it has been born alive.

Then the hairdresser, who was a lithe, petite man with an eye for his profession, took Shihab under his care: trimming the hair on his head, his beard, his mustache, and his sideburns with good quality razors and scissors. As he worked, he apologized to us for chewing gum, saying that he had eaten some garlic and leeks, a no-no for someone who works in his profession, since it requires that one have pleasant, sweet-smelling breath.

When we had finished, we paid what we owed to the keeper of the money box and tipped the janitors, the garbage-collectors, the fuel-stokers, the water-carriers, and everyone else who had served us at the bath and taken such eminently good care of Shihab. Then we took our friend, perfectly coifed and sweetly perfumed, back home, where a party complete with dancing and singing was hosted in a spacious room of the house. The table was laden with a variety of foods and drinks neatly arranged, including a meat dish known as haruniya and another known as harisiya which I had tasted something similar to once in the caliph's kitchen during my work in the fuel rooms there. It was among the dishes they used to serve us from the caliph's leftovers. Hence, I realized that Rita may have made it especially for the occasion. I myself had asked one of the palace chefs who was known for his skill—a man by the name of Kazim ibn Sabur—to tell me how it was made, and he said, "It is made from either rich beef or lamb. It has to be that of a young animal which has been skinned and from which the glands, veins, and nerves have been removed. It also has to be tender meat which does not crumble, and whose odor has not undergone any change. After it has been washed, it is soaked in salt water, then cooked well over a low flame until the meat becomes tender with the wheat that is added to it along with almonds, salt, seasonings, and galingale."

Kazim told me that this dish had been invented during the reign of a Persian monarch known as Khosrau Anushirwan.

In addition to this there were dishes native to Nawfara and Mosul, varieties of sour yogurt, kammuniya, and sheep's heads and trotters. As for sweets, they included abhazat, sesame rusks cooked with cheese, jawarish spiced with gum mastic, bitter orange, ambergris, sugarcane, and a sweet known as 'Ma'mun's dessert,' which had gained fame and popularity in Baghdad from the time when the caliph by this name ruled in the land. Besides all these there were roast sheep, tharid—which is a dish of meat, broth, and sopped bread—sweet drinks and drinks flavored with sweet basil and rosewater, and delicious kishk prepared with rice, vegetables, oils, and clarified butter and cooked with rich mutton. As such, it differed from the kishk I had known in Egypt, which is cooked with rich mullet fish or with the meat of migratory birds that happen to have landed on our territory, such as quails, flamingoes, and others.

It was then announced that the entertainers had arrived. When they took their places and began playing their lutes, flutes, tunburs, guitars, tambourines, cymbals, rebabs, and qanuns, people's spirits were refreshed by the magic of the music, while bodies relaxed in rapturous contentment. As for me, I was delighted beyond words at the arrival of Husayn ibn Falih al-Maraghi, whom I had not seen for so very long. We embraced, then lost ourselves in a long conversation about his affairs and mine and how things had gone for me since the time I parted with him after leaving the caliph's palace. The musicians stopped playing to have something to eat and drink before carrying on with their performance, and in the middle of our conversation, Husayn pulled me over toward a certain lutist and had me sit down beside him. I knew, of course, what a passion Husayn had for song and melodies, and before long I heard him asking the man about his lute, since he had noticed that it was strange and unfamiliar, having five strings rather than the usual four. In reply, the man told us that it was a Ziryabi lute, named after the person who had invented it, and that one would not find many of them in Baghdad. He explained that its fifth string had been added by the famed Andalusian singer Ziryab, and that he had bought his when he traveled once to the West. He said that this string was one of a number of Ziryab's musical innovations. The traditional type of lute had four strings in keeping with the four humors in the human body. Ziryab then added this fifth string, which he had painted red, and centered it among the other four strings. The zir, which is the highest string on the lute but which occupies the lowest position, is dyed yellow, thereby indicating that this string is to the lute what the bile is to the body. The next string is dyed red to indicate that it is to the lute what the blood is to the body. This second string is twice as thick as the zir, and is referred to as the muthanna, or double string. The fourth string, referred to as the bamm, is dyed black, thereby making it to the lute what the black bile is to the body. The bamm, he told us, is the thickest string on the lute and occupies the uppermost position. It is twice as thick as the muthallath, or triple string, which is left white to show that it is to the lute what the phlegm is to the body. This string, in turn, is double the thickness of the muthanna, which is why it is referred to as the muthallath. In this way, then, each string is placed across from its corresponding opposite in such a way that the lute is moderated and balanced just as the body is balanced by its various humors. The lutist went on to explain that Ziryab had added the fifth string because, although the four strings that characterize the traditional lute correspond to the humors of the body, they nevertheless lack a 'soul,' which is associated with the blood. Consequently, he felt obliged to add this fifth string and to dye it red in keeping with its blood-like nature, as it were. The fifth string has to be below the muthallath and above the muthanna in order to complete the energies of the four humors, or natures, of the lute, and in order for it to be to the lute what the soul is to the body.

Then he showed us his pick, saying, "It is made from the fore-feathers of an eagle's wing. This is the kind we were advised to use by Ziryab, too. It is more effective and produces a fuller sound than a wooden pick does, since, in addition to its lightness on the fingers, it also helps keep the strings in good condition when one plucks them with it regularly."

I found all this amazing and fascinating.

The musicians then went back to making their music, which was exquisite in both its harmony and its rhythm. Some guests got up to dance, full of hilarity and light-hearted fun and with a good feel for the beat. When the first dancers had finished and gone back to their places, a black slave girl got up to dance. With a long neck and locks of hair falling down over her temples, she moved with coquetry and refined grace, the sides of her body swaying beautifully to the rhythm of the orchestra. With a slender waist, lovely features, and everything in per-fect proportion, her robes flowed in a circular motion about her ankles as she moved, her breathing easy and natural. Then, taken by the subtle movements of her feet, the soft suppleness of her fingers and joints, and her rapid, shifting gyrations, Khalil al-Nassaj broke into song:

Young maids unveiled to us on Palm Sunday,
Would that gold and silver were as bright!
Their sashes embroidered with the greatest of care,
So comely in the final hours of the night.

Their tresses flowing
Like the swallow's tail,
Their movements weightless
As the gazelle.

However, no sooner had he finished than I saw Shihab's color change, and his face turn morose and stern. I suspect that everyone noticed the transformation that had come over him, since Yashkuri—who had been invited in my honor when Shihab had learned of our friendship—leaned over and said, "Could that man not have found some other verses to sing at Shihab's wedding? Does he not know that this song, that has become so popular in Baghdad of late, was composed by the caliph himself? He asked Ahmad ibn Sadaqa al-Tunburi to recite it to him on Palm Sunday, which is a holiday the Christians celebrate in the city every year. The caliph had twenty Byzantine maids-in-waiting who had been brought to him from near and far, and who were decked out in Byzantine brocades. They had gold crosses around their necks and reeds and olive branches in their hands the way the people of Jerusalem are said to have had when Jesus came into Jerusalem on the back of a young donkey. It was about them that the caliph composed the verses that Khalil al-Nassaj just sang. Does the fool not know that Shihab hates the caliph? After all, his family is from among the common people who live in one of the villages surrounding Baghdad. The caliph's soldiers have trespassed on their land, taken their crops, and stolen their riding animals, and the caliph has done nothing to protect their rights or punish the soldiers for their crimes. It is said that Shihab—though I am not sure it is true—has become associated with a group that is opposed to the Abbasids. Consequently, there are people here who might reproach Khalil for singing something like that, since there are bound to be some members of the group in attendance tonight."

I was astounded at what Yashkuri was saying, as it was the first time I had heard such a thing. It was something I had never known about Shihab despite my having shared his company and lived in his house since the time I left the caliph's palace. It was true, of course, that he left the house in the early mornings, and that I only returned there myself to spend the night. However, in the time I did spend with him, and despite the fact that he seemed disgruntled over the things happening in the country, I never noticed anything that would have indicated that he was connected with a group working against the caliph's government. Once I had asked him about the meaning behind the horseman with the spear in his hand atop the dome on Baghdad's wall, and he laughed, saying, "Now he is pointing it in the direction of Badhdh in Khurasan!" At the time I did not understand what he was getting at. However, I learned later from Yashkuri that Badhdh is the homeland of a man by the name of Babak who had declared rebellion against the caliph.

I did not comment on what Yashkuri had whispered in my ear. However, I thought to myself: Truly, "everything goes" in Baghdad, even old men getting married. It is the city of wonders and marvels with a thousand faces, and every time I think I have come to know it and unveiled them all, it reveals to me another that I had yet to see.

I was getting a bit woozy, as I had drunk some wine to be sociable, and in a show of joviality and contentment. Even so, I sat there grave-faced and pensive as my eyes followed the dancers' frenzied movements and revelry, especially when they began performing a type of dance known as dastanbad wal-ila. By this time I had begun thinking about Amuna, Suwayla, and Rita and the things that had happened between us. At the same time, disquiet over Rita was eating me up inside. I wondered what the days would bring her, especially given what I had just heard about Shihab al-Hallaj. After all, she had gone from the privileged life in a monarch's palace to life in the lowly dwellings of the monarch's subjects. She had left a royal residence and settled in an ordinary dwelling with nothing to set it apart from any other. She had once been a sought-after slave girl, only to become an ill-fated second wife. And I wondered to myself: Did I do her an injustice on the day when Fate placed me in her path after what happened in the caliph's palace, thereby binding her destiny to mine? Or was it something that had been foreordained for her before she was born? In other words, was it her ineluctable fate to emerge from the slavery of affluence into the freedom of penury, and from the gold-and-silver-brocaded ignominy of privilege to the dignity of life behind a veil, lived humbly from hand to mouth?

I left Baghdad several days later, by which time Shihab had made all the necessary arrangements for my exodus. He told me that my departure coincided with the conjunction of 'the head' and Mercury. Before leaving, I went to my sheikh's zawiya, where I performed two cycles of prayer and asked God Almighty to bless me on my way. Yashkuri, who was there to bid me farewell, gave me two tunics and an elegant Baghdad-made robe modeled on the type made for the caliph, which was as beautiful as any I had ever seen, to wear when I traveled. I gripped him in a long embrace and thanked him for the gifts, then mounted my riding camel, which was a robust workhorse that Shihab had presented to me. His wife Rawayihiya had given me a number of long-necked glass bottles filled with perfume that she said I could give to whomever I liked, use myself, or sell if I needed to along the way. As for Rita, she supplied me with some semolina cakes, which are a type of dry sweet well suited for travel. She wished me many blessings and stood there a long time asking God to keep me in His care and to grant me safety and success.

Having paid most of the money I had made during my employment at the stationer's shop, and which I had left in the safekeeping of Shihab's wife, to the owner of the caravan that would be overseeing my journey, I had just a few pennies in my pocket.

At the journey's outset the caravan only stopped long enough for us to rest or sleep until, two days later, we reached the city of Jerusalem. As I observed the city, I noted that it was built upon a mountain. At the time of our arrival it was raining hard, which we were told was normal for Jerusalem. The purpose for our stop there was to allow some of the merchants in the caravan to deliver some of their wares. When the guards granted us permission to go into the city's marketplaces, we were led to a location referred to as The Three Markets near the Mihrab Gate, which included a market for perfumers and druggists and another for fabric vendors. We then passed through the qaysariyat with their roofed marketplaces, bazaars, hotels, and merchants' inns with residences located above them, until at last we arrived at a large caravansary constructed from lovely pink stone. In the center of it there was a courtyard with the appearance of a roofed bazaar. We went inside and tied our riding animals. I learned later that this place was known as Khan al-Fahm, located on Khatt Dawud, or King David Avenue, which was the city's main thoroughfare. This street, which was the city's largest, ran from the Aqsa Mosque at Bab al-Silsila, that is, the Chain Gate, as far as Bab al-Mihrab, or the Prayer Niche Gate, which is known also as Bab al-Khalil, or the Hebron Gate.

Along the way I became acquainted with a man who traded in spices, and who appeared to be highly virtuous and well mannered. Near the beginning of our journey, during a rest stop in one of the villages located along the road that led out of Baghdad, I noticed him shooting me frequent, scrutinizing glances. Not pleased about this, I began feeling restless and suspicious of him.

"Sir," I said to him, "you keep looking at me. Have you perchance learned something about me that you disapprove of?"

"Certainly not!" he replied. "I have never seen you before. Nor do I disapprove of you on account of anything I see in you. However, I am a man with a discerning eye, and I know people well. You are going out in search of someone dear to you, and you will expend great effort and time in the process. This person is quite ill, though, and you may or may not reach him in time. Only God knows. However, on your way to him you will continue on the path you have set out on, and never turn back."

I was amazed at what the man had said. At the same time, I was gripped with a sense of dejection, fearing that some harm may have come to my beloved Thawna. When I asked him how he had perceived these things, he refrained from saying anything more, as though he were not willing to confide things about himself to someone like me. Consequently, I felt annoyed and offended at his self-importance.

So I pressed him, saying, "What you just said is nothing but superstition and trickery. No one knows the future but God alone. Have you never heard the saying, 'Astrologers lie even when they speak the truth'?"

Realizing what I was getting at, he retorted quickly, "I am not an astrologer, I assure you. Rather, physiognomy is a profound science. Have you never heard what the sheikh and philosopher once said about it? He said, 'Outward vision only sees perceptible entities when darkness is dispersed by the light of the sun, and when the barriers which separate vision from its objects disappear. So also with inward vision: It is not within its capacity to perceive the spiritual world unless the mirror of the heart has been purged of the lusts that prevent the divine light from being reflected therein.'"

Then he added, "I have 'read' what you are setting out to do through physiognomy. I have observed you as we have traveled, including your various tones of voice, the way your neck moves, the outlines of your nose and eyes, the condition of your hair, the odor given off by your body, the condition of your teeth, and the shape of your hands and feet. I have even observed the condition of your fingers, toes, fingernails, and toenails."

Incredulous at what he was saying, I recalled that a Hanafi sheikh from Harran had once come to Afif's shop requesting that he copy a book which he described as being precious and rare. He said that some time earlier, the caliph had asked his chief translator to find a copy of this book and to translate it for him into Arabic due to the great wisdom and knowledge it contained. The translator betook himself to the land of the Greeks beyond the Byzantine Sea and found the book, which was entitled *The Secret of Secrets*, in a pagan temple to the sun. It had been written by a sage of old by the name of Aristotle for a renowned king, although it had been copied from an ancient manuscript wrongly attributed to the thrice-great Hermes. In any case, the man came across a copy of the book in Persian, from which he then translated it.

As we were spending the night in the caravansary, a man who had just arrived in the city from the land of the Greeks informed us that the Byzantine emperor Nikephorus had advanced into Bulgaria and laid siege to its capital city, then defeated and sacked it. In the process, he had killed large numbers of people. So great was Nikephorus's barbarism, he said, that he had begun laying out young men on the ground and trampling them underfoot.

Then, after night had fallen and we had gone to sleep, we were all awakened by the sound of loud laughter and guffawing. We got up to see what the matter was, and what should we find but that one of the merchants was having a fit of laughter which he had no power to control. We tried every trick in the book to get him to quiet down: from reprimands, to curses, to beatings, to water poured over his head, to poking, to slapping, to pinching, to reciting verses of the Holy Qur'an intended to ward off evil influences, but all to no avail. Some of us thought he had gone mad. He remained in this condition for an hour, then died. Some of the elders who were with us suspected foul play. The man had brought an Ethiopian slave with him, so they took him aside for questioning. They tied him up and flogged him till he bled, and when he could not bear the pain any longer, he confessed that he had given the man a poison known as 'laughing poison.' When he was questioned as to the nature of the poison, he told his questioners how he had made it: He took twenty dirhams of cloves, one hundred dirhams of cinnamon, fifty dirhams of ginger, and fifty dirhams of pepper, then ground them all into a fine powder. Then he added five ratls of water and soaked the mixture in it for one day and one night. Then he took a ratl of saffron, ground it up finely and soaked it in the five ratls of water that had been mixed with the previously mentioned ingredients. This, too, he let soak for a day and a night, after which he allowed it to macerate. He then left the mixture until the solids had settled to the bottom, leaving the water clear. In this clear water he soaked another quarter of a ratl of saffron for one day and one night. He then repeated this process two more times until it had become a deadly poison. He said that he had given his victim two dirhams of the poison mixed with honey at his dinnertime, since his master had been in the habit of drinking honey mixed with water after the final evening prayer. What he had done, he said, was all on account of the fact that after accusing him of being remiss in his work, his master had threatened on more than one occasion to castrate him. The slave added that he had been afraid that his master was actually going to carry out his threat when the caravan arrived in Egypt.

The following day, they took the slave and handed him over to the city police chief. As for the dead man, we brought him grave clothes from the market, then washed his body and prepared it for burial. From the caravansary we took the deceased to the city's great mosque, where we prayed over him and buried him in a nearby tomb. As for his merchandise, we inventoried it and left it as a deposit with the caravansary proprietor until the man's family had been informed of his death.

Never in my life had I seen a mosque as magnificent as the Aqsa Mosque. Hence, when we left the cemetery, I excused myself from those who were with me and went back to get a better look at it, since my earlier exposure to it had confirmed to me that it was, indeed, one of the most splendid, extraordinary mosques in all of existence. A masterfully constructed edifice overlaid with gold and colored with pure dyes, it had numerous doors opening out from its three sides, and the entire mosque was wide-open space, unroofed anywhere but at one end. It had a spacious, rectangular atrium of exquisite beauty and delicate craftsmanship with colonnades of colored marble and mosaics that were more beautiful than any I had ever seen, even in the church at Antioch. In the atrium there was a large platform five cubits in height, with stairs that led up to it from several locations. In the center of the platform rested a huge, octagonal, lead dome on marble pillars. The dome was embellished inside and out with mosaic and colored marble. In the center of the dome was the rock to which people make pilgrimage, and on the edge of which one can see the footprint of the Prophet, upon him be blessings and peace. Beneath it was a grotto into which one descended by several steps and inside of which one could pray. This dome had four doors and to its east there lay another dome atop lovely columns called the Dome of the Chain. The Dome of the Ascension was likewise located on the platform, as was the Dome of the Prophet, upon him be blessings and peace. All of these rested on columns and were topped with lead. In the mosque floor, numerous basins and reservoirs had been dug, as the entire mosque had been built over a rock in which rainwater would collect. Consequently, not a single drop of it went to waste, and everyone could benefit from it.

I went on wandering around the mosque until after the midafternoon prayer. After I had performed my ablution, prayed, and uttered praises to God, I approached one of the walls of the mosque's atrium and sat down beside it. My roaming about the mosque, our walk to the cemetery, and insufficient sleep the night before had left me in a state of weariness. For some time I sat there ruminating, staring into the firmament that opened out above me and at the land that was visible to me in the distance, with its meadows, its tilled fields, its hills, and its houses. Then I began thinking about something my sheikh had said once as he spoke to us about his inner certainty:

> I found heat to be opposed to cold, and I found that the two opposites could never come together in a single place so long as their natures

are what they are. I thus perceived from their existence together that there is something that unites them, an irresistible power that conquers them contrary to their natural propensities. That which can be conquered is weak. Moreover, this weakness, together with the influence of that which conquers it, is evidence both of its temporal nature and of a being that brought it into existence, an originator that originated it. However, its creator or originator does not resemble it, because whatever resembles it must, ipso facto, likewise be temporal. Hence, its creator and originator is God, the Lord of the worlds.

I remained in this state for some time, reflecting on the cosmos and its grandeur, until my body grew lax and limp, my senses were dulled, and my consciousness began to grow hazy. Hence, I was tempted to surrender to my lethargy and take a much-needed nap to help me through what remained of the day and what might face me at the caravansary that night. I remained motionless for some time with my eyes open, staring into the heavenly expanse above me and meditating on the majesty of the Creator. Enveloped by a sultry breeze that refreshed my spirit and calmed my senses, I found myself slipping little by little into a contented, peaceful slumber. I do not know how long I remained in that state. However, I wakened to something which, for all I know, may have been a dream, or may have been a waking vision of reality itself. My beloved Thawna had come to me in the same form in which I had seen him once before while I was hiding in the marshlands of Egypt. As he had been the first time, he was standing atop a high hill with a staff in his hand. His face radiant with benevolence, he said, "Why the rush? Rather, remain in the city of the prophets until your spirit has drunk its fill and is indwelt fully with faith. Then come. I will wait until you get here."

I sat there for a while, speechless and disconcerted, uncertain what to make of what I had just experienced and the vision I had had of Thawna. But then God granted me guidance and opened up a clearer understanding to me. As a consequence, I made up my mind to do the very opposite of what I had originally intended. Getting up quickly, I went to the caravansary, where I found the caravan guide and informed him that I would not be leaving with the others the next morning.

Instead, I explained, I would be staying for some time in this city of the prophets. After bidding farewell to all those who had been with me on the journey, I gathered up my meager belongings and left. On my way out the gate, I met up with the physiognomist who had spoken to me before, and when I began bidding him farewell, too, he looked at me thoughtfully, then said, "Did I not tell you that you were about to embark on a path from which you would never turn back?"

I roamed about Jerusalem for some time thereafter. Winter after winter passed, and summer after summer. The city grew accustomed to me, as I grew accustomed to it. I would spend one night in a mosque, another in a marketplace, and still another in an orchard or a wilderness. The city had captivated me as no other city ever had, so much so that I could not part with it. It was as if there were no other place on earth where my spirit could find solace and comfort.

Some days I would spend in churches, and others in mosques. At other times I would go up to the fortress, then to David's Prayer Niche in the heart of the mosque that had been built on the west side of the fortress wall. An elevated spot to which one could ascend by a staircase, it marked the place where the Prophet David had sat, upon him be peace. I would linger there, looking through the large stone window where a mark had been left by his elbow when it sank into the stone, and I would marvel at the tile in which the imprint had been made. As for the Church of the Holy Sepulcher, its structures are among the wonders of the world. I would go there from time to time and gaze at the place where the Master, upon him be peace, had sat on the stone, and the rock-strewn spot where he was flogged and tormented, as well as the prison in which he was placed. I would remain there until the arrival of someone from the house of Nusayba or the house of Jawda—two Muslim families that had been given the keys to the church and entrusted with the tasks of opening and closing it.

I lived off what I received from people by way of alms and gifts, and most of my time was spent in prayer and worship. I preferred peregrination to anything else in this world. Sometimes I would go down to Dayr al-Musallaba, an old Byzantine monastery masterfully constructed of stones and lime. Situated gracefully in a sea of olive trees, grapevines, and fig trees not far from a village to which it was connected by a road, the monastery housed Greek iconographic paintings that had been drawn with the most exquisite skill and symmetry.

Other times I would go to an elevated spot that overlooked the Jericho Valley, the site of another monastery known as Dayr al-Siq, which in its turn looked out over green expanses and the River Jordan. Once there, I would be received by gracious, spirited monks, who would offer me some of what they had on hand by way of bread and fruit, then leave me to devote myself to meditation or prayer. The only people who would come their way were travelers for whom the monastery was their intended destination, or those passing through the farms in the valley beneath. As for the area above them, it was the site of a road that led to the red dune beyond.

One day I was passing through a valley known as the Valley of Jehosephat, where there is a spring of water. A group of women had come to the spring, and in their midst I saw a young woman who was one of the most beautiful I had ever seen. The other women pushed her into the spring, after which she took a drink and cast some of her clothes into the water. When, after she had done so, she remained standing on her feet, all the women cheered, applauded and let out trills of joy, saying that she was innocent and pure. Baffled by what I had just witnessed, I asked someone to explain it to me, and I was told that this spring was referred to as 'The Spring of the Virgin,' or 'The Spring of Accused Women.' Any woman who had been accused of not having conducted herself honorably would be brought to this place to be tested. If she was guilty of the accusation against her, she would die after drinking of the spring's water. If, however, she drank of its water and remained unharmed, this was evidence of her purity and innocence. It is said that the Virgin Mary, upon her be peace, agreed to submit to this test, drank of the spring's water, and thereby demonstrated her purity, since she neither died nor suffered any harm. And the spring has born her name ever since.

I do not know how much time I spent in the city of the prophets. All I know is that I would roam hither and thither within its blessed precincts for days and months at a time, my soul limpid and serene. Moreover, I lived a good life there despite the fact that I was without work, eating what I gleaned from the wilderness, drinking from springs, and finding my daily needs met through what people would give me occasionally out of the goodness of their hearts without my asking them for a thing. I would go to the meat or vegetable market in the city and ask to buy something cooked or roasted with the few pennies I had with me, only to have the person who had given me what I had requested push my hand away and refuse to take anything for it. On one occasion, a shop owner refused to take more than a quarter of a dirham from me in return for a plate full of meat and vegetable stew. And I was always amazed at the large numbers of marketplace restaurants in Jerusalem by comparison with Baghdad, where people rarely ate outside their homes.

It was in the city of the prophets that the strangest, most providential thing took place, something that seemed closer to fantasy than to reality. I was spending the evening in the Indians' zawiya next to the Samirah Gate, and together with a group of dervishes, I had just concluded a session of divine invocation and poetry recitation followed by dancing for the Beloved to the sound of the mizhar. We had reached a state of such intoxication and rapture that the dawsa had become an inevitability. Hence, we all lay down on the floor with all the weapons we owned—swords, spears, daggers, and knives—unsheathed. Then our guide and leader—a sheikh who had reached spiritual enlightenment and who had been manifested and purified, who had looked upon the Majesty and radiated Its light, and who had given himself over completely to the Divine and thus revealed Its glory—rode over us with his horse, which trampled our bodies, our spears, and our swords with its hooves. And throughout it all, our tongues were praising the Divine Name and our hearts were beating with adoration for the Beloved until at last we lost consciousness.

No sooner had we gotten up than there appeared a man at the zawiya door asking for a drink. His hair was unkempt, his clothing and body were covered with dust, and he appeared to be in a state of weakness and fatigue. As we rushed to bring him some water, I recognized him as Yashkuri the leper. Unable to contain myself, I fell upon him with hugs and kisses, thanking God for allowing me to see him again in this world. We brought him something to eat, then left him to rest and compose himself. After his condition had improved, we went out together to the orchards on the outskirts of the city, found a suitable spot in which to rest, then set about catching up on each other's news since the time we had parted in Baghdad. We talked until the dawn broke upon us and we were bathed in its blessed lights.

Yashkuri told me that Shihab al-Hallaj had come upon hard times in Baghdad and left with his two wives for the city of Marw, from which his wife Rawayihiya hailed. He also told me that the caliph had died and had been succeeded by an unjust, ignorant caliph who knew about nothing but weapons of war. The Zatt, a gypsy-like people who had originally come from the land of India, then settled in the rural area around the city of Basra between the Tigris and the Euphrates, had staged a major revolt against the new caliph after suffering poverty and distress the entire previous year without anyone to come to their aid. The caliph then summoned a group of Egyptians—whom his predecessor had settled in Antioch—to Baghdad to fight against the Zatt. Yashkuri explained that the Zatt had been waging war from boats on lakes into which the Tigris and Euphrates rivers empty, as a result of which the caliph's soldiers had been unable to go in and fight them. Hence, they fought them with javelins and slit open their bellies, after which the Copts encircled them and captured them, along with their families. As a result, they were defeated. They then requested protection and were granted their request, whereupon Ujayf, the military commander whom the caliph had assigned the task of waging war on them, led them away to Baghdad. They numbered approximately twenty-five thousand, including men, women, and children, and he put them on ships and took them as far as the village of Za'faraniya. Many of Baghdad's residents had come out to see them, myself included. They were in their boats and still dressed out for war, with horns to boot. When Ujayf brought them to Shammasiya, the caliph remained on a ship known as al-Zuw until the Zatt had passed by, still mobilized for war and blowing their horns. They were so numerous they extended nearly all the way from Qufs to Shammasiya. They remained aboard their ships for three days, after which they were brought across to the Eastern side, then to a town known as Khaniqin. It was said that they were going to be transferred from there to another location on the frontier by the name of Ayn Zarba.

When I heard all these things, my heard pounded wildly. I remembered Bakhnas ibn Ayyoub, my consternation over his unknown fate, and the total lack of news about his condition or whereabouts since we had parted on the Farama shore. I also thought about all the others who had been on the ships upon our departure from Egyptian soil and who had survived the trip to Antioch, at which point we had been sorted out, each of us to face his respective fate. I had learned that, on orders from the caliph, many of the Bashmourites who had not been sold had been settled on one side of the Antioch Lake in the marsh region north of the city given the similarity between the terrain there and that of the Bashmourite territories.

"And the Copts?" I asked excitedly. "Tell me, please, what became of them?"

Yashkuri gave me a bewildered look as though he found my question strange or offensive, and as though I had asked him about something that had never occurred to him before.

"The Copts?" he replied, taking off his turban and rebraiding his black, silky hair, which glistened in the light of the candles that were about to go out. "As I said, the caliph used them to wage war on the Zatt, but that is all I know about them. Perhaps they stayed in the locations that the Zatt had left, and took over their occupations there, such as fishing, buffalo husbandry, salt production, and gathering dung to make fuel and fertilizer for the agricultural lands. Maybe they took the Zatt's place in the marshy areas around Basra, such as Wasit, Najida, and Safiya. Your question is peculiar. No one else has ever thought about the Copts. As for you, you are still worrying about them, in spite of all that has happened to you, all the time you lived in Baghdad, and your decision to embrace Islam."

Then he added with a laugh, "I say, it seems you still have a Copt living inside you, or a pharaoh! The fact is, I have never thought about it before. Whether you are in Antioch, in Egypt, in Syria, or in Baghdad, it is all God's earth and the lands of the caliph, and we are all God's servants. I do not think any harm has come to them. If it had, the caliph would not have used them to fight against the Zatt. In the end, what happens to them happens to others, whether in Baghdad, Antioch, Marw,

Khurasan, or Egypt. At least, it is the same thing that happens to everyone who is defenseless in this world, and who has no recourse against
those who wield power and authority."

He stared solemnly into space for quite some time, his eyes clouded
over with sorrow and anguish. Then all of a sudden he cried out, "O
Beloved, O Answerer of prayer!"

Thinking about what he had said, I gazed out at the Jerusalem
horizon before me, then looked up at the stars that shone down on us
from the firmament. I felt troubled, since the reply he had given me had
not quenched my thirst for understanding. I sat there, still and speechless, my heart breaking over Bakhnas ibn Ayyoub. And I wondered to
myself: Did he reach Antioch safely after I parted with him in Farama?
And was he then taken to Baghdad to wage war on the Zatt? Was he
sold at the slave market in Damascus? Or did he meet his end on the
Byzantine Sea, only to be entombed in its boundless waters? My heart
was consumed with grief over him and all the others who had departed
on the ships. At the same time, I was certain that those who had perished
on the way to Antioch had been spared the further torment that awaited
those whom God had willed to remain alive. Then my mind quickly
moved to Thawna and to something he had said to me one day to the
effect that when they were at the height of their glory and brutal power
in Egypt, the Byzantines had used the Copts as fuel for their wars. They
even waged war once in a country to the north of the Byzantine Sea
and the land of the Greeks by the name of Switzerland, and when they
did so they took everyone with them, including pious Coptic women
who were given the task of caring for the wounded as physicians and
nurses. One of these women was a chaste, upright Jacobite who began
teaching the people of Switzerland the fundamentals of hygiene, how
to treat various ailments and the true religion. Eventually she was martyred, after giving her all in selfless service. Hence, the people erected
a tomb for her and drew her an icon, after which they built a church in
her name, which is known as the Church of Firina.

I was flooded with a sense of pain and bitterness and filled with a
noble sorrow as I thought back on all this. The sparrows of my longing winged their way toward the land of Egypt, while the force of the
nostalgia surged through my veins and my eyes welled up with tears.

Aching with the desire to return to my soil, my sky, my Nile, my sun, I began whispering some words that Rawayihiya, Shihab's wife, had given me one day. She had wanted me to write them for a friend of hers who was about to leave Baghdad for Ghazna with a man to whom she had been married from that city. As was the custom in Baghdad at that time, she wanted to embroider some of her friend's clothes with memorable phrases as a going-away gift. On the bodice of a silk tunic embroidered with silver and gold I wrote some verses to remind her of her family and her homeland in the Kufic, Nisaburi script that had gained such wide popularity in those days:

God waters the land of lovers with His blessed rain
And restores every alien to the land of his birth
He gives those of high station their hearts' desire and more,
And with the nearness of the beloved fills the lover with mirth.

I stayed in the orchard for some time after that with Yashkuri, who told me that he had come down to Jerusalem with the intention of staying there just a few days before his departure for Damascus, which he had chosen as his destination in the hope of working for some stationers in keeping with the promise he had received from the jeweler he met in Baghdad. He said he hoped to visit its mosques and the tombs of the prophets there, but that he would not be able to travel until after he had regained his strength and health. He explained that he had traveled a long way on foot after his mount got ill and could not bear to be ridden any longer. I suggested that we spend the night at the edge of the orchard we were sitting in, then try to solve his problem in the city the next morning, God willing.

We talked till nearly daybreak, with Yashkuri telling me about conditions in Baghdad and the things that had happened since my departure. He said things were not going well: that most people were in difficult straits and that there was an overall atmosphere of discontent, especially since the spread of vagabonds, troublemakers, and beggars. Poverty was on the increase, he said, to the point where most people had started eating nothing but mush made either from wheat flour or roasted barley mixed with dates similar to what the Sudanese eat, which was something that had never happened before. Another dish that had become the sole fare of many was harisa, on account of which certain wags had made up some verses that said:

How I love harisa, it pleases me no end
And habita I truly adore.
Mention some other sweet to me, and into raptures I'll go,
And if two others follow, I shan't seek more!

Poverty had become so ubiquitous that people began writing petitions to the caliph and government authorities, one of which read as follows:

I am beleaguered by the vicissitudes of Fate, its ordeals and tribulations, which have wrested away from me what the world had given. There is not an estate to my name that has not fallen into ruin, nor a river that has not dried up, nor a home that has not collapsed, nor wealth that has not gone the way of the wind. I no longer have a penny to my name. I am drowning in debt, with a wife and children to feed. At the same time, I am an old man, and no longer able to meet the demands upon me or bring in the income needed for my dependents. Hence, I look with hope to the Commander of the Faithful and his compassion, for I am in the state of the one who declared:

I have a house that is like a verse
of Ibn Hajjaj's from a silly rhyme.

What spider web could be so flimsy
Or as feeble as my mind?

A spot from which the sunrise is concealed,
I am in eclipse since it became mine!

Yashkuri told me that Baghdad's vagrant ruffians had become so powerful that they had begun stirring up riots and waging war on the police. They had even poured water on them and chased them down the streets. They had taken a particular fancy to harassing black servants, and' whenever they happened to run into one of them they would say to him, "Hey there, slave!" They had organized themselves into groups of ten.

Over each group of them there was a sergeant, over every ten sergeants there was a captain, over every ten captains there was a commander, and over every ten commanders there was an emir. The supreme head of their military organization had ten emirs under his command. Among their chiefs there was one called Nabtawiya, another called Khalawiya, another called Duwayl, and others called Daghghal, Abu Namla, Abu Usara, Dikawiya, and Mukharrami. It was said that they numbered more than fifty thousand in Baghdad. But whatever their exact number, there were so many of them, and they moved with such speed, that when they moved en masse from one place to another, some of them were bound to be trampled underfoot. They did not belong to any one particular race, though the majority of them were non-Arabs. Moreover, given the city's miserable living conditions, many artisans, traveling salesmen, and petty merchants whose goods were not selling had started joining them along with riffraff, former prisoners, and uneducated common folk.

Unaware of how long we had slept, Yashkuri and I awoke near noon to the sound of a loud commotion. When we were fully conscious, we realized that the owners of the orchard had come to work there and thought we were thieves who had come to steal their money and produce. We explained to them that we were not criminals, but just a couple of dervishes who had no end to seek in this world. When they had been convinced of our story and realized who we were, they treated us with generosity, feeding us some of the fruits of their land. We then asked them if they knew of a veterinarian who could treat Yashkuri's mount, and they directed us to one whose clinic was in the Jews' Quarter.

We pulled the beast along with us till we came to the Jews' Quarter, which is a lane that connects David Street with the city wall not far from the Zion Gate. I had never been in this area before, which was dotted here and there with a small number of houses. The neighborhood contained a few shops whose owners were either busy at work or standing at their doors, and most of them were visibly ragged and poor. We then turned down a narrower lane within the same neighborhood, which was known as Feather Lane. This was the lane to which the gardeners had directed us and which was our intended destination. We asked people about a veterinarian by the name of Nahman ibn 'Uwaydiya, and they directed us to his shop. When we arrived, the man welcomed us, and asked us what was ailing Yashkuri's mule. Yashkuri told him it was suffering from excessive movement of the head, poor appetite, and a runny nose, and that it had a rectangular protrusion behind its ear. He added that it was not strong enough to move about or engage in any activity. As the two of them spoke, I was examining the veterinarian's instruments, which I noticed were neither clean nor pleasing to the eye as is normally the case with physician's equipment. However, he was agile, with strong arms, albeit plump, and had an honest, faithful look about him. In one corner of his spacious shop were three large hammers which, by my estimation, may well have weighed more than seven hundred dirhams, and which appeared to be used for straightening nails and the like. There were medium-sized hammers for initial rappings and tappings and for straightening and adjusting most other instruments. There were also small hammers for clinching nails and straightening scalpels, the lightest of which in my estimation would have weighed one hundred dirhams. He had nine scalpels, some of which were light and delicate and others of which were heftier. In addition, he had tree stumps for working on, clamps, cauterization instruments, pincers, rings, probes, and two pairs of scissors, one large and the other small. He also had razors, needles, and wires of various sizes and shapes. It was quite an amazing sight to me, as I had never been in a veterinarian's shop before.

The man eyed the mule, patting it and coaxing it to open its mouth so that he could see its teeth and jaw. He examined its nose and nostrils, inspected its skin and abdomen, tapped lightly on its knees, as well as doing a number of other things that were necessary in order for him to complete his examination and offer a diagnosis. Then, after a bit more cogitation and inspection, he informed us that the mule was afflicted with an ailment known as ihlilajiya, the treatment for which was the dregs of seed oil or ground seeds in a bandage, and daubing with soap. If the boil erupted, he said, it could be treated through surgical removal, and he advised Yashkuri to go easy on the animal and not tire it out with too much walking until it had fully recovered.

Some time thereafter, Yashkuri bade me farewell and continued on his way to Damascus. In the meantime, I had made up my mind that before another year was out, I would be back in Egypt searching for my beloved Thawna in hopes of finding him before it was too late and we were separated by the final parting of friends and intimates.

Among the things that hastened my departure from the city of the prophets was that my personal condition had deteriorated and my money had run out. In fact, one night I got so hungry I ate mud. When I found myself in this state, I racked my brain, trying to recall whether I knew anyone who could offer me lunch or dinner, but to no avail. All the clothes I had to my name were a jubba and two tunics. Even so, I took off the inner tunic and sold it for a few pennies, then headed for the market where beasts of burden and transport were rented out. Then, after no little effort, I found someone who would agree to take me to Ramla for the little bit of money I had to pay. From Ramla, I reached a city known as Asqalan where there was a market and a lovely mosque. While there, I saw an old arch which, it was said, had once been a mosque. It was constructed of such large stones that if they had wanted to tear it down, they would have been obliged to spend a great deal of money. I left there and, on the way, came upon numerous villages and cities whose description would take up many pages. Then I came to a place called Tinah, which was a port filled with ships from which one could travel to Tanis. Having learned that a certain mariner with a kind look about him was heading to Tanis, I approached him and asked him to take me with him in return for my working in his fuel rooms. He agreed to my proposal. However, rather than employing me in the fuel rooms, he left me on deck guarding an elephant that had been brought from India and which was being sent by some merchants as a gift to the emir of Egypt. So there I remained, with the north wind stinging my face and the night spreading its frigid blanket over my head. All I had with me was a threadbare coverlet, a shabby quilt, and a few other necessities. I went on in this state till I began thinking back fondly on the mud I had eaten, and of which there was none at sea. A group of Coptic pilgrims had boarded the ship on their way back to Tanis after visiting Jerusalem and going to all the places a believer in Christ must visit there in order to receive the blessing he seeks. When they observed my isolation and the fact that I had nothing to eat, they offered me some of their provisions, including cooked cheese with honey, meat, and some fresh fruit. So I thanked them for their generosity and believed in God and His mercy as I recited the words, "There is no moving creature on earth but its sustenance dependeth on God." Truly has God spoken.

Shortly after the sun had risen above the surface of the water, Tanis became visible to us in the distance. When I glimpsed the land, the trees, the date palms, the mosque domes, and the church steeples rising in the distance, a shudder went through me, causing my arms and legs to tremble and blowing like a storm wind through my entire body. It was as though my eyes did not believe what they were seeing, and as though my soul doubted whether I had ever even gone away. Unable to contain myself, I broke into sobs that were audible to everyone around me. The elephant turned toward me and began nudging me sympathetically, as if to say that it understood my excitement and unbridled emotion. When the ship had come fully into port and I disembarked, setting foot on the soil of my homeland, I bowed down and kissed that which had taken my spirit away and given it back. Then I began picking up handfuls of dirt as my soul cried: This is the truth! This is certainty! Then I performed two cycles of prayer in thanks and praise to God.

I stayed the night in the Khurasani Mosque near Tanis's shore. After I had finished the final evening prayer and was telling myself to rest a bit before praying the tarawih prayers, I looked about me and pondered the place. As I did so, I saw a man who was seated and facing in the direction of Mecca as Muslims are required to do when they perform their ritual prayers, his walking stick and a copy of the Holy Qur'an before him. He wore a haircloth around his waist and his hair hung down over his back. Beside him there was an elderly man in tears, begging for the younger man's compassion, saying, "Your mother weeps out of sorrow and anguish!"

The younger man replied, "I will not darken your door as long as you occupy yourself as a money changer. I will wait until daybreak. Then I will enter the Nile up to my waist and throw off this haircloth."

The younger man continued speaking in this manner until he had extracted a promise from his father that he would desist thenceforth from all work as a money changer. Astonished at what I had heard, I realized that this man was an ascetic who had renounced the things of this world. Later I learned from the mosque attendant that this same man had lived for some time in a small shelter at the bottom of the minaret without having anything to do with a soul. When the commencement of prayers in the mosque was announced, he would emerge and pray. But as soon as the prayer leader had uttered his final, "May peace be upon you and the mercy of God," he would return to his secluded shelter. If anyone remonstrated with him, he would speak to his interlocutor while standing up after finishing his prayer. Meanwhile, his spiritual state was ever and always one of union in the midst of separation, nearness in the midst of remoteness, and intimacy in the midst of alienation.

I learned that this ascetic recluse had come from Marrakesh with his family some time before, after which he had made the pilgrimage to Mecca, then returned to Egypt and settled in Tanis, where he would only to speak to others out of dire necessity. He then set about renovating this mosque, which had been an abandoned ruin. He cleaned it up all by himself, got rid of the bats that had taken up residence on its ceilings, filled its cisterns with water, paved its surface with tile inside and out, plastered its roof, and began living in it.

In his heart of hearts he preferred the indigent and the widowed. He asked nothing of anyone, nor did he generally accept anything offered to him. He made a great effort to conceal his true spiritual state and was known for his frequent recitation of the Qur'an and reading of books. However, no one had ever seen him write anything with his own hand. No prayer rug was ever made for him, he never imposed a commitment on anyone, he never wore a skullcap, nor did he speak of himself as a sheikh or as someone who had renounced all but God.

I went to sleep in the hope that God would revive me anew the next morning, whereupon I would put my trust in Him and betake myself to Old Cairo to reassure myself concerning the well-being of the fathers at the church in Qasr al-Sham' and be blessed by the sight of Father Joseph, who was certain to know what had become of my beloved Thawna and be cognizant of his whereabouts.

I boarded a ship leaving Tanis and went down the Byzantine Branch, which is a much-traveled branch of the Nile that passes through the area known as Asfal al-Ard. I arrived in a town called Salihiya, which is full of blessings and the good things in life. When I arrived at its port, I saw numerous large ships under construction of the sort that can carry a cargo of more than one hundred homers, that is, around a thousand bushels. From there, goods were taken to Old Cairo and delivered to the doors of grocers' shops. While I was in Salihiya I met up with a Coptic man with whom I had become acquainted during my voyage to Tanis. I learned that he was on his way down to Fustat in search of a stationer who could prepare a book for him. He had written the book in Coptic about the various classes and categories of physicians, and was anxious to have the book translated into Arabic given the way this language had begun spreading in the country. When he learned that I was a Copt by origin and that the Bashmourite dialect was my native tongue, he was astounded, as he had thought I was an Arab by birth given the ease with which the Arabic language flowed off my tongue. Given this realization, he asked me to translate his book for him into Arabic, then to copy it for him as well, since in the course of our conversation it had become apparent that I had experience as a manuscript copyist as well.

He began telling me about part of the book, saying, "It contains things about all physicians, including a wise man whose name was known widely in ancient times, not only in connection with medicine, but, in addition, in the fields of geometry and the various other sciences. This man had come to Egypt in times of old and, specifically, to the City of the Sun, known in our day as 'Ayn Shams. He was accepted graciously there, and for a period of time he was subjected to a variety of tests. When his examiners could find no fault or remissness on the basis of which to reject him, they had no choice but to direct Pythagoras—which was the man's name—to the priests at Memphis to undergo even more rigorous tests. Those at Memphis agreed grudgingly to receive Pythagoras, whom they tested with the utmost rigor and the most probing of questions and, again, they could find nothing blameworthy in him nor could they cause him to stumble. They then sent him to the people of Diyusus, who likewise put him to the test. However, they were unable to refute him in his speech. Consequently, they imposed upon him demanding tasks that were in violation of those required by the Greeks in the hope that he would refuse to submit to them, thereby allowing them to reject him and deprive him of what he sought. However, he rose to the challenge and did all that was asked of him, thereby causing their admiration for him to exceed all bounds. Hence, news of his piety and integrity spread throughout Egypt until mention of him was made to Amassis, then king of Egypt. Amassis granted Pythagoras authority over the sacrifices of the Lord and all their offerings, something which had never before been granted to a foreigner. . . ."

At this point I apologized to the man, explaining that I had no time to spend on a project such as his. My return to Egypt had fanned the flames of my longing for my beloved Thawna, and the more I thought back on the words of the merchant and physiognomist whom I had met in Jerusalem—to the effect that I was going in search of someone dear to my heart, that I would expend great effort and time to find him, that he was very ill, and that I might or might not reach him in time—the more anxious I became. Hence, he bade me a regretful farewell, since it was a rare thing in those days to find someone who had mastered both the Coptic and the Arabic languages. There were many Copts who had learned to speak Arabic without learning to write it, and its manuscripts were not easy things to deal with. On the contrary, their contents were of such a critical nature that they could tolerate no error or lack of experience and skill. As we parted, I apologized to the man again, suggesting that he seek out the services of those in the churches and monasteries, since they had taken great care both to preserve the language of their religion and to master the Arabic language as a means of enabling the Church to preserve and protect its people. After I took my leave of the man, I continued thinking about what had transpired between us, as I had observed that many of those I had met in Salihiya and Tanis had begun speaking Arabic, albeit smattered with Coptic words.

Following this I performed the obligatory prayers, as well as a special prayer for guidance. The reason for the latter was that, despite my longing to see the fathers at the church of Qasr al-Sham', I also felt hesitant to go there for fear of the indignation they might feel if they learned of my conversion to Islam. At the same time, I needed desperately to know what had become of Thawna and to learn of his whereabouts. I then fell asleep in the gentle shade of a Christ's-thorn tree with a sultry breeze wafting over me, and as I slept, Thawna came to me in the same form in which I had seen him at the time I was fleeing from the caliph's army in the marshlands. Standing atop a high hill with a staff in his hand, he said to me, "Follow me to Wadi Habib."

When I woke up and began thinking back on this, my mind lucid and sharp now, I said to myself: By God, if I do not find him at the church in Qasr al-Sham', I will look for him in Wadi Habib even if I have to get there on foot.

Some people of good will advised me to go to Birkat al-Hajj, whence I could travel up the Nile to Fustat. Sometimes on foot, and other times transported by sympathetic wayfarers, I reached Birkat al-Hajj. It was filled with water, as was the waterway that led to it from the Greater Sea. Finding a number of ship and boat owners gathered there, I asked a certain fisherman to take me with him in his boat in return for my working for him, and he agreed to take me on in return for my helping him cast his nets and pull them back in throughout our journey together. At last I reached Fustat, and from there, Old Cairo, whereupon I hastened to the Qasr al-Sham' Church, and before long I was standing at its door. Then, just as I was about to knock and request permission to enter, there emerged a young man whom, judging from his attire, I took to be a deacon. Stepping up to him, I inquired of him courteously concerning my beloved Thawna, though without revealing anything concerning my own identity.

Examining me suspiciously, he replied, "Thawna? There is no clergyman by that name here."

His face betraying his curiosity, he fell silent for a few moments as he looked me up and down in an attempt to guess what sort of a mission I was on.

Then he added, "Perhaps you are referring to the monk Thawna the Most Humble, who is in Wadi Habib now at the Anba Macarius Monastery. Though I do not suppose that is who you are looking for."

The minute I heard those words, my heart leapt for joy. Thanking him profusely, I bade him a hasty farewell as he stood there, seeing me off with a look of surprise and bewilderment.

Alternately walking, resting, and sleeping, I passed through towns and villages, seeking shade beneath trees and date palms and allowing the clouds in the sky to be my mantle. Then at last I came to the out-skirts of Wadi Habib. The only clothing I had left was a waist-wrapper and a tunic and my only possession was a staff that I used as a walking stick. Whenever I caught a glimpse of myself in a brook or spring, I would realize how time had changed me. With gray now evident where my hair parted and wrinkles creasing my face, it was a certainty that I had passed from one era to another, and that manhood and middle age had taken the place of youth and its vigor.

A blazing sun that knew no mercy, as though windows of fire had been opened in the sky, accompanied me the entire way. I walked on, asking shepherds to direct me towards the monastery. Seeing the state I was in, they would assist me periodically with a drink of water or a swig of milk with some dates until, at long last, I reached the beginning of the road that led to the monastery. I sat down to rest for a while, then got ready for the sundown prayer by performing a dry ablution: I wiped my hands with the pure sand as though I were washing them, then wiped my face, forearms, and feet in the same manner as though I were perform-ing my regular ablution, albeit it without water, so as to purify myself for prayer. By this time the sun was seeking permission to depart, and when I had finished my prayer, I sat there contemplating the desert's boundless silence as the sun gradually disappeared from view, vanish-ing behind the magnificent knolls of sand. Captivated by the majestic scene, I thought about how weak and lowly man is, and how unjust, tyrannical, and infatuated with his own power and strength he can be despite the fact that, before God's might and grandeur, he is worth no more than a grain of the sands that surrounded me on all sides.

I got up and began walking, as I had been directed by the shep-herds, down a broad, expansive valley of sand. What remained of the evening sun had afforded me a fleeting glimpse of the monastery in the distance, and my heart danced with joy as I realized that I was about to reach my destination. However, it was not long before a thick darkness had fallen, engulfing the place in an impenetrable gloom. Not a single star shone, nor did the moon deign to show its face. My heart sinking, I was gripped by a feeling of lostness and desolation. Yet I kept on going, putting my trust in God. Every now and then I would collide with one of the ghostly cactuses that grew up here and there, or stumble in the fine sands over which walking was such an exhausting venture. And all the while, I called upon God to deliver me and bring me safely to my destination, that I might reach my beloved Thawna before I perished.

I do not know how long I went on marching. In any case, after some time there appeared a light that kept up a steady glow. At first I thought it was a distant star, however, as I advanced toward it, I realized that it was a large torch that had been lit atop the monastery walls to guide wayfarers or those lost in this vast, lonely wasteland.

At last I arrived at the monastery gate, which would surely not have been possible had it not been for that guiding light. As soon I found myself in front of it, I began knocking madly. From beyond the door there came a voice inquiring as to who I might be.

"I am a relative of the monk Thawna," I replied, "and I have come to see him concerning a matter of great import."

Some time later he opened the door for me, then led me down a narrow passageway inside the monastery. The monk who served as my guide carried a candelabrum holding a single candle whose light enabled me to cast my eyes about the place, whereupon it became apparent that it was a fortress of sorts.

I was brought into a spacious guest room which was surrounded by a number of darkened cells, and whose floor was covered with camel hair rugs. The room had bay windows constructed from fine wooden latticework to which one ascended by means of a wooden ladder that could be put up and taken down. The monk brought me water and dates, saying, "Go to sleep now. Tomorrow is another day."

I do not know how I managed to sleep, as my entire body was racked with pain. Even so, I did not awaken until dawn, to the sound of the church bell. When I heard it, I rose hurriedly without realizing what I was doing, since for a few moments I had thought I was still a sexton in the church at Qasr al-Sham' in Old Cairo and that I was late beginning my duties for the day.

I headed toward the bay window and looked out. Below me I could see the monastery and the desert enveloping it from all sides, as though it had been planted there deliberately in the midst of this barren expanse. Now I was certain that it was a fortress in truth: with its solid walls that rose aloft in the midst of the sand, its entrance, its diamond-shaped external structure, its lofty arcs, and its gargantuan iron-plated gate beside which they had placed huge piles of rocks which appeared to be used to ward off danger in the event that the monastery came under attack. In front of the gate there lay what looked like two large millstones which had been carved out of stubborn granite and which could be rolled up against the entrance. There was a winch next to the gate by means of which one could be hoisted up over the wall. Then there was the monastery's huge tower, the likes of which I knew to be used for the preservation of sacred books and manuscripts having to do with matters of faith, as well as for the storage of clothing, valuable containers and utensils, and foodstuffs such as wheat, oil, olives, and dates. In addition, the tower contained places where monks could go into hiding in times of danger. The monastery had one large, spacious courtyard and another small one. The monks' cells opened onto these courtyards, as did the mill and the bakery.

As I paused to reflect on all these circular forms, I noticed how similar they were to the buildings in Baghdad and Jerusalem, including both its Islamic and Christian quarters. Then I began thinking about how roundness is hallowed in virtually every three-dimensional art that our eyes behold. And I thought to myself: It must be on account of the sense of consolation and equanimity that's engendered by a curved, rounded line. Just at that moment, a plover passed by in song, warbling blithely with its captivating, celestial voice, and I felt a rush of joy. As I feasted my ears on its sweet voice, I wondered: Are not these rounded structures just a humble attempt to imitate what God has created? The sun is round and the moon is round, as are the leaves of trees and plants, or nearly so. Circularity is a state of timelessness and eternity that points to the fact that God is the First and the Last, the Beginning and the End. Hence, the tendency to employ circular forms in every art is simply a faith-inspired instinct placed by God in the human psyche without our being aware of it. Our eyes have seen and our senses have perceived the manifestations of His creation in everything that is curved, round, or nearly round, including even in the human form, the forms of animals, and droplets of water.

A group of monks then emerged from their cells and went into a room just off the courtyard. Soon thereafter I was approached by the monk who had received me the previous evening, and who had come to rouse me. When he found that I was already awake, he wished me a good morning and invited me to have some breakfast. I followed him to the room I had seen the other monks going into, and which turned out to be the dining hall. It was a long, narrow room with a domed ceiling, in the center of which there was a low stone bench in what appeared to be a shallow sunken area around which the monks had seated themselves. Once I had come in, greeted them and sat down, they began their meal, which consisted of coarse wheat bread, olives and olive oil. As we ate, one of the monks began reciting some verses from the Bible, so, like the others, I ate with my head bowed respectfully until he had finished.

I left the dining hall accompanied by the monk who was hosting me so that we could walk about for a while and talk. As we walked along, he informed me that after they had told Thawna my name and made certain that he knew me and wished to meet with me, I had been granted permission to see him. However, he added that Thawna was not in good health, and that he had been ill for some time due to his advanced age and a defect in his heart. Consequently, he explained, it was to be preferred that I keep my words brief. In addition, he urged me not to be alarmed or upset if Thawna did not respond to what I said or if his own speech was confused. When I heard this, I nearly wept. However, I assured the man that I would be a model visitor and abide by all his instructions.

They then ushered me into one of a group of cells in the fortress, which I was told had been occupied for some time by people from al-Marris, that is, from Upper Egypt. When I came into the cell, I found an elderly man reclining on a bed made of sycamore wood, with nothing beneath him but a camel's hair mat. No sooner had I made out his features in the morning light that was filtering through the cell window than I began to tremble. I stepped quickly toward him and knelt beside him.

In an agitated, eager voice I whispered, "Thawna! My dear Thawna!"

Then, to the monks' consternation and amazement, I broke into violent sobs, unable to contain myself.

For some time I went on whispering his name and calling to him, yet without evincing any response. Then I drew close to his ear and said with a trembling voice, "Thawna. It's Budayr! Did you not tell me to follow you to Wadi Habib? I have followed you, my dear, and here I am, kneeling before you."

Then I began weeping bitterly, it was so painful for me to see Thawna in such a state of unawareness. After all, this was the distinguished, sagacious nobleman whom I had known during one of the most difficult, yet precious, times of my life. As my sobbing grew louder, he turned his head toward me with considerable effort, saying, "My dear brother, Budayr! Are you here, alive and well? Is it really true? Or am I hallucinating in my old age?"

I reached out and placed my hand on his face in order for him to assure himself that I was real, and before long tears were streaming down his face as well.

Then he added feebly, "Praise be to God, for ordaining that I should see you again! It's a miracle from the Lord and a blessing from the martyr Abu Macarius!" He raised his hands with difficulty and began crossing himself. Then he began asking me questions about myself and what had happened to me after he lost me in the wilderness. So I proceeded to tell him the things I had been through and done.

After reminding us that Thawna should not speak too much for fear of stressing his heart, and lest he suffer one of his periodic attacks resulting from his illness, the monks withdrew and went their ways. Then he gazed at me for a long time, pondering my condition, and it seemed he was taken aback by the threadbare waist-wrapper and tunic I was wearing, not to mention the unkempt state I was in.

He fixed his gaze on my neck for a long time.

Then suddenly he said, "Where is your cross, Budayr? Why do I not see it on your chest?"

In a calm, confident voice I replied quickly, "This is another reason why I have come to you, my dear brother. I wanted to invite you to my religion, since you are one of the dearest persons to me in all the world. Islam is a religion of compassion and light, of love and righteousness, and under its guidance people are as equal as the teeth of a comb. I have found nothing in it but greatness, nobility, and goodness. These are the very qualities I have always found in you, my dear Thawna. God is my witness that you, of all people, are the closest to my heart and soul. Hence, it is my dearest hope that you might embrace what I have embraced, and believe in what I have believed in."

Despite his lassitude and illness, Thawna listened to me with attentive, open ears, and he seemed to be pondering every word I uttered. He did not interrupt me a single time, nor did he evince any anger or irritation.

When I had finished speaking, he remained silent for some time, then said, "It is not we who choose, Budayr. Rather, the Lord is the One who chooses for us. We are slaves to His will. I am happy that you are seeking to invite others to what you see as true and good. At the same time, I feel grieved that you have abandoned the religion of your family and forefathers, the paradise of the Church, and the path of Christ."

His eyes had grown moist with tears, and he seemed truly miserable and despondent. Trembling, I took his hand and began patting it as he went on speaking with difficulty: "I am saddened and distressed, Budayr. However, so long as you have found in your new religion that which places you on the path of truth and justice, you have the right to pursue what you see as right. As for me, beloved, I do not think I could ever abandon my religion, nor do I think I could embrace any other. I lived my entire life buffeted about by apprehensions, misgivings, and conflicting thoughts, my mind a battleground for competing philosophies, until I became an orthodox Christian, and in this faith I will die. May God have mercy on us all, my goodhearted son. May He forgive me and you, since it is He who has foreordained and willed what was and is to be."

I was deeply moved by what he had said, and a worry that I had harbored throughout my entire journey to him was dispelled: For I had dreaded these moments, the moments in which I would present him with my new religion. I was also aware of how difficult it would be for him to respond to the invitation I had extended to him. After all, Thawna was not a man who could be easily swayed. As such, he would never embrace a doctrine unless he had first examined it from every possible angle, nor would he doubt unless he was certain that there was a basis for such. He had never been someone to accept things uncritically.

I did not want to burden him with more words. At the same time, I sensed that he wanted to speak to me, that there was something he wanted to confide in me when he said, "You know, Budayr, after living all these years and reaching the age I have reached, I am no longer shaken much by what goes on around me. I have gotten so I think less about paths, and more about destinations. Since my escape from the marshlands, I have come to see that there is no good to be found in this earthly existence so long as there is no justice among people, and so long as mercy and compassion do not embrace the weak as well as the strong. I used to wonder, after all the unjust warfare I had witnessed with my own two eyes: Are not all these people its victims, be they Christians or Muslims, and do they not all deserve to be received into Paradise? Do you not think, Budayr, that the divine justice will embrace all those who have found no justice in this world? Those who have been hungry and naked, who have sold their children and families in order to survive? Do you not think, Budayr, that God will envelop them all in His bounty and compassion regardless of whether they are Muslims or Copts?"

Then he continued, "Look at the way you and I have ended up. I renounced and abandoned the world in order to be here and devote myself entirely to the service of Christ far away from people. And now you return to me after embracing Islam, clad in nothing but tunic and waist-cloth, and with nothing to your name but a staff to walk on. Tell me, for Heaven's sake: What is the difference between us? Is not your renunciation of the world the same as mine? And, my dear: Is it not the same rejection of the state of the world and its inhabitants that has impelled both of us to leave everything behind, realizing as we do that there is no hope to be found in this world and that there is nothing left for us but the love of God?"

Then, with his mind now lucid and his resolve strengthened, he began reciting some passages from the rule of faith in a low, reverent voice, saying, "Light from Light, true God from true God, begotten not made . . . Maker of heaven and earth, and of all things visible and invisible: God, Disposer of all, through Whom all things were made. . . ."

Then, after reciting for some time he concluded, ". . . and we look for the resurrection of the dead, and the life of the world to come."

I remained at the monastery for a number of days, during which time I was constantly by Thawna's side, ministering to him in whatever way I could. I could not bear to leave with him in such a frail state. By this time Thawna had informed the monks of the fact that I was a Muslim, and they treated me one and all with the utmost kindness and consideration. They even brought a clean camel's hair rug especially for me to pray on. The majority of them were men of obedience and humility, with sincere faith in Jesus Christ, who were committed to a life of asceticism and renunciation through fasting, prayer, and frequent recitations and readings from the Holy Scriptures and liturgies.

In response to an inquiry from me, one of them informed me that Thawna had managed to flee during the Bashmourite uprising and had been careful to remain in hiding until things had quieted down. After that, however, he had been loathe to return to the church at Qasr al-Sham', preferring instead to give himself to a life of seclusion and renunciation. Consequently, he had come to this monastery, where he had been consecrated as a monk. By the time I arrived he had spent many years there, not having left it for Alexandria or Cairo, nor even for the countryside. He was accustomed to remaining for long periods of time at the monastery's grotto, which was the site of relics from the patriarch fathers, namely, St. Mark, the first preacher of the Gospel in Egypt, whose head was found together with the sons of Fahd in the city of Alexandria and whose body was in Venice, and Ananyus, who was buried in the Church of St. Girgis at Pharaoh's obelisk in Alexandria. I was told that Thawna never went further than the cells nearby and those in the valley. During every prayer he prayed, he would burn incense over the holy relics, lighting a lamp for them every day and every night, and standing for long hours in a state of reverent worship.

One of the most astonishing things I saw at the monastery was the cell which had been named after the hermit father Dortheous, where not a single monk was permitted to utter the word "Hallelujah!" unless he knew the entire Psalter by heart. It was for this reason that the monks were all expected to memorize the Psalms in their entirety. I also saw a baptismal font where a miracle was witnessed on one night of every year: The font would be emptied of the sand that had accumulated in it over time, after which it would be filled with water, yet without anyone's knowing where the water had come from. And if someone guilty of some sin was immersed in the font, there would appear on his body a garment resembling the scales of a fish. Another miraculous phenomenon associated with the font was that even if many people were immersed in it at the same time, no one's body would touch anyone else's. The font was surrounded by the monks' cells, though without any trees or date palms nearby, nor did any plants grow there.

One year, after the twenty-fifth of Abib, the monks were informed that the Nile had not risen sufficiently. Hence, as was their custom, they prepared a bucket of water and prayed over it as they did on the Feasts of St. Paul and St. Peter. Following this, they took it and poured its contents into the sea, thereby causing its volume to increase. This was a rite that had been observed since ancient times.

Thawna became increasingly ill, and after every treatment had failed, we despaired of his recovery. The elder monks had tried numerous drugs, herbs, and potions, testing the movement of his heart and ascertaining the 'breath' of his heart from which the veins branch out all over the body. They would do this by applying pressure to the veins and placing their fingers on his head, his thigh, the tops of his hands, his rib cartilages, and his arms, since the heart, being the center of the body, sends out veins through all these members. They would also test his acid breath, which likewise flows through the body, in order to ascertain the extent to which his blood had deteriorated, particularly when he would drink water, because if the vein referred to in the ancient language as akhudh is blocked in the abdomen, the water goes to the ailing heart. Another thing they would test was the degree of congestion in his organs and whether they had fallen still as a result of the heart's turbidity and its mingling with the other organs. They employed these and numerous other ancient methods and sciences that were always practiced in monasteries, and which had been passed down by the monks from one generation to the next. Meanwhile, they persevered without ceasing in reciting passages from the scripture and the liturgy along with ancient magical formulas as they observed the four veins in the ears, since the breath of life is known to flow through the two veins in the right ear, while the breath of death flows through the two in the left.

They continued in this fashion for some time. As for me, I would spend my nights, awake and watchful, at Thawna's feet. And despite his deteriorating condition, he would always ask me to talk to him about my travels and the events and trials I had encountered. Hence, I went on relating to him everything that had happened to me. I told him how I had tried to heal Father Thomas by advising those at the Qasyan Church to treat his burns with the ancient formula that I had heard Thawna recite when a fire had broken out on account of ill winds that had blown across the grass huts of some ferry owners along the Nile. I reminded him of how we had gone to rescue the burn victims armed with potions, medicines, and this ancient formula of his.

He would also ask me to tell him more about my faith and my renunciation of the world since the time I had entered Islam. It seemed that I perplexed him, and on one such occasion, despite his mounting illness, he said with labored breath, "Tell me, Budayr, has your faith in God become more certain since you became a Muslim? Do you feel as though you have been cleansed of every sin such that you have peace and assurance in your heart?"

I did not know how I was supposed to answer this question of his. However, wanting to convey truthfully, and in the most forceful words possible, what I felt inside, I thought for a while, then said, "I can tell you honestly, Thawna, that every day that passed before I became a Muslim, I would wake up in the morning feeling burdened with worry, my thoughts in a jumble and my spirit tormenting me with memories of my early youth. The image of Amuna would never leave me for a moment, and when she appeared to me, I would be drowned in torment over the love I had had for her and my grief over her death. I was tormented even more when I remembered what had happened between Suwayla and me, and I would hate myself, despising my weakness, my recklessness, and my spirit's seeming inability to resist the lusts of the body. Before becoming a Muslim I had confessed my sins in the church numerous times. But confession did nothing to put distance between me and the pain, or to make me forget my sense of sinfulness and guilt. However, when I set out on the path of those who seek the knowledge of God and those who are wayfarers on the spiritual path, I arrived at 'There is no he but He.' When that happened—that is, when I forgot 'was' and focused entirely on 'is'—my inner torments disappeared and the distances between me and those things that had caused me pain grew vaster and vaster. After all, everything perishes but God's gracious face. Thus it is that the Revealing Light has come to me, my soul is at peace, and my worry and misery are gone."

Thawna listened to everything I was saying. Then, after what I suspect was a great struggle on his part, he uttered his final words to me in this world, saying, "When you bid me farewell and depart from this place, do not forget to say this to people, since this is what they need in order for their souls to find reassurance and their spirits, peace. Time always clouds people's memories, distancing them from their God-given instinct to live in faith. Tell them these things even if they beat you or persecute you, and be patient and forbearing toward them until they sense the trustworthiness of your faith and your certainty."

A few days later, my precious Thawna began entering the isthmus that bridges life and death. He fell completely unconscious, and it was difficult for us to give him even a sip of water to drink. Then, one day as the sun was making its descent onto the horizon and disappearing from the cosmos, God willed for his spirit to ascend. I had left him briefly to perform my ablutions and get ready to pray, and as I did so, the monastery bell commenced its mournful, rhythmic tolling. All the monks emerged from their cells to come to him and bid him their final farewell with gazes and prayers for his unblemished spirit.

Thawna's body remained where it was all that night, surrounded by candles. In keeping with our custom from times of old, a loaf of bread and a handful of salt had been placed beneath his head. The monks lingered about him, celebrating the Mass and reciting from the Scriptures and words of the Divine Liturgy. As they did so, I stood at a distance, murmuring what I could recall of the words of remembrance of the Almighty, All-Wise One, praying for mercy on Thawna's spirit and light in his soul, and calling upon God to usher him into the presence of the righteous.

After we had escorted Thawna to his final resting place I stayed on at the monastery for a number of days, as the monks had urged me to stay long enough for them to prepare me as best they could for my desert trek. They provided me with things to sustain me along the way, and with a nag to ride. I had requested their permission to keep something that had belonged to Thawna, something to remember him by. Hence, they allowed me to keep an old copy of the New Testament that had been his, penned on parchment, whose verses my beloved had read to me on so many an occasion and whose lofty meanings he had given me eyes to behold.

Once I had left the monastery and was on my own in Wadi Habib—which may have been one day in the month of Rabi' II—I hastened along until I came to a spot overlooking some inhabited areas. I entered a village, and as soon as I came within view of some young boys who had been playing in its streets, they stopped what they were doing. My disheveled, dust-covered mien and my shabby clothing seemed to have alarmed them and aroused their curiosity. They began gathering around me with laughter and taunts, after which they started pelting me with pebbles and stones. I urged my mount along to get away from them, asking God to have mercy on them and forgive them. Then, caught up in a state of ecstasy and longing, my limbs shaking from the force of the Spirit, I sang:

To those who pelt me with the stones of hatred
I owe compassion rather than dread.

God is my sufficiency, in Him have I trusted,
To the mighty He gives their daily bread.

No rest will they find who flee from Him,
Till to Him they flee instead!

SOURCES

I am indebted to the following writers and works, among others, for information and inspiration:

Abu Salih al-Armani, *Kana'is Misr wa adyiratuha.*
Al-Sayyid Taha al-Sayyid Abu Sudayra, *al-Hiraf wa-l-sina'at fi Misr al-islamiya mundhu al-fath al-'arabi hatta nihayat al-'asr al-fatimi.*
Salih Ahmad al-'Ali, *Khitat al-basra wa mantiqatuha: khitat Baghdad fi-l-'uhud al-'abbasiya al-ula.*
Zubayda 'Ata, *Iqlim al-Minya fi-l-'asr al-wasit.*
'Abd al-Latif al-Baghdadi, *Rihla ila misr.*
Martin Bernal, *Black Athena.*
Alfred Butler, *Egypt's Churches and Monasteries.*
Dawud al-Antaki, *al-Tadhkira.*
Al-Dumayri, *Risalat al-hayawan al-kubra.*
Nikita Elizov, *Tarikh al-sharq al-adna al-qadim.*
Imam Abu Hamid al-Ghazali, *Ahkam al-nikah wa qasr al-shahwatayn.*
Gamal al-Ghitani, *Hadith shifahi 'an al-dawsa 'ind al-turuq al-sufiya.*
Banub Habashi, *Misr al-qibtiya.*
Yaqut al-Hamawi, *Mu'jam al-buldan.*
Al-Hasan ibn Zulaq, *al-Durr al-maknun fi akhbar Dhi al-Nun al-Misri.*
Siegfried Hunke, *Shams al-'arab tastu' 'ala al-gharb.*
Ibn al-'Ibri, *Tarikh kanisat antukia.*

Ibn al-Nadim, *al-Fihrist*.

Anba Isidhrus, *al-Kharida al-nafisa fi tarikh al-kanisa*.

Sabir Jabra, *Nasib al-qibt fi taqaddum al-'ulum*.

al-Jahiz, *Risala fi shira' al-'abid*.

Ahmad Kamal, *al-Tibb al-misri al-qadim*.

Sayyida Kashif, *Misr fi 'asr al-wulah*.

Bahur Labib, *al-Athar al-qubtiya*.

Su'ad Mahir, *al-Bahriya fi Misr al-islamiya*.

Taqi al-Din al-Maqrizi, *al-Mawa'id wal-i'tibar bi dhikr al-khitat wa-l-athar*.

Yassi 'Abd al-Masih, *al-Lahajat al-qibtiya wa atharuha al-adabiya*.

Adam Metz, *Tarikh al-hadara al-islamiya*.

Al-Qalqashandi, *Subh al-a'sha fi sina'at al-ansha*.

Al-Qazwini, *Athar al-bilad* and *'Aja'ib al-makhluqat*.

Asad Rustum, *Tarikh kanisat antukia al-'uzma*.

Sheikh Yusuf al-Shirbini, *Hazz al-quhuf fi sharh Qasid Abi Shaduf*.

Munir Shukri, *al-Masihiya wa ma tadinu bihi li-l-qibt*.

Al-Suhrawardi, *Majmu'at musannafat Shaykh Ishraq*.

Al-Tabari, *Tarikh al-tabari*.

Al-Tifashi, *Risala fi-l-jawahir wa-l-ahjar*.

GLOSSARY AND NOTES

'abaya: A cloak-like woolen wrap.

Abu Muslim al-Khurasani: Instrumental in the success of the Abbasid revolt against the Umayyad caliphate, Abu Muslim al-Khurasani led the Abbasid armies against the Umayyads in the Battle of the Greater Zab in AD 750. Once the Abbasid dynasty had been established, Abu Muslim was stabbed to death, possibly under orders from the Abbasid caliph al-Mansur.

Akhmim: Once a major metropolis, Akhmim is located on the east bank of the Nile across from modern Sohag. To the northeast of the city is a rock chapel once dedicated to the worship of the local fertility god Min (hence its Coptic name, Khmin or Shmin), as well as a temple ruin to the west of the town dedicated to Min and the goddess Repyt, who was regarded as Min's consort.

AM: Anno Martyrum, or Year of the Martyrs. Coptic years are counted from AD 284, the year in which Diocletian became Roman Emperor. Diocletian's reign was marked by tortures and mass executions of Christians, particularly in Egypt.

'am'at: A pharaonic word referring to a certain herbaceous plant.

'Amr ibn al-'As: The Muslim general who entered Egypt in AD 639/AH 18. The Babylon Treaty of AD 640/AH 20, which marked the Muslim conquest of Egypt, stipulated that the Muslims would not take over churches or interfere in their affairs.

Anastasis: 'the Resurrection' in Greek.

Anubis: According to ancient Egyptian mythology, Anubis is lord of the dead and ruler of the underworld, and is usually depicted as a man with the head of a jackal.

Appolonarians: Followers of the teaching according to which Christ was solely divine because, rather than having a human soul, he was indwelt entirely by the Divine Logos.

Archiledes: Archiledes is a renowned figure in Coptic tradition who refused to see his mother in honor of a pledge he had made to himself never to look at a woman.

ardab: A unit of measure equal to approximately fifty-six kilograms for barley, and seventy kilograms for wheat.

Arianism: A term referring to the Christological view propounded by Arius of Alexandria (AD 256–336), a Christian priest who taught that the Son of God ("only begotten") was not co-eternal with or equal to the Father ("unbegotten"), but that before time began the Father brought the Son into existence, after which, working through the Son, the Father created the Holy Spirit, who is subordinate to the Son as the Son is to the Father. The conflict between Arianism and Trinitarian beliefs continued from one degree to another from the fourth through the sixth century AD.

Ba', nun, waw, mim, alif (pneuma): 'the Holy Spirit' in Greek.

Basta: The name of a town (Tell Basta) to which the Holy Family came after their flight to Egypt from King Herod. It is related that the town was full of idols, and that when the Holy Family entered, all the idols fell to the ground. Offended, its inhabitants mistreated the Holy Family, as a result of which they left the town and headed south.

Belbeis: A city in Egypt's Eastern regions of ancient origins that was the entry point for the Islamic conquest of Egypt.

black elder: Pre-Christian documents attributed healing, protective powers to the black elder, and in England it was considered bad luck to cut its branches lest one show disrespect for the mother elder, who was thought to inhabit the tree. In fact, the blossoms, berries, and bark of the black elder are known to have numerous healing properties and medicinal uses.

Byzantine Sea: The Mediterranean Sea.

carat: A unit of weight equal to somewhere between 0.234 and 0.264 grams.

Chalcedonian uncleanness: An allusion to the bitter rift that came about between the Church of Alexandria and the Byzantine churches following the Council of Chalcedon in AD 451. The Coptic Church is the portion of the Church of Alexandria that separated from the Byzantine churches after the Council of Chalcedon over the issue of the two natures of Christ, with the Chalcedonian formula holding that Christ was "one hypostasis in two natures," and the Coptic church holding that Christ's two natures, one divine and the other human, were united "without mingling, without confusion, and without alteration" (the Coptic Liturgy of St. Basil of Caesarea) in the "one nature of the incarnate Word."

dalnis: A type of small fish eaten by the poor of the Nile Delta.

dawsa: A practice once prevalent among certain Sufi orders, particularly in Egypt and the Levant, which consisted in the order's sheikh riding a horse over the backs of his disciples without causing them harm. A number of legal decisions have been issued by Muslim scholars prohibiting the practice, and even prescribing punishments for those who engage in it.

dinar: A gold coin weighing 4.20 grams, or approximately twenty carats.

Dionysius: St. Dionysius served as Patriarch of Alexandria from AD 248 to 264.

dirham: As a unit of weight, the dirham equals approximately 3.12 to 3.17 grams.

dragon's blood: A red, sap-like substance derived from the dragon tree, *Dracaena draco*.

dummaz: 'Kharaj' in Coptic.

Eis anatolas vlepsete: 'And look to the East' in Greek.

faludhaj: A sweet made from hulled wheat, honey, and ghee.

Farama: Known in modern times as Tell al-Farama, Farama was once known as Pelusium (from the Greek pelos, mud, or silt). Located thirty kilometers southeast of Port Said, Pelusium was historically of great strategic importance, having served as the entry point for numerous foreign invaders.

feddan: A measure equal to approximately 4,200 square meters.

". . . forbidden by a governmental degree to leave their lands . . .": During the time when the kharaj became so oppressive to farmers that many had to sell everything they owned, and sometimes even their children, in order to get themselves out of debt, large numbers of them began fleeing from their lands en masse as a last resort. As a result, there was no one left to farm the abandoned lands. In response, the state issued a decree forbidding all farmers to leave their land without its express written permission, thereby turning them, in effect, into serfs on what had once been their own property.

fuqqa': A drink made from barley that is fermented until bubbles appear on the surface.

Fustat: Close to Fort Babylon on the east bank of the Nile, Fustat was the capital of Egypt from the time of the Islamic conquest at the hands of 'Amr ibn al-'As in AD 640 until it was captured by the Fatimid general Jawhar in AD 969.

Gregory the Theologian: Gregory Nazianzus (AD 329–389) was a bishop of Constantinople who is honored as a saint by both the Roman Catholic Church and Eastern Orthodoxy, and who is widely quoted by Eastern Orthodox theologians.

Hanbalite: An adherent of the school of Islamic jurisprudence founded by Ibn Hanbal, who was known for the austere views he espoused.

Haydar: The name of a so-called Sufi sheikh who promoted the use of hashish among his followers.

indimansi: A piece of cloth on which there is a picture of Jesus being brought down from the cross for burial and on which the Host is laid. It may be used, with permission from the bishop, whenever a consecrated table is unavailable.

isba': A unit of length equal to approximately 2.5 meters.

Ishaq al-Turk: A propagandist for Abu Muslim al-Khurasani who was sent to the Turks of Transoxnia, Ishaq al-Turk declared a revolt against the Abbasid caliph al-Mansur after the latter gave orders for Abu Muslim al-Khurasani to be murdered.

Jacobite Coptic Church: The Jacobite Church was founded in the sixth century as a Monophysite church in Syria by Jacob Baradaeus with support from Empress Theodora. As such, it bears a doctrinal affinity to the Coptic Church; however, Copts themselves do not regard themselves as 'monophysites' in the sense in which monophysiticism was portrayed at the Council of Chalcedon. Rather, they maintain that since, as is stated in the Nicene–Constantinople Creed, "Christ was conceived of the Holy Spirit and the Virgin Mary," Christ thus had a single nature, i.e., that of "the Logos Incarnate," which comprises both full humanity and full divinity, whereas according to the Chalcedonian formulation, Christ was "one hypostasis in two natures."

jizya: The poll tax imposed by the Islamic state on its non-Muslim subjects.

John Golden Mouth: Born in Antioch, Syria in AD 347, John Chrysostum (Chrysostum meaning "mouth of gold") was a renowned Christian ascetic and orator known for his piety, his eloquence, and his erudite and thorough commentaries on the Christian scriptures. Eventually named Patriarch of Constantinople in AD 397 by Pope Saint Siricus, he ran afoul of the ruling authorities for his uncompromising stance on immoral practices then rampant in the Roman imperial palace. Having thus earned the enmity of Empress Eudoxia, he was stripped of his title and exiled; he eventually died in AD 407 while en route to preach in the village of Comana near the Black Sea.

jubba: A long outer garment, open in front, with wide sleeves.

kammuniya: A dish of Sudanese origin made from organ meats such as liver, spleen, lungs, etc., which are sautéed with onion, garlic, carrots, and other seasonings.

kardah: A Persian word referring to a certain fragrant flower.

Kemet: A name once used to refer to Egypt, meaning "land of the black soil."

kharaj: The tax levied by the Islamic state on lands conquered by force, or on lands concerning which a peaceful agreement had been reached with their owners.

khashkananj: A kind of cookie made in Egypt and Syria from semolina, flour, and almonds.

kishk: A dough made from bulgur and sour milk, cut into small pieces and dried in the sun, then used in the preparation of other dishes.

majdhub: Literally, 'drawn, captivated, charmed,' a majdhub is a Muslim mystic who has been so fully taken up into the presence of the Divine that he appears as a madman; he is "in the world but not of it."

ma'muniya: A semolina-based dessert associated with the Caliph Ma'mun which is eaten to this day in Aleppo.

matar: A liquid measure of Greek origin equaling thirty-nine liters.

Melkites: Unlike the Coptic Church, what is now known as the Melkite Church accepted the Christological formulation that emerged from the Council of Chalcedon in AD 451. However, it wasn't until near the end of the fifth century that it came to be called 'Melkite,' an appellation coined by its detractors in criticism of its fidelity to the Emperor ('malka' in Syriac) Marcian, who initiated the Council of Chalcedon. Under the Byzantine Eastern Roman Empire, Melkite patriarchs were appointed by the emperors as both religious leaders and civil governors; in this capacity, they oversaw the torture and martyrdom of large numbers of Copts who were persecuted for their refusal to accept the Chalcedonian Christological formulation.

mizhar: An ancient Arab variety of the lute.

mizmar: A single-piped woodwind instrument resembling the oboe.

Monarchianists: The Monarchianists, whose concern to preserve God's unity led them to deny the Trinity, were divided into two main groups: modalist and dynamic. Modalist Monarchianism has been better known as Sabellianism, according to which God exists in three 'modes,' namely that of the Father, the Son, and the Holy Spirit. These are three different forms in which God manifests Himself rather than three separate 'Persons' or hypostases. Sabellius was excommunicated by Callistus in AD 220, and Sabellianism was declared a heresy by the synod of Rome in AD 262. As for dynamic monarchianism, it is represented by the teaching of Paul of Samosata.

Muqawqis: Muqawqis (Qayrus), a Roman and a Coptic Christian, was appointed viceregent of Egypt by the Roman emperor Heraclius during the time when the dispute over Monophysitism was at its height (AD 631), particularly in Alexandria, the capital of Egypt at that time. Muqawqis appears to have been appointed to this position due to his willingness to cooperate with the Roman Empire's desire to oblige the Copts to adopt the teachings formulated at the Council of Chalcedon. When his efforts to change the Copts' doctrinal position failed, he resorted to persecution so fierce that historian Michael the Elder, Jacobite patriarch of Antioch, expresses the view that "therefore, there came to us from the south the sons of Ishmael to rescue us from the hands of the Romans." Quoted by Thomas Arnold in *The Preaching of Islam*, Delhi, Low Price Pub., Second Edition, pp. 54–55.

nida: A kind of starch-paste used by the poor in food preparation.

Novatianists: Followers of the sect established by the third century Roman priest Novatian (or Novatius), the Novatianists were orthodox doctrinally speaking, but differed with the Catholic Church on matters of discipline. Following the vicious persecution of the church under Decius, during which time some Christians apostatized or agreed to sacrifice to idols under torture, the Novatianists refused to reinstate such lapsed Christians into the fellowship of believers; nor would they permit Communion to those who had committed mortal sins. Novatius and his followers were excommunicated by a synod held at Rome in AD 251. Novatius is said to have been martyred under the Emperor Valerian (AD 253–260).

Nun, ya, fa', ya': spirit or soul in Coptic.

O Kyrios meta pandon imon: "The Lord is with you all" in Greek.

Osanna: The Greek transliteration for the Hebrew phrase, "Hosanna," or "Deliver us."

parasang: An ancient Persian unit of distance, equal to approximately 3.5 miles.

Paul of Samosata: Elected Bishop of Antioch in AD 260, Paul of Samosata aroused controversy with his teachings. Emphasizing the oneness of God, he taught that Jesus was born a mere man, but that at his baptism he was infused with the divine Logos. Hence, rather than being God-become-man, Paul saw him as man-become-God. Paul of Samosata's teachings thus anticipated those of Adoptionism. In AD 269, seventy bishops, priests, and deacons assembled at Antioch and deposed Paul as bishop; nevertheless, through support from Queen Zenobia, he remained in his post until AD 272, at which time Zenobia was defeated by Aurelian. At that time, he was forced to yield to Domnus, who had been elected his successor.

Paulinists: Followers of Paul of Samosata.

pole: A unit for measuring areas equal to approximately 3,733 square meters.

qadus: A unit of volume equal to 159.3 liters.

qandil: A special container for holy oil.

qanun: A stringed instrument resembling the zither with a shallow, trapezoidal sound box that is held horizontally in front of the person playing it.

Qarun: A figure mentioned in the Qur'an who rebelled against the Prophet Moses and who had been granted vast wealth (Qur'an 28:76–81).

Qasr al-Sham' at Fort Babylon: Thought to have been built by the Persians in the sixth century BC, then named after the original Babylon (though another theory has it that it was named after a neighboring city known as Babylion), Fort Babylon was restored by the Emperor Trajan in the first century AD. It was this fortress in which Muqawqis took refuge when a Muslim army entered Egypt under the leadership of 'Amr ibn al-'As. However, the fortress fell in the year AH 640/AD 20 after being besieged by the Muslim army for seven months. After the Arabs built the city of Fustat to the northeast of Babylon, Fort Babylon became an enclave for Coptic Christians and Jews, and to this day it is the site of six churches. This fort has also been known as Qasr al-Sham' (The Candle Fortress) supposedly due to the fact that on the first of each month, candles would be lit on one of the fort's towers.

qist: A unit of measure equal to approximately 612 grams.

Ra: The ancient Egyptian sun god.

ratl: A unit of weight equal to approximately four hundred grams.

rebab: An instrument resembling the fiddle, with one or two strings.

safidhabaja: A dish made from meat, chickpeas, galingale, and cinnamon.

sakamura tree: An aromatic tree which is said to have been brought to Egypt from Somalia by the Pharaonic ruler Hatshepsut.

sekanjabin: A mint and vinegar syrup made with either honey or sugar, which is diluted with water and drunk.

(Father) Shenouda: St. Shenouda the Archimandrite was a Coptic monk who served as abbot of the White Monastery (so-called for the appearance of the limestone from which it was built), located four and a half kilometers from modern Sohag, for more than fifty-six years in the fourth to fifth centuries AD. St. Shenouda was an indefatigable social and spiritual reformer who inspired many Egyptians to stand up in the face of tyranny, including that of the Byzantine Empire.

Subhan Allah!: A frequently recurring phrase in the Qur'an, "Subhan Allah!" means, "Glory be to God!" In a conversational context, however, it often expresses the sense of, "Amazing!" or "What do you know?"

Sunpadh: An eighth-century Zoroastrian cleric who promoted a syncretic heresy that melded Islam with Zoroastrianism. Sunpadh claimed that Abu Muslim al-Khurasani, who had been murdered under the caliph al-Mansur, had not really died and would return with the Mahdi. Sunpadh led a revolt against the Abbasids, but was captured and killed.

Tahouti: An ancient Egyptian deity viewed as the lord of the moon and light.

tannour: A pit, usually clay-lined, for baking bread; a kind of oven.

tarawih prayers: Voluntary extended prayers performed after the final obligatory prayer of the day during the Muslim fasting month of Ramadan.

tharid: A dish of sopped bread, meat, and broth.

theotokia: A hymn of praise and supplication to the Virgin Mary.

"Titi titi, zay ma ruhti zay ma jiti!": A light-hearted rhyme meaning, "You've gone and come back without doing what you set out to."

Thoxa Patri ke lo ke Ayjio Pnevmati: "Glory to the Father, the Son and the Holy Spirit" in Greek.

tunbur: A long-necked, stringed instrument resembling the mandolin.

uqiya: A unit of weight that varies widely, approximately 130 grams.

Ustadh Sis: Claiming to be a prophet, Ustadh Sis led a rebellion against the Abbasid caliphate in the mid-eighth century, but was defeated in a bloody battle against an army led by al-Mahdi, son of Caliph al-Mansur.

Valerian: Roman Emperor from AD 253–260, Valerian was kindly disposed toward Christians in the beginning of his reign. However, allowing himself to be influenced by opposition forces, he later took extreme measures against them.

whiba: A dry measure equal to approximately five kilograms.

white as a punishment: Given the fact that the color that represented the Abbasid caliphate was black, the governor's being forced to wear white amounted to a kind of public humiliation.

zawiya: A small cupolaed mosque erected over the tomb of a Muslim saint, with teaching facilities and a hospice attached to it.

zirbaj: A chicken dish consisting of chicken cut into small pieces and boiled together with salt, cinnamon, chickpeas, sesame oil, and vinegar. To this is added a sauce made from sugar and almond paste dissolved in rose water and seasoned with ground coriander, black pepper, gum mastic, and saffron.

VERSES OF
SCRIPTURE CITED

Verses are cited in order of appearance in the text. (Biblical quotations are from the Revised Standard Version, and Qur'anic quotations are taken from Muhammad Asad, *The Message of the Qur'an*, and Arthur J. Arberry, *The Koran Interpreted*.)

"Make a joyful noise . . ."	Psalms 100:1
"He who resists the authorities . . ."	Romans 13:2
"I will destine you to the sword . . ."	Isaiah 65:12
"Blessed is he who comes . . ."	Matthew 21:9
"Let not your hearts be troubled . . ."	John 14:1–4
"For this reason I bow my knees . . ."	Ephesians 3:14–21
"It is written: 'My house shall be called . . .'"	Matthew 21:13
" . . . and the gates of hell shall not . . ."	Matthew 16:18
"The Spirit of the Lord is upon me . . ."	Luke 4:18–19
"Any uncircumcised male . . ."	Genesis 17:11
"But of that day or that hour . . ."	Mark 13:32–37
"And as you wish that men . . ."	Luke 6:31–38
"Unless one is born of water . . ."	John 3:5–6
"You shall die . . ."	Genesis 2:17
"This at last is bone of my bones . . ."	Genesis 2:23
"But if Christ is in you . . ."	Romans 8:10–11
"If you would be perfect . . ."	Matthew 19:21
" . . . every sound tree . . ."	Matthew 7:17

"I am carnal, sold under sin . . ."	Romans 7:14–20
"The eye is the lamp . . ."	Matthew 6:22
"Do you not know that your body . . ."	I Corinthians 6:19–20
"Therefore, since we are justified . . ."	Romans 5:1–5
" . . . the Father of mercies and the God . . ."	II Corinthians 1:3–4
"Do you not know that he who joins himself . . ."	I Corinthians 6:16–19
"Do not love the world . . ."	I John 2:15–17
"Behold, we call those happy . . ."	James 5:11
"Behold, the Judge is standing . . ."	James 5:9
"The Sabbath was made for man . . ."	Mark 2:27–28
"One Sabbath he was going through..."	Mark 2:23–26
"Let no one be enrolled..."	I Timothy 5:9–10
"Even though I walk..."	Psalms 23:4–5
"Consider the flight of time!"	Qur'an 103:1–2
"And indeed, if you pay heed to a mortal..."	Qur'an 23:34
"O my father! Why dost thou worship..."	Qur'an 19:42
"And then he broke those idols..."	Qur'an 21:58
"And this was Our argument..."	Qur'an 6:83
"God is the light of the heavens..."	Qur'an 24:35
"There is no moving creature on earth..."	Qur'an 11:6

COPTIC MONTHS AND THEIR GREGORIAN EQUIVALENTS

Coptic Month	Starting Date in the Gregorian Calendar
Tout	September 11
Baba	October 11
Hator	November 10
Kiahk	December 10
Toba	January 9
Amshir	February 8
Baramhat	March 10
Baramouda	April 9
Bashans	May 9
Paona	June 8
Epep	July 8
Misra	August 7
Nasie (the 'little month')	September 6

Modern Arabic Literature
from the American University in Cairo Press

Ibrahim Abdel Meguid *Birds of Amber*
No One Sleeps in Alexandria • *The Other Place*
Yahya Taher Abdullah *The Mountain of Green Tea*
Leila Abouzeid *The Last Chapter*
Hamdi Abu Golayyel *Thieves in Retirement*
Yusuf Abu Rayya *Wedding Night*
Ahmed Alaidy *Being Abbas el Abd*
Idris Ali *Dongola: A Novel of Nubia* • *Poor*
Ibrahim Aslan *The Heron* • *Nile Sparrows*
Alaa Al Aswany *The Yacoubian Building*
Fadhil al-Azzawi *The Last of the Angels*
Hala El Badry *A Certain Woman* • *Muntaha*
Salwa Bakr *The Man from Bashmour* • *The Wiles of Men*
Hoda Barakat *Disciples of Passion* • *The Tiller of Waters*
Mourid Barghouti *I Saw Ramallah*
Mohamed El-Bisatie *Clamor of the Lake* • *Houses Behind the Trees*
A Last Glass of Tea • *Over the Bridge*
Mansoura Ez Eldin *Maryam's Maze*
Ibrahim Farghali *The Smiles of the Saints*
Hamdy el-Gazzar *Black Magic*
Fathy Ghanem *The Man Who Lost His Shadow*
Randa Ghazy *Dreaming of Palestine*
Gamal al-Ghitani *Pyramid Texts* • *Zayni Barakat*
Yahya Hakki *The Lamp of Umm Hashim*
Bensalem Himmich *The Polymath* • *The Theocrat*
Taha Hussein *The Days* • *A Man of Letters* • *The Sufferers*
Sonallah Ibrahim *Cairo: From Edge to Edge* • *The Committee* • *Zaat*
Yusuf Idris *City of Love and Ashes*
Denys Johnson-Davies *The AUC Press Book of Modern Arabic Literature*
Under the Naked Sky: Short Stories from the Arab World
Said al-Kafrawi *The Hill of Gypsies*
Sahar Khalifeh *The End of Spring* • *The Image, the Icon, and the Covenant*
The Inheritance

Edwar al-Kharrat *Rama and the Dragon* • *Stones of Bobello*

Betool Khedairi *Absent*

Mohammed Khudayyir *Basrayatha: Portrait of a City*

Ibrahim al-Koni *Anubis*

Naguib Mahfouz *Adrift on the Nile* • *Akhenaten: Dweller in Truth*
Arabian Nights and Days • *Autumn Quail* • *The Beggar* • *The Beginning and*
the End • *The Cairo Trilogy: Palace Walk, Palace of Desire, Sugar Street*
Children of the Alley • *The Day the Leader Was Killed* • *The Dreams*
Dreams of Departure • *Echoes of an Autobiography* • *The Harafish*
The Journey of Ibn Fattouma • *Karnak Café* • *Khufu's Wisdom* • *Life's Wisdom*
Midaq Alley • *Miramar* • *Mirrors* • *Morning and Evening Talk*
Naguib Mahfouz at Sidi Gaber • *Respected Sir* • *Rhadopis of Nubia*
The Search • *The Seventh Heaven* • *Thebes at War* • *The Thief and the Dogs*
The Time and the Place • *Voices from the Other World* • *Wedding Song*

Mohamed Makhzangi *Memories of a Meltdown*

Alia Mamdouh *The Loved Ones* • *Naphtalene*

Selim Matar *The Woman of the Flask*

Ibrahim al-Mazini *Ten Again*

Yousef Al-Mohaimeed *Wolves of the Crescent Moon*

Ahlam Mosteghanemi *Chaos of the Senses* • *Memory in the Flesh*

Buthaina Al Nasiri *Final Night*

Ibrahim Nasrallah *Inside the Night*

Haggag Hassan Oddoul *Nights of Musk*

Abd al-Hakim Qasim *Rites of Assent*

Somaya Ramadan *Leaves of Narcissus*

Lenin El-Ramly *In Plain Arabic*

Ghada Samman *The Night of the First Billion*

Rafik Schami *Damascus Nights*

Khairy Shalaby *The Lodging House*

Miral al-Tahawy *Blue Aubergine* • *The Tent*

Bahaa Taher *Love in Exile*

Fuad al-Takarli *The Long Way Back*

Latifa al-Zayyat *The Open Door*